ANIMAN:
Death of a Poacher

Antony E. Green

Copyright © 2015 Antony E. Green

Published by Peterborough Books

All rights reserved.

ISBN-978-0-9575164-3-4

This story is dedicated to my children – for whom I initially wrote the story - an elephant, a lion called Cecil and my late sister who would have edited this book had she survived long enough to do so.

Foreword

When Animan was first written, in 1994, it was in response to a similar event to that we've seen recently with Cecil the lion. In my case it was an elephant that I had 'met' a few years earlier in Tsavo while on safari.

The newspaper magazine article featured a picture of a fat businessman from Germany standing on the head of a prone elephant that he had shot with a high-powered rifle from 300 yards. He was the executioner of a very well-known elephant who had sired numerous herds over the years. The elephant had wandered out of Tsavo, where he was protected, into Tanzania where 'hunting' was legal.

There was no skill involved. There was no 'hunting', just simply driving around until something was found to kill.
Some bloody hero.

That lived with me for four years before I came up with the answer to this question: how could the animals get their own back?

I came up with a 'futuristic' solution with the express intent of not only bringing the world's attention to the problem of legalised killing, but to also try to do something about it.

As it was, I couldn't find a publisher so I put the manuscript away in a drawer but it never left my mind.

When Cecil's demise, at the hands of the dentist from Minnesota, hit the headlines I decided that Animan's time had come. There was a lot of work to be done to update and rewrite it and that is now complete.

If the book sells well, 50% of the profits will go towards my goals of developing tourism that will directly benefit the local communities in Kenya.

There are arguments in favour of legalising hunting and allowing wealthy individuals to spend ludicrous amounts of money to shoot animals, mostly with regard to bringing money into the local communities. That's all well and good but I, personally, don't see that the money goes to local communities. What I do see is that where there is money there is corruption and most of the money goes into the pockets of those who have little or no interest in those communities.

What I favour is that expansion of tourism should directly

benefit the people who need it most. It's also pertinent to note that they are also the ones who suffer the most when animals damage their villages and farms. By bringing in tourism and using that money to help to fund local development, especially of water and medical facilities, then the local communities are invested in supporting and protecting the wildlife that becomes their income.

At present, many of the safari companies are owned and operated by international companies with the substantial profits not benefiting the local communities at all beyond providing a few jobs for drivers.

That needs to change and I intend to help develop that initiative.

When I "invented" the technology I have used in the book it was something that I saw being achieved within 20 years. Some of it has been achieved some of it is yet to come, but when it all comes together you will find that there are dilemmas that arise way beyond the good that is being sought at the moment.

So reading this book will give insights into just what may happen but I don't think that it will be a case of forewarned is forearmed - I cannot see a way to stop it.

As that day approaches, and it will, it will become even more dangerous than when the first atom bomb was tested.

In my lifetime? Definitely.

Chapter 1

Fourteen years ago

Early August: the long rains had finished a week before and the floor of the Rift Valley in northern Kenya was as green and lush as anywhere in the world. The whole landscape had blossomed. Herds of zebra, wildebeest, buffalo and innumerable types of gazelles and antelopes were revelling in the abundance.

For the herbivores there was all the food they could eat, for the carnivores their larder was well stocked with new arrivals. And for the hunters and poachers there were good opportunities for profit from their gruesome, and largely illegal, trade.

Mtoto Abdebele had been following an opportunity for almost three weeks, to the exclusion of all else. His eighteen year old son and two hired trackers made up the poaching party. They had been following rumours and reports, seemingly around in circles, in and out of the Turkana game reserve, east of Lake Rudolf, finding evidence and trails of an elephant that everyone had been calling 'The Big One', only for the rains to wash away the trail.

Abdebele was not a patient man. He liked to find his target, disable it in the quickest and easiest manner possible, hack off the valuables and leave the rest, not caring whether it was alive or dead, and dash for the border with the spoils of his personal quest.

Once in a generation, however, something special would come along. The evidence he had seen and heard told him that he was following a lone bull elephant of around eight tons, standing about thirteen feet at the shoulder. The stories he had been presented with by his ever grasping informants, even allowing for exaggeration, meant that the shiny white tusks must be at least eight feet in length, possibly even ten.

His Chinese friends would pay heavily for such trophies. He would not need to take any risks for some considerable time if he could claim the biggest prize of all.

Abdebele had begun to think that the elephant, and his own informants, were deliberately leading him a merry dance when they came across a set of fresh tracks, the impressions were almost twenty inches in diameter.

"Hey, boss, come and look at this. This is one big piece of meat!" Shafiq Sanwar had a very big, very flashing smile emblazoned across his deep-black face.

Abdebele nimbly jumped down from the back of the almost new, but mud spattered and dust covered Land Rover - the result of his last successful venture into Kenya some five months before, when several elephants and rhinos had been less than humanely slaughtered.

The look on his face was pure greed and evil, the smile that cracked his face would not even have pleased his mother.

"Yes, my friend, it would look like we are getting very close now."

He stuck his fingers into a nearby pile of dung,

"Two hours old, no more than that. We have only one hour before dark. We may be able to find him, if Allah is with us, and be home again by morning. Come, let's move."

They leapt back into the Land Rover and his son gunned the diesel engine back into life. The elephant's trail was easy to follow for half an hour, and then a set of vehicle tracks appeared to cross and turn parallel with them.

"It looks like our quarry has some company, most likely in the form of wildlife rangers! What do we do now, boss?" Sanwar was a tall, well built young man, but he wasn't a brave man, he much preferred butchering animals to taking on men that could shoot back.

"We follow. We are too close to lose the trail now."

Sanwar didn't argue, he just swallowed hard, he liked even less the idea of being shot by Abdebele for disagreeing with him. At least the rangers were probably a few miles in front, not sitting beside him.

The trail was leading inexorably towards the tight knit jungle on the north eastern edge of the reserve. Assuming that the elephant could force his way in, it would be more difficult to follow him. The trail would be simple and obvious enough, but they would have to follow on foot. The chances of the Land Rover getting more than a hundred yards into the dense undergrowth would be extremely slim.

They had been losing time because of hanging back from the nuisance vehicle in front. For all of Abdebele's bravado, he didn't relish a fire-fight with the rangers either, it would not go down well with others who benefited from the spoils and helped him from time to time - even the corrupt officials who frequently arrange the early release from prison of convicted poachers don't relish having to face questions over murdered KWS rangers.

"I think we will have to follow him to the jungle and make camp for the night. At least he won't go too far tonight. Tomorrow will be the last sunrise he sees."

They set up in a clearing thirty yards into the trees. It was difficult to say how far in the elephant had gone, as he was following a trail that had been used by his kind before, only now it was wider. For all of its all-terrain ability the Land Rover would not be able to penetrate any further.

They had been asleep for the best part of three hours when they were rudely awakened by the sound of thunder, the ground was shaking and trees were crashing, Abdebele leapt from his makeshift bed and stumbled almost blindly by the dim light of the embers of what had been their fire towards the sanctuary of the Land Rover and the guns that lay quietly within.

Sanwar tried to run, but his legs remained entangled within his sleeping bag, he struggled like a seal out of water to get away from the ever closer sound of the approaching Armageddon.

Abdebele's son, Benji, a heavier sleeper than the others was being shaken and dragged by Zulfiqar, the other hired hand, when the rampaging elephant burst through into the clearing.

Abdebele was fighting with his rifle, the bolt, in his desperation, wouldn't work as it had thousands of times before. He turned on the lights of the Land Rover in an effort to help himself and his group, but only in time to see the massive dark shadow turn into the biggest elephant he had ever seen plunder its way through the middle of the camp towards Benji and Zulfiqar, the ear splitting trumpet of victory was accompanied by stomach-churning sounds of breaking bones and squashing of flesh as both men had their hopeless struggle to safety brutally terminated.

Abdebele ran in front of the rampaging elephant and with all of his strength hurled his rifle as hard as he could at the elephants head, the response was as savage as it was swift. The mighty tusks swiped at him as he tried to dive out of the way, the right tusk ripping into the flesh of Abdebele's right leg. The scream was even louder than the elephant's alarm call.

It was some minutes before Sanwar, the only one to remain intact had recovered enough composure to venture out from behind the Land Rover to help. He took one look at Abdebele's leg and fetched the first aid box, such as it was, from the front of the Land Rover. He cut off the ripped trouser leg and crudely but firmly wrapped the one bandage around the wound. The tear into the muscle was very evident but at least the pressure of the bandage staunched the blood flow.

Abdebele lay back, with his eyes closed while Sanwar performed his limited first aid and remained still for several minutes afterwards, before pulling himself upright and picking his way through the devastation to where the mess that was once his son lay, colouring the red earth black with his blood.

Zulfiqar had been caught flush on the back of his head by the elephant's knee and lay with his head back and twisted at an impossible angle, eyes staring through the canopy of trees into the black night sky.

Without a word being spoken, they took spades from the back of the Land Rover and began to dig a shallow grave for the two men. Abdebele's efforts were hampered by his injury but he still managed to keep pace with Sanwar through sheer willpower and burning anger.

As the sun quickly burst its gleaming shafts through the trees, they finished their sorrowful task. Abdebele looked up and swore to himself that he would find and very slowly kill the devil that had stolen his son. It was not meant to have been his son's last day on Earth. There was now a price to be paid beyond that of the removal of his tusks.

Sanwar was surprised that Abdebele had such an appetite as they ate their first meal of the day. Even then, two hours after they had completed the burial, no words had passed between them. The pile of earth that covered his son lay no more than twenty feet from where they sat, yet he ate as though nothing had happened.

The pain from his tightly bound leg would have been too much for most men to bear, but in spite of the damp, sickly, slowly growing bloody patch on the bandage and a pronounced limp there were no physical signs or sounds of complaint from the man at all.

Abdebele stood up, looked down at Sanwar, seemingly undecided as to whether any of the night's events were his responsibility, debating within, the future of the man's life. He turned suddenly on his heel and marched to the Land Rover and shouted to the slightly shaken Sanwar, "Well, come on then, we have much to do."

They set off with the sun at their backs, much to the surprise of Sanwar as the elephant's tracks clearly went south.

They drove in silence until they reached the fishing village of Ilaret on the shore of Lake Rudolf.

They hurled dust behind them as they lurched to a halt outside a large wooden single storey house on the north edge of the village. Abdebele raised his hand to Sanwar in instruction to wait and climbed out and limped across to the open door of the house.

An hour later he reappeared, still limping but fresh professional bandaging had been applied to his wounded leg. He was followed closely by two Kenyans dressed in army fatigues, carrying a rifle each and what appeared to be an ammunition box between them.

They loaded the box into the Land Rover through the rear door and then took their places in the rear seats, Abdebele resumed his position in the front seat and turned to Sanwar, "Now we are going to do some serious hunting."

He set his jaw, gritted his teeth and the engine barked into life.

The elephant had almost twelve hours start and they still had twenty five miles to get back to the trail. Contrary to Abdebele's conviction, Sanwar had a strong feeling that this ancient elephant had survived as long as he had because he was cleverer than the rest, maybe too clever.

Finding the trail again was not difficult, but although they were quite sure that they must be gaining, they managed, on several occasions, to lose the tracks, each time losing valuable minutes in the search. During the afternoon, they had passed through three villages, each one appearing to be giving somewhat dubious information concerning the direction the elephant was travelling in. More time lost. More trails found, more trails lost. How could they fail to find something that big, when they were so close behind?

The light began to fade on them again. Abdebele was giving more and more signs of desperation. He started to shoot at anything that moved, bloodlust was taking him over. The only time the animals, any of them, were safe was when he was driving.

By six thirty, the fire in his eyes was subsiding against the futility of the darkness. They made camp out on the savannah. They built four fires with the Land Rover in the centre of the square. Although they were supposed to take it in turns to keep watch,

Abdebele only closed his eyes to blink. He sat in the driver's seat with the door open and his loaded rifle across his lap.

Apart from the occasional scuffling and snuffling of the ngiri bush pigs, and other nocturnal creatures, the night was twelve hours long and quiet.

As the sun once again began to shed its light across the peaceful plains so the fruitless search for the devil-beast started once again.

As they moved south and east towards the Marsabit National Park, the desperation again returned to infest Abdebele's mind. The impression given by villagers was that their arrival was expected and no help was forthcoming from them. The two Kenyans sat silently in the back, ever watchful, but they could achieve very little on the open plains where tracks that were over a day old were being perpetually wrecked by the wandering herds of other animals.

The sun was at its zenith when something snapped. Abdebele stopped the vehicle no more than seventy yards from the edge of a herd of zebra. Carefully loaded a magazine into his rifle, stepped out onto the grass and carefully took aim at the closest zebra. The animal fell almost on the sound of the explosion, the others took flight immediately, but eighteen more fell before reloading was necessary. The eyes that turned their gaze back to the Land Rover were cold and vacant, and as they fell on the three occupants in turn, they spoke volumes as to what was expected.

They drove after the herds, and with the canvas roof rolled back there were three rifles pointing out and shooting at every living thing. Sanwar drove as though his life depended upon it. The carnage was terrible. A pride of lions, one adolescent rhino, a small herd of elephants, mostly young with three middle-aged females, countless zebras, gazelles, dikdiks, gerenuks, three monitor lizards basking on rocks, four hyenas and at least thirty warthogs were the victims.

The massacre only came to an end when Abdebele's rage and energy subsided along with the power of the sun.

They fetched one of the gerenuks skinned it and roasted it over a roaring fire. The crackling fat dripping and agitating the flames to even greater heights. The smell was reminiscent of a barbecue anywhere in the world. They ate well, Abdebele eating almost as much as the other three together.

The news of the slaughter was travelling fast though, it was the talk of every game lodge in the country. Several military units were dispatched with orders to capture or, preferably, kill the perpetrators and prevent more massacres. It had never happened before. Poaching, whilst it was not an everyday occurrence, was regular but always with specific targets, not wholesale slaughter. It had to be stopped.

By morning the mood in the camp had altered. Abdebele had shaken off, or worked out, his desire to obliterate everything in sight and was, more realistically, concerned with getting safely out of the country. It hadn't, however, deterred him from a dawn sortie to collect the bounty from the fly infested carcasses of the elephants and rhino. The spoils were meagre as the elephants gave up little and the rhino even less. It was just pointless carnage in terms of monetary value.

They had to travel a hundred and fifty miles due north to the nearest point of the border with Ethiopia, or almost two hundred miles to the Ethiopian border at the southern tip of Lake Stefanie.

The latter was the preferred destination as it was closer to home, but inevitably would be the most hazardous.

Four hours into their slow journey, keeping as close to jungle cover as possible, one of the Kenyan's tapped Abdebele on the shoulder and pointed across to the west to higher ground.

They came quietly to a halt under the shade of a jacaranda tree, climbed out of the vehicle and, with their binoculars, leaning on the bonnet, zoomed in to see a man standing by his own expensive-looking off-road vehicle searching for something. They could just make out the shape of three others in the car, one of them possibly a woman. The man wasn't looking in their direction, he was looking more towards the south.

"What do you think he is looking for? If they were looking for game you would think they would all be out, not just one," Sanwar offered.

"Maybe he has human game in mind. There are two Kenyans in his car, possibly Masai. Could be servants. Could be bodyguards. Could be anything. But what they could be is our passport out of here! Yes," he said, grinning, "it would look as though we have more hunting to do!"

One of the Kenyans fetched a map out of the back of the Land

Rover and pointed to the spot where the man stood. He was about two miles away, but with a magnification of forty times, they appeared to be less than a hundred yards away. The gorge behind them prevented any approach or escape from that direction. If they were to be successful they would have to make the approach on foot. The biggest threat to their operation, from such a distance would be if, when they were half way there, their prey decided to leave.

They watched and waited for half an hour. Then almost without warning the man got back into his car and drove south, still along the edge of the gorge, but crucially downhill, towards a group of trees. The car stopped as soon as it reached them and all of the occupants climbed down out of the Toyota Landcruiser and set about making a camp for the night.

"Excellent. They have given us the time, the cover and the opportunity. They are even making our beds for us. How kind."

The truly malevolent Abdebele had returned. Sanwar shuddered at the sight of him.

They had just over an hour to sunset, but importantly, they would only have to make the last mile on foot.

In spite of his strength, Abdebele realised that he would not be able to manage a cross country yomp with his leg and not cause it some serious damage. He dispatched the Kenyans and Sanwar to take the control of the camp, their instructions were clear, the white man and woman were not to be harmed, the Africans must be rendered harmless but not killed.

When he heard the shots he drove in to the camp to inspect the damage.

The two unarmed guides surrendered instantly when the warning shots were fired over their heads and had been tied up together with zip ties. The two whites were standing defiantly by the fire.

"Take them out and leave them for the hyenas," he motioned towards the guides. "For these two we will make a nice place here by the fire, where we can keep an eye on them."

Two strong stakes were cut from the copse and planted into narrow holes dug into the red-brown earth. The two hostages were firmly and expertly tied to them.

"What do you intend to do with us?" the white man asked.

"You are our passport out of here. We might even be able to get some ransom money for your safe return, pay for the trip!" Abdebele laughed a dry sickening laugh. No more words passed between them.

The chunky Thuraya satellite phone sat unnoticed on the floor of the Landcruiser. Four times it vibrated, demanding to be answered. The fourth time it was Sanwar who noticed the strange buzzing sound coming from the car.

He picked it up, looked at the strange device, and debated whether to answer the call. The decision was taken out of his hands when the vibrating stopped.

"Hey boss, look what I've just found!"

He met Abdebele half way to the fire and handed the phone over.

"Must be a satellite phone!"

He limped over to the white man and shoved the phone towards him.

"Who have you been calling?!" he screeched into his face, close enough for his acrid breath to make the white man wince away from him.

"Nobody, we haven't used the phone today. We didn't have time to use it before you attacked us," he replied truthfully.

Abdebele seemed satisfied with that and eased away.

"Someone has been calling you, can they trace your phone if you don't answer it?"

"I have no idea, I only use the phone to make calls to my company, or for them to call me if they need me," he lied confidently.

"That's all I needed to know, thank you."

He dropped the phone on the floor and smashed up the phone with the butt of his rifle.

Abdebele called Sanwar out of the clearing just before midnight, leaving the Kenyans to guard the hostages.

"We move on in the morning, if we make it to the border in one piece we can feed those two to the crocodiles in the river."

"But what about the ransom?" Sanwar was puzzled.

"To collect a ransom we have to expose ourselves to capture, I am not that desperate for money. Until then we will stay in the trees, I am not happy about that phone."

An hour later and the sound of voices and gunfire exploded into the night air.

"Soldiers!" Sanwar hissed.

"Quickly, we have the advantage of surprise."

They ran quietly towards the fire. Only one soldier, two others in the trees to their right, maybe more. They fired sustained bursts into the trees, Sanwar emptied his rifle in the direction of the soldier who was cutting the hostages free, the soldier's body erupted in a frenzy of red, and dark patches emerged through the woman's clothing. The white man was trying to struggle free from his bonds. Sanwar fired again, no result, empty. He ran to their Land Rover, more bullets. No time. Abdebele fired the last of his into the shadows in the trees, a gratifying scream returned. He ran across to the white man's stake.

"Come here, now!"

He and Sanwar hurled themselves at the back of the post that held the white man uprooting it, catapulting him forwards into the fire. The screaming started as he tried to roll away. Abdebele pulled a knife from the belt of one of the dead soldiers. Sanwar jumped into the Land Rover, started it and followed the limping figure of Abdebele away from the clearing, down to the soldier's jeep. Shots were fired in their direction, bullets bouncing off rocks or puffing into the dust. Abdebele reached the jeep and plunged the knife into the front nearside tyre and ripped the radio out from inside. He had bought some time. Precious time, and with luck, enough time.

Chapter 2

Present time

He sat alone in the gloom in his office, his long slim frame semi-slumped in his chair, the only light coming from the swirling screen saver on the large iMac that sat on his desk. It was late on a Sunday evening in November and things were not at all right in the world. The clock on the screen was showing 00:53.

He had again been to the struggling zoo to see what he perceived as the tormented inhabitants. For months he had been in danger of becoming depressed and obsessed with their plight, but things had changed, options were opening up.

A solution was forming in John's mind that would enable the zoo to stay in business and at the same time rescue the animals from the unnatural environment that held them prisoner.

Until that moment there had been no alternative.

John Hylton, cybernetic expert and designer of some of the most sophisticated commercial robots and prosthetic limbs, was turning his attention to the creation of a CyberZoo.

The technology was almost there, the materials were available and the will to achieve was being fanned from an ember deep within himself into a roaring flame of desire and ambition. The smile on his face was one of deep satisfaction that could only come from someone who knew that they could turn a dream into reality.

He burst into the lab like a whirlwind the following morning, the diminutive, dark haired Suzie Fielding, his partner, had already been working since seven but John was about to blow her schedule apart.

"Suzie" he exclaimed, the excitement was plain to see, "I want to change direction!"

"Hmm, forever the idealist. What's wrong with what we're doing?"

"Nothing, but there's something more important that we need to do."

"Is it going to be ridiculously profitable?" she asked without raising her head from her computer.

"Don't know. Probably. I don't care. This is far more important!"

"Have you been to that bloody zoo again?" she said, showing her irritation.

"What makes you think that?"

"Well, yesterday was Sunday and you're normally miserable on a Monday, having been to the zoo... so what do you want to do?"

"Something that could change the world," he said flatly.

Suzie reluctantly dragged herself away from her computer, raising her eyebrows in his direction. "Really? I suppose you are going to tell me what this is all about, whether I want to know or not, so we might as well have a coffee and you can have my full attention for a whole ten minutes."

She may have been small at just over five feet tall, but she punched way above her weight in terms of both intellect and personality.

She rolled away from her desk on her chair and left it half way to the coffee machine on the other side of the room.

John watched her as her slim frame shimmered under the close-fitting white lab coat. There had never been any sexual tension between them in spite of the fact that they had been so close in the same environment since they met and worked together at university almost twenty years ago. He valued her as a business and research partner too much to risk any impediment arising from a personal relationship. But it didn't stop him from admiring her athletic figure.

She lifted the coffee jug and nonchalantly poured the steaming black liquid into two mugs, added a teaspoon of sugar to one and walked across to the conference room while John produced a sheaf of papers from his brown leather briefcase.

The room was large and windowless with a long rectangular table and twelve chairs in the centre and a collection of soft furniture at one end.

They sat down together on one of the plush four-seater sofas, Suzie handed John his coffee mug and said, "Okay, let's have it from the beginning. Why are we going to change the world and how can we afford to do it?"

"We are going to build real animals, animals that walk, eat, sleep and make noises exactly like the real thing. Eventually we are going to use this facility to produce a complete electronic zoo," he said with total conviction.

"But we haven't built anything like that before," Suzie

protested. "Besides, what would we do with such a collection when we have got one, we've got nowhere to keep them."

"It really is quite simple, we replace many of the animals, just mammals, in the zoo and the current incumbents will hopefully be moved out to safari parks where they can lead a far better life than is available to them at the moment."

John spread out the papers he had placed on the coffee table in front of them.

"I have prepared a list of animals that we would need to make, the initial cost of production will be met from the next two years R and D budget and if this comes off we will have the most saleable asset that you could ever imagine. The possibilities are limitless."

"How many different animals are we talking about here?" the look on Suzie's face was one of total incredulity.

"Oh, we need just over seventy if we're going to cover both sexes!" John replied, smiling broadly. "Do you think you could produce the programs to cope with the random behaviour patterns that we are going to need?" he asked, more seriously.

"Good grief, John, you're not asking much are you!"

"Well, could you do it?" he asked again with obvious enthusiasm.

Suzie cradled her mug in front of her chin and thought quietly for what seemed like an eternity to John.

"This isn't the same as producing CGI for films or TV you know, it's far more complex than that."

"So, what will you need?" he said, his enthusiasm gaining momentum.

"It will very much depend upon the information you can come up with. If we video the animals and use a computer analysis over, say, a three or four week period to get the behaviour patterns, we may be able to translate that into a working program. It's possible, yes. Very time consuming though."

She paused again to reflect on what she was being asked to do. John waited patiently, there was no point in pushing her, that never worked.

"If we do that with the animals that are already in the zoo we can reproduce the exact patterns that take place during the study period which can then be randomised so that they don't always do the same thing at the same point of the cycle, or even the time of day," Suzie concluded. "We would also need to factor in responses to human proximity as well. We don't want to turn a tiger into a pussy cat!"

"Then I have some serious work to do. I'll have to start by persuading the zoo to allow us in to do the recording. If we start with the biggest first, the elephants, rhino and one of the big cats we should be able to produce prototypes within three to six months."

"What's your excuse going to be?"

"I'll say that we are doing research for a film and we need very detailed studies for the special effects."

"That seems a bit thin, they probably won't believe you."

"When I offer to pay them I am sure they will agree, they're almost broke according to last year's accounts."

"Don't give away more than you have to... money, I'm talking about," she said sternly. "I mean it. I know what you're like!"

John nodded, thrilled that it had gone down so well. "Okay, don't worry, but I need to make sure it's enough to get their attention."

He made an appointment to see the zoo manager for the following morning and, as his head was buzzing so much, failed to produce any work of meaningful quality for the remainder of the day.

He arrived promptly at nine o'clock and was shown into the manager's office and was told by the secretary that Mr. Jackson would be back in a few minutes.

Arthur Jackson's office did not portray the personality of a fastidious man. It was small, untidy and looked as though it had not been cleaned for weeks. The air was thick with stale tobacco smoke, not surprising as the large glass ashtray was full to overflowing.

"This must be the designated smoking area for the zoo," he said sarcastically to himself.

The computer on his desk looked as though it had come into the zoo along with the first animals, no doubt delivered by a man called Noah.

Lever arch files were arranged on three shelves in a haphazard order and appeared to contain paperwork from various periods over the last five years.

There was a large aerial photograph of the zoo in a cheap wooden frame hanging opposite the window, five years old and beginning to fade due to the constant exposure to sunlight

The view from the window was at least pleasant, overlooking the grassy picnic area and the flamingo lake.

Just as John was deciding that it was probably not an appropriate place to start the most important venture in years, Arthur Jackson breezed into the office.

He was not a tall man, some four or five inches below John's six foot one and he was definitely at least fifty pounds overweight.

He offered John his hand in greeting and the handshake was firm and dry, much to John's surprise, and indicated for John to sit in the wooden chair opposite the desk.

"Hi. I'm sorry to have kept you waiting but one of the keepers failed to show up this morning so I had to lend a hand for an hour. The animals tend to prefer to keep to their routines and they get a little restless if they aren't let out of their cages on time. Now, what can I do for you?"

"Well," John started slowly, he had been through his approach in his mind several times before he arrived, but it didn't seem to fit with the man who now sat before him. "We have been asked to provide some special equipment for a film that is slated for shooting in the summer of next year, but to be able to produce it we have to be able to study animals at fairly close quarters..."

John was interrupted sharply.

"I have a feeling that you have come to the wrong place Mr. Hylton, I'm quite sure that your presence here would not be beneficial. For either of us. My secretary will show you out."

Jackson turned his head towards the unruly pile of papers on his desk and made a great show of searching for something. Anything, it seemed to John.

"I think you may have the wrong idea, Mr. Jackson," John said warily, "we don't want to do an investigation into how well the zoo is run, we simply need to find out how the animals behave so that we can reproduce the same behaviour patterns in the animals we have to create for the film".

"Why don't you use CGI animals in the film, like everybody else?"

"Authenticity with the human cast. It always looks fake when someone is interacting with something that doesn't exist."

"So what's in it for the zoo? Assuming that we find your motives are genuine."

"We are prepared to offer you a fee for the facility of setting up cameras and computers to monitor the animals, for a four month period, possibly a little longer so that we can be as thorough as possible. We have to be accurate. If we can find some common ground on the financial aspect..." he let it hang in the air.

It never ceased to amaze John how easily the talk of money put aside the suspicions of most people, and Jackson was not going to be in the minority on this occasion.

"The problem that confronts all zoos is that whilst they carry out important conservation work, breeding endangered species, they cannot always look after the animals in circumstances that are self sustaining and beneficial to the animals themselves."

Jackson slipped quite effortlessly into sales mode.

"Informing the public as to the environmental disasters facing many species, as well as putting on a show for people who otherwise would have no contact with animals, apart from cats and dogs, costs serious money and we have to make the most of whatever opportunities we can, So I am sure you will understand that whatever figure we agree upon, the benefit will go entirely towards the welfare of the animals in our charge."

John glanced casually around the room and was quite sure that money was not wasted on the creature comforts of the human inhabitants of the zoo.

"The figure I have in mind," John suggested "is fifty thousand pounds and we will also recompense you for any time that we need from you or your staff as and when we need it."

Jackson leaned forwards, clasped his hands under his chin and tried to appear thoughtful.

"Hmm, it sounds like a lot of money, but I'm certain that should you have to set up on location it would cost you at least ten times that amount to get the information you need"

"That would be true, if we wanted animals that were out in the wild, but we don't. We need to see how captive animals behave. There are also a number of other zoos we could approach with a project like this that would be very interested to hear our proposition."

The game rules had been set. The opening moves had been made and both knew the other's strengths, whilst each was hoping they would not reveal their weaknesses to the other.

"I will have to give it some thought, Mr. Hylton. It would be somewhat unfair to expect me to make a snap decision on something that could be so important for the zoo. This could, long term, make the difference between closure and survival."

"Of course, I would expect nothing less," John replied.

"If we do co-operate with you and we can come to an acceptable arrangement over fees, we would expect due credit to be given for our assistance."

It was becoming clear to John that Jackson was beginning to see the benefits that a wide exposure could give him. With good publicity came government grants and wealthy benefactors.

"Naturally we would see to it that you were given maximum publicity for your part and I am sure that you would benefit in other ways as a result," said John.

"Then shall we meet here again the same time tomorrow morning? That should give us both sufficient time to consider whether your offer is an appropriate one," Jackson said, clearly pleased with himself.

"I think that would be best for both of us," John said, rising from his seat. "While I am here do you mind if I look around to see if I can get some idea of the scale of the task confronting me?"

"Yeah, sure. Feel free to wander. Should you need any information just ask any of the keepers."

They shook hands and John left the office quietly confident that they would reach a satisfactory agreement the following morning.

As soon as John had left the room Jackson rang the zoo owner, Eric Daniels on his private line.

"Mr. Daniels, it's Jackson. I have just had an interesting meeting. Right out of the blue yesterday morning I got a phone call from a chap wanting to meet to discuss the possibility of studying animal behaviour. I thought it could be of use as we may get some really good publicity from it, generate some additional income and make life a bit easier all round. When we met this morning he made me an offer of serious money just to be allowed to study the animals. At first I thought he was another nut that wanted to make trouble and have the zoo closed down, but it appears that he needs a study for a film that he has to produce some kind of special effects for."

Daniels only asked one question. "How much did he offer?"

"Fifty thousand!" Jackson replied enthusiastically.

"Films have big budgets," Daniels observed. "See if you can double it, but don't mess it up for the sake of being too greedy."

The line went dead. Daniels rarely wasted words on pleasantries and other non-essentials. Jackson understood why.

He had his instructions, simple, make it a hundred thousand. There was no stated threat but he shifted uncomfortably in his chair. He was clearly expected to improve the offer, but if he couldn't he would not be allowed to forget the failure. If he lost the deal? That really really shouldn't happen.

Meanwhile John was walking around making notes in his phone. The first thing that occurred to him was that he had overestimated the number of animals that he had to consider. Being in a positive frame of mind made all the difference, emotions only ever served to confuse a scientific mind and should be avoided at all times.

It was true that all of the big cats were clearly in the wrong place. The bears, both white and brown varieties, were also not happy. Herd animals would definitely be better off in their natural environments, along with the rhinos. The gorillas appeared depressed although the chimps and most of the other primates seemed quite content. Other creatures such as hippos and virtually all of the water dwellers seemed quite happy with their lot, the facilities for those were relatively good and in the short term, behaviour studies for underwater animals would be far more challenging.

As for the reptiles, which were not John's favourites anyway, they were not up for consideration.

To set up cameras around the pens for the land animals was not going to be a problem and using WIFI systems meant that they could locate all of their main equipment in one place anywhere within the zoo.

He was going to need forty six cameras and at least a dozen maxed out computers to process the data.

Well, maybe three years R and D budget would just about cover it, he thought with a rueful smile.

Having found a suitable building: a virtually empty single storey equipment lock-up at the rear of the tiger enclosure, he spent the rest of the morning organising and reorganising his thoughts and establishing priorities.

The more he thought about it, the clearer it became. All he had to do was to make sure that he didn't give too much money away to get what he wanted.

He drove his white convertible Audi A5 back across town to his office, his mind racing through the future and the problems they were going to have to solve. Not once did he concentrate on driving. The traffic was light which was probably a good thing as, when he arrived and parked the car in the underground car park, he couldn't remember anything at all about the journey.

"Thank god the autopilot's working well," he said out loud to himself, slightly concerned at what he had achieved.

The building housing Animagination was, from the outside, an averagely attractive anonymous three storey construction built in red bricks with bronze reflective glass, and could have been home to almost any type of organisation. The air-conditioned building itself did not give any clues as to the extremely hi-tech environment that lay hidden underground.

He walked twenty yards to the stairs next to the elevator and went one floor up to the main reception area at ground level.

Barbara, the receptionist, acknowledged his arrival with a smile and a cheery "Good afternoon, Mr. Hylton," and watched him place the palm of his left hand onto the security sensor to the left of the red leather faced door at the rear of the hall. A green light appeared on the display above his hand and the door opened with a quiet hiss as the two inch thick steel-cored door swung open to permit his passage into a six foot wide expensively carpeted corridor - specially made in the company's three shades of blue - that gave access to what he called the 'inner sanctum'.

His office was the first door on the right, but he walked straight past it and on past Suzie's office, as she was very rarely in there, down to the end of the corridor to the lab where he anticipated Suzie would be slaving over her array of computers.

The door slid open in reaction to his entering the passive beam two feet in front of it. The only person in the room was Alan Fisher, Suzie's right hand man. A short but powerfully built man who had been addicted to computers and programming ever since he was given his first gaming machine at the age of eight. The first thing he did with it was to complain that the games weren't very good and that he thought he could do better. He was a whizzkid in every respect.

He was sitting at the far end of the central island of computers, tapping furiously at a keyboard with his right hand and operating a mouse with incredible speed with his left, an ability that always amazed John.

"Hi, do you know where I can find Suzie?" he asked, not wanting to interrupt Alan's train of thought any more than necessary

Without lifting his head or acknowledging the greeting he simply said "She's downstairs testing out the new routines we developed last week."

With that John moved quickly to the door in the left wall of the lab which again slid open as he approached revealing a set of carpeted stainless steel spiral stairs that led down to a small anteroom, which in turn gave access to the working heart of the building. John galloped down the stairs, which after years of practice he could manage with the confidence of a mountain goat. He opened the door to the construction area with a palm scan of the right hand.

The floor was almost ten thousand square feet of the most impressive equipment ever assembled in one place. The room was lit by panels of LED lamps designed to give the optimum stress-free lux level for the designated task in that area. The floor covering was non-slip anti-static sheet flooring - everything in the room was very carefully planned. It was a lesson he learned at a young age from one of his uncles: measure twice, cut once. The one thing that John hated more than anything was doing anything twice as that meant something had gone wrong in the planning stage.

The main floor area was open with several distinct production sections, each one staffed by two or three people dressed in white all-in-one suits. The long wall to the left was lined with four dust free, temperature constant 'clean rooms', each one approximately thirty feet by twenty.

The floor was L shaped with the control room situated in the short leg of the L at the far end on the right, that was where all new robots were tested and improved. It was separated from the main construction area by a fully glazed partition with laminated glass an inch thick that could withstand an explosion from a hand grenade. Not that they were expecting any explosions, it was just a precaution in case something went wrong.

He could see Suzie through the glass and went straight to the door which obediently opened for him.

"How's it going?" he asked with considerable interest as she moved a robotic arm simply by asking it to achieve a particular objective, how it did it was entirely up to the robot - the processor was "thinking".

"This is working just beautifully. We have now got it to complete tasks without telling it how to do them. The other wonderful aspect of this is that it performs without jerking at all, it accelerates and decelerates so smoothly, we have got a real breakthrough," she said without breaking her concentration. "I don't think it will be long before we can produce autonomous machines."

John looked pleased "Good, because what I have in mind we are going to need this and a whole lot more besides. How long will you be before you are finished here?"

"Probably about two weeks," she grinned, acknowledging his disapproving look. "Seriously though, about another fifteen minutes, I would think. I'll call you when I'm done and I'll meet you in the restaurant. Okay?"

"Yes, that's fine. I'm going to see Bob, find out how far he has progressed with the tissue he has been developing."

He turned and left the way he came in.

Bob Ayres was located diametrically opposite the control room in the far end clean room, next to the door to the stairs.

He had been working on a project for one of the major teaching hospitals, developing artificial limbs for people unfortunate enough to have lost their own. The best that could be offered to such people, in comparison with the limbs they had lost, were jerky, slow mechanical versions. Whilst the patients were pleased with the result, the alternative being literally nothing, John was always looking for improvement, with the eventual target of total reproduction and integration.

John watched through the glass wall.

"Hey, look at this, I think you will be pleased with this little beauty. Watch this," came the voice from within through the speaker above the glass.

He had set up a test with a length of brown fibrous material held between two points. One point was fixed to a chunky steel bracket on the workbench, the other was attached to a hydraulic ram designed to pull against the tissue and place a variable load on it. That way the destructive strength of the tissue could be measured.

The digital display above the ram showed 0.00kg. Bob turned on the power and the ram pulled against the tissue. He increased the power until the gauge read 250kg.

"That's a 60% improvement on the last compound you used," John said, impressed by what he saw.

"Yeah, but this is the good bit."

Bob bit his lip and turned the power on at the other end of the tissue. The tissue tightened quite noticeably and the gauge at the other end slowly returned to 0.00kg.

"That is brilliant. Have you tested it to find the failure point yet?"

"I haven't wanted to, this has succeeded in every test I've put it through so far. The big bonus is that this fibre takes a much lower level of power than anything else we have used before, it is about 94% efficient, much more than that and we would have perfection."

John's adrenalin level was beginning to rise. "How soon can we use it for a prototype?" he asked urgently.

"I don't see any reason why we wouldn't be ready to put it to use in a week or two, I still have a number of tests to run on it to find any possible defects under chemical and heat attack, but essentially this is the best formula we have come up with by a long way."

Bob knew something big was on its way, John never pressed for testing to be completed. Hurrying test procedures only meant cutting corners, and that usually meant more problems than it was worth.

"But I would prefer to manufacture and test at least three more batches before you try anything serious with it," he added.

"Alright, point taken, I was getting more excited than I should, but this looks the part and the timing couldn't be better. Keep me informed on any progress or problems please."

Another piece of the jigsaw dropped into place.

John felt a tap on his shoulder.

"I'm ready if you are," Suzie mischievously said.

"Oh, I'm always ready for you," he playfully responded.

He smiled, moved immediately to his right and summoned the elevator to take them to the second floor.

The highest floor in the building provided the recreation, eating, showering and leisure facilities.

John had learned a long time ago that if you looked after the health of your employees, both mental and physical, the returns were far greater than the investment. They had installed a state-of-the-art gym with computerised exercise machines, all of them monitoring heart, breathing and metabolic rates. All of the employees used the facilities on a regular basis, morning, noon or night.

There was also a sauna and an eight seat hot tub, which John often used when he wanted to ease the stress out of his mind.

Then there was the party room, which could also be turned into a sixty seat cinema, often used for client entertainment and presentations, although it was also famous for some of the more raucous Christmas parties.

Christmas, he thought, is coming in more ways than one.

The room they were heading for was the company restaurant. They ordered their lunch and occupied one of the tables, complete with white table cloth and four place setting. The catering was contracted in and the food selection, although fairly expensive to the company, was excellent and provided the starving workforce with a very well balanced and appetising lunch. It would be true to say that no-one went out for lunch unless someone else was paying.

The chairs were extremely comfortable, sometimes he thought they were too comfortable for a workplace, as he often didn't feel like going back to work after a good meal.

"Successful morning?" she enquired.

"So far, so good, but we haven't reached an agreement over money yet, although his eyes widened noticeably when I mentioned fifty thousand pounds. We have arranged for a return meeting tomorrow morning, where I would imagine we will settle on something above that."

"Is it worth that much? That's a hell of a lot of money for study purposes."

"You're right, but in the context of a film it's not very much at all and I don't think I could sell the idea to the zoo that wouldn't arouse their suspicions any other way. Money is a great satisfier and I would prefer Mr. Jackson to be co-operative and actively help us rather than set his mind against us by trying to screw him down to the point where he resents our presence. After all we are going to have to be there for at least three months if we are going to get data for all of the animals I want to produce."

The food arrived and they both ate in silence for a few minutes.

"When do you want to set up down there, assuming that we reach agreement tomorrow?" he asked.

"The control program we have been working on is straightforward and almost complete, Alan should have it wrapped up by the end of this week I would think. He will be the one to put it all in place and make sure the programs are operating properly. So anytime after the middle of next week. I can get the systems section to assemble the hardware we are going to need by then as well."

John nodded his approval.

"As long as we can get the cameras I want, I can't see why, on that basis, we can't be up and running within three weeks. That will take us up to the first week in December, just about giving us time to get through the first phase by Christmas," she said matter of factly.

"Excellent."

Everything was working out quite neatly. John knew that she would have the entire installation set up and working on time, she was such a brilliant organiser. He also knew he was very lucky to have her as a partner.

"I think that it would be quite helpful to the cause if you came with me to meet Jackson tomorrow morning, your presence would probably take any possible edge out of the negotiating and keep things relaxed."

"As long as we are away from there by eleven, I can make it," she said pensively.

They finished their food in silence, both deep in thought about the monumental tasks that lay ahead.

Planning, John knew, was the critical part of any project, get it wrong and nothing that follows will work out without a battle.

He had considered a hundred different possible problems, and a potential solution for everyone of them, but there was something that was bothering him and he just couldn't see what it was.

They arrived for the meeting the following morning half an hour early to give Suzie the opportunity to look around the zoo first. It was a cold still morning, their voices carried easily on the sharp dry air.

"It's odd how you can come to a zoo and not take notice of how the animals feel," Suzie said, showing a surprising empathy. "I suppose on the occasions I have been here in the past I have considered it mainly as entertainment and only partially educational, without ever considering whether the animals actually enjoy being here, but when you come to see them for a purpose you look at them in a totally different way."

She was feeling the discomfort of the zoo and comparing how she thought she would feel if her freedom were to be suddenly taken away from her.

"The big problem with many of these animals is not just that they are in captivity but that they cannot be returned to the wild. A lot of them were born in captivity and most of the rest were brought there because their real homes were under threat or had already been destroyed. The best we can do for most of them is to find somewhere else for them to live. Have you seen enough for the moment?" John asked. Thinking about the life of a zoo animal only lowered his spirits, which was not what he needed at that moment.

"Yes, we'd better go and see if we can change the world," she said with a warm, sympathetic smile.

When they arrived at Jackson's office they found he was already waiting for them, they could tell that he was slightly apprehensive, which as far as John was concerned was an excellent sign.

Jackson greeted them with an over effusive "Good morning" and hearty handshakes all round.

John introduced Suzie as his partner and Jackson visibly appraised her appearance and it was quite clear from his reactions that he approved of her presence.

John smiled inwardly and thought 'Don't ever play poker Mr. Jackson, you'd be looking for a new shirt.'

They were ushered into Jackson's office and his secretary disappeared to collect an extra chair.

Jackson said "I hope you don't mind but I thought it would make life easier if Alice sits in on the meeting to take a few notes and it will also keep the balance in the beauty stakes."

Suzie looked at John with raised eyebrows and a slight smile.

John thought that it was a bit of a hamfisted compliment, but said nothing.

Alice returned with a battered looking straight backed wooden chair, which, on reflection, Suzie thought was only marginally worse than the chairs they were sitting on, with the foam padding grinning through the well worn grey cloth.

"Now then," Jackson started, "we all know why we are here. I have been doing some soul searching and I have decided that although the offer you put forward yesterday was interesting, we feel that..."

"We feel?" interrupted Suzie, sharply.

"Er, yes. I was, er, airing my views to Alice yesterday afternoon. I feel that the offer you made of fifty thousand, whilst it is a large sum of money, doesn't represent the value of the study to you for your film project. We would therefore expect you to considerably increase your offer before we can consider it fully," Jackson felt he had opened well.

"What sort of figure do you have in mind?" Suzie politely enquired.

"Well not to put too fine a point on it, we would be looking for nearer one hundred and twenty-five thousand... er, plus expenses, of course."

John let out a low whistle. "That, I am afraid is way beyond our budget, Mr. Jackson. We do have another zoo interested, but as we are both in the same city, it makes more sense to work with you if we can, but seventy-five thousand pays for a lot of travelling time."

"I am sure that it does, Mr. Hylton but what we are asking for is entirely justifiable under the circumstances."

"The circumstances being" Suzie interjected "that as films have large budgets we can afford to pay ridiculous sums of money to people like you that don't deserve it."

The look on her face was as scathing as the words she spoke.

"I am sorry you see it that way Miss, Ms. Fielding, but I am only trying to protect the interests of the zoo and do the best for the animals in my charge," countered Jackson.

"I think we can appreciate that," John was more conciliatory, "but I am afraid that we don't have the type of budget that you seem to think. You see, we had to bid for this work and we did not allow for that type of money purely for rent. The best we can offer you would be seventy-five thousand plus expenses, but the expenses would have to be limited to labour and materials for converting the store and no further fees for assistance with the animals."

"I see. Perhaps it would be better to put a definite figure on it to include the expenses, say a round one hundred thousand."

Jackson came to that figure a little too quickly and John immediately realised that it was the amount he had been instructed to try for. The expenses in converting the store would probably be no more than seven or eight thousand and they would have the improved facility when they had finished. John decided to stake it all on one last play.

"Ninety thousand all in. That is the absolute limit. If you can't accept at that we will have to go elsewhere."

Jackson squirmed in his seat. It had not gone quite as well as he had hoped, but he kept thinking about the reward he would receive if he came away with nothing at all.

"If I accept, we would expect fifty per cent up front and the rest spread over three months. We would also allow you to remain here until the end of May if need be."

Jackson was clearly sweating.

Suzie wound up the conversation.

"We will pay you twenty thousand within five days, then ten thousand a month starting next month and any balance when we leave."

The tone of her voice indicated that it was not negotiable.

"Hmm, I think we can work with that," Jackson relaxed almost instantly, clearly relieved that it was over. He hadn't got everything but he had got most of it and a much needed injection of cash immediately. He also began to regret welcoming Suzie Fielding into the meeting, very attractive she may be, but the woman was obviously made of granite.

"We will instruct our lawyers to draft a simple agreement, we will transfer the money as soon as your employer has signed and returned the agreement," John said, allowing a knowing smile to appear on his face and Jackson almost sheepishly acknowledged it.

At least he personally hadn't made any enemies, Jackson thought. Although as he offered his hand to Suzie he did wonder whether he wanted her as a friend anyway.

John and Suzie headed straight for the exit and John said "You played a bit rough in there, didn't you."

"He needed it. Besides, I enjoyed it."

"I feel like celebrating," John said with a grin

"Well I've got work to do and besides, this is only the beginning and we've got a long way to go before we do any celebrating," she stated in a way that wasn't open for discussion.

Tough lady, John thought, as he drifted back to earth again.

Chapter 3

During the course of the following week John divided his time between the office and the zoo. At the office his enthusiasm was becoming infectious, even though only Suzie, at that stage, was aware of the real reasons for the project.

His appearance at the zoo was accepted without question as it was expected that he would be in overall control of the project, although he spent most of his time there finalising the very long shortlist of animals they were to attempt to recreate. One animal that John felt very sorry for was a lone black panther, he decided that it would have to be the first one.

The whole installation was planned out very quickly by Alan, who had been given the project to control on site, and the zoo staff, who were quite used to executing building work at short notice, worked quickly and efficiently. Within six days the building work had been completed and the control room was complete with its new wooden floor and freshly painted walls.

It took a further three days to get the air conditioning and the final electrical installation completed.

The cameras were installed initially around the pens containing the panther, lions, rhinoceros, elephants, zebra and chimps. The external cameras were located so that every possible area was covered by at least two cameras and each internal sleeping house also had two cameras installed. The aim was to record and evaluate the behaviour of the dominant animal in each pen and that was achieved by the zoo vet implanting a small transmitter under the skin at the back of the neck of the designated beasts. That enabled the cameras to lock on to the signal and follow the same animal at all times.

The behaviour, sounds and expressions were going to be monitored twenty four hours a day.

John sat alone in the gloom in his office, it was Saturday evening, beginning of December, only three working weeks to Christmas. The mood was different though. The room may have been gloomy but the feelings were definitely up-beat. John had left the zoo that afternoon in a very different frame of mind to that of almost two weeks before.

He picked up the phone and called Suzie.

"Hi John," she answered almost immediately.

"Two weeks," he said "is a long time in science. It's been a long time since anything truly ground breaking happened, but what we are doing could change the whole face of industry if it came off.

"I agree, it seems as though everything we are working on at the moment has its part in the project. Maybe there is a grand design after all."

John laughed out loud.

"Well that's good to hear, it's been a while since I heard you laugh," she said with a smile in her voice.

"On Monday morning we will start for real. Alan will be monitoring the animals, recording and evaluating, Bob's finished the tests on the muscle tissue he's been working on and is really excited about that. How much longer before you've finished your programming?"

"It should be done by the end of the week. It's only an adaptation of our existing software, but I won't be able to do any more than test it in simulation until we have something built."

"Then the next part of the project is to work on building the skeletal structure of the panther, followed by the rhino and elephant, but that can wait until Monday morning, see you then."

"Goodnight, John, take a day off, don't go to the zoo tomorrow please."

"Yes, miss!" he said jokingly.

Suzie went to the zoo before going in to the office, so John went in to see Bob Ayres first. He was in his office, located at the far end of the ground floor beyond the design lab, through a door in the right wall bearing the inscription "Dr. Jekyll's Room".

Turning from his computer, Bob greeted John "Good morning. You look pleased with yourself today."

"I was just smiling at the thought of changing the sign on your door to "Dr. Frankenstein's Room", it might be slightly more appropriate after what I am about to tell you."

John sat six feet away from him on a spare chair.

"I'm all ears. And legs. And Arms." Bob laughed.

"Ok. Seriously now. What difficulties can you see in using the tissue that you completed last week."

Bob looked slightly puzzled. "That depends on what you want

to use it for. At the moment it has cleared all of the tests we have subjected it to. It is consistent, its strength is far better than human tissue, it has resisted virtually everything we have thrown at it except extreme heat."

"How hot does it need to be before it fails?"

"It will take up to 230° Celcius before there is any effect at all, but then it goes into total meltdown. So at the moment its uses will be limited by that. Endurance and recovery are as almost as good as infinite and immediate respectively, but it is a little early to say. We tested one sample for forty eight hours continuously without any reduction in capacity or change in the response time. I would say it is ready for a field test now. Got something in mind?" Bob held his breath in anticipation.

"If I said to you, I want to replicate an animal, what would you say?"

Bob sat bolt upright. "Actually go straight to producing a walking talking animal?"

John nodded.

"When do we start? What sort of animal?"

"We think we have almost all of the answers now, it appears that Alan and Suzie are close to completing the basic programming. What we are looking at now is turning those individual programs into sub-routines for the control system. So while they are working on that we can get started on the structure. We need to build a working skeletal system and then clad it with your tissue, switch it on and see if it works! Slightly simplified of course, but it seems as though we are almost ready for it. And as there is no point in messing about I thought we would start off with a panther!" John waited for a reaction.

"My God, you're not messing about are you?" The disbelief on Bob's face was entirely understandable.

"Well. if you're going to do something it might as well be a good one. I'll leave you to think about it for a while, I'll call back in an hour or so when I've spoken to the rest of the team."

Suzie was in the brightly lit control room at the zoo, leaning over Alan's shoulder and staring into one of six huge split screens that filled the entire end wall of the room, She was watching the computerised scan of the black panther. The program they had developed together received the pictures from the three cameras that were currently tracking the beast, converted the digital images into a single three dimensional image which the computer then could store as digital data and then allowed the operator to view the subject from any angle with free rotation and close inspection.

"I think that now we are up and running that I have to tell you just what the initial intentions of this project are," Suzie hesitated for a moment, unsure of how best to proceed.

Alan sensed her dilemma.

"You mean that we don't actually have a contract to produce special effects for a film," he said, supplying her with the starting point.

"No, we don't, but we do want to build some very special robots for our own purposes. We want to produce a number of different animals to replace the animals in the zoo that are entirely unsuited to being here, without destroying the zoo. The zoo does carry out important work and we don't wish to damage that work, it's just that a lot of animals here are paying the price for that work. We believe that we are in a unique position to change the situation to the benefit of all concerned."

"And nobody at the zoo suspects anything?"

"No, the less they know now the better it will be for us all. At the moment they are just pleased that they have been paid a lot of money and still have a lot more to come. As long as they concentrate on the money and don't have cause to feel threatened we should be able to complete our work here untroubled."

Alan looked pensive.

"So we continue with the original story until the time is right and we have something to show them."

Suzie nodded.

"If we don't they are bound to misunderstand our motives, especially having had to deceive them to get in here... and there wouldn't be another zoo in the country that would allow us through its gates."

"The only thing that puzzles me now is why you told me, you didn't need to tell me anything until my work here had been completed."

"There are three reasons why. Firstly, we trust you completely, secondly, you would you have to know sometime soon and thirdly, John should be bringing some physiological data this afternoon. The Natural History Museum has agreed to lend us their data on the muscular construction of all of the animals we are studying, it will save us a huge amount of work" she said, whilst appearing to concentrate on four sets of co-ordinates which were changing constantly in the top right hand corner of the screen in front of Alan as the animals moved.

All of the information was being continuously stored on Thunderbolt raids, one dedicated for each of the Mac Pros they were using. With that system they were able to monitor six animals, all tracked by RFIDs, for twenty four hours a day for the initial four week period without changing the setup at all. At night, when most of the animals were least active the storage used was minimal as the program they had devised only recorded changes in the images that were sent by the cameras.

"When John arrives I want you to integrate the data with the programs we are running so that we can digitise the animals completely, reduce the images to the level of the muscle structure and then we can analyse the muscle usage to program the animals we are going to make. This way the computers will do all of the work for us. They will effectively be creating an automatic brain so that movement becomes as much second nature to the cybers as it is to the real animals," she said.

Alan was completely nonplussed by what had been revealed to him that morning. Although he was used to working at the cutting edge of technology he seemed to be having some difficulty coming to terms with what they were now doing.

"Is this what we have been working on for the past fifteen months?"

Suzie turned back to face him and looked straight into his eyes "No, we have been working on this for precisely two weeks. In many ways this is a natural extension of what we have been working on throughout the company for the past two years or so, but this project is completely impulsive on John's part and wouldn't have happened at all but for his concern for animals."

She watched him visibly relax. she hadn't been sure how he would take the deception that they felt had been necessary, but she realised that it would have been better if he had been told the plan right from the start. Alan was intensely loyal to her but it had been John's project and he had wanted as little information revealed as possible.

Alan turned back to the computer, "It shouldn't take long to work through the program to give you a provisional construction set, if that is what you need to get started in the lab," Alan's mood was picking up by the second and the more he thought about it the more excited he was becoming. "Presumably you are going to want to build a prototype as soon as possible? If John gives me what I need this afternoon I could have an initial set for you by late tomorrow afternoon. There won't be any behaviour or character patterns but you should at least have a complete scan and muscle analysis. Which one do you want me to start with?"

"The black panther," she said flatly.

"Ooh, very symbolic" he observed with a wry smile.

Chapter 4

Jackson sat in his office picking at his fingernails and staring out of the window at the drizzly rain that was running down the glass. A lot of things had happened very quickly during the last two weeks. The organisation that had been displayed by John Hylton's people had been superb, there was no doubt about that, but what he couldn't quite get used to was the fact that there was something going on in the zoo that he had no control over whatsoever. Oh, it was true that the money they had been paid so far was going to be extremely useful and Daniels was going to allow all of the money to stay within the zoo, but he didn't like the fact that he appeared to have a no-go area within his zoo. The control room had a sophisticated entry system and alarm that he, Jackson, was not privy to. He had asked if he could be allowed to see what they were doing in there but Alan Fisher had politely but firmly declined to allow him in through the door. There had been no agreement for access to be provided, but there again there had been no agreement that it wouldn't be provided either.

Jackson concluded that he was only thinking that way because with just three weeks to go before Christmas he had the feeling that he wanted to be involved with something, anything.

Having divorced five years before, with no children, his parents both dead and no immediate relatives, Christmas was not a time to be cheerful as far as he was concerned. The only person he talked to on a regular basis was the bartender at the bar he escaped to every night after the zoo closed, which during December was 4.30pm and in forty minutes that was precisely where he would be heading.

John Hylton, by contrast, was enjoying his afternoon with Alan in the control room. They had loaded in all of the information that John had brought in from the Museum and the results were looking absolutely spectacular.

"It fits like a glove" Alan declared, "the data was assimilated far more easily than I expected."

They were watching the panther, not black anymore, pacing around in its compound totally naked, not even with the dignity of its skin. Not that the poor creature that had been laid so bare was at all concerned as the image had been created only by the genius of the computer. "Come back this time tomorrow and you shall have all of the information you need for Bob and his team to start working their little miracles," he enthused.

"These are exciting times, Alan, we are creating history, not just cybers. You had better shut up shop now, our friend will be wanting to lock up his charges for the night very soon. I'll see you tomorrow."

Jackson watched from his window as John walked past below with his coat collar pulled up against the intrusion of the cold wet weather. There seemed to be a bounce to his step in spite of the unpleasant precipitation.

"What has he to be so pleased about?" he asked out loud, "Things are clearly going well for the man."

He left his office and went down to the keepers' lodge where he sought out his head keeper Pete Thomas. It was an ancient brick and tile building with whitewashed walls inside. It was where the recreation and changing rooms for the keepers were located. The facilities were pretty basic and hadn't been improved since the nineteen eighties, but Jackson was quite happy with them, after all, he didn't have to use them.

He spotted his quarry coming out of the changing room, having returned to civilian clothing. He was a small wiry man in his late forties, with greying hair and a thin weasely face. He wasn't Jackson's favourite by any means but he was superb with the animals and his knowledge was far greater than anyone else's in the zoo.

"Pete, how's it going?"

"No problems, unless you want to sort out the plumbing in this place, it rattles and clanks like an old bus. You'll probably have to replace it this winter anyway if it freezes up again."

It was a familiar gripe, he complained at least once a week during the winter, generally because the keepers spent more time thawing and drying themselves out in the lodge during the winter months. The summer was completely different, the zoo was busier, there were far more jobs to do and apart from the occasional rainstorms the weather didn't affect them in the same way.

"I think you're right, the advent of our scientific friends has provided us with some unexpected cash, which at this time of year is very welcome. If you will do something for me, I will fund an upgrade to the facilities in here," Jackson said as he tried to smile benevolently.

The look on Pete Thomas's face was total distrust, he had been complaining for five years about the state of the lodge and here it was given to him on a plate. "What do you want me to do, break into Fort Knox over there?"

"Nothing illegal, I simply want you to find out as much as you can about the work our friends are carrying out, ask questions, keep your eyes and ears open and keep me informed. That's not much to ask, is it?"

"Alright, but I want to start on this place straight away, not leave it until after you find out what you want to know."

He had been given promises before that had not been fulfilled.

"No problem, you can spend five thousand on materials but you do the work yourselves at slack times. I'll leave it entirely up to you what you spend it on so make it go as far as you can on things that count!"

Jackson turned to leave, Thomas had a smile on his face. It dropped slightly when Jackson hesitated by the door.

"Do you think that you could plant a microphone somewhere so we can listen in on them?"

Pete could see his deal disappearing, shaking his head.

"Only if they let me into the building, there's no way in, now that they've put their security system in," he said, miserably

Jackson could see the enthusiasm that had been present shrivel in the man's eyes.

"No matter, just find out what you can, but carry on with this place anyway. Give it some thought though please," Jackson said amicably.

Thomas could hardly believe what had just happened and resolved to get a mike in there if he could.

Jackson let himself back out into the worsening weather. Pouring rain was fine for hippos and crocs, but not so much for the slight rheumatism in his hands.

He wished he'd had the sense to take an umbrella with him as he ran as fast as his unfit and overweight body would allow back towards his office. Just as he reached his door he saw the tail lights of Alan's Jeep disappear out through the gates and moments later he could hear the sound of Pete Thomas's car growl into life. He disappeared into the grubby reception area, ran his hand over his wet hair then wiped his hand on his trouser leg.

"Maybe we can tidy this up a bit as well, a lick of paint and a new carpet wouldn't go amiss," he said out loud. He walked over to the door on the far wall behind Alice's desk, opened it and punched the six digit code into the alarm panel on the back wall of the store cupboard. The system carried out its survey of the zoo automatically, checking each of the sixteen zones consecutively, a real pain, he thought, why can't it do them all at once and save me five minutes a day? He answered himself by saying "Because it's old and out of date like so many things around here."

The alarm finished its work and instructed him to leave the offices within two minutes. The final task he had to perform was to enter a second six digit code into the keypad by the back gate, which would automatically open to let him out and then slide the ten foot wide iron gate back into place, lock it and activate the entire alarm system.

He waited on the outside for the gate to close with its resounding clunk and then drove off to sink an ice cold beer or three.

Suzie and John at that time were enjoying a lukewarm cup of coffee in Suzie's office. It was a spartan room, without any indication of the gender of its occupant. The only picture frames hung on the wall were those containing her academic certificates of achievement and two certificates with winners medals attached for two triathlon races she had won some four years before. There were no pictures of children or family, she had never been married, she hadn't had the time. She had devoted her life to finding both her physical and mental limits and whilst she was still pushing back the latter she felt she had reached her physical limits, without impinging on her worklife, and at the age of thirty nine was quite content to keep extremely fit in the gym and explore the waters of the world whenever the opportunity arose. For her, her work stretched her mind, exercise stretched her body and scuba diving was the ultimate relaxation for both, whilst still providing a challenge.

"This is moving faster than you thought isn't it?" she asked.

"There's no doubt that we have achieved a lot recently but it is only because we have had a specific purpose and a focus for several different areas of our research simultaneously," he said, pausing momentarily. "The only thing that concerns me at the moment, is that there may be a moral side to this that we haven't considered properly. While we are not tampering with nature as the geneticists do, we are going to be in a position to replace nature with machines to some extent. I just want to make sure that we don't end up providing someone with the excuse to wipe out all of the animals because we have the perfect replacements. It wouldn't take some of the more unscrupulous nations of this world long to realise that they no longer have to keep to the international environmental agreements because we have given them the perfect escape clause."

The pained expression on John's face was plain to see. It was a major dilemma, that as long as the secret stayed within the company the problem would not arise, but without bringing their achievements out into the open they would be unable to use them for their own financial gain.

She contemplated what he had said for a moment and then argued with it.

"But as scientists we should not concern ourselves totally with moral issues, morals are for the people that use our products. Provided that we don't knowingly produce them for an immoral purpose then we can't be held responsible for those who eventually use them. Look, when we were approached by that arms manufacturer to produce robots for handling contaminated or dangerous material, we didn't have a problem with that and refuse to have anything to do with it. So in what way is this different? We can take a moral view, but it has to be a wide view. A cutlery manufacturer can't stop making knives just because someone gets stabbed with a steak knife."

"You're right, of course, but we will have to build in some safeguards otherwise we may end up providing someone else with a means to an end."

Suzie stood up, stretched herself up to her full height of five foot one, pushed her hands through her shoulder length dark brown hair and said "Well, I've had enough for one day, I'm going up for a workout. Do you fancy a twenty mile bike race?"

"Race against you? Not a chance. I wouldn't want to humiliate you," he said with a grin "but I'll gladly keep you company while you burn yourself out."

Chapter 5

Tuesday mornings, for Jackson, were reserved for the tedious task of management accounts. Alice for her part kept the books in a simple fashion on her computer, taking care of the revenue from the various shops and kiosks around the zoo and entering the purchase invoices.

It was Jackson's job to complete the accounts and produce forecasts, and decide what to do with any excess profits, not that there were any for ten months of the year. The zoo tended to run at a loss other than for July, August and holiday weekends, so at least with it only being December they would not begin to find things tight until April. He sat at his desk scrolling up and down pages of information on his computer screen when his telephone rang. It startled him at first as he had a standing instruction for Tuesday mornings not to be disturbed.

Alice apologised for bothering him but, as it was Mr. Daniels she thought that he had better take the call.

"Good morning Mr. Daniels."

"How are our friends progressing?" the voice was deep, flat and slightly unfriendly.

"They appear to be very pleased with themselves at the moment, but they have only been up and running properly for a day so far. They've installed a security system that we are not party to, so we can't come and go as we would like. I've asked Pete Thomas to keep his eyes peeled and ask questions whenever he can, as he has more contact with them than I do, but..." he was interrupted

"I want to know precisely what they are doing and what progress they are making. I want a full report by the end of the week."

The phone went dead.

Jackson sat looking at the phone in his hand, and wondered just why the man had to be so rude. The only time he had actually been pleasant to him was when he interviewed for the job six years ago. They usually only met two or three times a year, which was four times too many as far as Jackson was concerned. Usually when some new animals were about to be brought into the zoo. Daniels seemed to spend at least eight months of the year out of the country - most likely to avoid tax, he thought cynically. Although he had never denied him access to funds when they were desperately needed, he had always had to justify everything twice over. Daniels made everything such hard work.

Alan Fisher sat in front of his screen wall, carefully watching the panther. He had watched it for three quarters of an hour already and had seen it do nothing different from the previous day. The animal simply paced around his pen, first one way then back again. Occasionally stopping to peer out through the armour plated glass in the boundary wall, but it didn't do anything remotely interesting other than to climb up its tree in the centre of the enclosure. Alan was not particularly concerned about the animal at that stage but unless it did something a little more strenuous before the afternoon, the initial set he had promised John would be a little short on what he had anticipated.

Seeing that very little was going to happen to the solitary creature, he rose from his comfortable chair and went out to find the head keeper, the door automatically locking behind him.

He found Pete Thomas at the lodge, holding an informal meeting with the eight other keepers immediately under his control, discussing the refurbishment of the lodge - by far the most important event until the next feeding time at eleven o'clock.

As soon as he saw Alan walk into the room, he thought that he might soon get an opportunity to get some spying done, and briefly smiled to himself at the thought of it.

"Good morning. Mr. Fisher, isn't it? I presume you must be looking for me."

"Yes, one of the gardeners told me I might find you here. Can we talk somewhere? I have a small problem you might be able to help me with."

"Sure, come through into my, er, office."

He led Alan towards a door in the back wall of the main room, on his way past one of the tables he gathered up a coffee mug and turned to one of the other keepers and said "Make our guest a coffee, will you. We'll have to continue our meeting at lunchtime."

He continued on to the door and ushered Alan into a small room containing a table with an old computer, a telephone and an assortment of paperwork sat in a stack of three wire trays. There were also two cheap plastic chairs, one either side of the table. He motioned Alan to sit on one of them, he pulled out the other on the opposite side of the table.

"I'm sorry, I didn't want to interrupt you but I am on a fairly tight schedule at the moment and I'm a little stuck," Alan said apologetically.

"That's okay. So tell me how I can help you."

"The panther is our prime subject at the moment, and as he's on his own we can't see how he relates to others. He seems to be stuck in a rut, he appears listless, as though he wants to do something but has no prospects."

"It's his own fault. When he had a mate he went crazy and attacked her so we had to take her away. The only time he goes crazy now is at feeding time. It seems as though he can smell the meat as soon as we open the cold store door."

Alan was slightly puzzled.

"Yet when you fed him yesterday morning he was quite docile?"

"That was because we fed him first. Feeding time is in another half hour, you will probably get what you want if we feed him last, but in return, could you show me what you're doing in there, my curiosity will kill me soon?" he asked hopefully.

"I don't see why not," Alan was only too pleased to have a solution to his problem.

The door opened and a young man in a grubby keeper's uniform strode in through the door and placed a mug of coffee in front of Alan. He thanked him, although the state of the mug led him to believe that it might be safer not to touch it without gloves, let alone drink out of it.

"I wouldn't either," Pete said, reading his mind, "that boy probably lives like a hippo at home as well. I would suggest that you call in at the coffee shop until feeding time."

Alan took him at his word and went back out the way he came in.

Alan sat watching the screen showing the panthers pen. Each screen was divided into four sections with a camera image occupying each section. It had been ten minutes since the keepers started their rounds. They had deliberately driven their electric feeding carts passed the panthers pen first. The cat had immediately become more active and agitated in its movements and was beginning to get quite grumpy. Every time someone passed the windows it leapt as though it was in the jungle and the last antelope on earth was within its sight. Time and again it threw itself at the glass, snarling and growling, flashing its savage white teeth.

Damn glad I'm not in there, Alan thought with a shiver, but he was getting precisely what he wanted. He glanced at the corresponding computer screen and could see a flurry of activity, the three dimensional image was constantly changing, showing only the animal, without it's fur coat. Even those images transmitted the fury and immense power of the beautiful animal.

The panther had been 'complaining' for almost twenty minutes, but Alan could see from the monitors that its food was finally being delivered. The food was placed in a one way stainless steel chute next to the entrance to the pen. The keeper then closed the chute, pushed a small green button on a control pad to the left side, the chute then rotated to disgorge its contents into the pen on the other side of the wall. The panther braced itself some fifteen feet away from the meat, sank down on its haunches and in a blink of an eye was sailing through the air to land on its prey. It didn't immediately start eating, instead it ripped into the meat with its claws and teeth, shaking its head violently from side to side, in much the same way as a pet dog might play with a rag, only it wasn't play. It was pure violence.

There was a knock on the door, Alan glanced at the security monitor and could see Pete Thomas from both the side and front. Alan pushed himself up out of his chair and casually sauntered across to the door. He opened the door and saw the rear view of the head keeper.

"I was just admiring your handiwork, I heard the camera motors behind me. Very clever, is there anything you can't keep your eye on from in there?" he asked with a tone that suggested he did not welcome the intrusion.

"All of the cameras are programmed to follow their selected animals. To override that, if I wanted to, would mess up the surveillance data if I decided to follow something other than the nominated target. Nice thought, but entirely impractical." Alan immediately thought of pretty ladies on hot summer days, and then inwardly admonished himself for such unprofessional thoughts, but it didn't take the smile off his face.

He gestured for Pete to enter, closed the door behind him and led him across to the business end of the room and proceeded to explain what each of the monitors was showing.

"What type of effects are you going to produce with all of this?" Pete said moving his arm in an arc across the array in front of him.

"The idea is quite simple. We follow the selected animals with the cameras, digitise the pictures into one to produce a single 3D image, rather like a hologram within the computer. With the detailed studies we will have of the animals, we will know precisely how they move and react to a given situation. I don't know yet precisely what is going to be required of us, but I have a feeling that the footage we got just now of the panther is the type of thing I could do with from each of the animals. I'm not suggesting that you go and spook an elephant, but provided we get to see the elephants running in their field as well as throwing back its head and trumpeting, we can combine the two to show an elephant looking like it's on a charge. Put that into a 3D film and you will think that the elephant is charging right out of the screen and on to your lap," Alan smiled at the thought he had just planted in the keeper's mind

"I would have thought that they could do that sort of thing already," Pete stated, not appearing to be impressed.

"It's the level of reality that's required. Although current CGI is the best yet, it's just a bit too easy to tell it's not real. We want to take away the necessity to suspend disbelief and really make you jump out of your seat if a panther is coming in your direction!"

"Well that would be something if you can make that happen!"

Pete glanced at his watch and indicated it was time for him to leave.

"Thanks for showing me this stuff, very impressive indeed, but time to get back to work," he said, turning for the door.

"Sure, any time."

Alan opened the door to let him out and watched as he sloped off to report to Jackson.

John arrived after a slightly later lunch than he had anticipated, but, as he explained to Alan, he had just had to endure the most dreadful five-star lunch with his best client paying the bill.

"Some people are born to suffer. Next time let me suffer in your place," Alan gently chided him.

"Tell me what you have got so far then."

Alan proceeded to tell him about the encounter with Thomas,

adding only that he had seemed a little too pleased to see him and suggested that maybe he had been wanting an opportunity to look around.

"It's quite possible he is following instructions. I'll bet that Jackson's curiosity is biting his leg right now. After all he's not been in here yet. I think we'd better put on a bit of a show for him in a couple of days, something to really impress him that will keep him quiet for a week or two. Show me what you've got with the panther so far."

Alan played back the recording of the panther at feeding time.

"Oh, that's just perfect, exactly what we need. We wouldn't want to use that too often, it would frighten the living daylights out of most people, but it illustrates the likely response in a danger situation."

They skipped through the recordings on the rhinos and elephants, ignored the zebras for the time being, and downloaded the panther's data onto an external drive which John took straight back to the office and handed it to Bob Ayres.

"I think you should find this rather interesting. It's fascinating seeing an animal without its clothes on but the information you'll get from this should prove invaluable. How's the skeleton coming on?"

"Sally and her team are doing well. The bone construction should be completed in a couple of days or so. Using 3D printing made making the moulds for the bones so easy that she's already made a start on making them, I believe that she's seven down, a hundred and ninety seven to go. She settled on using Celazole reinforced with carbon fibre so it's lightweight and almost indestructible. The cartilage is going to be made with modified silicone to give a really tough, smooth connection and virtually friction free. We will have no trouble bonding the muscle tissue in place and by placing fibre control wires into the tissue you will have maximum flexibility and control built in. What are you planning to power it with?"

"I was discussing that with Suzie last night during a bike ride, we don't want to use anything hazardous, but we have to have enough power to last a few months. We concluded that, for now, lithium batteries, the same ones Tesla use, would probably be the best bet. We can pack them into the chest cavity along with the main processor as well as in some of the larger bones in the elephants and rhinos. That should probably give us three months use and should give us plenty of time to retrieve them for recharging. What I would like to do though is to try and incorporate a solar charging facility if at all possible."

"That would be tough under a layer of fur!"

"Yes, might have to skip that on the panther. Standard electrical charging port for him then. How about integrating something into the horns and tusks?" John asked.

"That might work as they would be permanently exposed to the sun, it would have to be something special though as normal PV panels wouldn't work there. There was an Indian company working on some prototype powdered material I read about a few months back, I'll see what I can find."

"It would be good if at all possible, but not essential. Have you had any further thoughts since yesterday?"

"I must admit I've thought of very little else, my wife was convinced I was on Pluto last night I was that far away. There are several points I think we need to look at quite carefully though. As far as the design and construction is concerned I don't think we will have any serious problems, Suzie and Alan will get the programming sorted, the power supply is set, and the rest will be complete by the end of this week, but what if it falls into someone else's hands? We have to be able to prevent anyone from taking it apart."

"You mean if someone decides to remove it from the zoo?"

"That would be fun, trying to get an elephant into the back of a truck that is programmed to stay where it is!"

"It doesn't have to be an elephant. If an EMP were used it could switch off the panther."

"So we make it a hardened system and put in enough spare capacitors to absorb the effects of an EMP. The cost would be very small, but would prevent anyone trying to mess with it unless it was deliberately disabled from here first."

"Fair enough but there are two other things we need to do. First, we make the sub-dermis from Kevlar, as that will prevent accidental damage as well as making it nigh on impossible for anyone to cut it open with normal tools, but also to provide a shell so that we can incinerate the internal structure. We know that the muscle tissue will melt down at 230°, so we can design everything to burn out at that temperature apart from the skin as that won't go down until at least 450°."

"Even that would be an advantage," John concluded, "as the inside could become an inferno without damaging the surroundings. The fuel cells could be programmed to provide a complete and instantaneous discharge, overloading the fibres which would superheat and start the reaction. I think that would give us a fair degree of protection."

"Is there any need for a sense of smell at this stage?" Bob asked.

"I can't see that would be an advantage right now but a small particle analyser would be possible later on if we need it. Hearing and sight will be taken way beyond that of the real animal, we can give telephoto vision and amplified sound capabilities."

"Are we building this to be autonomous or are we going to control it?" Bob interrupted.

"I think we have to have some of each, so that we can control it when we need to, either verbally or from our computers, but most of the time I want it to behave very much according to its own instincts. I would like to use it as eyes and ears for us as well. The capability will be there so we might as well be able to use it."

"So in a zoo situation," Bob could see a much bigger picture now, "it would behave in exactly the same way as the real thing, but when the keeper steps into the pen he could tell it to lie down and it would virtually switch off."

"Yes, otherwise it could follow the natural instincts it's programmed with and attack him."

"On the subject of zoos, one of the most interesting parts for the visitors is feeding time, how do we get round that?"

"I suppose the only way is to make it give the impression that it is eating. Probably an almost straight passage through with an internal receptacle, which it could 'eat' the food into, and then discharge out the other end when everyone has gone home."

"At least the keepers will still have to clean them out," Bob smirked.

"We could program them to dump their food into a container, that would be simple enough."

"No, leave it random, more realistic," Bob laughed.

"Very amusing, but this is in danger of getting down to schoolboy level. Container disposal it is. All right, change the subject. What about the last two senses, feel and taste. Without

53

those the processors won't be able to learn."

"As far as we need at the moment, I think we need touch sensors in all four feet, the head and tail, we can put touch sensors in the tongue but taste sensors will take a lot of time to develop. Taste certainly won't be necessary unless you have some other purpose in mind beyond the confines of the zoo."

"I don't know, we will have to see how the whole thing develops, I have tried not to think beyond the zoo stage yet, but as we develop the capabilities other uses are bound to present themselves. For now though, look through the data and let me know if you need anything else. I'll talk to you again in the morning."

Bob watched John leave the lab and head for the stairs back to his office. There are a lot of possibilities for this, he thought, and not all of them good. Plugging the drive into his computer he resolved to get on with the job and not to worry too much about what the future may hold.

The next three days saw the assembly of the skeleton and muscle structure of what was to be the black panther.

Suzie assembled the main logic board, formatted and programmed the array of solid state drives and interfaces while Alan continued with his work at the zoo. The entire experimental design team had been working round the clock on the project for three weeks and the prototype beast was almost complete. It was a sight that John would not have believed possible in so short a time. The black fur wasn't genuine panther though, that was synthetic, but the touch, feel and overall nature of it would have fooled even most experts. The one thing that it did provide that was most important was waterproofing for the porous Kevlar, otherwise the dangerous event that could jeopardise the 'animal' instantly was a good bath.

It was decided that the unveiling and activation would take place on the following Friday morning and that all of those involved would be present.

Nine-thirty on Friday morning and everyone was in the construction area, talking excitedly amongst themselves. The only ones to see the provisionally completed cat at that stage were John, Suzie and Bob although everyone, apart from Alan, had been involved in the physical construction at some point. Suzie was the last to come down from her office. The whole group were gathered around a stand some ten feet square with a white sheet draped over a frame over five feet in length, two feet wide and three feet high.

The buzz quietened while everyone waited with bated breath as John stepped forward and said in his Sunday best voice "Dearly beloved, we are gathered here to day to witness the joining together of many parts to recreate one of God's most beautiful creatures. Suzie, if you would be so kind as to unveil our little masterpiece..."

John stepped back as she moved forward to lift off the sheet concealing the most incredible looking animal with its black and glossy coat. It was impossible to tell that it wasn't real apart from the fact that it wasn't yet moving. The congregation murmured its approval, although some were stunned into anticipatory silence.

"Alan, please weave your magic and bring our new pet to life."

Alan moved quickly across to the computer console and with a flurry of activity set about making history.

As his hands moved across the keyboard so the beast slowly moved. At first it stepped off the dais and walked slowly around in a circle seeming to take in the surroundings. Nobody moved, it was almost as though they were afraid that they might draw attention to themselves and provoke some unwanted attention from this magnificent and, for appearance at least, dangerous animal. The cat made no attempt to investigate the human contingent present but instead carefully walked around the room, moving in and out of the individual work areas with total grace and nonchalance, surveying everything.

After a few minutes that seemed like hours, John broke the silence, "Come," he said loudly. The cat immediately turned his head and silkily approached the source of the command. Without any further instruction the big cat stopped two feet in front of John and lay down at his feet.

Collectively the congregation audibly exhaled, still not wanting to break the spell or to make any sudden movement.

Suzie was the first to find her voice and with a huge smile on her face she said "Well, it would appear that we can all be proud of what we have achieved, however there is one thing we have to do straight away. We have to give our new friend a name. Any suggestions from the floor?"

That smile, John thought, was worth every ounce of work that had gone into it and summed up everyone's feelings at that moment, although he had the impression that they all would have preferred a loud cheer.

Various names were put forward including Blackie, Simba, Sam, Beelzebub, but the one that got everyone's approval was Bagheera, from the Jungle Book. It seemed most appropriate as he was particularly friendly and helpful to humans.

"We'll call him Baggy for short," Sally chimed.

Alan quickly programmed Baggy to recognise his name and to respond accordingly. It was also decided that Baggy was only to respond to instructions from those who had worked on the project and not to attack any of those he responded to.

The next half hour was devoted to programming in visual and voice recognition so that everyone could be sure that they didn't have to keep looking over their shoulders.

Once Baggy was fully operational it was a simple matter of voice commands to introduce new friends that could be recognised as such without giving any extension of control. It was going to take a little while for them all to get used to having a panther roaming free around the labs, but at least he wouldn't be opening doors by himself.

While the staff of Animagination were waiting to go through the introductions, Pete Thomas was standing at the top of a ladder. Having decided where he needed to place his microphone transmitter, he carefully removed a dozen concrete roof tiles from the rear of the control room at the zoo, cut out two sections of tile lath, cut a square of underfelt away and eased himself off the top of the ladder into the roof space above the end of the room where Alan spent most of his time working. The compact little unit was capable of transmitting over a distance of four hundred yards and would be sending to a voice activated digital recorder. The salesman in the electronics store had assured him that the battery pack would last approximately four weeks. Ideal, he thought, just up to Christmas then we can change the batteries in time for the restart in the new year. Very simple, very efficient and very cheap. Once the equipment was in place, Pete crawled back out of the roof, fitted a new piece of felt over the hole and screwed the pieces of batten back on to the rafters, replaced the tiles and no-one would be any the wiser. He quickly slipped away with the ladder on his shoulder. Mission accomplished.

He went straight up to Jackson's office, where he let himself in, Alice wasn't in reception, it was too early for her.

"Better she doesn't know what's going on," he thought aloud. He plugged the recorder into the wall socket at the rear of Jackson's desk and placed the recorder upright on the floor in the corner. There was an array of lights on the front of it, a green one indicating that it was switched on and two others, a red one which would light up when it was recording, and a blue one to indicate that a recording had taken place and had not yet been played back.

It was only the size of a paperback so when the wastepaper bin was placed in front it was, to all intents and purposes, invisible. Extremely pleased with his early morning's work he set about the tasks that he was legitimately employed to do.

Alan arrived at the zoo shortly after eleven o'clock and went through his usual routine of checking through the night's recordings. That normally took about an hour, but with the morning's work to catch up on it kept him occupied until his break for lunch at one o'clock. Meanwhile, Jackson sat in his office frustratedly waiting for the recorder to spring into life. Unfortunately for him Alan was not in the habit of talking to himself.

He was, however, very pleased to see, at two thirty, the arrival of Suzie Fielding. She marched straight to the control room, placed her right hand on the sensor and opened the door.

Alan stood up.

"Hi, good to see you. How's Baggy settling in?" he said with a huge smile on his face.

"He's doing fine, it's far better than we had a right to expect. He's so good it's hard to remember he's not what he seems to be . For the next step we think it would be best to go for something smaller, this side of Christmas, moving on to something more sizeable in the new year."

Alan stayed quiet for a few seconds and then said "It's surprising, but from a programming and behaviour point of view, the smaller animals such as the chimps are going to be harder to work with because their lifestyles are so much more complex than that of the larger animals. I know, from a size point of view, elephants are more difficult to handle, but because they don't have the dexterity of the apes they are going to be simpler to work with. My own preference would be to work on the rhino next, at least it's midway between the two."

"How soon before you would have the initial set for the rhino?"

"It should be ready by the middle of next week. The only problem is that apart from the odd trot I've not yet seen it in full flight. I don't suppose you'd fancy driving your car at it and making it angry by any chance?"

"That would hardly be fair, why don't you just stick your head down and give it a charge, at least you're nearer its size, besides we could then have a go at rebuilding you afterwards. That would be far more useful," she retorted.

"Touché. I suppose I'll have to see if old Pistol Pete will lend a hand again. I wonder how you can make a rhino angry."

"Not easy, they're thick-skinned you know," she said, laughing at her own pun.

"The jokes don't get any better either. I'll see what I can do."

"I'll come in first thing on Monday" she said, "we have to make a decision by Tuesday at the latest or we won't have much chance of achieving anything this side of Christmas. See you later."

Alan watched her let herself out and wondered. Five years he had worked with her and he still didn't know her. Occasionally letting a sense of humour break through, but it was always business. The only other time he became close to her was when they were working out together in the gym and it was more often Suzie that would push the hardest, driving on when others would want or need to ease off. He supposed that that was why she was the partner. Her abilities as a programmer and developer were second to none but she had never seemed to have a private life. Always on the move, never relaxing, always on her own, never giving any clues as to the motivating factor behind it all. Unfathomable. Alan gave up and went out to find Pete.

He went out and headed towards the lodge as a starting point. On his way he passed one of the other keepers and was informed that he wasn't in the lodge and the last time he saw him he was going to see 'the boss'. Grateful for the information Alan turned and went back the way he came and continued on towards the offices. As he approached, the door opened and Pete appeared with a rather satisfied look on his face, which changed the moment he saw Alan looming large.

"Just the man I want," Alan said.

"Oh, yeah. What can I do for you?" Pete said rather defensively.

"You know the other day when you er, encouraged the panther, well I could do with a similar favour with the rhino."

"I don't know about that, slightly different kettle of fish, playing with the rhino." He appeared to be quite reluctant. "You see she's got the calf to worry about and I don't want to upset her. I can't see that there's anything I can do to help you."

"Is there nothing she's likely to break into a run for, or anything that she will play with?" Alan was struggling, even he couldn't visualise a rhino playing, it didn't really fit with the character of a rhino. A very serious beast, he thought.

"The only thing that I can do for you, but it would require Mr. Jackson's approval, would be to drive the ice cream cart past her field and play the jingle," he said, looking down at the floor.

"What would that do?"

"She gets a bit funny about that, I don't know why but she seems to take a dislike to the music, and I suppose with the moving cart she probably can't understand it and what she can't understand, well, she tends to take a bit of a run at. But you'll have to go and see Mr. Jackson, I can't go and do something like that without his permission."

"Is he in now?"

"Yes, I've just left him. You'll find me in the lodge if you get any joy. Coffee time. I'll make you one if you like."

"Er, no, I'll pass on that if you don't mind."

The memory of the last coffee he was given there was still fresh in his mind.

Alan went up to Jackson's office, Alice was not in her office so he knocked on the inner door.

"Come in," the voice shouted through the closed door.

Alan fought his way through the cloud of cigar smoke that was emanating from a brown torpedo the size of a loofah resting comfortably in the fat hand of Arthur Jackson.

"Good afternoon, sit down," Jackson stayed in his seat and gestured to the empty chair at the side of the desk.

Alan remained standing, determined to get out of the stinking pit as soon as possible.

"I need to ask a small favour."

Alan was slightly embarrassed, he didn't like not being in control and Jackson could so easily refuse with total justification.

"Fire away."

Very appropriate considering the burning bush sticking out of his mouth.

"I need a little help from an ice cream cart," he said sheepishly; it didn't feel very professional, but he explained how Pete had thought that it would give the rhino a little exercise and help speed up an important part of the research.

Jackson, surprisingly, agreed almost immediately. "I don't see why not, it's not as though we are doing anything that she doesn't do forty or fifty times a year. We do, however, make a point of not playing the jingle past her field. Have you anything interesting that you can show me? You see, I have to submit a report to Mr. Daniels, just to keep him informed. I'm sure you understand. Only sitting up here I don't really know what is going on out there. So I suppose you could call it a quid pro quo."

"As it happens, we had planned on putting on a little show for you fairly soon, so if you can ask Pete to arrange the cart for me now, I can show you around before we close up this afternoon."

"That would seem to suit us both then. It's three fifteen now, say I come down to you at four fifteen. Is that enough time?"

"No problem."

Alan stood up and quickly stumbled through the stinking fog into the fresh air outside. "How can he do that? If he can see through that lot he's got better eyes than me!" he said looking at the darkening skies above.

True to his word Alan found Pete in his broom cupboard of an office in the lodge.

Pete nodded towards the phone and said, "The boss says its alright to do it. Five minutes alright with you?"

Alan happily accepted and walked straight back to the control room.

He sat watching the cameras that covered the rhino field. The rhino was quite happily ripping up chunks of grass with her calf by her side. Her ears twitched at a familiar sound. Her large heavy head swung up and left to face the direction the sound was coming from. He hadn't been aware before that rhino's faces could have expressions but he had the very distinct impression that she was starting to get a touch angry, the eyes narrowed, the ears pointed forward and the head went down. The chiming jingle came over the speakers and so did the thundering hooves of a charging rhino, three tons of African black rhino with every intention of murder. As the rhino got within fifty yards of the perimeter wall, Pete switched off the jingle and smartly manoeuvred the cart away from the field. The rhino, with tremendous agility wheeled around six feet from the wall and, job done, trotted back to where her calf had remained. It was very amusing, Alan thought, just how light footed a rhino could appear, she appeared to be almost prancing along on her toes. Perfect. Exactly what was needed.

He left his chair and went outside to thank Pete for the help.

He found him parking the cart in a large garage with six other similar sized vehicles. That was clearly where they kept the summer vehicles in storage. What few ice creams and hot dogs they sold during the winter would be sold from the shops and cafes dotted around the zoo.

"That do you then?"

"That was terrific. Do they always charge that easily?"

"She does. The African Black Rhinoceros has a very short fuse and no manners. Like I said before, you don't play with them. White rhinos are much more placid, but they're also a lot bigger, they grow up to fourteen feet long and six feet at the shoulder, ours is a baby by comparison, but a very badly behaved one."

"Much appreciated, I'll be putting on a bit of a show at four fifteen if you want to accompany your boss."

"No doubt about it!"

Alan returned quickly to his lair. He had some work to do. It had to be impressive.

They arrived at four fifteen precisely. Alan welcomed them both in and showed them to the two waiting chairs in front of the screen wall. All of the monitors were now blank. Alan turned all of the lights down, leaving just enough light for him to see his keyboards.

"I would have thought that you would be using something a bit more up to date than that, can't you just talk to your computers to get them to do what you want?"

"We could quite easily do that, but I prefer to use this, I tend not to lose track if I input this way, not only that but talking to a computer is very literal, you can't talk normally to a computer it would misinterpret too many things you would take for granted, so in the long run I think this way is faster. Now sit back and enjoy the show."

The entire wall of screens now flashed into life to show not separate pictures but one huge one. The wall showed a black rhino contentedly chewing at bushes on the African savanna, the sun fairly low in the sky, it was late afternoon. Something had caught the attention of the rhino. The head swung left to face the intruder. A few seconds of complete stillness. The rhino turned its body to face the threat. Slowly moving forward, breaking into a trot, the head lowering, the ground shaking as the mass of armoured flesh and bone came crashing towards the two man audience, the rhino appeared to come right out of the wall into the room, the sound was deafening. The two men instinctively ducked down at the same time as craning their heads round to see where it was going. It appeared to run right over their heads and looking up they could see the underside of the great beast, they turned to face backwards and they could see the rhino disappearing towards the back wall. The room settled into darkness, no one moved. Total silence. A few seconds passed, they were still looking backwards when a familiar sound broke the silence. Quiet at first, growing louder, a horned head began to appear on the wall that gradually gave way to head shoulders and rampant legs. It was coming back. This time charging directly at them. Both men leapt out of their seats just in time for the huge apparition to leap back into the screen wall and disappear back to its original grazing position.

There was an audible sigh of relief as Alan switched the lights back on. Alan had a huge grin on his face, much to the embarrassment of the other two.

"Well, what do you think?"

Jackson was the first to recover some of his composure, "That was incredible. I knew it couldn't be for real but that didn't stop me be frightened half to death. How did you do that?"

"Quite simple really, there are four projectors, one in each corner of the room, plus the screens, at the point the rhino appeared to reach the screens the projectors kicked in and created the illusion of it coming out into the room, then I just turned it around and brought it back again the same way."

Pete Thomas appeared to be regretting having eaten that day,

Alan thought that he might have needed the bathroom, he was still extremely pale.

Half an hour later with everyone else having left, Jackson was in his office, window open, he couldn't face the smell of the cigar, not with the way his stomach felt. He was explaining to Daniels on the phone what had happened that day, including the taped conversation concerning 'Baggy', whatever or whoever that might be.

Daniels said very little, the odd grunt or "How?" Just his usual terse self. Jackson assured him that they would continue to press for information and ask as many questions as they could, but as there was only usually one person in the room the remote mike wouldn't yield anything most of the time.

Daniels didn't offer any suggestions as to how he might improve his efforts and, as usual, indicated his farewell by simply putting down his telephone.

The one way conversation Jackson had just had didn't do a lot for him either, but Friday at least meant an extended stay in Harry's Bar.

Chapter 6

Harry's Bar was an undemanding sort of place. It was a place to go and unwind, drink a few beers, talk about sport, any sport, it was full of 'experts'. Women were allowed in the bar, but it wasn't the sort of place to take a wife or girlfriend, the only women that frequented it were women in similar circumstances to the majority of the men: middle aged, divorced, needing company without obligation.

Arthur Jackson was precisely such a man and on that particular Friday night, having been half scared out of his wits, he needed both company and conversation - mainly to talk, not listen.

By nine o'clock the bar was quite busy, and, as Jackson had been putting the beers away since five thirty, his tongue was fairly loose.

"It was incredible," he said for the fourth time "this rhino, on a full charge came crashing out of the screen right over my head, and as if that wasn't enough after the damned thing had disappeared through the back wall of the room, it came straight back in and charged me again!"

Each time his voice was sounding even more incredulous "I swear that thing was so real that if I'd stayed in my chair I'd have been crushed to death."

"How big was the hole?" asked a bemused man suffering, and enjoying, the effects of alcoholic stupor.

"It didn't make a hole. It just went through the wall, turned round and came back again."

"What was it then, a ghost? I'm not frightened of ghosts," he slurred.

"No, it was an illusion, it didn't actually exist."

"Why were you frightened then? I wouldn't have been frightened."

Jackson groaned, the story got harder to tell as the evening wore on and that was about as hard as it could get. "Did you see the game on Monday night?" It just got easier.

All the time Jackson was telling his story to anyone who would listen, there was one man who was listening with both amusement and interest, and he wasn't drunk. This, he decided, could be the first of many interesting Friday nights in Harry's Bar. He didn't make himself known, he just sat and listened.

Friday night was also an interesting night for Jerry Grossman, but then Friday nights had been for the past six months. He had always held a fascination for cards ever since his father had taught him to play poker at the age of thirteen. His early baptism had been as a result of a game in which his father had been cheated by two men who had been working together.

The system was quite simple, the two players colluding, constantly raise each other to force other players out of the pot, making it more and more expensive to remain in pots and dramatically reduce the chances of the other players winning, even if they had the best hand.

Jerry's father, therefore, reasoned that his son would not fall prey to such a situation if he were 'educated properly'. He had not considered that without the introduction to the ways of winning at poker he would probably not be interested in playing the game at all.

It had taken Jerry almost two years to get into a reasonable card game since leaving university. There had been games there of course, but the majority of students had very little money to spare so the stakes were invariably low and the game was played more for the enjoyment of it rather than for profit. Not so in Jerry's case, he always played to win, and he enjoyed winning more than anything.

However, Jerry was about to experience a turning point in his 'career' as a gambler. Jerry's method of gambling had always been one of comparative safety, always gambling less than he could afford to lose, never getting sucked into thinking that the hand he held was unbeatable, not necessarily the fastest way to win, but it reduced considerably the odds of him losing. Jerry always considered himself to be a winner, because he very rarely lost and, as the log book he kept showed, he was several thousand pounds in front over the last six months. On the occasions he did lose, it was generally planned. The other players might refuse to play with someone who was as cautious as him if he always won and they had little chance to get their money back - the hook that worked for every gambler, the bait always being the money they had already lost.

The venue was the same as usual, the somewhat downbeat hotel in the centre of town, the cost of the room being split between the players, always eight of them. All of the players were known to each other, having played several times before. There was a pool of twelve who could play at any time, but some would play almost every week, others as and when they had funds available.

It was unusual to see a player who was not part of the pool, but it was up to a player who couldn't make it at the last minute to arrange a replacement. One of the regular players, Tom Bradbury, had been taken seriously ill, it was thought at the time, sent along his replacement with a letter of introduction.

"Well gentlemen, if there are no objections from you all, I will introduce our new player."

There were no objections, the letter saw to that.

"Then we will begin. We're playing pot limit, but we try to keep it reasonably friendly Mr. Phillips. First jack deals."

Sam Johnson delivered a card in turn face up to each of the seven players. The first jack landed in front of Jerry, who retrieved the cards and the deck, shuffled, passed the cards to his right for the cut, said "Ante up," whereupon each player tossed a five point chip into the centre of the table, he then dealt five cards to each player. The game was Texas Hold'em for the first of three two hour stints, Omaha for the second two hours and draw poker for the final two. There was a fifteen minute break in between and a five minute convenience break on the hour. The silence was deafening for the first five minutes.

The evening passed off without any major event, but in what turned out to be the third from last hand Jerry found himself sitting with a dead man's hand (two pairs, aces and eights - the hand Wild Bill Hickock was holding when he was shot in the back), and after the round of betting, before the change of discards, there were only three hands left in: Dan Phillips, Sam Johnson and himself.

Jerry drew one card, no change in two pairs. Dan Phillips changed one, as did Sam.

Sam bet fifteen, and after a suitable pause, Dan raised another twenty five , Jerry called the twenty five and raised a hundred and fifty, the biggest bet of the night, close to a pot.

Dan looked thoughtful and eventually decided to fold his three tens. It didn't matter whether he was folding the winning hand or not. It suited his purpose perfectly.

After the game had closed and the players were reflecting on the evening's entertainment and enjoying a final drink, Dan took

Jerry to one side. "You play a mean game of poker. You can't be more than twenty four but you play as though you've been playing all your life."

"Thanks for the compliment. I'm in front but not wildly so," he said, trying to act as calmly as he could.

"I only came along here tonight as a favour to a friend, I normally play in a more, shall we say," he hesitated to add extra weight and meaning to his words "competitive game on a Saturday night. You play so much better than the rest of them," he said glancing towards the others "I should think that it's hard for you to lose."

Jerry was positively gushing in response, "Well you know what they're like, you did even better than I did tonight. It's a bit like taking candy from a baby." Jerry felt at least four inches taller, and did his best to stretch his height beyond his five foot ten.

"Maybe you're ready for something a little more interesting then. How about you come along with me tomorrow night and play in a man's game. The stakes are not much higher but there's not so much loose money around."

Jerry suddenly felt a little uncomfortable, his father had constantly warned him about getting drawn into games with people he didn't know.

"Well, I'd really like to but I already have something on tomorrow. Maybe another time, perhaps."

"Yeah, sure. Look here's my card, call me."

It was a personal card, not a business card, with just a name and telephone number.

They stood in silence for a few seconds, Jerry slightly awkward, Dan biding his time.

"Are you some kind of dealer on the stock market? What do you do that makes you so cool?" Dan appeared to be genuinely interested.

"No nothing so glamorous, I just work in a research lab, designing computer circuits for industrial machinery."

"What sort of machinery?"

"Robots. Not the type you see in the movies, you know, more like the ones that build cars. What do you do?"

"Oh, import, export, that sort of thing. Look I've got to go. Call me if you change your mind about the game."

The group split up and confirmed their arrangements for the

following Friday night. Jerry thought that he was better off with the devil he knew.

About the same time Jerry was leaving the hotel, sober, Arthur Jackson was leaving Harry's Bar, quite drunk. There was very little traffic on the roads at two in the morning, which was probably better for the both of them. Jerry was driving himself without concentrating, his mind was wandering off to the new friend and the lure of a bigger game.

Jackson, however, was not driving, having left his car at home and at least had the common sense to be looking for a taxi. Not that he could see very far. After he had lurched into his third lamppost for support, he was beginning to despair of finding a cab to take him home and being lucid enough to realise that two miles was too long a walk in the cold damp air of December, sat down on the pavement to rest and dwell on his predicament.

A couple of minutes went by without any solution flashing into his woolly brain, when a voice from some where above him said "You look as though you could use a little help, my friend."

Jackson strained his neck to look in the direction the voice had come from and all he got for his trouble was a dark silhouette against the searing brightness (at least it seemed that way to him) of the streetlamp way above the voice.

"Yeah, well things might be looking up now." He burst out laughing at the unintentional pun. He turned his head again, "Things are looking up. Get it?" and he laughed again at his own joke.

A firm but friendly hand reached down and hooked underneath his right armpit, and the voice encouraged him to stand up.

"Come on, I'll take you home, you've had a real skinful. I bet you can't even remember where you live."

When he had eventually righted himself, Jackson did his best to look into the face that owned the friendly voice, what he saw as his eyes fought against each other for focus was the silent man that had occupied the end of the bar for much of the evening.

"Hey, I've seen you before" he slurred, "you were in the bar. That's alright then."

"Come on, my car's over there," he said nodding to a silver saloon on the opposite side of the road. "Careful, mind the kerb."

Jackson was quite pleased to have found a good friend at a time of such great need and obediently walked across the road, supported still by the left hand of the stranger.

He propped Jackson up against the car while he rummaged for his keys in his coat pocket and having opened the passenger door, unceremoniously dumped him on the front seat. He wasn't going to risk slipping a disc for this overweight hitch-hiker.

"Okay, where do you live?"

Jackson told him the address and included several misleading directions which the stranger/friend ignored.

When they arrived outside the requested destination, a small detached, bungalow with a small detached front garden, Jackson felt himself being dragged out of the front seat.

"For God's sake, make an effort or I'll never get you out of here," the stranger demanded.

He duly obliged and they both half flew across the lawn towards the front door. Jackson pulled out a bunch of keys from his pocket and made a good fist of getting the wrong key into the lock. The keys were taken from him and on trying the third key in the lock the handle turned and the door opened.

What happened after that was a mystery to him, but when he awoke the following morning he found himself on the bathroom floor, still with his crumpled suit on and the toilet bowl awash with alcoholic vomit.

"Ohh, never again," he groaned and crept out into the hallway where he could lie down away from the stench of the night before.

Jerry, by contrast, had had no such problems, being perfectly sober and arriving quite safely home.

However, as he lay in bed, trying his hardest to go to sleep, he couldn't get his mind off the card in his jacket pocket. He kept wondering what it would be like. Was he really as good as Dan had made him out to be. Of course he was. He had the figures to prove it. After the latest win he was over seven thousand pounds in front after twenty two sessions, an average of almost three fifty a time. Free holidays, he thought. It could be free cars next if he had the courage to take them on at the next level up. That's all it was, the next level. No different to leaving school and going to university, no different to starting work, no different to getting promotion. No different at all. A natural progression. But the butterflies were still there in his stomach, but they would soon go once he was determined to move up in the world. Maybe not tomorrow, maybe next week. The butterflies subsided, Jerry slept soundly until nine o'clock.

The first thing he did when he leapt out of bed was to fetch the card. He sat there looking at it for twenty minutes, inwardly debating, trying to make sure he was doing the right thing. When at last he had summoned almost enough courage to pick up the telephone and dial the number, he withheld his own number first, he found that the voice at the other end was inviting him to leave a message, assuring him that it would be dealt with as soon as possible. He said nothing and pressed the button on the phone, cutting the voice off, returning himself to the safety of the anonymous caller. His heart was thumping in his chest. It must have been a sign that it was not meant to be.

An hour passed, the card, lying on the bedside table, he felt, was staring at him, defying him to try again.

By eleven o'clock the tension was almost unbearable, he reached for the phone and pressed the redial button. It was answered almost immediately this time, by a female voice, not a natural English speaker, he thought. He asked for Mr. Phillips. He gave his own name in response to the enquiry. There was a short delay while the female voice went to find him.

"Hello, I didn't think I'd here from you so soon. Was it you that rang earlier. I was in the shower at the time and Maria couldn't get there in time."

"Er, no," he lied, "I've only just got out of bed," he told the truth."

"Well, what can I do for you?"

"I just rang on impulse really, I wondered whether you might be able to take me along to the game tonight, if the offer still stands that is."

He tried to be as cool as the beer in his fridge, but felt more like the jelly that sat alongside it.

"Yeah, why not. I'll have to make a call first though, just to confirm that it's okay. Give me your number and I'll call you back in five minutes."

Jerry thought about declining and saying he had to go out immediately and that he would ring him back later on, but seeing as how he had 'only just got out of bed' he thought better of it and gave him the number.

The line went dead and Jerry tossed the phone onto the bed behind him.

Dan read the paper and drank a cup of coffee, looked at his watch, thought another couple of minutes and rang him back at twenty five past eleven.

Jerry sat and stared at the phone as he let it ring four times before picking it up. "Hello."

"Hi. Yeah, it's Dan. Can't do it tonight I'm afraid. Big game on, even I'm excluded. This only happens once every couple of months. A couple of high-rollers are here, too good an opportunity, too good for us. Should be alright for next week. I'll ring you before you go out next Friday night. You want to take them for all you can next week. Get some stake money for Saturday night."

"Good advice, thank you. Oh, and what's the buy in on Saturday?"

"Fifteen hundred... that's not too rich for you is it?"

Jerry drew a very nervous breath. "No, not at all," he said desperately wanting to say that it was.

"Got him," Dan said to Maria.

"Is that good?"

"No, that's perfect."

Chapter 7

Monday morning couldn't come soon enough for Jerry, it was the start of the week and the sooner the week started, the sooner it would end and Friday would arrive. The day had started well enough, with a meeting in the lower conference room of all of the staff that were involved with the zoo project. Jerry had been involved with the design and manufacture of the power distribution and control circuits for the panther and was expecting to be involved in the new rhino that had just been announced. Everyone knew that it would be the next one to be created as Alan had been telling everyone of the way he had introduced her to the "two most unfortunate guys in the zoo. It had been a real pleasure!" he'd said.

But she would soon be brought to life in the same way as Baggy.

It was certainly going to be a more interesting year than the previous year when he had been fairly new to the company, having started working for them in early November. The first year after gaining his degree was spent testing circuit boards for a small specialist computer manufacturer, a job he couldn't wait to get out of. The opportunity at Animagination had presented itself by chance. He had gone with the maintenance engineer to carry out a series of tests on some problematic diagnostic machines his company had supplied to Animagination. Being a two man operation the tendency was to send out one qualified engineer and one in training. The problem was a fairly simple one to find but had proved to be a time consuming one to put right. As his assistance had only been needed for a short while Jerry found himself with three or four hours to kill. The first port of call was the very attractive receptionist, being about the same age it was an easy attraction. In between Barbara's duties they had managed to strike up quite a rapport. A date was arranged and they began to see more of each other.

Two weeks after they met, John Hylton decided that they were going to expand their manufacturing side to include all of the associated control hardware that they had previously been buying in. Barbara had been asked to sound out a list of people that he had provided her with, as prospective employees. Jerry's name hadn't been on that list but seeing an opportunity for him, she suggested that he ought to contact John to see if there could possibly be an opening for him in the new department. The interview had been a success and Jerry started work there four weeks later. The relationship with Barbara, though, was less successful. For her part she thought that she wasn't ready to be involved with someone she also had to work with day in, day out and the brief affair settled down to become a firm friendship.

Since Jerry had been playing regularly cards he hadn't had much time for the fairer sex though, something he regretted but there would be plenty of time for that once he had made it into the big time. The chance appeared to be presenting itself and he was getting more and more determined to take it.

He settled down to work with only half his mind on his current task of designing the circuit diagrams for a remote control unit for the panther when Barry Perkins, his immediate supervisor, and Alan Fisher came into the lab. They occupied the two iMacs at the far end of the central island from where he was working.

Jerry tried to concentrate on his work but continually found that his mind was wandering off to the coming Saturday night. He wondered where it would be. The thoughts that went through his mind were a mixture of excitement and dread. What would happen if he lost his nerve as well as all of his money? What would happen if was dealt four aces in a big hand? Would they let him get out alive if he took everyone to the cleaners on his first visit?

It was the third "Jerry", harshly snapped, that finally brought him back into the room with a jolt. The look on Barry's face wasn't exactly something he wanted to see again.

"Whoever she is, you'd better forget her until five thirty," he said with dark undertones. Barry was a tall, thin man whose angular face reflected a sharp, angular personality. Very heavy on his sense of duty and obligation, and very light on a sense of humour. "I want you to go down to the zoo, download the weekend's data, check all the cameras are functioning properly and bring the drive back here. You had better introduce yourself at the admin office, Arthur Jackson is the manager, and take your ID with you. You will also need to enter an eight digit passcode which I will give you in a minute and when you come out make sure you have everything you need as the code is a 'once only'. You will not be able to enter the code again, it will be deleted from the memory the moment you use it. Got that?"

"Yes, no problem." Jerry tried to look subservient as he took the note from Barry's permanently cold hands. He supposed that it must be because he was so thin that he couldn't keep the heat in his body.

Jerry smiled at Barbara as he approached her to sign out. It was a shame, he thought, that they hadn't made more of their friendship, she was certainly the best looking girl he'd been out with. She logged his departure into the database and he left via the lift down to the underground car park. His car was a two year old BMW, bought as a result more of his winnings than his salary. The extra three thousand it cost over the price of the Mazda that he had also been looking at, he felt, was more than justified in view of his additional 'income'.

The drive across town to the zoo took twenty minutes, he would have liked to have done it in less but it was impossible to break the speed limits in town without a photograph of the car and a request for a donation to the police coffers arriving in the following day's mail.

The prospect of traipsing around the zoo was less appealing and looming as large as the blackening skies overhead

Finding the zoo wasn't a problem, he had been there many times in his younger days, but the rain that had started as a fine mist in the wind was becoming more persistent as he parked his car in the staff car park. He took his folding umbrella out from under the passenger seat, opened the door, pushed the umbrella outside and opened it up. It looked woefully inadequate against the rain that was angling in against his body as he leapt out of the car. The locks on the car all snapped into place as he pressed the button on the remote and, in spite of the umbrella, he put his head down and ran in the direction of the sign pointing the way to the Administration Centre.

The relief on his face was clear for Alice to see as he burst through the door into the lobby of the reception area. He collapsed the umbrella, lay it down on the floor, brushed his hands down the sleeves of his jacket and walked purposefully towards Alice and her quizzical expression.

"I bet those flamingoes out there are happier in this than I am," he said lightheartedly.

She smiled. "How can I help you?"

"I'm Jerry Grossman, from Animagination," he said producing his ID card from his breast pocket. I was asked to check in here with you, before I go to the Control Room, as you haven't seen me before. Can you tell me the quickest way to get there from here, I don't want to spend any more time than necessary running around in the rain."

"It's quite easy. Go back the way you came, towards the lake. Turn right at the lake, follow the path towards the tigers and its the low building at the back of their enclosure."

"Thanks for your help, I shall only be here for about twenty minutes."

He turned, picked up his umbrella and headed off out into the rain again."

Jackson picked up his phone, dialled Pete Thomas's extension, which was answered immediately. "Get round to the computer room, there's a lad going in there. You might be able to find something out."

Jerry hurtled through the rain, water seeming to cascade into his shoes as he ran through the puddles. He arrived at the tiger pen just as Pete Thomas came walking round the corner in his oilskins.

Jerry called out "I'm looking for the Animagination control room. Is that it over there."

"Yes, I'll come over with you."

They galloped over to the door and Pete was surprised to see that Jerry didn't put his hand on the scanner, instead he took out a piece of paper with some numbers on it. Jerry made no attempt to conceal the numbers as he tapped them into the pad. Pete tried hard to remember them, thinking that he must write them down very soon. When Jerry opened the door, Pete hustled in behind him.

"I'm Pete Thomas, Head Keeper," he said, offering his hand in greeting. "Your Mr. Fisher put on quite a show for us in here last week."

"Yes, he was telling us about it this morning. He's an absolute genius when it comes to computers and graphics."

Pete decided to take his life in his hands and tried to sound totally innocent when he asked "How's Baggy doing?"

"He's doing fine. It takes a bit of getting used to with him wandering about freely. It's certainly different."

Jerry was looking at the array of Mac Pros in front of him and plugged the portable Thunderbolt drive into the first one, found the data files he needed, copied them and then repeated the process once more: one for the elephant and one for the rhino, while Pete looked on.

"That's it, I'm done here now. Time to get wet again."

Pete really wanted more time with Jerry, he certainly didn't appear to have any instructions not to talk to anyone. "How about a coffee? Have you got time?"

Jerry looked at his watch, started to agree and remembered Hal Perkins' face earlier that morning when only his mind had been absent for a few minutes.

"Nice idea but I think we'll have to make that next time. I have to get back with this data or I'll be holding up the program."

Pete couldn't think of anything else to say without making it obvious that he hadn't got a clue about what they had been talking about.

They left without further delay. Jerry back to his car and Pete straight up to Jackson's office.

"You had him! You let him go!" Jackson was pacing around the floor like a tiger. What did you think you were doing?!" he barked at Pete as he entered his office.

"I couldn't just ask him straight out 'What is Baggy?' I'd already made out that I knew what it was. To ask him anything else would have put him on to me for certain. At least he's not likely to go back and tell anyone I've been talking to him so he shouldn't give the game away that we know about 'Baggy', whatever it is." Pete was feeling rather defensive.

Jackson realised that his anger and frustration was due to a lost opportunity and there was nothing that Pete could have done about it. He was right, it would have been impossible for him to ask any further questions without raising serious questions, and they still had a lot of money to come from the project. The thought of losing the money and what Daniels would probably do to him if he did had a tremendous calming effect on him. "Yeah, you're quite right, you did as best you could. Hopefully he'll come back and you can talk to him again."

When he was alone again, Jackson rang Eric Daniels.

"It seems as though our friends are up to something. It may not be relevant to what they are doing here, but I have a sneaking suspicion that they have made something, they call it 'Baggy', not that the name gives anything away. We will keep trying and we still have the microphone in there so we should be able to find out eventually."

"You'd better have some more positive news next time or I'll take it out of your hands." The line clicked. It was apparent that the conversation was over.

Jerry took the drive straight back to the office, where they were gratefully accepted.

"Everything okay over there?" Alan enquired.

"Yes, all straightforward. I didn't see Mr. Jackson, but I did meet the head keeper when he showed me where our hut was."

Alan looked at Barry.

"I bet they are gagging for information over there!" he said with a laugh.

"Why didn't we just have a pipeline direct from the zoo to here? Save a lot of messing about if the data came straight into here?" Jerry asked.

"Simple. Cost. We don't need it for long and the bandwidth we'd need would have been humungous. Sure, it's not as convenient doing it this way, but a fraction of the cost though."

"Fair enough."

Jerry went back to his original task on the remote control unit.

The rest of the week was fairly uneventful. The zoo was closed to the public until after the new year, Alan hadn't seen Pete Thomas all week, and Jackson, as far as he knew, had stayed in his office, bothering no one.

On Thursday morning Suzie and John had a discussion about the forthcoming social events they were going to have to attend, mainly at the invitation of their clients and they also discussed the possibility of taking a well earned break, immediately after Christmas. Suzie suggested a trip to the Virgin Islands to do some diving. It was an idea that had serious appeal to John, both as relaxation and a reward that they were more than entitled to. It had been a long year and it would recharge their batteries for the long haul ahead.

After Alan left the zoo on Thursday afternoon, Pete Thomas went over to the control room and stood frantically tapping numbers into the screen next to the door. He was convinced that he had written the numbers down correctly and was mortified, when, on the fourth attempt to input the numbers the message 'This console is now disabled. Contact the administrator' appeared on the screen. He had bided his time all week, expecting to be able to snoop around some more and it had all gone wrong. He looked around him, there was nobody there to see him so he scurried off. He'd have to pretend that he knew nothing about it. He certainly couldn't tell Jackson about it, he'd go nuts!

On Thursday evening, John had been shopping for food at his local supermarket. He was about to go home when, as he reversed out of his parking space, there was a resounding thump and the sound of mangling metal and breaking glass. He had reversed straight out into the path of another car. He couldn't understand how he could have done something so stupid, so elementary.

He got out of his car to meet the victim of his error.

She was extricating herself from her seat belt, apparently quite shaken by the event. He walked over to the small Ford and opened the door.

"Look, I'm very sorry, it was clearly my fault, I couldn't have been paying attention."

His victim had a very attractive face with long blonde hair, late twenties probably, but was unable to determine much else.

She sat and looked up at him for a few seconds and then said, "You have just saved yourself from the stream of abuse I was going to hit you with! It's hard to be angry with someone who has just apologised so profusely," she said, still apparently shocked by the collision.

"Can I suggest that we park up the cars, they aren't too badly damaged and then go into the coffee shop in the supermarket and exchange details out of the cold?" he suggested.

He found himself wanting to find out more about her and he had the perfect opportunity. She readily accepted the offer and after scraping some of the broken glass from her headlight into the carrier bag he offered, they headed into the store.

It turned out that she was quite tall, slim and even better looking than he had been able to make out in the gloom outside. With heels, she was almost looking him straight in the eyes.

Every cloud has a silver lining, he thought.

They exchanged names, addresses, insurance and licence details. In just a few short moments they had given away more information about each other than they would normally have done in several social meetings. Delilah Sampson, it transpired, was a fashion journalist, she was twenty-eight, unmarried, deliciously attractive, with bright blue eyes, long natural blonde hair and a beautiful smile. She lived on her own in an apartment in one of the better areas of town, had a pet cockateel called Joe and a wicked sense of humour.

"Were your parents particularly religious," he carefully asked. "Your name would suggest a certain biblical connection?"

"On the contrary. My parents were not at all religious, but my mother, when she was young, went to a Tom Jones concert. She was a really big fan of his. She even confessed to taking off her knickers and throwing them at him on stage. She was such a big fan that she decided then that she would call her daughter Delilah, after one of his biggest hits, and she didn't change her mind when I came along. I've always been known as Dee-Dee, so people don't usually get the opportunity to make the connection."

They talked briefly about getting the cars fixed, John offering to pay outright for the damage, rather than involve insurance companies, and then John decided that he might as well take the plunge.

"I don't suppose that you would allow me to take you out to dinner, by way of an extended apology, on Saturday night, would you?"

She smiled, she had enjoyed his company.

"I think that would be very nice. I don't think that my car will be fit for a few days though and I hate driving strange cars. I'll have to leave it here tonight as well because I'm not going to drive it with only one headlight."

"Then as I have your address already I will take you home. Do you need anything out of your car now?"

"No, I was going to do some shopping when you changed my plans. I'll do it when I collect the car in the morning instead."

The three minute drive to her apartment was quiet and smooth.

He hopped out of the car and skipped round to open the door for her.

They shook hands politely and John said, "Then I will call for you at eight, in my dented chariot."

"I shall look forward to it. Goodnight"

"Goodnight."

John had no reason to doubt that his fortunes had changed in recent weeks. As for Miss Sampson? He would have to wait and see what Saturday night would bring.

Chapter 8

Friday was a nervous day.

It started badly when Alan arrived at the zoo and noticed the small red light on the screen outside the control room door. He hadn't seen it before. He touched the Reset Functions button and the 'Console Disabled' message was displayed. Someone had, for the first time he concluded, attempted to get in. He placed his palm on the scanner and opened the door. Quickly checking around, everything was in its place. The Macs were all up and running. Nothing had been disturbed and all of the screens were operational.

No one had gained entry, so that could only mean that someone had thought they had known what the code was and tried to use it to get in - and failed.

Alan took out his phone and called the office. He asked to be put through to Jerry.

"Jerry. It's Alan. Tell me precisely what you did when you came here the other day."

He proceeded to tell him about his arrival in the rain at the zoo; his introduction to Alice; the directions she gave him, meeting up with Pete Thomas and the helpful attitude he displayed...

"Was he with you when you entered the code for the door?"

"Yes, he was stood right next to me."

"Could he have seen you enter the code?"

"I suppose so, it couldn't do him any good though."

"He must have thought he could get in because someone tried to use a code to get in sometime after you left, but on the fourth unsuccessful attempt it locks out. Did you let him in the room?"

"Well, he followed me into the room, I didn't see anything wrong with that as I knew he had been in before, and it was chucking it down with rain outside."

Jerry was starting to feel uncomfortable.

"I want to know exactly what you talked about."

"We didn't talk about anything really, I wasn't in there more than two minutes. He offered me a coffee, but I hadn't got the time to spare. He must be a bit bored now that the zoo has shut for a couple of months, because he seemed a bit disappointed that I couldn't stop for a chat."

"Did he ask any questions about what we were doing here?"

"No, not really, he only asked me how Baggy was doing and that was it. I said he was fine and then I left."

"Okay, that's fine. I'll see you later."

Alan was more than concerned. It wasn't Jerry's fault Thomas had been talking to him, Jerry hadn't been appraised of the situation and he hadn't been told to avoid talking to anyone. What was puzzling him though was the reference to Baggy. Nobody had told them about Baggy. It was reasonably serious, but it also meant that whatever they did know it was not enough for them to know who or what Baggy was.

Alan reached for his phone again to speak to Suzie and the more he thought about it he couldn't remember talking to anyone one on the phone about Baggy. The only time anyone had talked about Baggy in the room had been when Suzie had called in last Friday afternoon. So they must have been listening in somehow. Fortunately they couldn't have gained any real knowledge or Pete Thomas wouldn't have been fishing.

Alan had nothing on site that could detect bugs and the place was too big to carry out a visual search, the thing could be hidden almost anywhere. He had two options, not discuss anything in the room or feed disinformation. He thought about it for a few moments and decided it was probably easier and safer to keep quiet.

Arthur Jackson, however, had been listening to the telephone conversation, or half of it anyway, and was sweating quite profusely, pacing up and down the office again. They had blown it. Pete trying to get in was, more or less, understandable.

"Oh God," he said out loud. "If they work out that we've been listening in we are going to be in massive trouble!"

He almost fainted when he remembered that the next payment was due in five days time. He stopped pacing and flopped down in his chair and stared blankly at the wall.

"Why? Why did it have to happen now? This was going to be the best Christmas in years and now we've buggered it all up!"

The only thing that entered his head was the opening line of the Tale of Two Cities: It was the best of time, it was the worst of times. Was he heading for the worst Christmas ever?

He leapt out of his chair and unplugged the recorder. He didn't want to hear any more about anything. He didn't care what they were doing in there. He just wished that Pete hadn't tried to get into the building, he'd feed him to the lions, one leg at a time for that.

Jerry wasn't worried about the conversation he had just had with Alan. He hadn't been warned not to speak to anyone, and besides, the fact that the keeper had tried to get in using the code only served to warn them that they might be up to something. So instead of it being a bad thing it had probably done them some good. Forewarned is forearmed, as they say. He got back to thinking about more important matters, he had a game in a few hours, his last game in the little league.

Arthur Jackson was still slightly nervous as he drove home that night. Some things in life just weren't worth the risk. The first thing he did when he got home was to phone for a cab to call for him at six o'clock. Harry's Bar would relax him, he thought, and you never know what might happen in there on a Friday night, he might just get lucky.

He showered, shaved, splashed on too much cologne, put on his best suit and poured himself a stiff whisky while he waited for the cab to arrive. It was going to be a better night than the day had been.

Jerry Grossman also showered, shaved and splashed on too much aftershave. Jerry preferred to have his own car outside the hotel and he certainly wasn't going to drink. He wanted all of his wits about him. It needed to be a big night. He checked through his gambling records for the last six months and noted that his best night had been a win of just over a thousand pounds. He was going to have to do better than that if he wanted a decent stake with no risk attached.

Just as he was putting his ledger away the phone rang.

"Hi, Jerry. It's me, Dan." The voice was big and friendly. "You ready for the game tonight?"

"Yes, I'm looking forward to it. It feels good, I'm going to take them for everything tonight."

"Good. You will need five thousand for tomorrow night. That's the minimum sit down money. You ought to bring more than that though, you can do that much in one bad hand if your lucks out."

Jerry suddenly went cold, Dan was talking about almost all of the money he had carefully won in the last six months being lost in one hand!

"What sort of stakes do you play for?" he didn't sound very convincing.

"Ante's only twenty, then the pot's the limit. Nothing for you to worry about. You can handle that."

"What happens if you run out of money during a big hand? I've heard of people being frozen out," he said, trying to sound knowledgeable.

"That doesn't happen in our game, we either accept markers or the pot freezes and the remaining players continue with a separate pot. We don't want anyone to go broke with a winning hand, it's a fair game," Dan replied lightly.

Dan was upbeat and cheerful. Jerry was reassured.

"I'll pick you up at eight thirty. Where do you live?"

Jerry thought quickly, he didn't want to tell him, he preferred to be a little anonymous. "It will be better if I meet you there, I won't be here tomorrow, I'll be coming straight down from my parent's tomorrow evening. Tell me the address and I'll meet you there."

"You wouldn't get through the gate without me. Come to my house and I'll take you from here."

Jerry agreed and he gave him the address, settling on seven thirty so that they could have a relaxing drink beforehand and Dan could run through the house rules so that there could be no chance of misunderstandings.

Arthur Jackson arrived at Harry's Bar feeling fairly good but in definite need of company, preferably female. He was a little disappointed when he arrived to see that the opportunities right then were zero. He sat at his usual stool at the polished mahogany bar, was greeted effusively by Harry who invited him to have the first drink on the house, Arthur accepted and ordered a large fillet steak with salad and an ice beer.

He casually looked around and around the corner at the far end of the horseshoe shaped bar he saw a man that he didn't know, but somehow looked familiar. The man nodded by way of greeting but remained seated. Jackson, puzzled, nodded in return and also remained stationary. The music in the bar was subdued and not particularly to anyone's taste.

Jackson took a deep draught from his beer, stood up and took his drink over to the stranger at the other end of the bar.

"Hi, I've a feeling that I should know you, but I can't think where we've met before. I'm Arthur Jackson."

"Pleased to meet you Arthur, I'm Keith Boscik and we have met before. Last week we were both in here."

Arthur groaned "It wasn't you that er..."

"Assisted you in your hour of need?" he offered.

"It would be appropriate, I think if I were to offer you a drink by way of thanks," he said somewhat embarrassed.

"I will gladly accept your offer and I think that we need not mention it again. But perhaps you would care to join me. I must admit to being more than interested in the story you were telling, it sounded quite fascinating."

Harry motioned to Jackson that his food would be ready in a couple of minutes as he walked over to one of the booths along the side wall to lay out the cutlery and napkin for him.

"Have you eaten yet?"

"Not yet. I'll join you over there." He ordered a steak sandwich and fries and two more beers, which Jackson instructed Harry to put on his bill.

They both settled down into the red velvet upholstered booth. It had high mahogany backs to it with a rectangular table in between two very comfortable bench seats. Unless someone was standing at the open end or was leaning over the top of one of the sides it was quite private.

"I gathered from your exploits last week that you had been the victim of a charging rhino, unless the drink had got the better of my ears."

"No, you heard correctly."

He retold the entire story.

"That really was quite something. What has happened since then?"

"It's been quite quiet since then, I've kept out of the way."

He was debating whether he should confide in him, when he suddenly realised that he knew nothing about the man sat opposite.

"Tell me, what do you do?"

"Nothing particularly interesting. I work in a small private hospital, just around the corner from here."

"Doing what?" Jackson thought this was like pulling teeth.

"I work in the operating theatre, assisting with operations, that sort of thing. You know what it's like, long hours without a break. Gets a bit depressing at times, particularly when you lose a patient on the table. Not really the sort of thing to talk about on a Friday night."

He looked away into space as if to emphasise the point.

"Yeah, I can imagine. I don't think it's something that I could handle. The only meat I want to cut up is that which is on my plate and it's coming right now."

The food was delivered by Harry's daughter who also did the cooking. She was an attractive red-headed young girl, early twenties, wearing a very short tight skirt, unfortunately also very much off limits to the customers.

Jackson had a quick look round the room, but to his dismay there were no other females anywhere to be found.

Overcoming his disappointment, he returned to the plateful of food in front of him and got stuck into it with the voracity of an alligator that hadn't eaten for a month.

Jerry arrived at the motel on time at eight o'clock, the others were arriving at the same time. There's a full complement tonight he thought, pleased. The more the merrier. With seven others that meant there was at least seven thousand to be won. He quickly decided that a third of that would be his target for the night.

Everyone quickly settled down into their usual places, collected their chips from the suitcase that Sam Johnson brought with him. Everyone's cash was put into the room safe as a precaution against unwanted intrusion from outside. Not that anyone had ever tried to rob the game, but it had not been unheard of at other places and it was a simple precaution.

The cards went round face up and Aaron Goldberg, who sat two places to the left of Jerry was delivered the first jack.

The betting was very little different to the normal games they would play, but it was noticed that Jerry was a little more aggressive and stayed in a little longer than he was wont to do.

As the evening wore on, Sam Johnson realised that Jerry was a man with a mission. Jerry appeared to be about fifteen hundred up and looking for more. At that rate, Sam thought, he will take out at least one of the players. Not good for the game.

At eleven thirty Sam called for a break to recharge the batteries and get a breath of fresh air.

Two of the other players went out with him on to the verandah.

"I don't know what has got into our friend tonight, but whatever it is, he is winning far too much for our little game. I don't mind losing but I think it's time to change the strategy. We can't stop him winning but we don't have to play with him. We'll do to him what he has been doing to us all these months, we'll play cagey. Call early when he's in, play on when he's out. Simple. Prevent the pots from getting too big and he'll get the message. Good luck gentlemen."

The other two nodded their approval and they marched back in to do battle.

Their ploy worked as successfully for them as it had previously worked for Jerry. Although, with four others not in on the arrangement it did mean that Jerry continued to accumulate his profits, but at a much slower rate.

Jerry didn't pick up that it was tactics that had caused a slow down in his success, he just assumed that the cards weren't running as well for him and he took the rough with the smooth. Sam Johnson noticed that there had been a marked upturn in his own fortunes and instead of finishing up seven hundred down, he ended the night only one hundred and twenty five down. Jerry had cashed in two thousand eight hundred and twenty in chips and looked very pleased with his evening's work.

"Same again next Friday, Jerry, give us a chance to win back some of it?" Sam asked cheerfully.

"Yes, I don't see why not." Losers, he thought uncharitably, you'll get more of the same more like.

Jerry went home, showered to get the smell of cigars out of his hair, flew happily into bed and slept like a log.

Arthur Jackson and Keith Boscik were having a steady evening, consuming three beers an hour and Jackson doing most of the talking.

He eventually decided, in his three sheets to the wind state, to confide in his new found friend.

"You know, I had a difficult day today. Pete Thomas my head keeper got into a bit of trouble. On Monday I asked him to go down to the computer room with this young chap, Jerry, from the company, just to see if he could find out a bit more about what was going on, nothing heavy. When Jerry was tapping in the code to open the door, Pete watched him and tried to remember the code. Well, the idiot obviously got it wrong, because when he went back there yesterday he put the number back into the keypad and it wouldn't have it. After the fourth attempt to do it the damned thing seized up on him."

"So what's the problem with that?"

"The guy that works in there normally opens the door with a hand scan, but this morning he noticed a red light that told him someone had attempted to get in."

"So he came to you and demanded to know what you had been doing."

"No, he just rang his office and asked Jerry if anyone had been in there with him, and had he let anyone see him put the door code in. He then found out that Pete had been with him."

"Like I said, what's wrong with that?"

"Well, nothing really, we could have passed it off as one of the keepers getting nosy and as they didn't get in it was a good test of their system. I know it sounds a bit weak but it wasn't really worth arguing about. The problem will come when I'm asked about Baggy."

He looked quite depressed at the thought.

"Why? What is Baggy?"

"I haven't got a clue."

"So what's the problem?"

"The problem is that Pete asked the kid how Baggy was doing. Pete doesn't know what Baggy is either, he just thought he might be able to get a bit of information."

"That's no crime."

"No it's not, but we're not supposed to have even heard of Baggy. We, Pete, that is, put a microphone transmitter he bought in town into the roof space above the end where they work most of the time, so we were able to listen in to their conversations. Every time anyone said anything a recorder in my office switched on and we didn't miss a thing. But it appears that what we did find out, next to nothing by the way, could jeopardise the whole project. And lose us an awful lot of money. Daniels will have my balls in a sling if that happens."

"Who's Daniels?"

"He owns the zoo. He's a right miserable sod."

"What have you done about the microphone?"

"The mike's still in place, but the batteries will run out sometime over Christmas. I've disconnected the tape recorder. I've learned my lesson. If Daniels wants to know what's going on he'll have to ask them himself. He can't sack me for not being able to get information but he'll kill me if I lose the money and I'm not risking my neck!"

"Best decision. Stay out of it. D'you want another drink?"

Chapter 9

Saturday evening was fast approaching and there was more than one person feeling nervous. John's day had been quite hectic, after he realised that most of what could euphemistically be referred to as his wardrobe was at least five years out of date, he hadn't even bought a new pair of shoes for at least a year, he decided it was time to go shopping. He thought that by the end of the afternoon he must have been into every shop in town. He'd spent enough money, he was convinced, to have bought at least two of them.

Stepping out of the shower, it occurred to him that he was behaving like a sixteen year old. He'd even bought the biggest and most beautiful bouquet of white lilies he'd ever seen.

He even suffered the type of panic attack that affects virtually every male teenager that has ever walked the earth: the fear of rejection. What happens if she says: "Hey, this is only you buying me dinner because you banged up my car. Do you really think I'm attracted to you?" What would happen if she said that?

After a while his nerves settled down and he decided that he would proceed as planned. He would give her the flowers, he would take her out to dinner, and if she said thank you for a nice time, but I don't want to do it again, then at least he would have had a pleasant dinner with a beautiful lady, and that is more than he would have had if he hadn't smacked into her car. Nothing ventured, nothing gained.

By seven thirty he was ready to leave. He started his car and drove as slowly across town as he could and he still arrived ten minutes early. He parked at the end of her street and waited for one minute to eight to arrive. Palms sweating, stomach churning.

"I'm thirty nine, for God's sake! Calm down!" he hissed at the roof of the car.

Jerry had also arrived ten minutes early. He sat opposite Dan's house in his car taking in an impression of his surroundings. It was certainly an affluent area and Dan's house was one of the biggest. It was set, he guessed, in at least an acre of grounds with a six foot high brick wall facing the road. The pair of curved wrought iron gates were about eight feet high in the centre from where they swept down either side to the substantial piers they were hung from.

The gates were closed but he could see an intercom on the right hand pier just below a camera. There were lights on top of each pier. He could also see the hydraulic rams attached to the back of the gates, meaning that they would be electrically operated, probably from the house and his car. How the other half lives, he thought.

He restarted his car and pulled up to the gates. The gates silently swung open as he debated whether to get out of his car to operate the intercom. The tarmac drive led straight to the centre of the old Victorian house, with its red bricks, tall windows and slate roof. Trees lined the drive which must have been at least seventy five yards long, with large areas of lawn behind them. The driveway widened out in front of the house to allow a car to turn full circle around a small ornamental pond with a stone fountain in the centre.

The front of the house was well lit by floodlights positioned on the lawns either side of the driveway at the end of the trees. He drove around the pond and parked to the right hand side of the house. When he arrived at the front door it was already open and a young woman wearing a knee length close fitting black dress was waiting for him.

"Good evening, Mr. Grossman, I'm Maria, please follow me."

She led him across a large hall, which accommodated a large sweeping oak staircase, to a pair of large dark carved oak doors. She opened the left door into a large comfortable room with large comfortable looking furniture. He stood in the middle of the room debating whether he should sit down. She went across to a tall dark cupboard which opened up into a very impressive bar. There must have been at least fifty different bottles in there, as well as four or five dozen glasses. "Drink?" she asked with a turn of her head.

"Yes please. Tonic water and ice would be fine, thank you."

"Mr. Phillips will be down in a minute. Please sit down."

He chose a slightly worn looking wing backed chair that had seen better days, but then all of the furniture was old, so he presumed that the furniture was probably antique and was therefore probably worth more than his own house.

'Mr. Phillips, he thought, not 'Dan'. Can't be his wife or girlfriend, must be his PA or maid.

He wasn't given much more time to think as Dan walked briskly into the room. Maria poured him a straight whisky, handed it to him and left the room.

"Good evening Jerry," he said holding out his hand.

Jerry stood up and shook the hand that was offered and sat back down as Dan settled into an identical chair to his own some eight feet away.

"Looking forward to the game?" Dan asked cheerfully.

"Definitely, although I am a bit nervous. I had an excellent game last night, I came out just over eighteen hundred in front," he felt that Dan should be impressed.

"Good. Don't lose it all in the first hand or the night will be quite boring waiting for me to finish."

Jerry came back to earth with a bang, eighteen hundred was peanuts.

"How much cash have you brought with you?"

"Seven thousand. I hope that will be enough."

Jerry felt a little sheepish. He realised that he would be playing with men who had far more money than he had. Still, if he didn't take a risk he wouldn't be able to get the sort of money they had.

"So do I, I'd hate to think you would go home empty on your first night."

"What game do you play?"

"Usually seven card stud."

It was a game Jerry had played a every second or third week when they mixed up the games, he mainly played Hold'em or draw, Omaha Hi-Lo was his particular favourite, but they'd mix it up and play some Omaha or Stud as well. He was quietly confident though, after all, he had successfully stepped up his game the previous night

"Drink up we'd better be moving we've quite a way to go. A word of advice, don't drink when we get there, these guys are extremely good."

All the way there Dan was asking questions about Jerry's work, what sort of robots they produced. Jerry told him about the industrial robots and briefly mentioned the zoo project and the work they were doing for the film

They arrived at a modern mansion-sized house set on a clifftop overlooking the sea. The approach to the house was down a long winding private road. There was no high wall time to keep out intruders, unlike Dan's, but there did appear to be several men walking around outside. There were no trees within fifty yards of the house. Just lawns. Nothing for anyone to hide behind, thought Jerry. Privacy wasn't going to be provided by trees and walls out there. Anyone going there would be there for a purpose.

Dan pulled up by the steps to the white house, left the engine running, got out of the car to be replaced by a thick set man dressed in a dark suit, white shirt and dark tie. Not the sort of person that would be top of the list for invitation to a garden party. Jerry followed Dan into the house, the car was driven off to some invisible parking place.

All very impressive and all very intimidating, thought Jerry. He thought about the seven thousand he had in his pocket and felt inadequate. What am I doing here? This is way above me! He started to feel panic rising up in his stomach. He wanted to leave, but knew he would have to go through with it, no matter what.

Dan called him forward to be introduced to their host. He was a short fat man with dark hair, his left hand supported about as much gold as it would take to anchor a small ship. Big fat rings on every finger, the biggest gaudiest wristwatch Jerry had ever seen and the right wrist was home to the gold anchor chain, but the fingers on that hand were devoid of decoration. It was Lorenzo Lanfranco. Jerry didn't know quite how to respond. It was clear from the reaction of the others that this was a very important and probably a very powerful man, but Jerry had never heard of him. He simply shook the offered hand and said it was a pleasure to meet him. He refrained from making any further comment or observation for fear of making a fool of himself.

He was casually introduced to the other players as well as to two extremely beautiful girls, both aged about twenty, both wearing plunging long dresses, one dark haired, one blonde, both very distracting. Dan told him that they would look after their refreshment needs. Jerry was thinking of other needs at that point in time. They were ushered into an oak panelled room with a single circular table in the middle. The table was also dark oak with a four inch border of oak encircling green baize. There were six packs of unopened cards in the centre of the table, six piles of chips, one at each place determined by six chairs evenly spaced around the table.

Dan ushered them in and gave the instructions.

"Gentlemen, please deposit your funds with the ladies, you have five thousand in chips waiting for you at the table, you can request more chips as and when required. Drinks are not permitted on the table, there is a stand between each chair for those. No-one leaves the table during a hand. You may only rejoin the table between hands. The game is Seven Card Stud, pot limit with an ante of twenty. First jack deals. Our newest player will select the first deck."

They all handed large bundles of notes to the girls who counted the money and entered the amount against each players name in a ledger. Their places had all been decided beforehand with Dan sitting next but one to Jerry's right and Lorenzo sat two places to his left.

Jerry chose the pack that was the furthest away from his appointed place and handed it to Lorenzo, who broke the seal, riffle shuffled the cards, offered the cards to the man on his right to cut and dealt the cards. The first jack landed, second time around in front of the man sitting on Jerry's left, whose name he had already forgotten.

For the first dozen hands Jerry played cautiously, he only completed the hand on three occasions. Each player being dealt two cards face down and one face up. After the ante, bets are placed after each card is dealt face up. When each player has four cards face up the final card is dealt face down At each betting stage players can fold their hand if they feel their cards are not good enough to continue with. Jerry folded six times with two cards up, three times after the third card, known as fifth street and bet three times after the seventh street. He lost each one.

After an hour and a half he was fourteen hundred down, and the way he was playing there was only one direction his pile of chips was going and that was down.

John Hylton, on the other hand, felt that he was holding a fist full of aces. At exactly eight o'clock he pulled up into the car park of the apartment block. It was relatively small, only six apartments in all and Dee-Dee's was on the ground floor. He walked to the entrance, somewhat self-consciously carrying the flowers, pressed her number on the intercom and the door clicked immediately, he let himself in and was greeted by Dee-Dee at her open door dressed magnificently in a knee-length, pale lemon dress with a deep cut neckline. She had a white lace stole around her shoulders partially covering her intriguing bosom. She was dressed to kill,

John thought, and she had just knocked him stone dead.

She looked at the enormous bunch of flowers he had in his arms smiled and said "Come in, we must put these in water before we go, they are absolutely beautiful. Would you like a drink first?"

All John could think was 'Wow'. It took him a few seconds to recover his composure. He followed her through to the kitchen, where she found a vase that was barely large enough to cope with the garden he had brought with him. After she had squeezed them all in and put the plant food into the water she set them in the middle of the low table in the living room, stood back and admired them.

"They're gorgeous, I'll split them later so I can have some in my bedroom as well. What would you like to drink? I don't have much of a selection I'm afraid, whisky, gin, Bacardi and Pernod."

"A small whisky will be fine, thanks, with nothing in it. You have a very attractive apartment here. Have you been here long?"

"Nearly two years," she said over her shoulder as she poured their drinks "I've just about got it how I want it now. Sit down, make yourself comfortable."

John had the choice of a two-seater sofa, three-seater sofa or a matching chair. He quickly decided on the chair, safe, but at least it cut out the chance of him being left alone on one of the sofas.

His choice of seat both dismayed and impressed her at the same time. Not what she would have preferred, but at least it displayed consideration and respect.

A game of chess. The opening gambits were made and responded to, the moves being made with a view to uncovering the other's intentions.

She handed him his drink, he found it extremely difficult to keep his eyes above neck level as she bent towards him, the room seemed to get five degrees warmer.

She retreated to the comparative safety of the three-seater, putting the flowers and the table comfortably and properly, but not completely, between them. She was totally at ease as she leaned back, sideways, into the softness of the sofa and brought her feet up to rest on the seat beside her.

Confident and secure, he thought, as he tried to interpret her body language. He decided that the only way forward was to be the perfect gentleman, forget any lustful thoughts, it was only a reparational dinner date, he told himself, falling something short in the conviction department.

"Where are we going tonight?" she asked.

"Well, if it's alright with you, I've booked a table for nine o'clock at Pierre Luigi's and, if you want to after that, I thought we might go on to The Dancing Slipper... if you like to dance that is. It's ages since I've been there."

He looked for confirmation in her face.

"It sounds wonderful, I shall look forward to it."

"Maybe not as exotic as some of the places you get to, I would think. You must travel around quite a lot."

"This time of year is relatively quiet, it won't pick up for a couple of months or so until the fashion houses start to unveil their spring collections, then we really get into the season with the shows in Milan, Paris, London and New York. It gets very hectic then, flying all over the place. It's like an enormous circus really."

"And very glamorous as well."

"It is for those involved with it all, but for journalists and writers like myself, we are really only hanging on to the coat tails and getting dragged around with the circus."

"Don't you go to the endless parties and dinners, mixing with the rich and famous day after day?"

"We do get invited, but only because if we didn't it would be so much harder for them to get the publicity they crave. With us in there with them they tend to put on an act for us. It's all a bit shallow really. I much prefer to be with interesting people, rather than famous designers and models. They have a tendency to be totally absorbed in themselves and mostly only reflect the image that they portray in magazines: two dimensional, and superficial."

"Well, that has certainly exploded any preconceptions about the fashion world I had!"

"Good, I didn't want you thinking that I lived the so-called 'high-life'. I'm just a straightforward uncomplicated working girl," she said with a semblance of a smile.

If that's absolutely true, he thought, I'm a monkey's cousin.

"Shall we go?" he asked, looking at his watch, it was just after eight thirty.

"Definitely, I could eat a horse."

"No problem, half of the menu's French, so I'm sure it will be on there somewhere," he said, grinning.

She smiled but didn't reply. It should be a good evening, he thought.

When they arrived at the restaurant it was very busy. The head waiter saw them come through the door and hurried over to greet them.

"Good eevening Meester Hylton, how nice to see you here tonight."

He clicked his fingers and immediately he was attended by a young boy wearing a dark blue dinner jacket and black bow-tie who offered to take their coats. Dee-Dee slid out of her long off-white cashmere and handed it carefully to the boy. John pulled off his black Crombie, half folded it and handed it over without reverence to the boy who was finding it very difficult to repress a smile as wide as the Atlantic at the sight of the yellow goddess who stood uncloaked before him.

"That will be all Henri. Thank you," the maître d' snapped.

The boy, chastened, turned and walked off with his burden, but he couldn't resist looking back over his shoulder, only to see a very black look on the maître d's face.

"I shall have words with him later, he will regret his insolence, Mademoiselle."

"Please don't, there is really no offence."

"Thank you for being so gracious," he said, half bowing to her, and held out his arm to indicate the way to their table.

Safely seated at a table for four, set for two, in the centre of the restaurant, they were instantly attended by a waiter brandishing two menus and another waiter, wearing a red dinner jacket, wishing to take their order for drinks.

"Do you come here often?" she asked quite innocently.

"Are you trying to pick me up? What kind of question is that to ask a gent?" he replied with mock indignity.

She laughed.

"Probably two or three times a month," he said seriously.

"I should think that the head waiter was surprised to see you here with another girl this evening then," she teased, yet looking a little disappointed.

"I should imagine he was very surprised. You're a little different from my normal dining companions."

He returned the teasing, and immediately regretted it.

"I'm sorry, I should explain. I normally only come here for

lunch, very rarely with a lady, and even then only when she is accompanied by her business colleagues. This is the first time this year I have had been here for dinner."

The smile and warmth came back into her eyes.

From her reactions, John hoped it was going to be a special evening.

Jerry was definitely having a special evening. He was being taught a poker lesson. He was getting caught time and again. He was running with hands that didn't have a prayer and folding hands that could have won, being frightened off by the betting, bluffed almost out of existence.

By eleven thirty Jerry was almost four thousand down. He had had only one success about an hour before that ended his longest period without winning. He took the opportunity to take a break with a visit to the bathroom at the top of the hour.

He stared into the mirror above the basin and questioned the sanity of being pulled into the deep end and feeling unable to swim with the sharks. It was a hard lesson he was learning, the players he was up against were far better than anyone he had ever come up against before and he was paying for the privilege. The worst hand he had gone with had been a big bluff, that gave the appearance of a straight, but was in fact only a pair of nines. He had been beaten by two small pairs and lost a thousand for the pleasure. It meant that they could read him like a book.

He no longer had to consider the expression on his face, the face staring back at him from the mirror was permanently set as that of a loser.

At eleven forty Dan dealt him another one of those hands that promised a little but would probably cost him a lot. He had a pair of fives in the hole - the face down cards - and a four on top. The betting was light. The other cards were, clockwise from himself, an ace, a queen, an eight, another eight and a six. Every one of the face cards was greater than his pair of fives.

The next delivery saw the arrival of a ten for himself, then in order from there a queen for the ace, a four for the queen, a two for the eight, a second eight giving a pair, and a king on the six.

The pair of eights led the betting with fifty, everyone called.

The third face-up card was dealt, it provided Jerry with a six, the ace-queen with another ace, the queen four with a jack, the eight-two with a three, the pair of eights with a nine, and the king six with another six. That meant that there were three pairs showing on top and three apparently weak hands.

Jerry would have folded but the betting led by the pair of aces to his left was only a hundred with everyone calling except for the eight-two-three that folded, he decided that he could stay in another round, maybe the cards would fall for him, there were no other fives on top. The sixes and eights were weak, with others out on top, the aces were the obvious danger but he didn't go for the kill early, so he thought that they were about all there was in that hand.

When the sixth street, the final face up card, was dealt he received another four, better but nothing to get excited about with two small pairs. The aces didn't improve visibly, nothing to be learned there. Lorenzo received a seven, possible straight or flush, the pair of sixes received a king, giving two pairs, as did Dan with his pair of eights.

The betting increased to two rounds of a hundred, with Dan having raised on his pair of eights. Everyone called, including the aces.

The pot stood at two thousand three hundred and twenty.

The seventh street was dealt face down and Jerry saw a third five giving him a full house of fives over fours. Jerry didn't take it in at first, which was probably his saviour, because if he had, he would almost certainly have given the game away. His pupils dilated, his heart began to race. No one was paying any attention to him, they were watching the rest of the cards fall.

He glanced around the table: Kings and sixes, but with only one king and one six remaining he was sure that he had that beaten. The Aces hadn't improved on the top but with three cards face down and no other Aces out it was possible he could be beaten, but the player hadn't raised at all throughout the hand so it was unlikely he had anything else and was just hoping to hit something on the final card - he immediately flashed back to his thought about what he would have done with four aces and his stomach started to churn.

The best Lorenzo could do was a straight or a flush, but couldn't be a straight flush as Jerry had his six of hearts, so no matter what he had he couldn't win unless he had three of a kind in the hole making four of a kind with one showing... massive odds against that happening.

Unless Dan had a pair of nines or Jacks in the hole, he couldn't win.

The aces opened up with a hundred, Lorenzo raised to two hundred, the kings and sixes called the two hundred, Dan folded, he hadn't got two jacks in the hole, Jerry took his time and reraised to four hundred.

The betting returned to the aces who re-raised two hundred more. Lorenzo called the four hundred. The Kings and sixes folded, Jerry surprised everyone by calling the two hundred and raising another six hundred. The pot had increased to four thousand nine hundred and twenty, the aces responded by calling Jerry's re-raise. It was, four hundred to Lorenzo to call, but he raised again by six hundred.

The betting was back to Jerry, the nerves were beginning to show, his palms were damp, he hesitated briefly and asked for his remaining two thousand in chips as he only had another two hundred and forty in front of him.

"Going out in a blaze of glory, kid?" Lorenzo asked disparagingly.

"Something like that," he said, struggling to hide a quiver in his voice.

The chips duly arrived. He paused and then re-raised all in. He didn't have enough to bet the pot.

The hand had gone on for almost fifteen minutes and until Jerry's big move showed no sign of finishing with the three of them believing they had the winning hand.

The aces eventually called. With almost eight thousand in the pot, he couldn't fold and called.

When Lorenzo called, the pot had grown to a huge eleven thousand six hundred and forty.

As Jerry was the raiser who was called, it was his obligation to reveal his cards.

Ostensibly he had only a pair of fours showing, but one by one he turned over the three fives he had face down. The shock was audible.

Dan clapped and congratulated him. The aces, which turned out to be an ace high club flush looked as though he could kill and Lorenzo who had a jack high heart flush just smiled quietly and said nothing.

Jerry was still shaking while the next hand was being dealt. He really didn't feel up to any more just yet. He accepted his cards, glanced at them, nothing out of the ordinary, received two face up cards and folded at the next bet. At the end of the hand he asked for permission to sit out for a while to collect his thoughts. The battle had taken its toll. It wasn't for the want of leaving the table in a winning state, he was simply drained of energy. He left the room to go to the bathroom, only to be followed by the blonde.

She was five foot four but looked taller in her high heels.

"That was a very good hand you won back there. The others had you out for the count, particularly Michael."

Jerry looked puzzled.

"You know, the one that went with you and Lorenzo."

"Oh. Yes. He didn't seem best pleased with the result. Is there somewhere I can sit down and have a drink?"

"Yeah, sure, in here. I'm Jacqui by the way."

She opened the door to a small sitting room. Compared to the rest of the house it seemed out of place. It had an antique fireplace with a large brass dog grate that had been stacked full of logs, most of which were, by then, three-quarters burnt through. Opposite the fire was a brown leather two-seater sofa with a big old armchair at each end angled in towards the fire. He sat in the centre of the sofa, giving Jacqui the option of sitting next to him or taking one of the chairs. Instead, she turned and went back out of the door, returning two minutes later with two very large brandy glasses with very large brandies inside. She stood in front of him, with her back to the fire, the glow penetrating through the thin material of her cream dress, perfectly outlining her gorgeous silhouette.

"Let's drink to success," she said "in whatever shape it comes."

"I'll drink to that!" he said, looking at the shape that stood in front of him and thinking only of success.

She sat down beside him, put her hand gently on his neck and lightly stroked him.

"How come you got involved with this game?" she asked quietly.

"By accident really, I happened to be playing in another, much smaller game last week and Dan stood in for one of the other players. At the end of the night he asked me if I would like to play in a more competitive game, and here I am."

"You don't gamble for a living, I can tell that, so what do you do?"

Her voice was soft and persuasive.

"Nothing exciting really, I design controls for robots."

"What? Like in the space movies?" she asked innocently, her eyes bright and enquiring.

"No mainly for industrial purposes. Although we have just started building robotic animals."

"Wow, what are they going to be used for?"

"I don't really know, I've not been that closely involved with it, I'm just putting together the remote controls for one of them at the moment.

"Gosh, that must make you one of the cleverest people I know."

She closed her eyes and leaned forwards so that her lips were a fraction away from his face, he could feel her soft breath on his cheek. He turned and slowly, gently kissed her full lips, parting as they touched his.

There was a cough, from somewhere over her shoulder, as Dan stood in the doorway, with a somewhat disgruntled look on his face.

"I think it might be more appropriate for you to return to the game, I think our host might take exception to running off with both his money and his daughter!"

Jerry jumped up like a scalded cat.

"Oh my God, I'm sorry, I didn't realise, I just thought... " he didn't finish the sentence.

"Don't worry, you go back and take the rest of their money instead," Jacqui said with a positively wicked look in her eyes.

The rest of the evening was pretty much an anti-climax, in every sense of the word, Jerry lost sixteen hundred over the last two hours, but still remained three thousand in front. He didn't see Jacqui again until they were packing up. She came in to see if any more drinks were required, and she didn't even look at Jerry.

On the drive home Dan remarked that it was an extremely dangerous thing to have tried to take advantage of Lorenzo's daughter. Jerry protested his innocence, that he had been the one that was being seduced, besides, they had been interrupted before anything could have happened.

"I don't think Lorenzo would see it that way somehow. I was sent to find you, I don't want to be sent to find you again. Do you understand?" he said with undisguised menace.

Jerry thought that he understood only too well. He felt extremely relieved when he was safely back in his car and driving home. At least they didn't know where he lived. He took a very circuitous route home, just to be on the safe side. He didn't like the idea of being followed, no matter how unlikely. Maybe it would be safer if he stopped playing cards for a while.

By contrast, John and Dee-Dee had enjoyed a very pleasant evening, no stress, no tension, just enjoying each other's company. They had left the restaurant just after ten thirty, the food and wine had been excellent. John left his car in the restaurant car park and they walked the two hundred yards or so to the Dancing Slipper.

They danced together for most of the night, breaking occasionally for a drink, but mostly locked in each other's arms.

They left the club at two thirty, feeling relaxed and comfortable with each other. Holding hands on the way back to the car.

John opened the car door for her, but before she could get in he put his hands to her face and kissed her softly.

She looked up at him with smiling eyes, said nothing and got into the car.

The journey back to her apartment was made in silence. When they arrived, he quickly got out of the car, walked round and opened the passenger door. They walked slowly to her door, hand in hand, she opened the security door to the lobby and stopped in the doorway.

"Can I see you again, soon?" he asked.

"I don't know. I've really enjoyed this evening, but there are other complications. Let me give you a call sometime during the week."

Before he could reply, she quickly leaned over and kissed his cheek, turned quickly away to her own apartment door, put her key in the lock and opened it.

"I've had a wonderful time tonight. Let me take it all in. I'll call you, I promise."

She closed the door.

John was stunned for a few moments. His brain was in total disarray. What did she mean when she said "but there are other complications"? Is she married?

Totally confused, he let himself out of the security door and walked slowly back to his car. His feet suddenly felt like they were made of concrete. It was not how he wanted things to be. He had felt alive at the end of the evening only to be replaced by feeling completely numb.

Limbo was a difficult place to be.

Dee-Dee was also confused, it was not at all right. She didn't want to get involved, but it would be so easy and yet it would be so wrong.

Chapter 10

The telephone disturbed the silence, the ringing was an unwanted intrusion.

"Well?"

"I don't want to continue."

"You've started it. You'll have to finish it."

The connection closed. The silence was restored. Discussion was neither required nor permitted.

Chapter 11

Nine o'clock, Sunday morning, John's head was still spinning. He decided that the best solution was to ring Suzie and go for a long hard run, something they hadn't done together since the summer.

"You've only just caught me, another five minutes and I wouldn't have been here. Come over, I'd be delighted to have the company."

"I'll be there in ten minutes." He put down the phone, pulled on his running clothes and was in his car in less than two minutes. Six minutes later he pulled into Suzie's driveway.

"Hi. What's brought this on then? Your head need unscrambling again?" she asked unsympathetically.

"You always know how to hit where it hurts don't you?" John wasn't in a mood for confiding and Suzie wasn't the best person in the world to get advice from. She was too self sufficient, too much in control of herself, but she was a great one to draw strength from. "No, I just felt that after a good night out the best thing for me was to come out and give my body some punishment. Where are we going?"

"I was planning to go up into the hills, it will be cold and the forecast is for dry weather until late on this afternoon. A fifteen mile circuit should get the heart working. We can grab a light lunch back here and go for a nice bike ride this afternoon."

John knew what her definition of a bike ride was, fifty miles minimum. "I was just about with you until the bike ride, let's see what's left of me after the run first please."

They drove out in John's Audi to a spot five miles out of town, which, had it been summer, would have been extremely busy with walkers and tourists. The paths criss-crossed the hills, with colour coded markers denoting the more popular routes. It was a breathtaking place to be on a clear day, but the cloud was low and the tops of some of the hills were shrouded in mist. Unless the wind picked up the mist would stay there for the rest of the day.

He parked the car in one of the many small parking areas that had been cleared at the side of the road, loosened up with stretching exercises for five minutes and then set off at a steady pace. They ran along in silence, side by side where the path permitted, Suzie in front where it did not.

Five miles out and John was beginning to unwind, his running had settled into a rhythm and his mind had broken free from the shackles of the previous night's events. In the cold light of day, things were more in perspective. After all, he hardly knew her, Dee-Dee had only come into his life by accident, literally, and one night out, no matter how enjoyable, doesn't make a romance. Must be going soft in my old age he thought.

"Come on, slow coach," Suzie called from twenty yards in front, "are you getting tired already?"

"Sorry, I wasn't concentrating."

"I'll race you to the top of the next hill. I'll give you a hundred yard start."

John looked ahead, it must have been best part of half a mile away, with about a three hundred foot rise. "You're on, loser buys the beer."

He accelerated smoothly away from her, Suzie ran on the spot until he was far enough in front, and then set about the task of hauling him in.

John was setting a good pace, but as they started to climb John realised that he wasn't quite as fit as he thought. His calf and thigh muscles were beginning to pull tighter and as he drove his legs into the path to push harder he knew that if he was to beat her to the top he would be running on fumes when he got there.

He glanced over his shoulder with no more than a hundred and fifty yards to go and was met with the sight of Suzie, seemingly floating over the ground, drawing closer with every stride. John with a gargantuan effort managed to hold her twenty-five yards behind him, but with a hundred yards to go Suzie closed the gap and comfortably beat him to the top by thirty seconds, the last part of the climb John finished at walking pace.

Suzie was still moving when he arrived, she was stretching, doing star jumps and squats.

John just looked in amazement. "Where do you get the energy from?"

"How many times have you done this since the summer?"

"None."

"You have your answer then, I do this every weekend, twice when the weather is good."

"Point taken."

There was no real surprise involved. There was a big difference running on a machine in the gym and running out doors on uneven ground an conditions that were less than ideal.

He sat on a large rock to get his breath back, at least the run back wouldn't be too difficult. After a couple of minutes she sat down next to him.

"Want to talk about it?" she said with genuine concern in her voice.

"No, it's nothing serious. I was just feeling a bit off that's all. I thought the exercise would do me some good."

"Hmm, I know you better than that, John Hylton. Stay in control at all times please."

Yes, miss!" he said, doubting whether he'd be able to do that.

"Okay, we'd better get moving or your muscles will get too cold and in this weather you can pull something quite easily.

Unfortunate choice of words, he thought ironically.

They stood up and moved easily across the top of the hill and started the long easy descent down the other side, circling around to the left to begin the route back. They had taken forty five minutes to run out, a six minute stop and fifty eight minutes to run back. Not championship times for a thirteen mile run, but for a Sunday morning cross-country it had been a good work-out. Precisely what John had needed.

Monday, 15th December, only ten days to go to Christmas and the atmosphere in the office was picking up. Hardly anyone was working late once the party season was getting into full swing. John was invited to several during the course of the day, friends and clients alike were inviting him to their parties, two of which he accepted invitations to on behalf of himself and Suzie during the week and two others for the weekend which he said he would let them know later on in the week when things were more settled.

The first two were for clients and Suzie was invited in her own right, but those events they normally attended together.

The two weekend parties would be all-nighters and it was necessary to be in the right mood or they would seemingly go on forever - Dragging the Night Away, make a good name for a song, he thought. He would decide on those much nearer the time. They wouldn't miss him if he didn't go; there would probably be more than a hundred and fifty at each party anyway and by midnight nobody would be in a fit state to consider who was or wasn't there.

Having spent most of the morning fielding social calls, he went down to the construction area to see how the rhino was coming on.

It turned out that the skeleton was almost complete, it would soon be time, literally, to put some flesh on the bones.

He went through to see Barry Perkins. As he opened the door he was greeted by Baggy and he bent forward to stroke his head.

"We'll soon have a job for you," he said thoughtfully to Baggy. "How's the remote coming on?"

"Jerry's almost done with it," he gestured with his head towards Jerry who was working at a computer with a monitor displaying a facial close up of John, looking, rudely he thought, straight up his nose. John realised the cat was sat down and looking up at him.

John was impressed.

"Very good. Presumably we will be able to turn this on whenever we want?"

"Yes. And we can also use voice commands through here as well as introducing new routines if we want to change his behaviour pattern, wherever he is and whenever it is necessary without recalling him."

"Excellent, and I presume that this will also go straight into the rhino."

"Yes, it should be ready to install along with the main processors later this week."

Barry looked pleased with himself, he had good reason to be.

"Have you finished with Baggy now?" John asked.

"Yes, we don't need him in here anymore."

"Good. Come," he said looking at Baggy.

John opened the door and left the room with Baggy following close behind.

As he left, Jerry said, "Barry, do you realise we have the purrfect peeping tom? Any of the girls wearing a short skirt with Baggy around could be in serious danger of exposing herself right here on the screen!" Jerry had a lecherous smirk on his face.

"If you do that, you're fired!" he said, trying to be serious.

But Barry couldn't avoid a small smile to himself.

John was quite getting used to Baggy following him around, the cat almost seemed to be developing a personality. He put it down to the programming from the cat in the zoo. They were still adding data from Alan, but most of it wasn't activated, after all they didn't want Baggy ripping someone's head off just because it felt like the right thing to do.

The preparation of the control data had been much more complete for the rhino and Suzie was running tests on it when he walked in with Baggy in tow.

"Good morning, how's yer legs, partner?" she asked.

"A little sore, but able to hobble better than I did first thing this morning. It looks as though we may be ready for setting up the rhino on Friday if everything goes well. Have you seen Bob this morning?"

"Yes, he's well advanced, the tissues are already half way there. As soon as the skeleton's complete he can start attaching. The control system has already been built in, the Kevlar underskin is being made right now, so we appear to be right on schedule. Any thoughts on a name? I thought we could put out a suggestion box and give a case of champagne to the best one, that should put some extra party spirit amongst them. Closing date tomorrow lunchtime. Okay?"

"Fine by me, the sooner we have a name the better, much less cumbersome than 'the rhino'."

The names flew in thick and fast, some were silly, some were imaginative, some were rude, but the winner was "Rhoda", The champagne went to Sally. She chose the name because she had an aunt who was big, fat and frightening. Three of the bottles were opened that lunchtime and everyone had a glass to celebrate the Christening of "Rhoda the Rhino". Slightly strange that she should be Christened on the Tuesday before she was officially due to be 'born', but nobody complained.

Tuesday evening was supposed to be Jerry's quiet night in, doing all of the household chores that he chauvinistically called 'woman's work'. He hated cleaning, changing sheets, washing clothes and the occasional flick round with a duster, but he couldn't justify paying someone to come in and do it for him. He wasn't exactly houseproud but he did prefer things to be relatively neat and tidy.

He didn't hear the phone ring at first, above the noise of the vacuum cleaner, it was only when he was right next to it that he saw that it was ringing.

"Hello."

"Jerry," the voice was big and friendly, "I'm glad you're in," said Dan Phillips, "we've got a game on Thursday night. I'll pick you up at seven thirty."

"I don't know. I don't think I'll be able to play, I'm supposed to be at a party." Jerry's brain was racing, nervous, trying to sound convincing.

Dan was more forthright, slightly ominous, "I don't think a party is as important as this. I know where you live, I'll pick you up at seven thirty. You can carry on with your cleaning now. Bye."

Jerry stood looking at the phone in his hand, trying to let the implications sink in. He heard a car start up outside, ran to the window only to see Dan's car moving slowly away. He must have been watching through the window, the curtains had been open, he wouldn't have even needed to get out of the car.

Jerry suddenly felt extremely vulnerable and more than a little concerned. All because of a game of cards. What had he got himself into? He should never have moved out of his league. Dan had been helpful and friendly at first, now he was distinctly worrying.

Who was Lorenzo? What was his business? Why did he need men patrolling outside his house? Was he legitimately wealthy or did he live in fear? The questions raced through his mind. The only conclusion that he could come to was that he would have to lose the money he had won the previous Saturday, and probably double. At least he would be no worse off than before he had played on the Friday night, no real lasting damage done.

He resolved that Thursday would be his last ever game. It wasn't what he'd set out for, just some fun and a little extra money, no harm in that, but it looked like these people didn't play for fun. Then it occurred to him that it might just be a ruse to get him back to the scene of his indiscretion with Jacqui.

"Oh God, I hope not," he said out loud. The thought made him feel distinctly uncomfortable. Not something to dwell on.

The rest of the evening was a blur. He did the rest of his jobs without concentration and at eleven o'clock he stepped into the shower, feeling drained, somewhere warm and somewhere to wash away his worries, he thought hopefully.

He considered not being at home when Dan called. How did he

know where he lived? He had avoided telling him and the players at his Friday night game only knew his telephone number. That worried him. If they knew where he lived they probably knew where he worked, they would probably follow him to make sure he didn't run off somewhere.

Then as water and soap cascaded from his body, he came to the conclusion that he was probably over-reacting and that Dan just wanted to make sure they got their money back, after all, he hadn't been invited to the first game with them expecting him to win. The compliments Dan had paid him had felt a little bit over the top at the time, now they seemed quite obvious: egos had a habit of misting the vision. That would be it, they just wanted his money.

Somewhat relieved he got out of the shower and dried himself. As he got into bed he decided that he could comfortably afford to lose five thousand out of the seven thousand he would take with him and consider it a lesson well learned.

Suzie and John attended the first of the parties they had been invited to. A taxi collected them from their respective homes ensuring there would be no restrictions upon their freedom to enjoy themselves, always considering that they had to work the following day. It was a good party, thrown by a small but rapidly growing chemical engineering company for its staff, customers and major suppliers. Held at the city's largest hotel, it was a lavish affair with thirty tables, each seating ten people. The function room had been beautifully decorated with balloons, flowers and streamers everywhere. There was even a net suspended above the dance floor containing a thousand balloons that were released just before the end of the party at one thirty.

A twenty piece band provided the music right through the evening and, apart from when the food was being served, the dance floor was packed from start to finish.

It was a relaxed evening, with both John and Suzie enjoying it. They danced with at least ten different people each and talked to at least fifty more.

When they returned home in the cab, they were both relaxed, comfortable and very slightly drunk. Saturday night seemed a thousand years away as the cab dropped off Suzie first. John gave her a peck on the cheek and thanked her for her company. Suzie smiled, said "Goodnight" and left John in the cab.

When he reached home, out of habit, he checked his answer machine. There was one message for him, he pressed play, there was a click, three seconds of silence and then another click. Someone had clearly been in two minds as to whether to leave a message or not. He wasn't too bothered until it occurred to him that it might have been Dee-Dee. Accepting there was nothing he could do about it at two in the morning he flopped into bed and slept like a log until the alarm rudely awoke him at seven o'clock.

Chapter 12

Alan, having completed the studies of the rhino and panther, took down the cameras surrounding their pens and moved them to the chimpanzees and brown bears. He thought the bears would be a simple enough part of the project but the chimps would probably take the longest of all, given their extremely complex behaviour and society structure. There would be a lot to learn if they were to be successfully replaced.

He hadn't seen anyone from the zoo for several days. No one had tried to get into see him, Pete had kept himself tucked away in the lodge: the refurbishment work had given him plenty to do for the past week or so. Unusual, though, that he hadn't been seen at all.

The two and a half days had been as quiet as a cemetery at midnight. Excluding the animals, he hadn't seen a living soul at the zoo. Maybe they had found out more than he thought possible.

Not wanting to take any further chances, he left the zoo and headed back to the office.

He went straight into see John.

"Call me paranoid , John but I haven't seen anyone at the zoo all week. I know they've been busy refitting the lodge, but there's usually someone poking around asking questions. This morning I took down the cameras from the rhino and panther pens, put them back up on the chimps and bears and nothing, nobody. There'd normally be at least two of them come over to see what I was doing, I think they've been ordered to stay away."

"Do you think that this has anything to do with Jerry's conversation with Pete last week?"

"I can't think what else it could be. When I spoke to him on the phone, I tried not to say too much, but if they were listening in somehow they must have known that we were onto them. How else could they have heard about Baggy?"

"And you think that because they are listening in they don't need to ask questions any more, is that it?"

"It's the only thing that makes sense."

"But given that there is very little that is actually said in there, unless you talk to yourself all day long, they can't know very much at all? Unless Jerry let on more than he told us."

John picked up his phone, called Barry Perkins and asked him to send Jerry up to him straight away.

A minute later Jerry appeared at the door, John and Alan remained seated.

"Think back to last Friday morning when you went to the zoo. Is there any little detail that you didn't tell us about? This may be very important. Think carefully," Alan said

Jerry felt a little uncomfortable. "I told you before everything that happened. We hardly said any more than ten words to each other. I didn't have the time or the inclination to talk to him, I was in a hurry to get back with the data, and it was pouring with rain," he said defensively.

"Okay, thanks Jerry, that's all for now."

Jerry gratefully left the room for the sanctuary of the lab.

"That means that they have to be listening in to us, it can't be the phone as we only use our mobiles, not the line they provided for us and they haven't been in the room with an opportunity to do anything since we've been there. I'll go into town and see if I can get hold of a frequency scanner, if they have planted anything in there I should be able to find it easily enough."

Alan had a determined look on his face, it was annoying him to think that his privacy had been invaded.

The phone on John's desk broke the temporary silence.

"Yes Barbara?"

"There's a Mr. Keith Boscik on the line for you."

"Thanks, put him through. Keith, how are you? Long time no see."

"I'm fine thanks, but it's you that concerns me."

"There's nothing wrong with me that your surgeon's knife can cure," John laughed, albeit slightly uneasily.

"I didn't mean in that way."

Keith went on to describe the conversations with Jackson and his shenanigans, emphasising that Jackson had half been frightened out of his wits at the prospect of being found out and losing the money - being more frightened of the boss than anything else.

"It couldn't have been a more opportune moment for you to call, you have just answered a whole load of questions and saved Alan a lot of work. I owe you. Let's get together sometime soon, I'll buy you the best dinner in town. I'll call you straight after Christmas."

"Make it the second week in January, I'm having a

reconciliation trip to New Zealand and Australia with Marcia over Christmas and New Year, try to rescue what's left of our marriage. You look after yourself and have a good Christmas."

"Good luck."

"Thanks."

John put the phone down. "Well, it seems as though out friend Jackson has got you bugged, but when you guessed something was going on he panicked and pulled the plug at his end. The transmitter is somewhere above your chair in the roof void. Still activated but no longer in use."

John relaxed, the threat was gone.

"I'll get up there this afternoon and find it. There's an access hatch in the ceiling at the opposite end of the room, I can get in there. I'll call you when I've found it."

Alan was sporting a huge grin. "And then I'll give Jackson back his lost property, he'll probably need to change his pants when I drop that on his desk."

"Go for it. Send me back the pictures!" John said with a laugh.

Honour would be satisfied, he thought.

It took Alan only five minutes of crawling through the roof space across the ceiling joists, just avoiding putting his knees through the ceiling, to find the device and only another thirty seconds to work out how it came to be in there. Pete Thomas had left the cut out piece of felt on top of the ceiling where he had come in through the roof. Very clever, he thought, at least it had only been a recent entry, it couldn't have been in there from the beginning or they wouldn't have had to break in through the roof.

"Now for the fun," he said to himself with a smile.

He climbed back out of the roof with the bug in his hand, disconnected the battery and put the device, not much bigger than a matchbox, into his jacket pocket.

Walking briskly across to the office, he burst in, ignoring Alice completely, and presented himself to Jackson, appearing to be full of anger.

"What the hell do you think you are doing?"

Jackson looked dumbfounded, but wasn't given a chance to answer.

"We pay you and your crumby zoo a small fortune and you repay us like this. Well, I've been doing some fumigating!"

He slammed the bug down on to the desk. Jackson looked absolutely petrified, quite unable to speak.

"Do you know how I found this?"

Jackson shook his head.

"By sheer bad luck. It had been interfering with the signals coming back from the zebra pen. That's three weeks work down the pan thanks to you and your big nose. Most of the data is scrambled, it'll take ages to sort it out. You stupid prat!"

Alan was beginning to enjoy it, but Jackson looked as though he would have been happier jumping out of a plane without a parachute.

"Don't expect to get paid this month's money. And we may not see out the rest of the agreement either. That will very much depend on how well you can grovel to Mr. Hylton."

Alan turned smartly and left Jackson feeling as if he had just been through a hurricane. It was a good job he had been sitting down or he would probably have fallen over with the impact.

"Alice," he called with a very shaky voice, reaching into the bottom drawer for his bottle of whisky and a glass. He put the glass back, unscrewed the top and took a long pull from the half full bottle.

"Yes Mr. Jackson?"

"Take a letter. Write this in the most pleading tone you can manage. You've got a job, and a life, to save... mine."

Alan called John and related the event to him who seemed to enjoy it every bit as much as Alan had done.

"I think you will probably get a letter from him apologising as abjectly as he can. I don't think he's got the courage to talk to you."

"It will be interesting to see what he claims his motivation was. I would think that Daniels was the one that put him up to it. He's probably more scared of what he might do to him, if what he told Keith is anything to go by. Well done, at least that's got that monkey off our backs."

John put the phone down and it immediately rang again. "Hello."

"Have you had any more thoughts about the Virgins?" Suzie asked.

"Yes, it should be illegal for anyone over the age of nineteen!"

He laughed, he was in a good mood.

"Very funny. Typically male. I'm going to book a flight for the 27th, that's a week on Saturday. If you would like to come I would be glad of the company, if not it doesn't matter, I'm quite used to holidaying on my own."

"Okay, you've talked me into it. Flying back the following Saturday, yes?"

"Yes, we'll get the New Year celebrations and festivals, no work, no stress, plenty of diving, you won't regret it. I'll talk to you later."

John rocked back in his chair, put his feet on the desk and felt better about life than he had done in a long time.

Thursday afternoon saw the personal delivery of an envelope marked for the private and confidential attention of Mr. J. Grossman. It was handed to Barbara by a tall black haired man with a hard, unkind face. The sort of man some women would fall for in a flash and spend the rest of their lives regretting it. She had just met Dan Phillips.

No, he didn't need to see Mr. Grossman, just to give him the letter as soon as possible. He left as quickly as he'd arrived.

Barbara called Jerry, who was working on Rhoda's controls with Barry at the time. She told him that it was an urgent delivery. Jerry couldn't imagine what it could be, but went up to reception five minutes later.

He started to open the envelope on his way back to the lab. It contained a playing card, the Ace of Spades. Nothing else, no message. The card itself was enough. They knew where he lived and now they showed that they knew where he worked. Why? What use could he be to them, a small fish in a very big ocean. He hadn't got enough money to make them rich, he didn't have access to state secrets. Why?

As he stood pondering, John walked towards him in the corridor, saw the ace on his hand and said "Not allowed to play cards in working time," with mock seriousness and continued on past him.

Baggy trotted on behind, he was becoming inseparable from John. He greeted him every morning like a dog upon the appearance of his master come down for breakfast. John was becoming more convinced the cat was developing a persona as each day passed. Nobody had considered the emotional aspect when they were programming her. Emotions weren't something you learned either, they were something you felt, or were they? Maybe a mixture of both. Social conditioning plays a part in the development of people, so the same logic could easily apply to Baggy.

John didn't know whether it was a good thing or a bad one. A cat with a human personality? The concept stretched the human understanding beyond its boundaries. John concluded that he must be imagining it, the animal could only be reflecting what it saw, not interpreting it, nothing to worry about, was there?

Barbara received the second visitor of the afternoon. She was the complete opposite of the previous caller. Tall, long blonde hair, very attractive figure, the type men fell for in a flash and spent the rest of their lives wondering what hit them. Maybe not so different after all.

Barbara smiled her professional smile, "How may I help you?"

"I've called to see Mr. Hylton, if he's available."

"And you are?"

"Miss Sampson."

"I don't have an appointment for you Miss Sampson. Can I ask you what it's about?"

"It's a personal matter," Dee-Dee said without being evasive.

I bet it's personal, thought Barbara, with your looks it wouldn't be much else.

"I don't think he will be free at the moment, Mr. Hylton has meetings all afternoon."

"Would you please check with him, it really is quite important."

Barbara reluctantly picked up the phone and after a few seconds began to speak to John, inaudibly to Dee-Dee. The look on Barbara's face said it all. Disappointment.

"Mr. Hylton will be out to see you in a few minutes. It will have to be brief as he is very busy. Perhaps you would care to take a seat in the waiting area."

Barbara gestured to her right towards an archway leading to a room with several easy chairs placed around a coffee table.

"Would you like a coffee while you are waiting?"

Dee-Dee nodded.

"Milk and sugar?"

"Just milk please."

Sweet enough already, Barbara thought bitchily.

Dee-Dee waited patiently, glancing through the selection of magazines on the table, all of them current, a good mixture of technical and general, giving an insight into the type of business establishment she was in.

The coffee didn't arrive until four seconds before John arrived, Barbara hurrying across just in front of him.

"Would you like a coffee as well, John?" she asked with obvious and unprofessional familiarity.

"Yes please, I could do with one," he said somewhat lamely.

John thought he detected an air of disdain about Barbara, but couldn't think why it should be.

"Hi, nice to see you again."

He meant it.

"Yes and you. I'm sorry about," she broke off as Barbara re-entered with John's coffee and pointedly waited for her to go before finishing the sentence, "Saturday night," she continued.

"There's nothing to apologise for. We went out, we, I had a marvellous time."

"You were right first time, we had a marvellous time. I suppose I enjoyed it so much that it just frightened me a bit that's all."

Her whole attitude was that of an apology. It was clear to him that she meant every word of it, either that or she deserved an Oscar for her performance.

"That's alright, I must confess to being a bit shaken by the abruptness of the end to what had been a perfect evening, but there was no offence taken."

He smiled gently at her, not wanting to make another forward step for fear of being rejected again.

"Then I feel a lot better for that. How's your car?"

"I should get it back tonight, how about yours?"

"I picked it up this morning, all sorted. Look, would it be possible to see each other again this weekend, pick up where we left off?"

He could tell that she would have been hurt if he turned her down. It had taken a lot of courage for her to come and see him, although he didn't know why.

"If you don't mind coming to a party on Saturday night where you will be among two hundred people you don't know, then I would be delighted to take you."

"As long as you don't mind me sticking to you like a leech," she peered out from under her eyebrows, her head tilted down slightly.

"Not at all, the pleasure would be all mine."

"I will look forward to it," she smiled, the relief showed on her face.

"I'll pick you up at eight again, you can introduce me to Joe this time," he said, returning the smile.

"It's a deal."

She held out her hand, he shook it, he would have preferred to have kissed her, but Barbara would probably have had a seizure, judging by her previous performance.

Dee-Dee smiled and waved to Barbara on her way out and didn't give a hoot about her sitting in her chair, seething.

John had a definite bounce in his step on his way back to his office. Life was looking up and he was now looking forward to a party that only the day before he had convinced himself he wouldn't attend.

Jerry was pacing up and down in his living room, lights off, curtains open. Able to see out, not wanting to be seen. It was seven thirty-five, maybe he wasn't coming after all, but that would be too much to hope for. The lights showed along the street as Dan's car pulled up in front of his small house. Dan didn't get out, he clearly expected Jerry to come to him. Good dog, thought Jerry, as he bitterly opened his front door to obey the unspoken command. He briskly walked down to the car, trying to put on a brave show. He didn't feel brave. He felt like a condemned man going to meet his executioner.

"Hi, Jerry, glad you could make it."

The smile on the face of the tiger, Jerry thought ruefully as he opened the car door and saw the gleam in Dan's eyes.

"Wouldn't miss it for the world," he lied. "I'll go Christmas shopping tomorrow with the winnings," he said flatly and totally without conviction.

"Yeah, me too. How much have you brought with you?"

"Seven thousand, same as last time."

"Well, as we know you now, we'll accept markers if you need some more," Dan said with a hint of hidden meaning.

"I'm sure that won't be necessary."

The rest of the trip was made in silence.

They arrived, without incident, back at Lorenzo's house, the men were still patrolling the gardens. Jerry wondered if they were ever allowed inside the house, or whether, like most guard dogs, they had their own kennels at the back somewhere. He was thinking cynically and was aware that he had become resigned to his fate, whatever it might be.

He was not, however, prepared for Jacqui, who bounded over to meet him in the hallway, in a dress that was cut far too low to be decent and her ample cleavage was on display for all those foolhardy enough to look at it. Jerry was feeling very foolhardy, he thought he might as well be hung for stealing a sheep as much as a lamb. She threw her arms around his neck and gleefully said "Daddy said you would come back tonight, I didn't think you would after Saturday, but as usual, Daddy was right. I put this dress on specially for you. Do you like it?"

He felt that the entire world was watching him, waiting for a bad move, ready to pounce.

"It would be a pleasure to see you in almost anything."

He tried to be gallant and noticed that he wasn't as shaken as he expected. His confidence started to rise, Daddy surely wouldn't do anything to harm his daughter's current favourite?

"Well, that dress is almost nothing," Dan said clumsily, staring at her breasts, and laughed at his own crude observation.

The withering look he received from Lorenzo would have fried a chicken at ten paces. Dan wished he had kept his thoughts to himself. Jerry had definitely scored points with Lorenzo there, any more like that and Lorenzo would probably let the kid win tonight.

Drinks were offered as they were led into a large well lit, contemporary white living room. There were works of art all over the walls. There was an impressive swimming pool painting by Hockney that was hung on the wall to Jerry's left as he entered the room. Opposite were large sliding glass doors that took up almost the entire wall. The doors, had the weather been appropriate, opened on to a patio surrounding a swimming pool exactly like the one in the picture. He wondered which one had come first, the pool or the picture. He guessed the picture as the pool looked too new. Even in the middle of winter it was open and illuminated, presumably, therefore, heated. The retractable, telescoping, sliding walls and roof were parked at the far left end of the pool.

Jacqui moved him on to what she described as "Daddy's

favourite". It was, to Jerry, a strange affair full of triangles, circles and other geometric shapes hanging above a huge modern fireplace. Jacqui explained that it was an abstract expressionist painting by a man called Kandinsky. Jerry didn't want to ask what that meant as he got the feeling that Jacqui wouldn't have known either.

After the guided tour of the room, Jerry was invited to go to the card room along with the others.

He took up the same seat as he had on Saturday night, the only difference was that the pair of aces had been replaced by a timid looking man, small in stature and looking like a summer breeze would blow him away. He was nervously cleaning his spectacles when he was invited to choose a deck of cards from the six in the centre of the table.

Lorenzo looked at Jerry and announced, "Mr. Jones here is a senior manager for one of the country's most important financial institutions. He is brilliant with figures so be warned, Jerry, he will be calculating the odds faster than your computers!"

Jerry was taken aback by that: Lorenzo seemed to be warning him. Maybe he had nothing to fear after all. He also noticed that it was the new player that was offered the choice of deck, just as he himself had been a few nights before. The man Jones had replaced, the pair of aces, had lost heavily on Saturday, maybe, he thought, they like to play games in more ways than one, with their chosen prey. Maybe there is more than one purpose to it; maybe there is a hidden agenda; maybe there is a danger, but maybe not at the table for me tonight. Fortified and not worried by his string of maybes, Jerry resolved to play for all he was worth, hoping that he wouldn't lose all he was worth.

The evening was fairly slow and uneventful for the first couple of hours or so, with each man almost taking it in turns to win a series of small hands. Then, after a short break, just after eleven o'clock the cards seemed to take a dramatic turn, but not for Jerry.

It was a big hand, Jerry's first four cards were so random it would have taken a miracle for him to have made anything of it so he folded before he took his fifth card. When the fifth card had been dealt the others all had something promising on top, the weakest hand appeared to be Jones's, a pair of fours. There were two other pairs showing and Lorenzo with a possible straight flush, Dan had a pair of eights. The hand started to look very familiar to

Jerry.

He noted that Jones didn't have the six of hearts that would be needed to prevent the straight flush, he had the ten of diamonds and he already had the pair of fours that Jerry had had when he played the hand previously. The pair of aces from last time, this time were queens with an ace, the other meaningless hand was there and so was Michael with his pair of sixes.

Jerry realised immediately what was going on. He had been let out. That was the fate that should have befallen him on Saturday night. Why had they allowed him to win? Was it down to Jacqui? He looked across to her, she was sat in an easy chair in the corner to his left. She smiled knowingly at him. He knew now. He hadn't won that hand, he had been given it!

He somehow doubted that the same fate was about to visit Mr. Jones.

Jones was looking fairly calm as he stayed with the betting. He received the six, but it wasn't the six of hearts, it was the six of clubs. They had him!

The betting was heavier than Saturday had been. They were raising two fifty at a time and there was already over five thousand in the pot and still two cards to go. Jerry worked out that the cards were going to leave Lorenzo as the only threat to Jones, and what a threat!

Michael sat there with his pair of sixes and a king showing, two other kings had been and gone, Jones had a six in front of him, the chances of Michael getting the remaining king and six as his hole cards were extremely remote, but then they only needed to beat him with one hand, not two.

The final cards were dealt and as Jerry expected. The queens hadn't improved, Lorenzo looked open for the straight flush, although needing two cards to complete it. Dan folded during the betting of the previous round so that just left the three of them. The queens had also folded.

The betting was getting heavy. After three rounds, Jones called for the rest of his chips and shoved all in, bar two thousand. The pot was over fifteen thousand. The other two also asked for an additional five thousand chips. It was clear to Jerry that Michael stayed in as it hiked up the betting and reduced the chances of a call. That was what his father had warned him about all those years ago... and he had been so close to getting caught, saved only by the whim of a girl.

Lorenzo pointed out to Jones that markers were acceptable should he need to use the facility, immediately prior to raising Jones's shove by twelve thousand.

"I think that I will take advantage of that offer. Twenty five thousand will suffice please."

"Okay. Jacqui, will you do the honours please?" Lorenzo asked calmly.

A pad was offered, with the amount entered. Jones signed it and was presented with another pile of chips.

"In which case I will raise you to twenty seven thousand," he said very confidently. Michael folded.

"Do you want to go again? Make it another, say, thirty five?" Lorenzo asked politely.

Jones as confidently as before replied, "Make it fifty and I'll call you."

"So, that's seventy five thousand total? Are you quite sure?"

"Absolutely!"

"So be it. Jacqui? Again please. Just put your marker in the pot, Mr. Jones, that's fine."

Jones, very hurriedly, turned over one four from his first two cards and the fourth four from his final card, four of a kind. He was grinning like a madman.

His hands shot out to take the pot, but even faster than a striking rattlesnake, Lorenzo's hand grabbed his left wrist to stop him.

Lorenzo looked disgusted with him.

"Mr. Jones, you have just made three cardinal errors. Firstly, you turned over your cards when it was you who called me, but that can be forgiven in the heat of the game. Secondly, you have reached out greedily to claim a pot that you do not know to be yours."

He hesitated for maximum impact.

Jones gulped.

"And the third?" he said very shakily.

"You have lost."

Those three words seemed to hang in the air like a spectre at a funeral.

Jones went totally white as Lorenzo turned over first the five and then the six of hearts. The straight flush was there.

"Holy Mother of God!" Jones didn't need to say anything else. He was down by eighty two thousand. He slumped back in his chair.

The tension was broken by Jacqui who stood up and enquired "Would anyone care for a drink?"

Jerry sat stock still, not daring to make a move, not wanting to give any impression that he understood that Jones had just been cheated out of a large fortune. For all of his intelligence, it had been the greed of the man that had led to his downfall. He and Jones were now the only ones left seated at the table and feeling that he didn't want to be associated with Jones on any level, Jerry stood up and left him to contemplate his fate. From the look on his face, total and utter bewilderment, it crossed Jerry's mind that just maybe Jones hadn't got the kind of money he had just lost. He didn't even want to think about it. There but for the grace of Jacqui…!

He turned round looking for Jacqui, he saw her bouncing towards him, again with two large brandy glasses, with very large brandies inside and an extremely lascivious look in her eyes.

"Would you like to join me in front of the fire?"

It wasn't so much a question and he certainly didn't feel that no was an option. They quietly slipped out of the room and into the same sitting room that they were in when Dan so rudely interrupted them.

The large white furry rug on the floor, he surmised had, in better days, belonged to a polar bear. It now belonged to Lorenzo and his daughter. Far more dangerous than a bear he thought as she pulled him down onto the rug..

As she wrapped her arms around him he struggled slightly and protested that Dan would soon be looking for him.

She spun him over onto his back so she was sat astride him. "Don't worry about Dan. He and Michael will be taking Jones home to make sure he doesn't kill himself on the way back."

"What about your father?"

"Why do you think you're here? He's saved you for me."

She unzipped the back of her dress and allowed it to fall to her waist, revealing everything that Jerry had been lusting after earlier in the evening.

Jerry groaned and gave up. If that was what fate had in store for him he might as well enjoy every wretched moment of it!

Chapter 13

The following morning Jerry awoke to find the clock on the bedside table reading 9:32. He nearly died. Although the night before he thought he had been in heaven, the irony of the situation was lost on him in his state of panic.

He leapt out of bed, looked around the room for his clothes, nowhere to be seen. He heard the shower door slide open in the room through the door to the right of the bed. He dashed in to find Jacqui, drying herself, he stopped for a second to take in the breathtaking naked sight in front of him and then the panic started to take over again.

"Where are my clothes, I've got to get to work, I'll get killed if I don't get in this morning?"

"Don't worry, lover, it's all taken care of," she said calmly.

"What do you mean?"

"You are in the local hospital recovering from an attack of food poisoning. The hospital rang your company this morning and informed them that you should be released sometime this afternoon when they have completed the tests and can be sure that you won't have any further problems."

"But what happens if they ring up to find out how I am, they'll find out."

Jerry was calmer but still clearly worried.

"No problem, the registrar is a personal friend of my father's, it has all been taken care of. As far as the staff are aware you are in a private room and being attended to by one of the staff doctors. So relax, we have all day, we don't have to get up yet, no-one else in the house will surface before eleven. So lets have some more fun."

The look in her eyes would have made Superman shake in his boots, there was nothing else for it, he would just have to grin and bare it!

Over a very late breakfast, Jerry was quizzed quite ruthlessly by Lorenzo. Michael had returned to the house, but there was no sign of Dan. It turned out that Michael was Jacqui's brother, Dan was just hired help.

"What are you building these animals for?"

"I don't know the ultimate purpose, I've only been involved on the periphery really."

"How do they function?"

"They can be autonomous or they can be controlled remotely by computers or by voice commands."

Jerry felt there was very little point in denying Lorenzo any of the information he had, as the animals would be of no value to him unless he was planning on starting his own zoo. And if he was, then the company, he reasoned, would benefit from a very lucrative contract to produce them. As far as he was concerned, Jerry thought that he was doing the company a big favour.

"What do you mean by autonomous?"

"The animals in the zoo have been studied very thoroughly with cameras connected to the computer system which has analysed the movements and behaviour patterns. That means that the animals we recreate can be programmed with that behaviour so in a zoo situation the animals take the minimum supervision and attention whilst still providing a totally authentic display. That would be a tremendous advantage over conventional animals for anyone that already owns a zoo or even for someone thinking of starting one."

Jerry was feeling quite pleased with himself, the sales pitch, he thought, was very professional and would be bound to benefit the company.

Lorenzo nodded his head, and said no more. It appeared that he now had all of the information he required. He probably knew more about Jerry than he knew himself, the confirmation of the zoo project was the detail he needed.

"I'm going to show Jerry around this morning, take him down to the beach, as its quite a calm day, then we'll grab some lunch and I'll take him home. Is that alright with you Daddy?"

"Whatever you want sweetheart is absolutely fine with me."

They left the dining room and Jacqui pulled him towards the stairs. "We'd better put some warm clothes on, it's fairly cold outside."

She dragged him upstairs but it was more than half an hour before they came down again.

Jerry was eventually dropped off at his house at five thirty, Jacqui wanted to come in with him but Jerry protested that as he was supposed to be recovering from food poisoning it wouldn't look good if John or Suzie came by to find a beautiful young woman in very close attendance.

Accepting his explanation reluctantly, she kissed him passionately and watched him walk up the path to his little house.

Jerry was relieved to see her go, he was absolutely shattered and all he wanted to do was to go to bed. Alone.

At least he wouldn't have to face anyone until Monday morning, maybe it would be better to go up to his parents for the weekend, they would be pleased to see him, it had been nearly four months since he had last been.

Friday had been a brilliant day for Rhoda's team. The construction team had worked non-stop all week and the fruit of their labours was standing in the centre of the room. They all stood marvelling at the stunning creature. John suggested that Sally should be the one to 'switch her on' as it had been her name suggestion and she had done "probably the lion's share of the work", atrocious pun, but it did get a laugh "in making the skeletal structure."

Sally duly obliged, although Rhoda's legs were not part of the initial procedure. They simply couldn't take the chance of her lurching into the equipment that surrounded her. They decided that that part should be reserved for the car park - preferably empty.

Rhoda was deactivated and the whole ensemble, including Baggy, who stuck to John like glue, moved upstairs to the refectory where they were presented with the most sumptuous lunch of the year, complete with fine wines and champagne. John and Suzie had decided that a celebration was long overdue.

"It's a pity Jerry isn't here, he's really missing out," Suzie said with genuine concern. "I hope his food poisoning isn't serious. It isn't much fun being stuck in bed in the middle of the day."

John, Suzie and Alan had decided that Saturday morning would be the ideal time to find out how well Rhoda would move, they would be the only ones in the building and they would have the car park clear by leaving their own cars at the front in the visitors car park.

Rhoda had been constructed on a low platform with twelve small rubber tyred wheels, electrically driven so that she could easily be transported between the various departments that needed to work on her, the final stage being the addition of the skin, put in place in the main construction lab, where she had originally started out as a pile of bones.

Alan smoothly guided the trolley through the insulated steel doors that led to the car park in the back left corner of the lab. The lights were on and the exit doors were closed.

Alan stood back from the trolley, he pressed a couple of keys on the laptop he had brought with Rhoda and her head began to move, appearing to survey her unfamiliar surroundings.

John spoke to Rhoda, a little unsure of the precise commands to use, one slip and three weeks work would be down the drain. They were all aware that the instincts of the rhino were predominantly to charge at anything it didn't understand. Alan had isolated parts of the data but had warned at the same time that they might just have a problem with her. Because she had been with her calf all of the time they had been studying her her entire temperament had been one of protection and aggression, it would not be possible to isolate all of those tendencies and therefore there could be some risk attached to giving her the use of her legs.

"Rhoda," her head moved to acknowledge the direction of the voice "move forwards off the front end of the trolley and stand still when all four feet are on the floor."

The three tons rhino lumbered slowly off the front of the trolley, did precisely as she was told and looked to John for further instruction, much as a young child would do when playing a new game for the first time. The humans all looked at each other, the tension in the air was evident.

"Move forwards at walking pace only, walk around the perimeter of the area, do not touch anything with your body or your head. They were more concerned for the safety of the animal than possible structural damage to the car park. Alan had done a good job, the programming appeared to be flawless, the bad tempered beast was behaving quite placidly, until just twenty feet away from Suzie on its return, Suzie sneezed. The sudden noise and the convulsive movement appeared to awaken something deep within Rhoda's electronic brain, in a fraction of a second she had moved from a slowly moving behemoth into a fully charging rhino.

Before John and Alan could react, she reached Suzie and with her momentum picked her up on her head and was charging straight at the wall that was in front of her, Suzie was helplessly stuck on the front of Rhoda's head above her horn. Six feet from the wall John and Alan both shouted "Stop!" as loudly as they could, Alan was also thumping the computer in an effort to turn her off, when with only inches to go the juggernaut abruptly halted, as quickly as it had set off, Suzie, flew off the rhino's head and crashed sickeningly into the concrete wall, slid down and crumpled in a heap on the floor.

John and Alan both rushed over to her, there were no obvious signs of damage, no external bleeding, although Suzie was shaken up quite badly she was only unconscious for a few seconds. As she came to she started to sit up, arched her back sharply as though in considerable pain.

"Call an ambulance!" John said to Alan.

"No, wait," she said, "I think it's just bruises, my breathing's not a problem, so no cracked ribs, I can move my legs, I'm fine."

She tried to stand and her legs gave way underneath her, John and Alan supported her, moved her onto the rhino trolley and back into the lab.

"What do we do about her?" Alan asked, nodding towards Rhoda.

"Bad girl, she can spend the weekend in the garage as punishment!"

Suzie laughed painfully, "I'm pleased I'm not one of your children, you'd be locked up for cruelty."

Alan called for an ambulance anyway, they met the paramedics in reception with Suzie still resting on the trolley. They transferred her to their own gurney and into the back of the ambulance.

"What happened to her?"

John thought about the truth and decided they wouldn't believe it in a million years.

"She walked behind my car as I was reversing in the car park."

The explanation was readily accepted and they whisked her off to hospital. They reacted quickly and didn't give them the option of travelling with her.

"It appears that we still have a way to go with Rhoda," John said. "I think it would be better if we got her away from the car park, we don't want any more accidents on Monday."

"It shouldn't be too difficult to sort out, I will have to program a long list of things that shouldn't be attacked under any circumstances. I can take care of it on Monday morning."

They encouraged Rhoda back on to the trolley, took her out of the car park and returned her to where she had started from. Alan temporarily reprogrammed her only to respond to direct voice commands from John and himself to, hopefully, prevent any more mishaps in the meantime.

"It's a damn good job it wasn't Baggy that had attacked her," John said. "He would have gone straight for her throat and that would have been Goodnight Vienna."

The thought sent a shudder right through them both.

They locked up and went off to the hospital to see how Suzie was.

When they arrived they found her sitting up in bed looking as well as ever. She already had a visitor, in the shape of Dr. Boscik. He stood up the moment they entered the room.

"What's going on John, I don't hear from you for months and then it's twice in a week, I hope the problems aren't bigger the next time we meet."

He held out his hand and John shook it warmly.

John introduced Alan and enquired after the patient's wellbeing.

"They tell me that they are going to keep her in for observation overnight, in case of concussion, there are no breakages and the opinion is that if Suzie hadn't been so strong and fit she could have easily have been seriously injured. How fast were you going when you hit her? It looks more like she was hit by an elephant than a car."

Keith was being quite serious.

Suzie burst out laughing, until the pain caught her breath and reminded her why she was there.

John remembered as he drove home from the hospital that in a few hours he was due to be collecting Dee-Dee for the party. He didn't exactly feel like going to a party after the scare they had just been through, but his curiosity wouldn't allow him to cancel the date. He needed to know what had been going through her mind on the previous Saturday night.

The afternoon seemed to pass like a tornado, there one minute, gone the next.

At seven fifty five he drove into the car park outside her apartment. As he did, another car, a large, dark coloured Mercedes pulled away. John thought that he had seen the car somewhere before. There weren't too many big Mercs like that around. He couldn't place it though.

He pressed the intercom for her to open the door for him, the buzz of the door lock opening was the response a few seconds later. As he walked over to her door, she opened it. She looked a little apprehensive, worried even.

"Good evening, young sir, and to what does a lady of my standing owe the pleasure of this visit?" she asked nervously.

John couldn't think straight immediately, it had put him right off guard. He recovered his composure and replied "I think this wandering knight would request the pleasure of the company of the most beautiful lady in the land to accompany him to the ball and banquet of the King of this realm. He would be most honoured if she would not find it beneath her to lend dignity to the invitation by bestowing her acceptance upon it."

"Well requested most brave and handsome knight, any less an invitation would surely have resulted in a negative response."

They both laughed. The ice was broken. He followed her into the hall, "Do you want to be introduced to my flatmate?"

It took John a moment to realise she was referring to Joe, the Cockateel.

"Yes please."

She led him through to the dining room, where Joe stood on her wooden perch in front of a magnificent, large gilded cage.

"She's a Josephine really, but I named her after another of my mother's favourites, Joe Cocker, a singer from the sixties and seventies. Joe didn't do a lot, she shuffled from one end of the perch to the other and back again, put her head on one side and looked at him. She then shuffled back to the other end again, took a peanut out of the bowl fixed to the end of the perch, took it back and offered it to John.

"You're a hit, she approves! Not many people she does that for at first meeting."

John tried to take the nut from her, but she moved her head quickly away. "Oh, well, can't win 'em all."

They moved through into the living room, where he was offered and accepted a scotch.

He smiled.

"Two parrots sitting on a perch, and one said to the other 'Can you smell fish?'."

Dee-Dee looked puzzled, handed him a drink and didn't know

quite what to say, so she put her arms up around his neck and kissed him.

It was John's turn to be puzzled, but responded gently. The clinch lasted only for a few seconds and Dee-Dee broke away.

"There, I think I owed you that from last time," she said a little sheepishly.

She sat down on the sofa, he sat down beside her. "You didn't OWE me anything, and you don't owe me anything now. Let's just go out and enjoy ourselves, and whatever may or may not happen to us I will just be happy to have had you in my company."

It was the most sincere thing he had ever said in his life.

The emotion was welling up inside her, she couldn't think of a response, only to kiss him again. This time it was longer, more passionate, more searching.

They separated, and John said "I think we had better go to the party or we're never going to get out of here."

He stood up and pulled her to her feet by her hand. She looked straight into his eyes and smiled.

"Thank you," she said and kissed him on his cheek.

The dress she wore was bright peacock blue, made from crushed velvet, with thin straps and a low front and a deep cut back. The single aquamarine pendant that lay between her breasts complemented the colour of her dress and matched her eyes perfectly, bright and dazzling. She fetched the cashmere coat she had worn the previous week and without further conversation they left for the party.

The party was a wonderful vibrant affair with the attending throng all in a Christmas mood. There was even a visit from Santa Claus at midnight, when all of the ladies had to go and sit on Santa's knee and tell everyone how naughty they had been before he would give them a present. They danced together and they danced occasionally with others, there was no shortage of men wanting to dance with the fair young maiden attached to Sir Lancelot's arm. There would probably have been a riot, had she not consented to the occasional foray into the massed ranks of the serfs that lay in wait.

At four o'clock the party was still going strong, although there were an increasing number of bodies prostrate on the floor, mostly inhabiting the land of alcohol induced dreams, so John and Dee-Dee thought it wiser to leave while they were still standing.

John phoned for a cab without any success, it seemed that no-one was prepared to answer the call at that God forsaken hour. Much against his better judgement, he decided to drive home. At least it had been over two hours since he had last had an alcoholic drink.

They arrived back at her apartment. She leaned across and kissed him with feeling and tenderness.

"I would invite you in for coffee but I think it's too early."

"For coffee? I'd never get to sleep if I had coffee now!"

"No, not coffee," she responded coyly. "Besides, I haven't got anything to offer you for breakfast."

She looked at him almost apologetically, hoping he would understand.

"I am deeply in your debt already. I have enjoyed two wonderful evenings in your company and can honestly say that both of us need to retire and get some sleep. However, I would like to invite you for lunch on Monday or Tuesday, if you are available."

"Monday would be fine. I'll look forward to it."

"Come to the office around one, the food we have there is amongst the best in town, and I can show you around, you'll enjoy it, I promise."

"Gladly."

She kissed him again, opened the car door and disappeared in to her apartment.

As he drove away he felt quite intoxicated, the high he was on was far better than any alcohol induced one he could have had.

The big Mercedes moved smoothly away, unnoticed, from the side road behind John and went quietly in the opposite direction.

Chapter 14

Monday morning was memorable for a number of reasons.

Jerry arrived into work with a smile on his face that the devil couldn't have removed - having recovered from his food poisoning which had concerned quite a number of the staff.

Alan had spent the first two hours since his arrival at seven o'clock programming and reprogramming Rhoda. He told everyone about the mishap with Suzie, and no-one went within twenty feet of Rhoda in spite of the fact that she was switched off.

John was feeling lean, mean and ready to take on the world and all of its troubles, although nobody quite knew why, and when Suzie walked carefully into the lab at nine thirty you would have thought that she had just won the Olympic gold medal for the hundred metres from the cheer that went up.

All-in-all it was an excellent start to the week, and furthermore, there were only another three days to Christmas, and just one more working day to go. John had left the organising of the office party very much in Barbara's safe hands, she had booked the band, the catering (not difficult as they used the same caterers every day), the vast quantities of drink and a cabaret act. The invitations were restricted to the employees, thirty six of them, their partners and two friends, giving a maximum number of one hundred and forty four, although one hundred and twenty two was the anticipated number.

Barbara's thoughts were rudely interrupted, she considered, by the arrival of the "personal" Miss Sampson, who said that Mr. Hylton was expecting her for lunch.

Barbara sent a text to his phone: 'There's a woman here to see you.'

John got the message and immediately ran up the stairs and through to the reception, where Barbara was doing her best to freeze-dry Dee-Dee with her best cold-shoulder.

"Hello, glad you could make it," he leaned forwards and kissed her cheek, much to Barbara's annoyance. "Come on through."

Barbara was totally dumbfounded. It must be serious, she thought, he never, ever takes anyone into the back unless they are paying serious amounts of money for something to be built, and even then it's done reluctantly.

They arrived at John's office. He stopped at the door, "There's someone I'd like you to meet, don't be frightened, there is absolutely no danger whatsoever. Trust me."

He opened the door and entered first. As Dee-Dee followed him he said "Come."

The silky smooth shape of Baggy came around from behind his desk and sat down immediately to John's left, with Dee-Dee, mouth dropped open, on his right.

"Baggy I'd like you to meet Dee-Dee, the cat slowly appraised her from head to toe, storing every detail in his memory banks. "Dee-Dee, please say hello to Baggy."

"Er, yes, er hello Baggy."

She didn't look very convinced, nor did she sound it.

"Touch him," he said gently, "he likes having his head stroked."

Dee-Dee looked even more uncertain as she slowly reached across him, risking her fingers with every inch they travelled.

"Is he always this calm and docile," she asked as she grew more confident.

"He is, unless I want him to be otherwise. I should explain. Baggy isn't a real panther, he's a cyber, a machine. Built, programmed and controlled by us, but I think he must be developing his own mind because he has attached himself to me out of preference to the others."

Dee-Dee couldn't think of anything sensible to say. She just bent down and stroked him, looking at his face. Then she noticed that his chest wasn't moving, he wasn't breathing. Then she believed and understood what she had just heard.

"It's incredible, absolutely incredible. He is so real."

"Lie down," John said, and the black cat behaved like a black dog returning immediately to the far side of the desk.

"Well, I'm pleased you showed him to me before you told me about him, I wouldn't have believed it possible!"

"It wasn't until a few weeks ago. We have been studying the animals at the zoo for just over four weeks, learning how they behave, making it possible to reproduce them perfectly. What you have just seen is the first tangible evidence of that study."

"Surely it has taken you longer than a few weeks to develop the technology for this?"

"Oh, yes. This just happens to be the culmination of three quite separate developments that we have been working on right since we set up the company fifteen years ago, but specifically for the last three years. Baggy just happened to be in the right place at the right time to be created, an accident really."

Dee-Dee stiffened, slightly at the mention of "accident". Her head was beginning to spin. She was feeling distinctly uncomfortable.

"John, can we talk, there's something I have to tell you."

"Okay, we'll go up for lunch, I've got plenty of time now that things have come together over the past few days."

They took the lift up to the refectory, John pointed out the other facilities on the way.

"You've certainly done it in style, this is very impressive."

They chose a table in the corner by the window. John offered her the menu, which was equally impressive. They both chose and ordered their food, John selected the wine.

"John, there's something I have to tell you." She paused, took a deep breath and...

"There you are. Barbara told me we had a visitor."

John stood up.

"Dee-Dee, I would like you to meet my partner, Suzie Fielding. Suzie this is Delilah Sampson, known as Dee-Dee. Will you join us for lunch, we've only just ordered."

Barbara sent a text to Suzie the moment they went upstairs, she told her that John was lumbered with a visitor he would rather not be left alone with.

Suzie to the rescue. She found him as soon as she could, hoping that he wasn't suffering too much!

Some suffering she thought, as she looked at Dee-Dee. Then as the conversation progressed, she realised that the only person that didn't want John to be left alone with Dee-Dee was Barbara. Poor, jealous Barbara. Fortunately Suzie had no such feelings towards Dee-Dee, in fact she quite enjoyed her company. They ate their lunch in a very convivial atmosphere, all comfortable with each other. Dee-Dee put her burning desire to talk to John alone to the back of her mind. There would be other opportunities, but clearly not just yet.

The meal was concluded and Suzie made her excuses and left.

John walked to the lift with Dee-Dee, forewarning her of the next project he was about to introduce her to.

The lift arrived, and as the door closed she threw her arms around his neck, kissed him fast and hard, hugged him tight for a second and then let go as if nothing had happened.

John had a silly grin all over his face

"I'm sorry, I shouldn't have done that here. I just couldn't help myself."

"Not a problem for me, I assure you," he said, trying to straighten his face before the lift landed two floors down.

They walked out of the lift into the construction room, a large area of the room had been cleared, leaving plenty of clear space around Rhoda. Alan was working nearby on a computer, he was the only one within forty feet of Rhoda.

John took hold of Dee-Dee's hand and guided her towards the dormant rhino. They walked round to the front of her and John nodded to Alan who activated her senses, but not her legs.

"Rhoda, I would like you to meet Miss Delilah Sampson."

Rhoda blinked slowly and appeared to nod her head at Dee-Dee.

"Now I've seen everything. This is just mind-blowing."

"Don't damage that, brains are something we can't replace just yet. It was Rhoda that gave Suzie such a hard time on Saturday, but Alan is confident that the problems are now solved, aren't you Alan?"

Alan smiled in acknowledgement, but didn't want to commit himself in front of witnesses.

As they walked away from Rhoda towards the stairs, Dee-Dee's mood seemed to change dramatically.

"I have to be going shortly, I have a Christmas show to cover later this afternoon and then it will have to be in the New Year before we can meet again. I'm spending Christmas away with my father, we're leaving tomorrow evening. We will be back on New Years Eve, but you will be away with Suzie and your virgins."

She tried vainly to smile.

They went through the door and up the stairs to his office, where Baggy appeared to be asleep.

"I had been hoping you could keep me company tomorrow night at our party, but if it's not to be, then I can live with that if I have to. I very much want to see you again, I have a feeling that Christmas will seem so much emptier without you, but the New Year will be so much more to look forward to. I haven't even had a chance to buy you a present," he said, trying very hard to lift the mood.

She looked into his eyes, put her arms around his waist and pulled herself close to him, burying her head into his shoulder. They stayed like that for a while, she holding tight, he stroking her hair.

Then abruptly, she pulled herself free. "I really must be going, I have enjoyed meeting your friends," she said, looking at Baggy, still 'asleep' on the floor "and I will try to sleep between now and the New Year."

John looked at her, not quite understanding what she meant.

"If I sleep, it will come so much more quickly. Merry Christmas, Mr. Hylton."

"Merry Christmas, Miss Sampson."

Dee-Dee turned and hurried out of the door, down the passage and out past the slightly stunned Barbara into the cold crisp December air.

John followed to watch her disappearing out of the small front car park. As he turned back, Barbara, who had been watching the events with interest, quickly looked away and appeared to be very busy talking into the telephone, with a somewhat embarrassed look on her face.

The party the following evening was quite a raucous bash, everyone was really letting their hair down. The previous five weeks had been so intense and pressured, largely as a result of the animals robbing other projects of much needed hands.

Suzie, much to John's surprise had invited Keith to the party as her consort for the evening.

John took the opportunity of dancing with her early on to find out what was going on.

"You might have warned me. Last week when I spoke to him he told me that he was going off to New Zealand with his wife for Christmas, to try and save their marriage. This won't exactly help the situation."

His concern for them both was quite evident.

"The situation changed on Saturday evening. He took his wife out for what he had intended to be a romantic dinner, and half way through the main course she announced that she wouldn't be going to New Zealand after all. In fact she had had never intended to go with him, she had simply chosen the most expensive trip she could find, included all the stopovers she could and left it until the last minute before telling him, so that he couldn't cancel and get his money back."

"Nasty bitch!" John was stunned. "That's horrible."

"She left him sat in the restaurant, went home and by the time he arrived she had already packed and left a note to say that she was leaving him for an accountant, he was boring, rich and didn't work all the hours god sent."

"An accountant, that would hurt his pride, it might at least have been someone interesting. Probably a lie though."

"When he came in to see me on Sunday morning, before I was discharged, he just looked as though he needed to talk to someone and I happened to be available."

John thought back a week to when he needed to talk to someone, but Suzie didn't seem to be the listening sort. All the years he had known her… maybe there was a softer side to her after all.

"So I invited him here to get him away from his normal surroundings. I don't think that he's particularly emotionally devastated by his wife leaving him but it's going to take some adjusting to. So, if you'll excuse me, I'd better be getting back to my guest."

Well, well, well. Whoever would have believed it? A real turn up, he thought to himself.

The party had been going well, the food and entertainment superb, John had mixed and mingled all night. He had danced with at least twenty different women to keep Dee-Dee out of his mind. At one o'clock, he quietly slipped out of the party and went down to his office.

He had taken a bottle of scotch from behind the bar and decided that it was time for some peace and quiet.

He went into his office without turning on the light. He sat gently down in his soft, high backed leather chair, poured himself a strong one, his first alcoholic drink since the champagne at the start of the evening. He stared at it for a minute and then took a big slug out of it, settling back in the chair with his eyes closed. He smiled at the thought that it was the third time in the last few weeks he had sat alone in the dark in the building after midnight; contemplating the future and each time the mood had been different: ambitious, triumphant and finally contemplative.

"Oh, Baggy, what a strange place the world is."

Baggy raised his head at the mention of his name, sat up and rested his chin on the arm of John's chair.

He could hear the rhythmic thumping of the music coming through the thick concrete ceiling above him, there were no other sounds to be heard. He finished his drink and poured himself another. He unconsciously stroked Baggy's head and thought it strange that he should be drawing comfort from a machine. No, it was not a machine, it was Baggy, the second most important thing that had happened to him in years. It would be impossible to explain to anyone, but Baggy felt as though he was somehow a part of him, and would have a very large part in his future.

Baggy's head lifted and looked towards the door, he had heard footsteps on the carpet outside, somewhere down the corridor. John swivelled his chair round and turned on the light with the switch on the wall behind him. The atmosphere was broken. The door opened and Suzie was stood there, clutching her drink.

"I wondered where you had gone to, I looked all over for you, and when the barman told me you'd swiped a bottle from behind the bar I knew I'd find you here."

"I'm just worn out after all these parties. I'm getting too old for it. Can't take it anymore," he grinned as he lied.

"Yeah, yeah. I don't quite know how to put this, but...."

"Our trip to the Virgins?" he raised an eyebrow to emphasise the question.

"How did you know I was going to talk about that?"

"See all, hear all, think a lot! It's logical, that's all, and I don't mind. Keith's a good friend, you're the best friend I've ever had and I think I know you better now than I ever have. Go and have fun. I wouldn't be the best company for you this Christmas anyway. Enjoy it. Don't do anything rash, but you have nothing to lose."

He smiled in an almost fatherly way. She deserved some real fun in her life, it may not work out long term, but life isn't always for living in the long term.

"Thank you. Stand up please."

He stood up, she came over to him put her arms around his waist and buried her head in his shoulder and hugged him tight. It was getting to be so frequent, he thought, that it's in danger of becoming a profession. He kissed her gently on top of her head and she relaxed her hold, but didn't let go.

"There was a time, you know, when, deep down, I wanted it to be you I would spend my life with, but I also understood that we would never be able to work and live together. It had to be a choice. It was a difficult choice, you are a very special man, John Hylton and I love you deeply as a friend. Whatever happens in the future, to either of us you, will always have my love."

That was the side of her that she had compressed and repressed, she might well be a tough lady but not all the way through.

He couldn't think of anything that he could possibly add, for once he was lost for words. He simply wrapped his arms around her and squeezed her tight.

"Hey, that's enough now," he said brightly " you'll have me crying in a minute, and there's a party going on upstairs. Our party, remember?"

He held her at arms length, and she wiped the tears from her eyes with the back of her sleeve.

"Yes, quite right. Merry Christmas Mr. Hylton," she smiled.

"Merry Christmas, Miss Fielding."

He thought at that moment that if anyone else said that tonight, tomorrow he would join a monastery.

The party broke up shortly after two o'clock, John and Suzie were the last to leave, Keith was waiting for her outside in his car.

John punched the numbers into the alarm and locked the doors, said goodnight to her and wandered down to his own car.

He sat for a few moments in a vague effort to collect his thoughts before starting his car. As he turned the key he sensed he was not alone in the car, but before he could react he felt a sharp stab at the back of his neck as the needle went in and three seconds later he was unconscious.

Chapter 15

It would have been two o'clock in the afternoon, had they still been in the same time zone. It had been twelve hours since John had been driven away from Animagination in his own car. The abduction had been ruthlessly efficient, but made easier for the fact that all of the cars had been outside in the visitor's car park instead of the underground park.

As he started to come round he became aware that whilst he was probably unhurt. His head felt like it was made of cotton wool with a jackhammer somewhere hidden inside that was disorientating him. He tried to lift his hand to his head but he soon found that he was unable to move his arms or legs.

He fuzzily tried to examine the cause of his disablement and was at least relieved to see that it would not be permanent. His forearms were strapped to the arms of his chair by means of a Velcro band that was wrapped over and fastened for the length of his forearm. He couldn't see his legs, but presumed that they were held in a similar fashion.

As his eyes began to focus and the throbbing in his head gradually began to subside he deduced that he was somewhere up above the clouds in a large private jet aircraft of some description. It wasn't the type of plane that multi-national companies would have for transporting globetrotting directors around in, it was much larger. More like an older commercial plane.

He had been awake for fully ten minutes when a late-middle aged man appeared, possibly around sixty years old, he was around five foot ten in height, dressed in a dark suit and wearing a hat that John hadn't seen outside of fifties movies, the dark frameless glasses that he wore added to his threatening air. He was in control. There was nothing John could do.

"Good afternoon Mr. Hylton. I'm pleased you have joined us. I'm afraid you have been out for just over twelve hours. Unfortunately, we could have no idea of the amount of alcohol you would consume, so the effect of the drug was only a best guess, so to speak. Either you were very tired or you must have drunk a fair amount as we had only planned on you being out for six to eight hours at the most."

He sat down in a vacant seat some five feet away, opposite John.

"Lucky for me, then. I don't suppose you would care to tell me what is going on."

John wasn't quite sure how he should react. He felt outrage at the thought that someone would kidnap him and hold him prisoner. He was confident that there was a purpose to it and that that purpose meant that there was no immediate threat to his life… for the time being. So he quickly opted for indignance and curiosity.

"As you are no doubt aware, we are flying. We are currently somewhere above the Mediterranean Sea heading towards Egypt, where we will be making a short stop for refuelling. This is necessary because we still have a good distance to travel on from there and this old 727 doesn't quite have the range to make it in one hop. We should be landing in approximately forty minutes. I'm afraid that until after we have left Cairo you will have to endure your captivity. Then, subject to your guarantee that you will not misbehave in any way, I will remove your bonds and you will be free to move around the plane as you wish. You will not of course be permitted access to the flight deck."

He stood up to leave.

"Are you going to tell me what the hell I'm here for?" John was beginning to get angry.

"All in good time, Mr. Hylton, all in good time."

He disappeared back through the door that separated his section of the plane from the rest. He tried to work out how big the plane was and what else might be on board. He could see that the compartment he was in stretched from just behind the wings, where he was sitting, to just in front, so there was at least as much again fore and aft of him.

Craning his neck around, he could hardly move his shoulders due to the restraints keeping his forearms fastened to the arms of his chair, he thought that the bathroom facilities must be behind him. It was getting dark outside, there was almost nothing he could see anyway, the cloud base was sparse and several thousand feet below, but the angle he was at to the window he couldn't see any more.

Whether it was the effect of the drug or the hangover, he wasn't sure, but he suddenly felt very thirsty. Thirsty? Thirst means drink, drink means full bladder, full bladder means bathroom, bathroom means a degree of freedom. John began to shout. At first there was no reaction, then just as he thought he was about to lose his voice, the door opened to the foreward section. Not far, just enough for a small Chinese-looking man to put his head through. John could hear voices on the other side of the door. The voices seemed to be arguing, male and female, couldn't tell what they were saying.

"Boss says you be quiet. You get nothing till after Cairo. You wait one hour."

The door was closed and the only sound he could again hear was that of the engines outside.

He tried to concentrate on the voices he had heard, his head was still too fuzzy to replay what he had heard accurately, but there was something about the woman's voice that he thought he recognised.

He sat quietly for several minutes, then he knew. He went very cold, sweat began to break out on his forehead. It couldn't be. He didn't want it to be, then in desperation he roared at the top of his voice "DEEEEEEE - DEEEEEEE!".

"The door opened immediately, the man in the hat reappeared through the door, quickly closing the door behind him.

He sat down again in the chair, he seemed more weary than before, still in control but definitely with a noticeable reduction in confidence.

"Well, it looks as though I have been a little careless," he looked around the cabin, giving the impression that he was either looking for inspiration or just for the right words to use.

John wanted to demand to see her, but his need for information was greater and chose to see what was about to be offered. He was feeling stronger, seeing the other man visibly weakened by the outburst.

"I had rather hoped that this wouldn't be necessary until after we had taken off again. You see I am presented with two options at the moment. I can either spend some time with you now and give you some of the information that will be revealed to you in the fullness of time, or I can make use of Fong Hu's admirable services again and allow you to sleep until we reach our ultimate destination. It really is quite a dilemma. Don't you agree Mr. Hylton."

"Oh, yeah, life's a bitch, full of difficult decisions," he snarled, trying to be as scathing as he could under the circumstances.

"At least with you quiet I can deal with other more pressing issues, on the other hand I don't think that my daughter would be very pleased with me."

John suddenly felt extremely ill. The enormity of his situation hit him with the force of a herd of charging elephants. He felt as though his entire world was falling apart around him. His head began to swim. Everything that had happened to him during the past two weeks came back, flashing into his head. He felt that he must have been the biggest fool that had ever lived. Not only had he been falling head over heels for the woman, he had been showing her all of his secrets. He had blown it. Blown everything. What a fool. Show him heaven and deliver him to hell!

"Get out of here you bastard and you can tell that lying, conniving bitch she can rot in hell with the rest of you!"

His anger had been vented. His head rocked forward onto his chest. At that moment he had nothing to live for and nothing to die for either. He didn't care about anything anymore.

"I don't think that it would be very fair to my daughter. She is not the reason you are here. In fact, quite the opposite. You are here in spite of my daughter."

John wasn't listening. He didn't want to listen to anything. He just wanted to crawl under a stone and get away from the world and all of its deceptions.

"You see, Mr Hylton, she has tried very hard to obstruct me and prevent me from gaining access to you. Oh, she couldn't do anything physically but she did try to blackmail me emotionally into leaving you alone, but I'm afraid that she and I are made from different material. Perhaps you would like to see her now."

John looked up, a sneer had crept into his eyes.

"Why? She can't do you any good now, she had her chance and she took it. What was it that you wanted from me? Baggy? Rhoda? What was it you bastard?" John was beginning to think again. He needed to know how much he knew. The reactions would tell him everything.

"Yes, it has been an interesting game Mr. Hylton. Unfortunately until Saturday we were always at least two steps behind you."

Saturday? Saturday? John was trying to piece together the past few days. Dee-Dee hadn't been into the workshops and met Baggy and Rhoda until Monday! What the hell happened on Saturday?

John decided that he needed to play the game out.

"Then you are still at least two steps behind me."

"No, I don't think so. You see we are quite confident that you have produced at least one cybernetic animal, and probably two. Unless I miss my guess, you now have somewhere within your building a rhinoceros and a panther."

There wasn't the look of triumph on his face that John would have expected from such a revelation had the man been certain of the facts, and he hadn't reacted at all to the names of the animals. Saturday. He was actually telling the truth. She hadn't told him a damned thing. But that still didn't tell him what was going on.

"What makes you confident enough to arrive at a guess that is mildly accurate, but still a long way from the mark?"

"It seems that we are playing games with each other, Mr. Hylton. There are certain advantages that I have over you at present, but I must congratulate you on your recovery. There are not many men that could recover from such an emotional ordeal so quickly. That must be put down to a high degree of intelligence and ability to see through the fog that others would simply stumble around in."

"Cut out the crap and get to the point."

"I shall take that as an assent for us both to be straight with each other," he said smoothly. "The advantage that I have over you is that you don't know who I am. My name is Daniels, Eric Daniels."

He let it sink in.

"Good god, the zoo! I assumed that your name was Sampson. Christ, her cover was good. The driving licence, the car! Jesus," it hit him like a bullet, "the accident, it was all a setup! She was brilliant, I couldn't work out at the time how I had managed to hit her. I didn't - she hit me!"

"Yes, and that was where it started to go wrong for me. The dinner was perfect, it allowed her to get to know you, to get inside. Unfortunately, human emotions are a bit of a nuisance as they are somewhat unreliable. The dinner and dancing was too perfect. I lost the arrangement we had started with. I tried to persuade her to continue, that it could be crucial to my work. If what I thought you were doing was correct, then it would present me with the biggest leap forward for twenty years. The deception that was necessary for her to continue with, I'm afraid, was emotionally beyond her capabilities."

John was intrigued, he also knew that the man presented no

danger whatsoever, neither now, nor in the future.

"So how do you arrive at the conclusion that we have produced the animals you have referred to if Dee-Dee hasn't told you anything."

"Elementary my dear Watson."

Daniels allowed himself a small smile, he was right.

"Firstly, you have been studying the animals in my zoo. You frightened poor old Jackson and Thomas half out of their wits with your display. They were impressed, but I'm afraid that that technology has been around for quite some time, and I am quite sure that you wouldn't have needed such a thorough study even if you had wanted the film effects to be so realistic. No, you had to be doing something else. Last week, your Mr. Fisher took down the cameras from around the rhino and panther pens. That meant that you had finished gathering the data you required. We also know from the display you put on you had enough information at that stage to make full use of it, and yet you still kept the cameras up, that meant there had to be more than just films. You are also specialists in robotics and two and two makes four Mr. Hylton."

John sat quietly, neither confirming nor denying anything. He still didn't know for sure that they had actually produced anything meaningful.

"And then came last Saturday," Daniels paused for effect. "On Saturday, not an unusual day for you to work, but for the three most important people in your establishment to be there together, and no-one else, something serious had to be happening. The first clue was when you all parked your cars outside, refraining from using the underground car park. It was logical to assume therefore that you were going to were going to use the car park for some other purpose. As much as I would have liked, I had no way of knowing what you were doing and it was left very much to a most unfortunate and regrettable event that gave us the missing piece of the jigsaw."

John supplied the answer.

"Suzie's accident."

"Precisely. We were watching when you were back above ground and saw the ambulance arrive. It was then a simple matter of asking after the lady's health in the hospital and finding a nurse talkative enough to tell us how it had happened. The story she gave me, we knew immediately, was false as it was purported to be your car that did the damage, but as we know that was outside at the time and nowhere near Miss Fielding, so that simply wasn't possible. We therefore concluded quite rightly that you had had an accident with the rhinoceros. Incidentally, I assume now, that Rhoda must be the rhinoceros, but Baggy? That one has been puzzling us for quite some time. It didn't help the situation when Thomas opened his mouth and put his foot in it."

"No, Jackson's letter of apology provided us with a great deal of amusement. I hadn't realised it was possible for one man to grovel so much! Baggy, is short for Bagheera."

"I see, how stupid of me not to work that one out," he said with resignation. "Now that almost everything is out in the open, I assume that you would like to be released from your bonds."

John nodded, almost wearily.

"Would you also like to see my daughter, if not for your own sake, then for hers."

"I think I would like that very much."

The restraining straps were released. John stood up slowly, not daring to either move too quickly or stretch too far, in anticipation of some associated pain that it might bring.

Daniels disappeared through the door, John heard the murmuring of low voices on the other side and then the slow emergence of Dee-Dee's tear streaked face.

"I'm sorry, so sorry, I wanted to tell you yesterday, but I didn't have the chance, every time I started to say something we were interrupted. I'm so sorry. Please, can you ever forgive me?"

Her bloodshot eyes were pleading with him. It was absolutely impossible to feel angry with her, for anything. She had embarked on what must have felt like an adventure at the request of her father and baled out of it at the first opportunity. She was the one that deserved the sympathy and the understanding. And the loving.

He walked towards the dishevelled bundle that stood before him, leaned forward, took her face in his hands and kissed her so tenderly, it made him feel as though he wanted to cry with her. They had been through such a lot in such a short period of time. They held each other for what seemed like hours.

The captain, however, had other ideas. The speaker announced that they were beginning their descent into Cairo and would all passengers please take their seats and fasten their seatbelts.

"Good grief, no sooner do I get out of the damned chair than I have to get strapped back into it!"

His laughter brought an enormous smile to her face.

They sat in the seats on the opposite side of the aircraft to the one in which John had served out his captivity.

"Merry Christmas Mr. Hylton."

"Merry Christmas, Miss Sampson. Or should that be Miss Daniels?"

"No, you were right first time. My parents didn't marry until I was six and I had always been known as Delilah Sampson, it was on my birth certificate and even after my mother married my father she kept her maiden name. A sign of the times I suppose. I didn't lie to you once. Not about anything. I didn't even lie to you about the accident, you came straight up to me and told me it was your fault. I just didn't argue with you!"

"No, but it wasn't a very honest way to get to meet me."

"If you hadn't insisted that it was your fault I was going to apologise to you for not looking where I was going, but you were so nice about it I didn't want to spoil it all by arguing with you."

He leaned across her and kissed her again. In spite of everything, he realised that he was falling desperately in love with her.

They landed safely at Cairo airport. As they were only refuelling they were not allowed to make use of any facilities at the airport other than the washrooms. John and Dee-Dee didn't bother to leave the plane, they simply opened the door to breathe in the night air.

The stop was over in just under an hour and they were given clearance to take off again. Destination Nairobi.

They returned to their seats and shortly after take off were joined by Daniels who suggested that as they had a considerable amount to talk about they would probably be more comfortable in the forward cabin.

It certainly was more comfortable. The seats in the back were more or less regulation flight seats, eight pairs of seats, set in four groups of four, two pairs facing each other across a low, wide table. The forward cabin was more like the furniture in an upmarket house, wide comfortable chairs set around a low circular table that looked as though it could be raised for dining.

"Please, take a seat."

John and Dee-Dee chose to sit next to each other, with Daniels sat opposite John, a space between him and his daughter. Poignant and ironic, John thought.

"If I tell you what I have been doing for the past thirty years, you must tell me what your original intentions were when you set out to recreate my animals."

"Agreed."

"For years I have been waging a war against poachers and the destruction of the environment and wildlife of eastern and central Africa. I have not been doing this unaided. In fact my earliest excursions were simply to persuade the governments of the countries where the poachers were most active to clamp down hard on them, properly protect their National Parks where they were already set up and to establish new ones where there were none. A simple enough task... if the governments were not involved with the poachers.

"The biggest single problem is that most African governments are dictatorships of one kind or another: having either come to power by force, having been elected in one party elections, or two party elections where one party has had its supporters so badly terrorised, most often through tribal rivalries, that no-one dare to vote for it. There are few exceptions to this within Africa, and none in the area in which I have been working.

"Initially, we were having some success, but then it became apparent that the poachers were, with government protection, simply moving to other parts of the country where they could continue with their activities unnoticed for a while. I then started to receive 'inside information' from people within the government who were supportive of my efforts. I was told that the poachers were receiving help and information concerning my efforts and in return for military protection the poachers were depositing large sums of money into numbered foreign bank accounts on behalf of these people. The problem is, Mr. Hylton, that these people do not expect to stay in power for ever. They are realistic enough to know that they will eventually be removed from their positions in the same manner in which they arrived at them. They will almost certainly have to flee the country and to ensure that they have sufficient funds they are quite prepared to be paid by the lice that deal in the blood of the animals.

"After years of trying, with a certain amount of success, to eliminate the poachers legitimately, it was quite clear that the only way to deal with these scum effectively was to eliminate them illegally. No government, no matter how much they had supported me in the past was prepared to openly associate themselves with, what the rest of the world could pompously call, murderers. I have had a lot of support behind the scenes and I do receive a lot of information, but for everyone that is helping me, it would appear that there are at least two being paid to help the poachers.

"Then, fourteen and a half years ago came the attack on my wife and I. We had been out searching for one particular poaching party who had left a devastating trail of slaughter after, we were told, being attacked by a lone rogue elephant. The only thing that I could see was that the elephant was clever enough to take the fight back to the poachers. There were never any reports of the elephant being found, dead or alive. The man responsible for the carnage was also responsible for murdering my wife, and..." he removed his hat, showing a badly scarred head with little hair on it and a forehead that would have done a Klingon proud "... for this also. I owe it to myself and my wife never to give up the fight against these people, whether they are poachers, the Chinese who fund and arm them or their supporters in government."

"That's a very sad story and I'm sorry for the loss of your wife in such terrible circumstances. But where do I fit in to all of this?" John said with genuine sympathy.

Dee-Dee squeezed John's hand and looked appreciatively at him.

"I think that you fit in quite beautifully. You have made the breakthrough that, I think, will enable us to eventually wipe the poachers off the face of the earth."

"I'm sorry, I'm not quite with you. I originally made these animals with the intention of replacing zoo animals, so that they could be allowed to live out their lives in better, more appropriate surroundings."

"Very noble and commendable. I cannot disagree with you at all, but I have at least been able to rescue my animals from what otherwise would have been destruction. If your animals are up to the task, my intention, only with your co-operation of course, is to release some of your animals into specific areas as a target for the poachers. We would then be able to leave them out as bait, roaming wild and free and a very big temptation. We would be able to confine the animals to a given area and know that we would be in striking distance when the poachers showed themselves."

John threw back his head and laughed.

"What is so funny? Can't it be done?" Daniels was perplexed.

"Oh, it can be done all right. We can do a lot more than that. We won't even need to go anywhere near them. Rhoda would probably win a battle with a tank corps! She would be more than capable of taking out a few shabby little poachers, furthermore they should be allowed to escape, initially. What would they tell their employers? Sorry boss, a rhino trashed the jeeps, we shot it at least a hundred times and she still kept coming. I don't think they would be quite so keen to go back after that had happened a few times. It doesn't just have to be rhinos either. How about an extremely bad tempered old bull elephant or two, a few cheetahs, leopards, chimps, lions. God, we could have them so damned frightened they wouldn't dare go to a zoo!" John was beginning to be carried away on a wave of euphoria.

"You can do all of this?" Daniels asked, barely believing him.

"No problem at all, the rhino can leave whenever you want, nasty tempered old boot that she is. Suzie for one would be pleased to see the back of her!"

"Then the purpose of our journey has changed. I think that we will spend Christmas in Nairobi. I will introduce you to some of my dearest friends and we will go out on some game drives that will make you fall in love with Africa."

John looked at Dee-Dee and thought that there couldn't be room for any more falling in love just yet.

He was proven quite wrong. The time they spent in the game reserves, particularly at night when the animals came wandering down to the waterholes, was so incredibly magical that it simply heightened the feelings he and Dee-Dee had for each other. One night, they counted the elephants in: thirty four of them arrived over a two hour period. John had always been an animal lover but it was a completely new dimension. Also the number of different animals that came down to the water hole was amazing: lions, elephants, antelope of numerous varieties, wildebeest, gazelles, the list was endless. It was as though at night there was a truce between them. The hunters and the prey arrived at their appointed place, seemingly without fear of attack, although the lions did make the dik-diks nervous, being snack-size for a lioness. That really was worth preserving, there could be no doubt about that. What was beyond his comprehension was how anyone could possibly see a profit in the destruction of such magnificent scenes. The world would be an extremely barren place if it were allowed to be ruined.

Chapter 16

While they were in Kenya, John and Dee-Dee saw so many wonderful sights, from the hippos at Mzima Springs to the flamingoes on Lake Nakuru, but there was also the work of the poachers, hunting down and leaving their trail of destruction along the Kenya-Tanzania border. One of the biggest problems facing Eric had been the unwillingness of the Tanzanian government to ban hunting within its own borders and its capacity to ignore the presence of the poachers. The animals, of course, don't recognise borders and the elephants of Tsavo and Amboseli frequently wandered out of the relative safety of the reserve straight into the hunters and poachers bullets. At other times the poachers would not be prepared to wait for them to stray so they would enter the reserves to kill them wherever they were to be found. The carcases would be found with gaping holes where the tusks or horns once were, slaughtered for no other reason than to satisfy greed and the forever demanding markets in China and Asia for "traditional" medicine and aphrodisiacs.

John wondered if it would ever be possible to educate the people that gave the murderers their outlets, but concluded that thousands of years of so-called culture would be impossible to overcome before the animals were driven to extinction.

No, they had work to do. They would be able to provide a balance against the weapons of the hunters and thieves and, maybe, provide a platform for them to build on to drive the poachers to extinction.

Time was of the essence, they had the facility to let Rhoda loose onto the plains, to seek out and at least destroy the confidence of some of the poachers, but it would take a lot of time and a lot of money to produce sufficient numbers of animals to make a difference.

It was decided by Alan, more than anyone, after their return on the 2nd January, that the best solution would be to set up a monitoring centre on board Eric's plane. It could be installed easily and could be transported anywhere it needed to go with very little notice. Alan would also be able to keep track of events by a secure satellite link to the plane, no matter where it was so that any problems that might arise could be dealt with remotely.

It was also decided that nobody outside of their group should be informed about the operation. There was too much money to be lost by the poachers and their supporters in the governments, police and military to be certain that someone wouldn't change sides for twenty pieces of silver.

On the sixteenth of January, Eric Daniels and his crew flew back to Kenya, his plane carrying a whole host of computers and enough new technology to keep track of an army, and, as they were going in to battle, that was precisely what was needed. She was a tight squeeze getting through the forward door, but there was also a rhinoceros in the hold.

And there was an additional passenger on board. There had not been adequate time to train anyone new to operate the equipment that didn't have a relevant background, and as it would have been impossible for Alan, John or Suzie to have gone out with it, they decided to offer Jerry Grossman the opportunity to be the eyes and ears on board the plane. Jerry was, at first, reluctant to go. John assumed that the nature of the job, in a potentially hostile environment, was an intimidating prospect, but with three days to go before the scheduled departure, Jerry suddenly changed his mind and it seemed that nothing would be allowed to prevent him from going

Jerry's Christmas had been one that he would never forget. He had hardly left Jacqui's side during the two weeks they had been together. He was rapidly coming to the conclusion that she was insatiable, but was, nonetheless, enjoying every moment of it.

He had experienced the finer things in life that only vast wealth could provide. On the day after the office party, Jerry had been casually informed that they would be flying down to the Maldives for Christmas, Lorenzo owned a small island there and it was less crowded than the Caribbean. Jerry had, he thought, been treated to a lifestyle that only royalty would be privileged to know, and all because of a game of cards and a woman.

The return home on New Years Eve had been something of a comedown for him. He had been getting very used to the idea of a life of luxury and all of life's pleasures that had hitherto been denied to him. But then, Lorenzo's attitude towards him had altered perceptibly. Nothing definite, but the smile that had always been resident on his face was seen with less regularity. There had been the occasional raised voice, not with him, but with Jacqui. It appeared as though Lorenzo was tiring of the indulgence he had permitted her over the previous two weeks.

As Jerry returned to work, Lorenzo's question sessions became more frequent and more detailed. Jerry felt that he was expected to make himself available at all times. He had only been to his own house three times in over three weeks. The trip to Africa, when it was originally proposed, hadn't really appealed to him. The conditions would be poor, the hours would be as long as the day, he would also miss Jacqui's attentions and the luxury that was attached to her.

By the twelfth of January, Jerry was beginning to feel claustrophobic, he was no longer free to come and go as he pleased and the thing that disturbed him the most was Jacqui treating him as one of her possessions.

On one occasion she coldly informed him that he needn't bother coming back if that was all he thought of her, when he told her that he would quite like to spend some time at his own home. He invited her to join him, but it made no difference. The conclusion that he arrived at on the thirteenth, when he told a delighted Alan that he would go, was that if he stayed any longer, he would have been owned lock, stock and barrel by Lorenzo, and the good times would only continue as long as Jacqui tolerated him.

The realisation also struck him that Lorenzo collected people. He had learned that Jones the Unfortunate hadn't been able to make good on his marker and that he would be forced to repay his ever spiralling debt by feeding Lorenzo with inside information on companies that he dealt with allowing him to make a killing on a large number of deals on the stock market.

Jerry had no doubt that Jones was only one of many. No wonder that Lorenzo felt the need to live in an isolated house with men patrolling constantly outside. The intruder system had to be seen to be believed!

On the sixteenth, Jerry left the house as normal, not telling anyone of his imminent departure, least of all Jacqui, who had a habit of sleeping in until well after he had left anyway. He had stood and looked at her for one final time as he dressed. Beautiful lady, shame about the attitude, he thought.

It had been decided that Rhoda would be released in Tsavo West, a game reserve under the shadow of Mount Kilimanjaro, right on the border with Tanzania. Before they left the lab they increased the size of Rhoda's horn. John wanted to make sure that the sightings of her would attract a great deal of attention.

By guiding her into the vicinity of the game lodges and villages it would ensure that her presence was being flashed up on the sightings boards all over the reserve. Three days into her journey, Eric sent two of his crew out to the lodges to check the boards. Every lodge has one, giving information on the sightings of the 'big five' animals on every game watcher's list. The system also provided the same information to would-be poachers and hunters. Sure enough, there had been sightings posted in each one of the lodges they visited, the location varying depending upon the time that the group saw her, but from the location and times given it was quite possible for her general direction and route to be approximated.

The first sighting of the poachers came on the fourth day as Rhoda was wandering along the border. There was only one Jeep, with four Africans inside. They were extremely excited when they saw her, very impressed with the size of the pot of gold stuck on the front of her face.

Jerry was sitting in the back of the plane, watching the screens in front of him as Rhoda stood in a wide open space, the nearest cover was two hundred yards away. At first she stood quite placidly, appearing to be curious about the presence of the men, getting closer at only seventy yards away. The poachers were not there to take prisoners. The Jeep stopped, one of the men standing up at the back pulled his rifle up to his shoulder, resting his elbow on the roll bar. It was going to be easy, head on, straight between the eyes, not even bothering to move, so easy.

"Heh heh, even you can't miss from here, Andwele!" the driver said, almost salivating at the prospect of a big payday.

As Andwele cranked the bolt on the side of the rifle Rhoda swung quickly to her left, running at an angle of forty five degrees away from the Jeep, towards the safety of the trees, the cover would be sparse but it would interfere with aim of the hunters.

"Damn!" the driver said as he set off after the rhino.

Andwele fired off a shot as he aimed at her left side. Even with the Jeep bouncing about he could hardly miss with the entire flank to aim at, but miss he did. Or at least he assumed he did, as the thirty mile an hour gait of the rhino didn't falter.

As she reached the edge of the trees, the Jeep was running almost straight at her closing the gap. At the point at which Andwele had decided he would fire again, Rhoda abruptly changed direction, straight back into the path of the Jeep. The driver could hardly believe his eyes, a sixty mile an hour impact with a three ton rhino was not his idea of fun!

"NO NO NO NOOOO!" he shouted in desperation.

The others were hanging on and shouting for all they were worth but the rifle that had been ready to fire suddenly found that it was pointing away from the rhino as the driver swerved hard left away from Rhoda. Too late!

Rhoda hit the jeep hard and low, hooking her horn into the back tyre and with the momentum of the jeep in her favour swung her head as hard and fast as she could, throwing the jeep onto its side, scattering the poachers all over the ground. With a snort of approval Rhoda scanned the scene of devastation in front of her and then rammed the Jeep underneath and tipped it fully over. Job done, she turned quickly and trotted off into the bush, seemingly bouncing along on her toes. Somewhere in her memory an ice cream cart jingle was playing...

The poachers were not seriously hurt but their jeep was beyond repair and upside down.

They picked themselves up and watched Rhoda disappear into the bush.

"What is it with you? Anyone could have hit that rhino?"Jamil, the driver, ranted.

"I swear I hit it! How could I miss? Maybe the bullet was faulty and didn't have enough power to get through her skin?" Andwele pleaded to be believed.

"A likely story, you're useless! And now we have..."

With a final crash, the roll bar that had been partially propping up the Jeep collapsed.

"...nothing! We have to try and get our guns out at least. Go and find some wood that we can use as levers to lift up the side.

Their weapons and water were trapped underneath and being faced with a long walk back to the hole in the ground from which they crept, all in the heat of the midday African sun, water was something that they needed even more than guns.

Leaving the poachers to live to tell the tale ensured that the stories would be circulated very quickly when they returned. It would be a tale that would get a lot of attention even if Andwele's reputation was shot to pieces: he couldn't hit the side of a rhino at fifty yards!

Jerry had seen the entire sequence of events from the safety of the plane, some hundred miles away and enjoyed every second of it. It was he that gave the instruction for Rhoda to hit the Jeep a second time. The satisfaction was immense, and no doubt Eric would be ecstatic when he reviewed the footage when he returned from Nairobi.

What he had also managed to capture was the pictures of four poachers who, hopefully, would be identified by the authorities. They would not be able to pass on the details of how they came by the information but Eric would certainly make sure that the pictures got into the right hands.

Round one to Rhoda.

John had been working long hours ever since his return from Kenya and had seen more of Dee-Dee as a result of her spending more time at his office. She acted as a liaison between John and her father. John still found Daniels difficult to get on with, mainly because the man seemed to have trouble communicating with anyone on the same level, always wanting to be in control, never wanting to take no for an answer.

John decided that the best solution was for Dee-Dee to act as a buffer particularly as she was not busy with her writing. She wanted to be involved, partly to repay John for what had happened to him and partly just wanting to be able to be with him. It was also an opportunity to participate in the mission to avenge the death of her mother.

The news about Rhoda's first encounter, when it came in from Jerry was received to tumultuous applause. The film was played through three times for all the staff to watch, and each time they saw Rhoda spear the jeep the 'Ole' that went up as she did it became even louder, it would have graced the arena at a Spanish bullfight. John wondered how a suggestion of replacing the bulls would go down... and thought better of it.

The encounter with the poachers, though, made it all

worthwhile. The Revenge of the Rhino... that would make a good film title, he thought.

Suzie had returned from her trip to the Virgin Islands looking very tanned and relaxed. She was looking good, very happy, everyone remarked to John how they had never seen her that way before, it was like she was a completely different person. She didn't work any less hard, nor was she any less dedicated, it was just that she had a permanent smile on her face. Whatever had happened in the sun had clearly been very good for her, and, John thought, not before time. She deserved something more in her life other than permanently driving herself to the physical and mental edge, life wasn't just for achieving, it was also for living.

On the twenty third, a week after Jerry had left for Africa, Barbara took a phone call from a man trying to contact him.

"I've been to his home, but it seems as though he hasn't been there for a while, we had an appointment last week which wasn't kept, I wondered if you would be able to tell me where I can reach him?"

"I'm not sure that I know myself, all I know is that he had some leave that he was due for, so he decided to take a break whilst we are a bit quiet, we always are in the post-Christmas period. Perhaps if you leave me your name and number I can find out when we are expecting him back and I can let you know."

"No, that's alright, I won't be available until the middle of next week, I'll ring back then. Thank you for your trouble."

As Barbara put the phone down, the penny dropped. She had heard the voice before, it belonged to the man that delivered the letter for Jerry before Christmas. There was nothing that could be done until Jerry came back, so she made a note in her message book for when he returned.

Dan was not pleased, it looked as though Jerry had just disappeared. He hadn't been seen for a week, he hadn't been in to work, to his home or to his parents and from what he had just learned it would seem that he probably wasn't even in the country. The only thing they could do would be to wait until he returned, but would Lorenzo be satisfied with that? Most unlikely.

Dan was quite right, Lorenzo was furious. Jacqui wasn't in

much better humour either, she was much more used to finishing with her boyfriends on her own terms, it was something quite new for her, and she didn't like it.

Lorenzo had been carefully building up a picture of the work that Jerry had been involved with and he didn't appreciate the interruption to his planned schedule. He would wait one more week, he had no other option and a lot to lose by jumping in with both feet. He still needed more information before he could make any moves and Jerry was still the best way to get it.

Chapter 17

Jerry was having the time of his life, all thoughts of Jacqui and Lorenzo had vanished on the way into Kenya. Most of the flight had been overnight and consequently there had been nothing to see, but the dawn breaking over Kenya as they flew in towards Nairobi had been one of the wonders of the world.

Just before five o'clock, local time, there had been a glow to the distant edges of the clouds that lay a few thousand feet below them, and in minutes the whole carpet was gleaming white, but the sight that stunned Jerry and all of those that were awake to see it was the appearance of the peak of Mount Kenya spearing through the clouds. It was the most breathtaking sight he had ever seen, something he would never forget as long as he lived. With its snow lined top it stood proud, almost powerful, against the dawn, dominating the whole skyline. Welcome to Africa.

Since their arrival, Jerry had spent the majority of his time on board the plane, parked forty miles west of Nairobi at the end of a red-earthed runway, watching through the eyes of the rhino. There had been several sightings of tourist safari buses during Rhoda's search, Jerry made sure that she was seen at a respectable distance, giving those hunters that only shot with cameras the thrill of seeing a 'real live rhino' in the wild. Considering how few there actually were in the park the chances of them actually finding a genuine one were extremely remote, so Jerry and Rhoda were probably making the high point of their holiday. They were also ensuring that the notice boards would be full of even more reports of the rhino sightings.

On the morning of the twenty second of January, Jerry and Rhoda spotted a mini-bus out on the plain, Rhoda moved out into full view. The driver of the safari mini-bus decided he was going to try to take a closer look, to get his camera happy customers really close. Jerry thought that it would be a good opportunity for a little fun.

Rhoda was jogging along as the bus approached cautiously from her rear, as the bus got within thirty yards the cameras were clattering away like it was the finish line at an Olympic track final. Rhoda looked over her shoulder and turned slightly to take her path across the front of the bus. The driver slowed down, not wanting to alarm the magnificent animal and then Rhoda increased her pace, crossing over to the left side of the bus, circling round so the she now faced its side, smartly accelerated, head down, the driver reacted as best he could but the bus was not the swiftest vehicle on a road, let alone across the dustbowl of the plain, with five yards to go and the tourists starting to say their prayers, except for two that were intent on keeping their videos going.

Jerry veered Rhoda to her right and allowed the bus to escape unmolested. Left to her own devices, Rhoda would have put a hole in the side of the bus and left the driver very much regretting his bravado.

Rhoda's reputation as the bad tempered rhino with a habit of charging anything on four wheels would be legendary in the bars of the safari lodges by the end of the week and the driver would be dining out on his story for years to come. A real bonus for any driver is a genuine claim that he gets his customers to the sharp end, literally, of the safari.

Jerry thoroughly enjoyed the sport, it would be a holiday to remember for the six people in the bus and the videos taken by the two brave ones would be the best souvenirs of them all.

For two and a half weeks Alan, Bob and Sally had been working all hours to get the next two animals ready for the journey to the sun, there was a playmate for Rhoda, she one was going to be called Rhonda and then there was Elvis.

Elvis was would be the star of the show, he could really rock and roll. Elvis had big ears, big legs, big tusks and was just generally big. He stood thirteen feet at the shoulder, weighed over seven and a half tons and his feet were twenty inches in diameter.

Elvis the bull elephant was going to make a real splash at the waterhole. He was scheduled to fly out on a transport plane along with Rhonda from a private airfield, owned by one of Eric's few friends, with an ultimate destination logged as Sudan. The cargo had been registered as farm tractors and cultivating machinery. Elvis and Rhonda had been shipped out at night in a truck that had been driven to the gates of the underground car park.

Dan Phillips had been watching from the safety of the bushes in the gardens at the front of Animagination, but had been unable to see what was actually being loaded, but eleven o'clock at night on a Sunday was a very strange time to be loading anything into a truck.

It was, unfortunately for him, not possible to get down to see precisely what was going on as it would have meant walking directly down the roadway with absolutely no cover whatsoever. The only other alternative was going to be to follow the truck to its destination and hope for better luck there.

Dan was watching as well as he could, he had night vision binoculars as well as standard twenty by fifties, but the only things he had been able to identify had been John, Alan and the woman, whom he presumed to be Suzie. She was the only woman and she was there late, couldn't be anyone else. He was also taking photographs of everything he could see.

The truck left the car park just after twelve thirty. Suzie was already on her way to Nairobi on a scheduled commercial flight that had departed on time at eight forty five. Due to be met by Eric at the airport the following morning, she was going to assist Jerry for a few days. Having one animal to keep track of was relatively simple, having three would not be too difficult but they couldn't afford any mistakes early on, and it was a good excuse for her to go and join the fun.

Dan followed the truck for seventy miles before they arrived at the airfield. There was only one plane out on the tarmac and the truck drove straight up to the back of it. The tailgate of the plane was already down, ready to receive the cargo. The truck reversed towards the tailgate so that the back of the truck and the ramp into the back of the plane were only ten feet apart. The truck driver climbed down out of his cab, walked to the back of the truck, opened the doors, pulled out a pair of ramps and stood back to let his mighty cargo out. John had travelled in the cab and was standing on the far side of the truck.

Dan could see that he was calling into the back of the truck, but couldn't tell what he was saying. Then the rhino made her appearance out of the back and walked gently up the ramp into the hold of the plane. John followed her in and a few seconds later returned to the rear of the truck. He called again and almost immediately the massive shape of Elvis materialised.

Dan gasped, he couldn't believe what he was seeing, it had to be the biggest animal that he had ever seen and it was walking like a puppy to John's commands. His camera was also working overtime taking pictures of the Animagination creations, only now the photographer knew what they were. Lorenzo would be very pleased. It more than made up for Jerry's infuriating departure.

For six days he had been watching the comings and goings with very little to show for his efforts, other than to be able to confirm that Jerry was nowhere to be seen. Now he had hit the jackpot, he had identified the most important people, got clear photographs of them all and of the two most recent creations. It filled in just about all of the gaps that Jerry had left. He had told them that they had been producing robot animals, he had told them that they were powered by lithium fuel cells, but he had not been able to tell them what they were going to be used for or what they would be capable of. At least they now knew the scale of the animals and Lorenzo would be able to find out from one of his many 'suppliers' where the animals were heading for. They had the aircraft number, its departure time and place and they knew its cargo, the rest would be simple.

When Dan drove to Lorenzo's in the morning, he'd had only three hours sleep. He had arrived home at just after four and the alarm, to his disgust, had woken him at seven thirty. He decided that it would be better, in spite of hardly being able to open his eyes, to see Lorenzo as soon as possible. He needn't have bothered rushing, Lorenzo didn't appear until after ten.

The news, when it was eventually given, was well received. Lorenzo immediately made two telephone calls, and with the second came up with a rather surprising answer.

"It looks like our friend is not exactly being honest with the authorities. The flight is logged with a destination of Sudan, which is a very odd place to be taking the cargo you described, but not for the cargo that they have admitted to carrying, which is down as being agricultural machinery. Our friend is up to something and that gives me an edge."

Lorenzo looked very pleased with himself.

John arrived at the office rather later than usual, without Dee-Dee who had gone in to her own office at the magazine to find out more about a story concerning the antics of one of the more eccentric French designers who had been making the news.

He spent what was left of the morning going through the next part of the Africa project with Bob and Sally, both of whom looked like they needed another holiday already after only three weeks back at work. John and Eric had decided that they could do with some more animals out there that would be information gatherers. Rhoda had been doing a wonderful job getting herself noticed, but as yet they had only had one run in with the poachers. The place for Elvis had been elected as the Kenya-Uganda border area, where the poachers had been quite active during recent weeks, while Rhonda, after two or three days in the same area as Rhoda, was going to head into Tanzania. They had to spread themselves over a wider area.

They were therefore going to build a giraffe and three chimpanzees. The chimps, initially would be solitary animals, moving around the forests, trying to locate any camps or trails that the poachers might be using so that they could send information back to Jerry and Suzie to divert the three targets in the poachers direction, or to alert the KWS if they were too far away. After the initial success things had gone quiet for Rhoda, and she was not the ideal creature to be moving around in the forests. The giraffe would wander around on the plains simply being a lofty lookout, he would be of no value to the hunters and should not attract too much attention.

The telephone call from Lorenzo was as unwelcome for the intrusion as much as the content.

Barbara explained that the man was insistent to the point of being rude when she put the call through.

"Excuse me while I take this," John said to Bob and Sally.

"Mr. Hylton, my name is Lorenzo Lanfranco, I doubt that you have heard of me, but I do have a considerable interest in your current project."

"And which project are you referring to Mr. Lanfranco? We have several under way at present."

"I think that it would be better if we met to discuss my proposition face to face. I have a project of my own in mind that will earn you a considerable amount of money. Are you free for lunch today?"

"I'm sorry, but today is absolutely impossible. I'll put you back to Barbara who will be able to arrange something for next week."

"I'm afraid that wouldn't fit in with my plans and it wouldn't be at all advantageous to you either," Lorenzo said with a touch of menace.

John was trying to thinking quickly. Who was he, what could he possibly know? What could he possibly want?

"Mr. Lorenzo, we try to accommodate all new enquiries, but at the moment we are very busy..."

"I understand but I must insist that we meet today or tomorrow. It really will be beneficial for you."

John felt no option but to capitulate.

"Tomorrow would be easier."

"Fine, we'll meet at the Ristorante dell'Artista at one o'clock. Just ask for my table. Goodbye Mr. Hylton."

"Goodbye."

John was perplexed and worried.

"That man was confident, too confident. He must know something, or he would have wanted to meet here not in a restaurant. Have either of you ever heard of him?"

Bob and Sally both shook their heads.

"Do you think he's referring to the animals? Even if he is what possible use could they be to him, they're not exactly toys."

"No, it's strange, but the timing would make me believe that it can't be anything else. Nothing for it other than to meet the man, see what he's got to say."

Suzie had been enjoying the change of scenery, she'd never been to Africa before and seeing it through the eyes of a rhino was quite an experience. She had spent a lot of time talking to Eric, who was not at all bombastic with her; she had a certain rapport with him, although she didn't know why. She learned a lot about him in the first two days she had been there.

When he had first tried to get help from the various African governments he had met with an awful lot of opposition, not officially but from individuals, he had also learned that talking was going to achieve very little. He had been responsible for the setting up of an anti-poaching task force to patrol the national parks in Kenya but they had been woefully underfunded by the government, often not having enough fuel to make more than one day trip a week. It had not been easy carrying the fight on his own. The poachers were well organised and well funded, the money they could earn from one dead elephant would have kept the entire task force in supplies and vehicle parts for a month. It was a bitter struggle.

He had set up schemes to help villagers to benefit from the tourism that came with the protection of the animals, so that instead of the people wanting to be rid of the animals because they ate or destroyed their crops, they learned to live with them so that they could benefit more from the tourism. It also meant jobs and comparative prosperity. They came to see the animals as an integral part of their future and not something that was trying to destroy it.

He told her that in the nineties they had experimented in cutting off the horns of the rhinos and the tusks of the elephants so that the animals would have no value to the poachers, that worked to a degree. The elephants had certainly been safer but the poachers were still hunting the rhino as there was still enough horn left on them below the surface for them to justify killing them and the price they were getting for the horn increased threefold. Simple economics of supply and demand. It was a hateful business.

Suzie hadn't asked about his wife, but he volunteered what was probably the worst story of all.

"Almost fifteen years ago, my wife and I were on a patrol to find some poachers that had been running riot in the Marsabit National Park, killing virtually every animal they came across, there was no pattern to the killing, they simply slaughtered everything they found. Zebra, wildebeest, rhino, elephant, lions, giraffes they all went the same way. Everything. It was simply vandalism of the worst order. What we eventually found out through talking to the few people who would talk, was that it was being carried out by a poacher called Mtoto Abdebele who originated from Am Timan in Chad. He had been making occasional forays out of southern Sudan into the north of the country with his son and a few followers. They had been moderately successful, mainly killing elephants. They had been following the trail of a big old bull whose tusks had been reported to be over eight feet long. Tusks of that size would fetch an absolute fortune in Japan or China. The group had camped for the night when, without any warning, the old bull came rampaging through the camp. The first victim was the son, his chest was trodden on and crushed, the father was gored in his right leg as he tried to get out of the way and one of his trackers was also hit by the elephant and killed. The elephant got away unharmed and was last reported heading south towards the Marsabit reserve, never to be seen again.

"The poacher buried his dead, got himself patched up and a few hours later set off in search of the elephant. By the time they arrived, the elephant had long gone. News travels fast and almost everyone had heard the story and many enjoyed the thought of a poacher getting what was due to him. Consequently there were very few people who were willing to help the man in his quest for vengeance.

"As a result he took out his anger on every other living animal that he came across."

Suzie sat as still as a rock, totally transfixed.

He continued.

"We were not the only ones looking for him, all of the rangers were out and several army units, but the Northern Frontier district is a very large place. Finding a small group out there requires a good degree of luck as well as skill.

Unfortunately our luck came in the form of bad luck. We stopped at the top of a ridge so we could get a good view of the gorge below us and the land to the south, but while we were looking for them, they had found us. We had only just set up a camp when we were attacked. Our two guides were stood searching the plains below with their binoculars when warning shots were fired at close range. They naturally surrendered immediately. The poachers had come up on foot and it seemed that their purpose had been to take us hostage, so they could bargain their way out of the country. Until that time they hadn't killed or hurt any people.

"My wife and I were both securely tied to large stakes that they cut and planted into the ground by the fire we had built, we were no more than six feet away from it, our guides had been trussed hand and foot and, as far as we could tell, had been left to their luck some distance away from us.

"I found out afterwards that my satellite phone had been tracked and a small squad of soldiers came quietly to find us. They had been told of a reward for the poachers, dead or alive. They clearly thought that a surprise night attack would get the job done and that there was a very good chance that they would get us out as well.

"When they did attack they moved in swiftly and took out two of the poachers, but Abdebele and one of his men had not been with the other two, they were several yards outside the clearing on the opposite side and so escaped the main attack. The soldiers, realising their mistake, left one man to set us free, while they went in search of the others. The soldier that was cutting my wife free died in a hail of bullets and my wife was badly injured at the same time. The poachers had evidently used what bullets they had in their guns, because when they came in to finish us off, the guns were empty. They went to fetch more ammunition from their Land Rover, but before they could reload they could hear more soldiers coming. They hadn't time to kill me, so they simply charged into me from behind, uprooted the stake and I fell forward into the fire. The soldiers arrived within seconds, but my hair was on fire. I was lucky. They put out the fire quite quickly, but my the top of my head and forehead was badly burnt, which is why I prefer to wear my hat and glasses, not for any other, more sinister reasons."

"And your wife?"

"I'm afraid that my wife didn't survive the journey to the hospital."

"I'm sorry."

She meant it, it was the most horrific story that she had ever heard, she was almost in tears.

Eric took a deep breath.

"The worst of it is that the scum that killed her escaped into the night, the other two were killed, but as far as I know, he is still out there somewhere. Perhaps one day I will be treated to his company, then I, and the animals, will be able to sleep in peace at night."

The arrival of Rhonda and Elvis lifted everyone's spirits. Elvis was truly magnificent, there was no doubt that he was the King, even if it was only of the jungle.

John and Alan had programmed him to travel up through the Masai Mara, towards the north.

"How did John know where to send Elvis?" Eric asked Suzie.

"He took on board your story and decided that the north would be a good place for him to start. He could hardly have him wandering around with the rhinos in the south or the game would soon be up and the poachers would move elsewhere."

"Well, it would appear that we are on the same wavelength. It would be a tremendous bonus if Elvis could flush out Abdebele! Wishful thinking no doubt. He's probably already died in some opium den in Cairo by now, I couldn't be that lucky."

Rhonda was sent south to Tsavo and double up with Rhoda. It was a typical January Tuesday in Kenya, hot, dry and slow. Nothing moved fast, unless it was either hunter or hunted, but Jerry hoped that there might be some action coming up soon.

Chapter 18

John spent Tuesday morning trying to find out what he could about Lorenzo Lanfranco. An internet search had thrown up very little on him, apart from a connection with a charitable foundation. He called a few friends but most had never heard of him, but two that had, only knew enough to tell him that he was extremely rich, probably made by illegal means but he had never been caught with his hand in anyone's till and that John would probably be best advised to steer clear of him.

John called Keith Boscik on the off chance that he might be able to give him some help.

"Lanfranco, you say, it certainly doesn't mean anything to me, but I can give you the name of a man that should be able to help you, he's a fraud squad detective. If the police have an interest he should be able to tell you. His name is Alex Benson, Sergeant. How's Suzie?"

"She's absolutely fine, I don't know what you two got up to but whatever it was, she hasn't stopped smiling since. She should be back in ten to fourteen days if everything goes well. I must admit I could do with her here, we'll start falling behind with the paying customers if she stays too long."

"Give her my, er, best regards when you talk to her next, and good luck with your man today."

"Thanks."

John didn't make the call to the sergeant, he couldn't work out how to give the man a plausible story and ask for information that should be privileged. Even if he had mentioned Keith's name it still seemed an unbalanced request. If the police were interested in him it was always possible that he could get hooked up in an investigation that he really didn't need. The request had to come from Keith if at all.

John rang him again at the hospital.

"I'm sorry Mr. Hylton but Dr. Boscik has just gone into theatre, he is expected to be in for at least two hours. Shall I get him to call you when he's free?"

Two hours, one thirty. "No it's okay. I'll call him back this afternoon."

Forewarned is forearmed, he thought, but not much to go on. Have to play it by ear.

The Ristorante dell'Artista was a fairly typical, but upmarket Italian restaurant, most of the tables were small, square four-seaters, with a red and white checked undercloth and a starched white table cloth laid diagonally on top. The atmosphere and decor was very authentic; there was no doubt that Mr. Lorenzo Lanfranco would be in his element.

John asked for his table and was led smartly to a corner table set for two, Lorenzo was sat waiting for him, drinking a glass of Frascati - the bottle was in the ice bucket on a stand at the side of the table.

"Mr. Hylton, I am so glad that you could come, please sit down."

John noticed that he didn't offer his hand in greeting, maybe it wasn't going to be an easy meal to enjoy.

"Please help yourself to some wine."

John accepted the invitation and poured himself half a glass.

"Mr. Lorenzo, you inferred on the phone that you had a proposition for me," John said matter of tersely.

"Yes. I can see you are a man who doesn't like to waste words. That is good. I am sure that we will do business together."

John didn't like the smile, it smacked of something nasty. The man knew what he wanted, and John got the distinct feeling that he wouldn't want to give it to him.

"My sources tell me that you have produced something a little special."

He paused to let his words sink in.

"I am informed that you have made some excellent reproductions of zoo animals, let me see, a rhino, an elephant and a panther. I think that is right. Do you agree, Mr. Hylton."

"I think that your sources have misinformed you."

The man clearly knew something, but whatever it was the information was not complete. They had made two rhinos, not one.

"We have made some mock-ups for a film. Special effects, the majority of the action sequences will be produced inside our computers, not tangible machinery."

"Yes, I understand that that was your story for the benefit of the zoo, but what I want is for you to tell me that you have actually produced working, walking versions of these animals."

"I can tell you want you want to hear, Mr. Lanfranco, but it wouldn't be the truth."

"I can understand your reluctance, you obviously have the ability to produce something truly remarkable but you are not yet ready to unveil it to the world, and here am I sitting in a nice friendly restaurant telling you that I know of your inventions. Shall we order?"

John didn't really feel like eating, but knew that he had to find out what was going on in this man's head, he also knew that this man would, sooner or later, have to tell him what he wanted.

John spent several minutes studying the menu, his mind racing, but realising that the only information that could be imparted would have to come from the man opposite. John eventually ordered a green salad for starter and tortellini for a main course.

"Now, Mr. Hylton. we can sit here talking all day, me telling you that I know something and you sitting there denying it all. So I think that you had better look at these."

The photographs might as well have been a nuclear bomb. John could not deny the existence of the elephant and rhino. Elvis and Rhonda were there for all to see. Date and time printed on the photos. The first pictures were of the truck, its front end sticking out of the entrance to their car park. The second set, timed two and a half hours later were of the animals walking out of the truck into the plane. There were eighteen pictures of each of them, each a second apart, showing them progressing out of the truck and down up the respective ramps. There was no argument. How could he have been so stupid? But why should he have taken more precautions, the only perceived threat had previously been from Eric, and now that they were firmly on the same side, there had been no need for extreme caution. He had no answer to them. They had clearly been followed on Sunday night. They had done nothing wrong, there was nothing to worry about from a few photographs.

"So what?" he replied, with nothing to lose.

"At least we are now out in the open, Mr. Hylton, or may I call you John? I think its so much more friendly doing business on first name terms, don't you?" The smile was sickening.

"Mr. Hylton will do just fine. Mr. Lanfranco."

"Have it your way. But at least we are making progress."

The starter arrived. John ate and didn't look up from his food until he had finished. It was not going to be an enjoyable meal

"What I want from you is to build for me something similar to what you have been building for someone else. I understand that these animals are of your own design, by that I mean that they were not commissioned by another, so we don't cross any legal problems. I am prepared to offer you a very large sum of money, simply for producing two such creations to my own specification. I tell you what I want them to be capable of doing, you produce them in the same way you have produced the others. Nothing difficult abut that, nothing illegal, and I'm sure that you won't sniff at fifteen million for each of them."

John was shocked. Thirty million for two animals. When he originally thought that they could make serious money out of the project, he hadn't necessarily been thinking along those lines.

"That's a lot of money. I assume that you are a businessman to be able to spend that sort of money. So where is the return on your investment. It certainly isn't going to be in starting a zoo, at that rate you couldn't cover the interest."

"My purpose is my own affair."

The main course arrived. The pasta was perfection, al dente.

"Before I could consider any such proposition I am afraid that it is a company policy to know precisely the purpose of any project, if we don't like it we don't build it."

"At this stage, Mr. Hylton, I am not prepared to give you any further information. I think that thirty million is a sufficient inducement for you to change your rules, but even so, I am only wanting an agreement in principle at the moment. Once I have established that the proposition is viable I have to consult with my partners."

"Well I'm afraid that I also have to consult with my partner, so I can't give you an answer right now. The only thing that I can promise you is that we will consider your proposition."

Before turning it down, he thought.

"More wine, John?"

The afternoon was moving slowly, John was feeling uncomfortable. Keith had been operating almost non-stop since the morning, he had finished the routine operation only to find there were two emergencies waiting for him when he came out, one after the other.

It was ten past four when Keith finally rang him back.

John told him all that had happened with Lorenzo earlier, and when John told him the sort of money that had been bandied around Keith could hardly believe it.

"What do you suppose he wants for that sort of money? Whatever it is it could hardly be legal."

"I don't know, but what I do need to know is what sort of businesses he is in to, he may be legitimate, but I doubt it. Will you talk to your man and find out if they know anything about him, if they have an interest it may just be that it could tell us what he wants."

"Is there a time limit on this?"

"He wants to meet me again for lunch on Thursday, but I've told him there's no chance of me having any sort of answer for him by then. He wasn't deterred, he still insisted on meeting me, told me that he had something else to encourage me. I really don't like him, but I've a feeling that this whole business could get nasty if I don't go along with him."

"I'll see what I can do."

Suzie and Jerry had had a quiet, pleasant afternoon watching their pets wandering through the bush and plains. Plenty of tourists and other animals but nothing that resembled trouble. The early evening had been the best time of all as Elvis lumbered his way down to the waterhole at Yathabara (Waterhole of the Leeches) in the Aberdares National Park.

It was already crowded with other drinkers. One or two of the others moved out of his way, but probably only because of his size, none of them perceived him as a threat. Even the other elephants appeared to ignore him, which was something of a surprise to Jerry. He expected some sort of aggressive action from a couple of younger bulls, but apart from a few glances and the occasional trumpet, they left him alone. Jerry guessed that as Elvis probably didn't smell like an elephant they had no reason to try and pick a fight with him. Probably a good thing as Jerry would have had no option but to withdraw him, when what he really wanted was for him to be seen.

Rhoda and Rhonda had a quiet day, Jerry had them together for a while, roaming close to Salt Lick Lodge. Talk of the two of them together would have reached right around the park in a flash, but they had later gone their separate ways, with Rhonda heading down towards the Tanzanian border.

Rhonda was 'resting' in thick bush when she heard the sound of the Jeeps, there were two of them, still over a mile away, but with her amplified hearing, and sound travelling well over the still night air, they were easy to hear.

Jerry decided that it would be best to leave her hidden, try to gain information. It was a long term project, they were not there just for a week's fun. The jeeps didn't appear to be hunting, they were too steady, they must be returning rather than going out in search of their prey. Then it became apparent that they weren't going to be going within half a mile of Rhonda. He had to make a decision, confront them or follow them, doing nothing wasn't an option. Jerry chose to follow, see what she could find out, at least under cover of darkness the poachers wouldn't expect to be tracked by anything on four legs - four wheels maybe.

The trip lasted just under half an hour, by which time Jerry had sent for Eric and Suzie, he didn't want to handle it on his own.

When they arrived, he quickly apprised them of the situation and told them what he thought was happening.

The trek had gone almost ten miles inside Tanzania, they had gone across some rough dusty land, very little cover for Rhonda, but at night she was invisible unless they turned their search lights directly on her.

The Jeeps pulled into a narrow cleft in the rocky landscape. It was only perhaps twenty five feet wide, with overhanging walls to the east and west sides thirty feet high, the length of it being a couple of hundred yards before the width tapered off to nothing, only one way in for vehicles, with a climber's way in or out at the back. Excellent cover, very difficult to spot from the air or land unless you came at it from the north, but not an easy place to defend if attacked. The security came in its invisibility.

Eric certainly didn't like the idea of Rhonda going in there on her own, so they settled her down a quarter of a mile to the northwest of the entrance, while Eric made some phone calls. They had a precise location, all of the animals were fitted with GPS trackers, and could place her to within five yards on the map. Jerry tried to listen in to the poacher's conversations but at that range, not being in a direct line to the entrance to the cleft all he managed to pick up were some very faint and indistinct voices mixed in with the night sounds of the plains: insects, and what sounded like several hundred small predators scuttling around in the rocks and brush.

Eric came back looking very disappointed, the Kenyans weren't interested in crossing borders but had said that they would make representations to the Tanzanians in the morning if Eric would give them the precise location of the poachers. Eric declined, it would be more likely that a warning would be sent out and the poachers would scurry off to a town where he wouldn't be able to get at them. No, he would have to try and deal with it himself.

"How long would it take for Rhoda to join Rhonda down there?"

"She's over thirty miles away at the moment, it would probably take the best part of two hours for her to get there, what have you got in mind?" Jerry asked, starting to feel the adrenalin rise inside him.

"To be perfectly honest, I'm not sure. I've never had the luxury of hunting with rhinos before. The one thing that is absolutely certain is that we are not in a position to take prisoners, but by that I don't mean that we have to kill them either. I think that we have to get Rhoda there as quickly as possible and that will give us some time to decide on what to do."

"When are they likely to start hunting again?" Suzie asked.

"They will normally set off just before dawn, to the places they suspect the animals will have spent the night. They will never attack at the water holes as there are too many people within range, either the military, rangers or tourists. Either way, they would not be able to carry out their gruesome tasks undisturbed. They will wait nearby and then trail the animals until they are far enough away for them to move in for the kill safely. Or they will do the reverse, and hunt just before dusk as the animals return to the waterholes. There is nothing to be gained, apart from sunstroke, from hunting in the middle of the day."

"Then if they are always leaving or returning in the dark would it not make sense for us to hit them when they would least expect it? Right on their doorstep? Not in there, where it would be almost impossible for us to avoid killing them, but just outside in the open?" Suzie offered.

"I think you have just made the decision for us, young lady. If they come out in the morning, it's likely to be anywhere between four thirty and five thirty, sunrise is just after six. Depending on how far they are going to travel for a morning kill, we should have some action soon after four thirty. Jerry, can you take Rhonda in for a closer look, say to within fifty yards of the entrance, try to see how many vehicles there are in there and if there are any hidden problems, such as deep holes in the ground that could be either a nasty surprise for us or something that we can use in our favour, and get Rhoda moving as soon as possible."

"I'll send her down at a trot, there's no hurry, it's still five hours before she has to get there, she'll use less energy at a trot than if she belts down there in two hours."

Rhonda quietly moved off towards her prey, the ground was fairly flat without any real features. Just beyond the entrance there were a few sizeable rocks strewn around, off the main track in, nothing to create a problem for the rhinos but they would certainly cause a Land Rover to come to grief if it struck them. The land held no difficulties beyond a hundred yards out for either man or beast, and so it was determined that Rhoda and Rhonda would attack in the first fifty yards, they would be able to charge out from among the rocks at the side, with the Land Rovers only able to move backwards or forwards. They would need an awful lot of luck to get away to the sides, and hopefully by the time the rhinos had finished with them they wouldn't be going anywhere.

Rhonda continued her mission into the entrance, using her eyes they could see quite clearly into the heart of their camp. There were four wooden buildings, each approximately twenty feet long and ten feet wide, one across the end, facing north, and three down the left hand side, facing west. There were three Land Rovers or Jeeps and a very old half-tracked vehicle. the building at the end appeared to be windowless.

"That must be the store, probably for fuel as well as the spoils," Jerry pointed out. "All of the others have two doors and at least three windows. It probably means that the buildings are split internally."

"They're probably sleeping quarters in one end and living quarters at the other in two of them and the other is probably used for cooking and eating. Those two much smaller buildings to the right, probably for washing and latrines," Eric suggested.

"If most of the poachers are out in the two Jeeps, there should only be four or five left behind and they would almost certainly come out to find out what is going on. If they come out in the other Land Rover, then we can give them a champagne reception as well," Suzie said. "If they come out on foot, then Rhoda and Rhonda can go in past them and wreck the vehicles where they stand, and then go through the buildings."

Jerry had a massive smile on his face.

"I think that we can work with that!"

It was going to be a night to remember. He was going to enjoy it more than anything that had happened over Christmas!

Eric brought them down to earth "And suppose they don't come out at all for a couple of days, then what? We can't afford for both of them to stay out there. I suggest you settle Rhonda down, you can leave it so that she gives you a wake up call if she detects any activity and then we can all go and get some sleep."

Jerry did as he was told. Eric was quite right, there was a chance that they would be out in the morning, but no more than that. The adrenaline level settled down to normal.

At four fifteen the rhino alert on the iMac broke the silence and woke him from his light sleep, his eyes opened on the first beep. He left the bed that had been set up in the control centre for whoever happened to be on duty during the night and leapt across to the screen. He was completely awake. Rhonda was still lying down, eyes staring in the direction the sound was coming from. Welcome Rhoda!

Jerry thought that it was a good job he hadn't woken them all up for that, it would not have been a popular move. Jerry could see them both, looking at each other - each one on a different screen. Jerry told them both to move off to their appointed places, each fifty yards off to opposite sides of the entrance.

By five thirty both Eric and Suzie had returned, along with the flight crew and Fong, Eric's personal assistant. The air was thick with anticipation, but by ten to six they all realised that it was not going to be the time. Jerry recalled them both and sent them in different directions, Rhoda back into Kenyan territory, Rhonda further into Tanzania.

"Why don't we bring them back late this afternoon, we can be waiting for them a couple of miles back into the bush and pick them up on their way out if they go out tonight? At least that way we would be able to hit them before they get a chance to do any more damage."

Jerry was almost pleading.

"Yes, I take your point. We don't want to take any chances with our pets, but we don't want to give them a chance to go hunting tonight either."

Eric wasn't quite sure how to deal with it for the best.

It was Suzie that again came up with the best suggestion.

"Wouldn't it work if we sent one of them straying in towards the camp, leave the other one back outside in the edge of the bush. Surely if they see a rhino wander in they are going to think Christmas has come again. They would come after her, chasing her straight back to the other one who can then charge in? The surprise element would probably be higher, and we would probably get all of the vehicles out together. They wouldn't want to let this one go. If we did it around midday, they wouldn't be very well prepared and the temperature out there in the open would be at least a hundred and twenty."

Eric seemed satisfied with the idea.

"What do you think Jerry?"

"I'm all for anything that gets us in amongst the scum. And after we've taken care of the vehicles we should be able to go back and waste the camp without any trouble!" he said with gusto.

"Okay, bring them back. We might as well take care of them while we can. In the meantime, let's have a look to see how Elvis is getting on."

Eric was looking forward to getting Elvis further north, but it would take at least another three days yet to reach his ultimate destination, Lake Turkana on the Ethiopian border.

Chapter 19

The information that came back to John on Wednesday morning was confusing to say the least. The police had investigated Lanfranco on two occasions in the past. The first one had been on a suspected case of insider dealing. Lanfranco had made a real killing three days before a hostile takeover bid for an electronics company had been announced. He had bought several million shares in the well-known company in the space of twenty four hours and when the bid was announced and the price went through the roof Lanfranco quickly unloaded his shares. The suspicion had been that Lanfranco had heard of the bid from inside the aggressor, but as he had no known contact with the bidder, or the target of the acquisition, the investigation had to conclude that Lorenzo had been both shrewd and extremely lucky, but very few people believed it.

The second occasion was four years later concerning an investigation into a claim that he was blackmailing a senior executive in a bank. The allegations were never substantiated as the claims were withdrawn quietly after a confession that the man had been under a great deal of stress and had been embezzling money to feed a burgeoning gambling habit and had simply wanted to try to blame someone else for his problems. The executive was subsequently tried and imprisoned for five years. He was released after three for good behaviour and six months later he left the country, whereabouts unknown.

Lanfranco was also a great supporter of deserving charitable institutions, everything from orphanages to hospitals, schools to overseas projects. Whatever anyone else thought of the man, he had certainly been extremely generous in his donations. The odd thing about his donations to schools and hospitals was that he always insisted on privacy. He had never had a school, a hospital or even a ward named after him.

John cynically thought that the last thing a man like Lanfranco would want is publicity, whatever the source.

He felt like asking for a list of the recipients of his generosity, but wasn't sure that it would tell him anything anyway, he was sure the police or the stock exchange would have looked into that already. There was nothing more he could do until after he met him again, something he would rather not have to do but the feeling was that it might make things more difficult if he didn't show up.

At least lunch with Dee-Dee would be a different kettle of fish, she was due back in after two days out working for a living. He could forget about Lanfranco until tomorrow.

Elvis was getting along quite nicely, he had completed his journey through the Aberdares National Park and was heading up towards Lake Baringo. The abundance of game they all saw on his travels was quite remarkable. From monitor lizards doing nothing in the sun to jackals in search of a meal and when he arrived at Lake Baringo they met with some pretty mean looking crocodiles.

Eric explained that while crocodiles could be found in several of the lakes of the Rift Valley, there were only two that contained and supported a significant population, Turkana (or Rudolf) and Baringo. Elvis was going to visit both of them.

"Won't the crocs have a go at Elvis?" Jerry asked.

"No, their food is too easily caught in the lake, they have absolutely no need to take a risk on anything out of the water. They wouldn't attack an elephant anyway, they would quite simply come off second best. But a hungry croc could lie in wait for an antelope on one of the game trails as it came down to the lake. Baringo is stuffed full of fish like tilapia and barbus, while Lake Turkana is full of giant Nile perch. The crocs don't have to work hard to catch a fifty pound fish, so they certainly wouldn't be interested in chasing after you. Having said that though, when I first came here in 1978 an eighteen footer fetched a fisherman out of a boat, and when they caught the croc the following day and cut him open only his legs were recognisable. It was slightly unusual in that crocs normally like to store their kills for a while to tenderise them. It must have been hungry!"

"We don't have to go up there, do we?" Jerry wasn't too sure that he wanted to leave the plane.

"Not unless Elvis comes across a something we can't deal with from here."

"What about the other lakes, why don't they have crocodiles?"

"Most of the lakes are too alkaline, they are virtually liquid sodium carbonate and there are very few fish that can survive the conditions. Naivasha is the most significant exception. It has vast fish stocks, mainly of carp these days, but because of its altitude, at six thousand feet and prone to frosty mornings it is not a suitable place for saurians which require an all year round warm temperature. It does, however, have one of the richest bird concentrations in Africa, with fish eagles, pelicans, kingfishers and herons all feasting on the fish that breed in their millions in the lake."

"That I would like to see before I go home," Jerry said.

"Leave Elvis to cool off, he'll want to wash the dust off as well. Have you ever seen a red-brown elephant? Let's see where Rhoda has got to."

Rhoda was almost back to the bush where Rhonda was waiting, just about half a mile away from the camp.

"Okay, send Rhonda in, a nice steady, curious trot, just until she gets seen." Eric was beginning to enjoy it.

She set off at jogging pace, it was just before noon, there was nobody out in the heat so Rhonda was going to have to give them a bit of an alarm call. There was a pile of oil drums, presumably diesel for the vehicles. They should make a din when they go over, thought Jerry. He guided her in towards them on the west side, about forty yards before the huts started on the opposite side, carefully nudged her towards them, he didn't want her to charge at them, just to lean on them a little, make it look like an inquisitive rhino was getting herself caught up a bit. Rhonda did his bidding beautifully, there were twelve drums in all, seven on the ground, five on top.

She nudged three of the top ones off, all of which were empty, and made quite a racket. Rhonda looked startled when they came crashing down, but not as startled as the man who came running out of the hut to find out what was going on, only to find himself looking at a black rhino no more than eighty feet away. He ran back into the hut shouting his head off. Seconds later, with Rhonda making her escape, eleven men came hurtling out of the huts, rifles in hand to see the rhino apparently running for all she was worth out of the camp and north east towards the bush. The two Jeeps were hurriedly started and were revving furiously, wheels spinning, trying to turn round to get a run out of the narrow canyon. The Land Rover soon followed. Rhonda had to slow down or she would have disappeared before they had got themselves sorted out, they needed them to see her go into the bush.

"If we can take the first and last ones out, leave the middle one to work out what's going on. With Rhoda hidden in the bush, we can get her to hit the first one from the side as soon as the last one enters the bush and Rhonda to hit the last one straight after, the one in the middle will be trying to go in two directions at the same time, then both of them can hit that one together" Eric was talking faster than a machine gun, he knew precisely what he wanted to achieve.

The first jeep came in precisely where Rhonda had been, but the second and third, went right and left, the second one went directly at Rhonda who had very little option but to stand her ground and meet it head on. The driver didn't even see her until it was too late, Rhonda took three steps forward and buried her head in the radiator. The driver went straight through the windscreen and crashed onto Rhoda's back, he wasn't going anywhere else that day. The other three who had been standing up, went flying over the top and landed painfully in the bush. Rhonda in pulling her head out of the tangled mess of the front of the jeep stepped back on to one of them, breaking his left leg in the process.

Rhoda, hit her Land Rover perfectly as planned. She hit the front left side at full gallop and the driver seeing her coming, tried to swerve into her but it made no difference, she heaved it over on to its side and then on to its open roof. One of the men was crushed under the roll bar, two were thrown clear and landed dazed on the dusty ground. The other one was unconscious under the wreckage.

The middle Jeep that had gone to the left was coming up behind Rhonda. Two guns were blazing away, all to no avail, she spun round to meet them and it was only when Rhoda came charging through the bush that they realised there was a bit more to the game than they first thought. That was all the thinking they managed to do as they were hit from the right side and the front simultaneously. It was game set and match to the ladies. The driver smashed his face into the steering wheel and somersaulted over the windscreen, one of the men jumped out just before impact and the third went down with the ship. The one that escaped joined up with the others who were trying to hide in the bushes. Two were dead, two missing, one with a broken leg and six scared to death and clueless as to what to do next.

Jerry instructed the ladies to find as many guns as they could and trample over them before going off to make firewood of the camp.

The next thirty minutes saw vandalism of the highest order take place and even the rhinos looked as though they were enjoying it. When Rhonda went into the dining hut, without opening the door, the roof came crashing down on top of her, but with a shake of her powerful head she appeared through the wreckage with what Jerry would have sworn was a smile on her face. By the time they'd finished there wasn't a vertical piece of timber in the canyon.

With total satisfaction they headed off towards the west and the plains of the Serengeti.

"Congratulations, Jerry that was a wonderful piece of work," Eric said slapping him on the back. "By the time we have finished here the Rift Valley will be a better place to be."

Jerry was beginning to like him, at first he seemed to be a bad tempered old man with a chip on his shoulder the size of Kilimanjaro, but he had softened noticeably over the past forty eight hours. Jerry thought that it was probably because he not only had other people working with him that he could trust but that they were actually inflicting some serious damage for a change.

Suzie called John to tell him what had happened, she was brimming with excitement.

"Oh John, it was fantastic. We'll send you the film to watch over there, your babies are just incredible. The poachers just didn't stand a chance, they're unbeatable. With these two we can take care of this part of the country so easily."

She was on a real high.

"Slow down. You will not be able to solve all of the problems by beating up a few poachers. For a start, sooner or later they are going to get suspicious. Rhinos don't hunt people! You've got away with it this time, and you may manage it once more, but they can't be travelling together all the time. What you have done today is tremendous and a real stride forward, but if too many of them are attacked by the rhinos too soon then as a long term plan it won't work. You will have to let them be found not provide them on a plate as you did today. Find the poachers with the monkeys and the giraffe and watch where they go but if you go in and demolish them again, they will know that there's something seriously different about the rhinos."

She sighed. "Point taken, but promise me you'll watch it, it really was tremendous fun."

"Alright, I will. When are you coming back?"

"Probably the week after next, it depends on whether Jerry wants to come back for a break, it may be later."

"So what do you want me to tell Keith, he sends his love."

"Did he actually say that to you?" she didn't quite believe it.

"Let's say I read between the lines."

"Tell him that I miss him, but I've got work to do here first. Can you get him in so I can talk to him?"

"If he's not busy, I'll try to get him here at this time tomorrow."

"Thanks. Thanks for everything. I owe you a lot."

"You owe me nothing, partners don't have debts between them. If they did I'd have been bankrupt years ago. Go on, get on with your work."

He was beginning to feel awkward.

"This is more like play than work, it's pure enjoyment."

"See that it stays that way."

They disconnected and returned to their separate worlds.

Suzie went back to wallowing with Elvis in Lake Baringo, watching the other animals venturing carefully down to the lake, ever watchful for the hungry dangers that lay within the clear waters.

John went back to his problem with Lanfranco. What could it be that was worth so much money to the man?

There was no doubt that the money would fund an awful lot of work in Africa and the zoos, but what would be the price elsewhere?

Lorenzo and his right hand man and eldest son, Michael, had been discussing their ever increasing problems. Some of the suppliers, as they were known euphemistically , were getting restless.

"I really don't know what else we can do about Noel Sanderson, we have threatened him with exposure to his bosses, we can't threaten his family because they won't have anything to do with him and he doesn't care about them. He's on the point of a breakdown and if he gets to the stage where he really doesn't care about himself then we have little choice but to take care of him permanently. The worst of it is that he's not the only one. We can't take out four of them, or sooner or later the pieces would fall into place and the finger would be pointing at us."

Michael was out of his depth. Blackmail and extortion were his strong points but when someone really couldn't give a damn any more then there really was nothing more that he could do.

"What if I told you that I really do have the perfect answer. It's so ingenious that it would have to be the perfect crime."

Lorenzo was smiling, not at all worried by the potential disaster that was confronting them.

"There is no such thing as the perfect crime, at least not one that would solve our problems."

"On the contrary, the solution we need can be provided by our new friend, John Hylton. He has the technology, we have to be ruthless in persuading him to use it for us."

"Are you serious? How can a few animals take care of our problems?"

"Who said anything about animals?" Lorenzo was looking extremely smug.

Chapter 20

Thursday morning was a turning point, Elvis had left Lake Baringo and was heading for the south shore of Lake Turkana, where he would follow the east side through to the north. He hadn't been seen by anyone since leaving the waterhole at Yathabara, and there had been no sightings by anyone on the route to Baringo.

Rhonda and Rhoda split up when they arrived in the Serengeti National Park in Tanzania where Rhonda remained. Rhoda headed north towards Amboseli in southern Kenya. There were plenty of sightseers in both parks who were all extremely excited to see a rhino, an increasingly rare sight, and particularly one with such a magnificent horn, whether it be Rhonda or Rhoda.

The day was long and hot with absolutely no cloud in the clear blue sky, Rhoda had been meandering along with no clear instructions other than to be seen, when the ground beneath her feet suddenly disappeared, the covering of red dust over a mat of branches and leaves had been almost indistinguishable from the surrounding land. She crashed headlong onto the darkness of a pit that was ten feet deep, ten feet wide and twenty feet long. The sides were sheer and afforded no means of escape, even to Rhoda with her additional capabilities.

She had been in the pit for just over ten minutes before Suzie checked on the whereabouts of the two rhinos, she had been enjoying the view that Elvis had been providing.

"Oh, my God!" she couldn't understand it at first, she thought that she must have somehow wandered into a cave, "Jerry, Eric, come here," she shouted at the top of her voice.

"What is it?" Eric was the first to arrive. Jerry was asleep in his proper bed at the time having been up most of the night.

"I think we have got ourselves a major problem. Look."

"Oh hell and damnation. How on earth has she ended up down there."

Rhoda was looking around, almost wistfully, at the top edges of her predicament.

"She obviously can't climb out of there, what do you think, can she dig her way out?" Eric asked.

"How?" Suzie couldn't quite grasp what he was suggesting.

"If she digs away at one end of the pit, two things will happen, firstly she will create a pile of earth, which will reduce the depth and secondly she may be able to burrow into the wall so that the earth above collapses in and provides a slope for her so that maybe she can climb out. Unless you can think of anything better."

Jerry came charging in, having been woken by the sudden commotion and Suzie's rather loud exclamation.

"What's the problem?" he said, tugging his shirt down over his head.

Eric quickly explained and Jerry, having no better suggestion of his own, set about trying to get her out of trouble.

For two hours she prodded and scraped, but in fact achieved very little. There was no sign of any activity in the area, but they all felt that time could be running out.

Suzie tried calling John but his mobile phone went straight to voicemail. She called the office and Barbara told her that John was out for lunch and wouldn't be back for a couple of hours.

John was to meet Lorenzo Lanfranco in the same restaurant at the same time and, he had no doubt, the topic of conversation was going to be the same.

When John walked in he was surprised to find that Lanfranco was not already there waiting for him. The head waiter, recognising him, ushered him to the table they had occupied two days earlier, offered him a drink, which John declined, and informed him that Mr. Lanfranco had been delayed but expected to be no more than fifteen minutes late.

John waited in frustration, feeling that he had far more important things to do rather than waste time waiting for a man with whom he had no intention of doing business.

He was on the point of leaving when Lanfranco came bustling in through the door, his bodyguard parking himself at the bar. The other diners, being somewhat disturbed by the noisy and unruly intrusion into their normally tranquil eaterie, turned to deliver their distinctly disapproving glances at the loud man who was bowling quite briskly through the tables.

"I'm sorry to have kept you waiting," he announced when he was still more than twenty feet from the table "but I was delayed by a very interesting gentleman from Customs this morning."

He held out his hand, which John reluctantly shook, and sat down.

"Now, have you considered my proposition?"

John was caught somewhat off guard, he had simply intended to tell him that he had no interest in working for him at all, but all of his instincts were telling him that that could be a mistake.

"It is very difficult to make a judgement on any proposal without knowing all of the details, money in itself is not a proposition."

"At this stage there are two things that you need to know, one is the amount that I am prepared to pay you and the second is that it would appear that you have been a little less than honest with your declarations in the export of your agricultural machinery. The international export of live animals and endangered species is subject to a considerable amount of legislation and you have transgressed just about all of it."

He waited for his words to hit home.

"The gentleman I recently left, whilst he doesn't have any detail at present, is very interested in the possibility that someone may have been breaking a great deal of the laws that come within his jurisdiction."

"And I suppose that you have shown him the photographs?" John was feeling very uneasy.

"No, not at this stage. Of course, you and I both know that the animals are nothing more than machines, but the fact that you lied about the nature of the cargo, whether live or not, could give you an awful lot of trouble."

John said nothing. He couldn't deny it and he also had no doubt that the "gentleman from Customs" would probably be 'owned' anyway.

"So we return to my proposition. Thirty million is the offer, for two creations. I don't know what your costings are but I would imagine that they would be covered several times over at that."

"What do you want me to produce?"

The look of resignation on John's face said everything.

"Two animals... Of the human variety."

"What?" John could hardly believe it, it was certainly not something that he had ever considered, but why not, it was blindingly obvious, or at least it was to someone who could put such creations to work. John suddenly realised that his simple idea of almost three months ago had the most incredible implications, it shook him to his roots. "I'm sorry, but that is just not possible."

He was trying to think, his brain racing through a million uses for a 'real' human, and not one of them legitimate.

"Now you and I both know that it is entirely possible, don't we? The offer is thirty million Mr. Hylton, I don't expect it to be refused."

The malice in his voice made it even clearer to John that he couldn't possibly produce probably the most lethal weapon of all time.

At that point John began to regret ever starting the project, but that was probably the true nature of science: start out on one path and end up walking on another, never knowing where it is going to lead, Chinese fireworks to nuclear devastation, the good to the bad, all started innocently enough, but nonetheless changed the face of the world. For the better? Only history can decide that.

"I am afraid that you have overestimated our capabilities, Mr. Lanfranco, whilst we can produce a cyber in almost any form, there is a big difference between a rhino and a man. An animal has distinct behaviour patterns and lives in a limited environment, the possibilities for variation are very limited indeed. To produce a man that would pass off in society is probably twenty years away at least."

"Very good, but I think that you are being too modest. I know that you are producing the most sophisticated and realistic robots ever seen, but I don't want something that can pass off as a man for long periods and interact with others, I merely need servants, I simply want two servants that will do my bidding, nothing more than that," he said with a benign smile.

"I'm sorry but I am not prepared to do it. The risk of letting loose human cybers with the capabilities that we currently have are just too great. I suggest that you come back in twenty years, when we can control them precisely."

John stood up to leave.

"Please sit down Mr. Hylton."

John stayed where he was, looking down at him, the contempt was rising within him, but he didn't want to show it.

"If you do not do business with me, it will be a big mistake. I can cause a lot of problems for you."

"If you are talking about the photographs, you're wasting your time, I've no doubt it would waste some of my time as well, but it isn't something I can't handle."

John was bluffing, the last thing he wanted was for his secrets to get out into the open, but the problems posed by Lanfranco would be far worse than Customs poking their noses in.

"Very well, but we will meet again soon, believe me."

John turned his back on him and walked as calmly as he could out of the restaurant.

By the time he got back to the office, the despondency was beginning to take its toll. Why had he started it, why hadn't he realised at the outset what it could develop into? It could very rapidly get out of control. He had to stop the project, destroy it all, but to what end? The cat called Baggy was already out!

Barbara almost jumped out of her chair when she saw him. "Mr. Hylton, Miss Fielding has been calling you for the last hour, something about a problem with Rhoda, they need your help urgently!"

"Thank you."

John didn't feel very urgent, but he put the call through.

"John, thank God you've called. We have got a serious problem. Rhoda has fallen into a pit, and in spite of all her attempts we are not having much luck in getting her out."

"How far away is she from you?"

"About eighty miles"

"What has she done so far?"

"She has dug into the side of the pit to try to make a slope so that she can climb out but it's so hard it will probably take her two days constant work to make it, it looks as though the pit was originally dug out by machine."

"What machinery have you got out there?"

"Almost nothing that would be of use, we haven't got an excavator or anything like that, and even if we did have there is no way we would be able to get it out there, this plane needs a proper landing strip, it's not like a Cessna that you could almost put down anywhere."

"Well, I suggest that if she hasn't got herself out of there by morning, then you will just have to burn her, sooner if the poachers return. With the power left in her you should be able to destroy her completely. On second thoughts, don't waste your time, do it now. It's probably for the best anyway."

Suzie instantly knew there was something else, John was never negative, he always looked for the positive in any situation,

"What's wrong? Something's happened?"

"Nothing that you can help with, you've got your own problems, I'm okay. Call me when you have resolved yours."

"Don't shut me out John, I'm your partner, what is going on?"

John didn't reply, he disconnected the line.

Suzie was angry.

"Shit! This I don't like, something bad is happening, and I can't do anything to help from here. Eric, what's the earliest I can get home from here?"

"I'll get the pilot to contact Nairobi airport." Eric disappeared forward.

"Jerry!" she shouted. And waited. No reply.

She walked into the forward cabin, looked out of the open door and saw Jerry and Fong driving off in a cloud of dust in the Land Rover.

"Where the hell is he going when I need him?" she shouted. Then she realised what was strapped onto the roof rack, he had taken the loading ramps from the truck.

"Oh, how stupid! He'll never get her out that way, they aren't long enough," she said out loud to herself. They were probably not much longer than the pit was deep. What would happen if the poachers came back while he was there? She felt quite helpless. Couldn't stay, couldn't go.

Eric came out of the cockpit and saw her standing in the doorway.

"There is a plane leaving in three hours, there are seats available, you're only an hour's drive away. Do you want me to book you on it?"

"Do you know where they are going?"

She nodded towards the cloud of dust on the horizon.

"From what I have just been told, they are planning to rescue Rhoda. Jerry was going on his own, Fong wouldn't have the authority to stop him so no doubt he decided it was better to go with him. Do you want to speak to him on the radio?" Eric didn't much like the idea of frying Rhoda, he liked her too much to do that to a friend, even if she was bad tempered.

Suzie was resigned to staying, she couldn't leave Jerry to his fate, John was more capable of looking after himself than Jerry. Whatever John's problems were, they weren't going to be life or death!

She went through into the cockpit, the co-pilot, Chris Harris, handed her the radio handset.

"Jerry, what the hell do you think you are doing?" she was almost smiling, she didn't want to fry Rhoda either. Maybe in the end they would have no choice, but at least they could try their hardest for her.

"Going on a long voyage, to see what lies over the hill and I might never come back."

He was being silly to cover up his nerves, she thought.

"Jerry, have you any idea of what you could be getting yourself into? You could end up getting yourself killed?" Suzie was seriously concerned.

"Any chance of sending the cavalry to meet us?"

"What? Rhonda? I don't see why not. She won't be there to meet you, she's too far away, but I'll get her there as soon as I can. Keep in contact every fifteen minutes, we haven't got the facility to track you I'm afraid, so keep me posted. We'll give you the precise co-ordinates to find Rhoda. Good luck."

"Thanks, but I'm sure we'll get her out without any problem. See you for breakfast."

As he said it, Jerry realised that they had come without any food, but at least water wasn't going to be a problem, they always kept a five gallon container in the back.

Elvis had been enjoying a peaceful day on his northward journey to Lake Turkana, mingling in amongst zebra, wildebeest, oryx, Thomsons gazelles, giraffes and ostrich but he had kept a respectful distance from a herd of elephants. The late afternoon gave him his first opportunity to cool his soaring body heat, the warm water of the Lake was precisely what he needed, a few crocodiles scattered and swam out of his way as he lumbered down into the water, he stopped with only half of his massive girth out of the water, he swished his trunk back and forth, sucking up and blowing water out over his back, every inch an elephant thoroughly enjoying himself in the relief of the water. He remained there for half an hour before, reluctantly it seemed to Suzie, dragging himself out of the water and away on his journey north, keeping the water on his left. He still had another eighty miles to travel, which moving on through the rest of the day and night he should be able to complete by mid-morning the following day.

John didn't say anything to anyone about his current dilemma, it was something he had started and something he would have to finish on his own. He felt sorry for Suzie, he didn't want to shut her out, but it wouldn't be fair to burden her with the problem.

As far as Lanfranco was concerned, he decided that he wouldn't make any pre-emptive move, there was no point in contacting Customs as he couldn't be certain that Lanfranco would carry out his threat, and if, as he suspected, it was his own man inside it wouldn't make any difference anyway. Better to let the situation develop and deal with it accordingly.

John reflected that his laissez faire attitude was dictated by the fact that he hadn't got a clue as to what else he could do.

"When will our friend have the device ready?"

"It should be ready for delivery on Saturday morning, as scheduled. What made you so certain that he wouldn't agree to your proposal first time around?"

"Much of the work his company does is about helping people who are in trouble. We don't quite fit into that category and he's a moral man. The money this time had to be big enough to overcome any moral objections. I wasn't certain that he would be sufficiently motivated financially so I planned ahead, that's all. Are you sure that it will do what we want it to."

"From what Jerry told us we know that the cat basically lives in the construction area in the basement. We know that Bob Ayres is in charge of that department. The parcel should be received by Hylton, Fielding, or Fisher on Saturday morning as they are usually the only ones in the building. So whoever receives it should take the parcel down there. The cat then has two whole days to get within three feet of it. The low level radiation given off by the fuel cells will trigger the device. There are sixteen razor discs built in, four to each side of it, none in the top or bottom, so that no matter which way round the box goes, or whether it is placed on the floor or a table, at least two of the discs should hit it and bingo the cat is in pieces. These little babies will go through it like a knife through butter, and they will be hot."

"Good, maybe this will teach him a lesson and we can convince him that his refusal to co-operate is a mistake."

Jerry programmed the GPS in the Land Rover so that they could be sure that they were taking the most direct route, provided that they didn't run across any insurmountable obstacles. They were making good time across the scrubland and leaving a trail of dust that seemed to stretch forever behind them. The GPS estimated that it would take them the best part of two hours to reach the burrowing rhino. It was two and a half hours before sunset. Time enough, they hoped, to get her safely out of there.

Rhonda had set off from the Serengeti where she had been having an entirely uneventful time and was expected to arrive sometime around half past five, just after Jerry and Fong.

With ten miles to go, a pair of binoculars was trained upon the dust trail on the horizon, they were two miles west of the trail on top of a hill. The man with the binoculars steadily followed the progress for ten minutes wondering what could be driving so hard, so late in the day. It was the wrong trail and too fast for it to be tourists. It couldn't be trailing anything at that speed. The shoulders shrugged and continued to watch. Could be military. Could be bad news.

As Jerry made rapid progress, oblivious to the observer so far away, he was only concentrating on one thing: how to get a three ton rhino out of a hole in the ground, he couldn't possibly allow her to remain there forever.

"The only thing I can think of is to find something to build up a platform at the bottom, probably two to three feet high, place the ramps on top of it and get her to walk up the ramps, the only problem is that we don't know whether she can go up such a steep gradient."

"Maybe we pull her up the ramps with this," Fong offered, tapping the dashboard with his hand.

"Hmm, excellent idea. We'll still have to build a base, but if we help her up it shouldn't make much difference how steep it is."

They drove along in silence for the remainder of the journey. Satisfied that they had the answer.

The man behind the binoculars was becoming more and more curious, they were definitely travelling for a purpose. What could it be?

When the dust finally stopped, he could tell that there were two men in a Land Rover. He couldn't see what they were looking for. The voice over his shoulder asked "What are they doing? They will end up in our trap if they are not careful. Maybe that is what they are looking for."

"The way they drove here, they came for a purpose, maybe they have been told of the pit. Maybe they have been told there is something in the pit. When was it last checked?"

"Two days ago. Maybe something wandered in there yesterday or this morning. But how would they know? Nobody else has been here."

"Maybe we should go and find out what they are up to."

"Maybe we can rob them and steal their Land Rover and put them in the pit." He laughed, that was a good idea.

They could not approach directly, the slope of the hill and the terrain was against them. They had to circle around to the south and approach from the west, a journey that would take them half an hour if they were not to be seen. At least they would have some trees and brush for cover for most of the way.

Rhoda heard Jerry and Fong approach, Suzie made sure that Jerry could find her easily , by instructing her to snort as long and loudly as she could.

"She's over there somewhere," Jerry said pointing towards an old sun-parched fallen tree. They ran across and thirty feet beyond the tree was the pit. With the helpless rhino pacing around in the bottom, although she could only just turn around in the width.

They stood at the edge looking down. She looked very big down there and Jerry was wondering whether the ramps would be able to take the weight. Three tons is quite a lot more than a Land Rover, which was what they were designed for carrying, but the angle, he guessed, would effectively lessen the load.

"You'd better bring the wagon over here, Fong. We've got a lot to do."

They took the ramps off the roof rack and lowered one down into the pit, only two and a half feet of it stuck out above the top edge of the pit. Jerry did some rough calculations in his head. "We need a platform about eighteen inches high to give us an angle of forty five degrees, two to two and a half feet would be better. We had better collect some logs and rocks, anything large." It wasn't exactly Jerry's forte, and Fong didn't seem to have any other ideas of his own. It seemed to Jerry that Fong's only purpose in life was to fetch and carry and drive the car.

For a small man he certainly carried a lot of weight, he outperformed Jerry two to one over the next twenty minutes.

When they had got what seemed to Jerry like two tons of rocks collected at the top of the pit, he decided that it would be best if he were to be the one to go down to the bottom to construct the platform. He started quite slowly, Fong was dropping them over the side at the end and Jerry collected them from where they fell and carefully arranged them in a square about five feet across. He then proceeded, painfully Fong thought, to build up a solid base, filling in gaps wherever he could with smaller stones. He also used some of the debris that Rhoda had managed to scrape out of the wall as infill.

The light was beginning to fail in the pit, it would only be a matter of half an hour or so before the light would disappear altogether. The platform was coming along quite nicely when Fong thought he heard the sound of a branch rustling in the brush somewhere behind him. He remembered that they hadn't called in to Suzie for over three quarters of an hour, although she would be able to see what Jerry was doing she had no means of communicating directly with them. He left Jerry to his labours and climbed aboard the Land Rover.

"Fong here. We okay. You okay?"

"Yes, thank god you've called. You are going to have some company soon. Rhonda picked up the sound of a jeep travelling in your direction ten minutes ago, it could be trouble. Be careful. Rhonda will be with you in another ten minutes."

Fong didn't get the chance to say anything else before the muzzle of a rifle was pressed rudely into the side of his face. He didn't move a muscle. The gun was withdrawn and the ebony face of a poacher motioned for him to get out. The other poacher appeared and said in Swahili "The other one is already in the pit. You won't believe this but he's down there with a rhino! Big horn, worth plenty. Tie this one up."

They spoke in English to Fong. "Get down on the floor, face down, now."

Fong did as he was told. They took his hands and bound them expertly behind his back. "Don't move or we will shoot you. You will not move again."

The point was well made and not at all misunderstood.

They walked quietly over to the pit where Jerry was still working away. He heard footsteps above him.

"Two more minutes and we'll be ready to get her out of here."

"You will not be going anywhere my friend, you are already in your final resting place."

The white teeth in the black face flashed as he threw his head back and laughed.

Suzie thought her worst nightmare had just come true. Rhonda was only two minutes away, but two minutes might as well be two lifetimes unless Jerry could keep them talking.

"Why is this rhino allowing you to do this. You should be dead."

"She belongs to me."

Jerry was also aware that Rhonda couldn't be too far away, the light was failing rapidly, she should hopefully arrive before dark.

"What do you mean she belongs to you? She is a rhino not a cow."

"I brought her into this world, she is my friend."

"Very good. I like that, and now you have brought your friend to play with us. Well we are going to play a little game with you. First we are going to shoot her, so that you don't have the worry of getting her out of there. I think we will probably have to shoot you as well. Then we can take her horn to a man that really knows how to appreciate a rhino properly."

"I don't think that you will want to do that. You see, my friend will help me out of here in a minute and you will put down your weapons and leave peacefully."

Jerry was growing in confidence, Rhoda was nodding her head, Suzie was telling him something, Rhonda had to be very close.

"I think you must be a fool, your friend is already tied up, he will not be helping you do anything. Say good-bye to your friend."

He raised his rifle and aimed straight between Rhoda's eyes. The shot cracked as flame shot out from the rifle. Rhoda stood and shook her head and looked up at the man as he looked down, open-mouthed, reloaded his rifle and took aim again. He carefully squeezed the trigger, it was the last shot he would ever fire.

He neither heard nor saw the mass of rhino that slammed into him and speared him with her horn straight through his right kidney and up into his heart. Rhonda shook him off her horn like a fly and turned to see the other man leap over the fallen tree and run away, his rifle slung over his shoulder, towards his jeep. He ran towards Fong, only because it was the shortest route to safety. Fong lay on his back, pulled his knees up to his chest, rocked back onto his shoulders, threw his legs forward and sprang on to his feet. The poacher tried to react with his rifle to use it as a club, but as he raised the gun over his head Fong jumped and crashed his right foot straight out, toes pointed, into his solar plexus. He dropped like a stone to the floor, unable to breathe, unable to move. It had taken less than two seconds. Rhonda galloped around the tree and the Land Rover to see if there were any leftovers. All she saw was Fong standing at a right angle to the prone poacher who clearly wasn't going to be any further trouble.

Suzie hadn't been able to watch Fong's performance, she could only see the result. She turned to see Eric beaming all over his face,

"He is good, very good. That is why he works for me. Nobody ever takes any notice of him, until it's too late!"

Suzie wondered how she could get a round of applause out of a rhino.

Jerry climbed up the ramp and out of the pit. He walked over to Fong who was struggling in vain against his bonds and saw the poacher unconscious on the floor. "How on earth did you do that?"

"Me? No. He fell down, very careless, should watch where he run."

Jerry couldn't work it out, and shaking his head, untied him. Together they finished off the platform and with a rope tied around Rhoda's horn and the Land Rover's towbar they pulled her gently and steadily out of the pit. They looked at the poacher on the floor, nodded to each other, picked him up and slid him down the ramps to the bottom of the pit. Jerry decided to leave the dead poacher to the scavengers and left him dangling over the fallen tree.

They pulled up the ramps, loaded them back on the roof and drove off to the jeep that Rhonda had found for them, two hundred yards away hidden in the brush. The keys were still in it and enough fuel to get back to the airstrip south of Nairobi. Fong hopped into it and followed Jerry along the track home.

Rhoda and Rhonda trotted off happily into the night together.

Suzie called Jerry on the radio.

"Don't you ever sneak off again like that or I'll sack you."

She paused.

"Well done, just get back here in one piece. Eric says don't bring the other vehicle back here, disable it somewhere, we don't want any possibility of a connection being made."

"No problem, I hope you enjoyed the show."

"A bit gruesome for my taste, but rather them than you. Thank you, I didn't want to desert her either."

The emotions were beginning to rise within her. Hey, this isn't me, she thought, snap out of it!

Chapter 21

The drive back had been much slower than the drive out. The creatures of the night were frequently frozen in the headlights of the Land Rover, so Jerry drove at less than half speed, not only because of the animals but because he needed more time to spot potentially crippling potholes, rocks and crevices that could appear from nowhere.

When they finally arrived it was almost midnight and Suzie greeted them by the plane with such relief.

"I never thought I would be so pleased to see you. That was a crazy thing to do, and you should be whipped for your stupidity, but I can't thank you enough."

Jerry just stood and grinned, he couldn't think of anything sensible to say. Fong was his normal inscrutable self.

"Come on in, I've got the champagne on ice, after what we've all been through, I think it has been earned."

The following morning Suzie wanted to call John but the time difference meant that she had to leave it until ten to catch him at the office, so she checked with the airport and confirmed her departure on a flight scheduled to leave at eight fifty that evening.

When she finally got through to him he sounded less worried than the previous day, but still refused to say what was going on. When she told him that she would be back the following day, but probably wouldn't surface until sometime in the late afternoon, he accepted the news without a reaction. That worried her even more. She expected him to be pleased that she was returning. It almost seemed to her that he would prefer her not to come back.

Consequently she couldn't wait to go, but was helpless to do anything more about it.

John was feeling more uncomfortable as the hours passed, he was waiting for something to happen, but nothing did. No phone calls, no unexpected visitors, no letters. He didn't believe that Lanfranco was bluffing, the man was too sure of himself for that. Whether he would use the Customs threat or whether he had some other plan he had no idea. The waiting was the worst side of it.

Better to produce some decent work than sit around metaphorically chewing fingernails. He also couldn't decide whether Suzie's imminent return was a good thing or whether it could make the situation worse. Under normal circumstances he would have welcomed her with open arms, but the situation was far from normal.

John called Keith Boscik at the hospital to give him the news.

"That's great, that's better than winning the lottery. When will she land?"

He was as excited as a puppy, John thought. He wished he could as pleased.

"Sometime in the early hours of the morning, I'll give you the flight number. Do you want to meet her off the plane? She'd like nothing more," John said, trying to sound encouraging.

"That would be a total pleasure. I wouldn't want to miss it for the world."

At least that was sorted out. John wouldn't have to see her, probably, until Monday. Keith would look after her.

John took a call late on in the afternoon from Suzie who rang to confirm that everything was on schedule. He said that someone would be waiting for her at the airport when she arrived.

"Someone? Not you. Keith?"

She sounded like a little girl who was about to see her favourite uncle.

"I don't think you will be disappointed. Have a good flight, and have a good weekend, I don't want to see you this side of Monday morning."

"Thank you. You're an angel."

"Just as long as I don't have to wait till I get to heaven to get my reward."

His voice softened, he relaxed in her happiness.

The evening was slow, nothing had happened during the day at all, Dee-Dee was away on a four day assignment and wouldn't be back until Sunday afternoon. The television held no interest for him, he didn't want to go out for a drink or a meal, so he spent the early part back at the office in the gym, working against all of the machines in turn, gradually increasing the loads on each circuit. He carried on for three hours until just before ten o'clock, when he felt sufficiently exhausted to know that he would be able to sleep when he arrived home.

Nothing followed him on the homeward journey and John began to conclude that nothing was likely to happen until Monday at the earliest. After all, no matter what Lanfranco could infer from the photographs, there was no likelihood of him being subjected to armed police raids at dawn, even if they believed the story that he was trading in endangered species. How many people would believe that an elephant and rhino were being kept at an electronics factory, it would be about as believable as a bull keeping guard in a china shop.

He slept well, breakfasted well and travelled into work in a far better frame of mind than had existed the day before, a little later than usual.

Alan was already in his lab when he arrived.

"Morning, boss. You look better today."

"Thanks, I tried to kill my body last night," he said, pointing upwards "fortunately I failed, but I feel much better for it anyway. Suzie should have arrived home in the early hours of this morning, so I have no doubt that next week will be quite hectic as she tries to catch up with events here. How's the chimp doing?"

"Very difficult, there is a lot more to them than meets the eye. The facial movements and expressions are very complex. Even though we've had a lot of help, it is going to take a long while before we will understand them thoroughly enough to install them in a zoo."

"How about for letting loose in Africa?"

"They could be ready in a little over a week, provided you want them on the same basis as the others, with basic functions and to control them when you need to. If so, then all we have to do is to build them."

"At the moment that's all we do need. We could do with more eyes and ears in the forests and along the rivers. Hopefully then we can try to find out where the poachers have been getting their assistance. Although we have had some remarkable successes in the short time we have been out there, it really is only the tip of the iceberg."

"Oh, by the way there was a parcel delivered for you this morning, I put it on your desk."

Alan turned back to his work.

"What time did it arrive?" John felt uneasy.

"About twenty past eight."

"Was there anything unusual about it? Was the van here when you arrived?"

"Nothing unusual, standard courier delivery, I arrived at seven thirty."

"Where's the paperwork?"

"He didn't leave any, I just signed his scanner. I presume that the consignment note is in the box."

"Thanks."

He walked out and down the corridor towards his office, hesitated outside for a few moments and then went in. The package sat in the middle of his desk. It was about two feet by one and seven inches high.

There were no company markings on the outside at all, nothing to indicate the contents, just his name on the label on a plain brown box.

He stared at it for a while and then picked up his phone. Alan answered.

"How heavy is this package?"

Alan realised that he was seriously worried about it. "Only a couple of pounds, nothing much at all. Do you want me to come in?"

"No, you stay there, thanks all the same."

He put the phone down and sat looking at it.

What on earth could it be, addressed 'For the personal and private attention of Mr. J. Hylton'.

For five minutes he sat there debating whether to open it or send for the bomb squad. Then it dawned on him. Ripping off the brown paper wrapping, he remembered the two dresses he had bought for Dee-Dee on Monday. He had asked for them to be delivered discreetly on Saturday morning because he wanted them to be a surprise for when she returned on Sunday.

He took them out of the box and felt quite foolish. hunting for ghosts and finding shadows.

He picked up the phone again to speak to Alan.

"Hi, problem solved, I remembered what it was. It's just that I'm not used to receiving personal things here on a Saturday. Sorry."

He put the phone down. He was extremely relieved, as well as angry for letting Lanfranco get to him so badly.

The buzzer went for the front door. John clicked on the CCTV icon on the desktop of his iMac and brought up an image of a young lady in a courier's uniform holding a large box at the front door.

He went through to reception and smiled at the courier through the glass as he placed his hand on the scanner to unlock the door.

"Parcel for Mr. R. Ayres, Animagination," she said with a smile.

"Who's the sender?" John asked warily.

"Aurag Electronics, urgent delivery."

One of their regular suppliers. John signed the parcel scanner and took it from her, it was about two and half feet by two by two high, quite heavy. Unusual to have two deliveries on a Saturday morning, he thought to himself. Don't start ghost hunting again, he chided.

The door closed automatically as he moved away.

He walked to the back of the reception, placed his left hand on the scanner while balancing the box on his right knee, the door opened, he performed the opposite task at the other end of the corridor, right hand, left knee, to let himself into Alan's lab.

"Need a hand with that?" Alan offered.

"No it's okay I can manage and I haven't said hello to Baggy yet this morning.

He skipped down the stairs and into the construction area. Baggy came bounding over to greet him.

The explosion wasn't particularly loud but the effect was devastating.

John was blown half way across the room, he was covered in blood from top to bottom, there was very little left of his arms which had taken the bulk of the force. His legs were ripped and bleeding profusely.

Alan came roaring down the stairs. The sight that greeted him made him retch. Just managing to control himself he dropped down to where John lay, his head was propped at a strange angle against the plinth of one of the platforms. He quickly realised that there were bits of John scattered all over the room. Although John was losing a lot of blood , the heat of the explosion and the steel appeared to have cauterised some of the tissue.

Alan leapt to the phone, called for an ambulance, checked that John was still alive, hauled him onto a trolley and vomited profusely when he picked up John's arms that were still inside his jacket sleeves and put them on the trolley.

Fighting back the retching once more, he moved him into the lift, took him upstairs to reception and waited for the ambulance to arrive.

Alan was completely helpless, there was nothing he could do to help the man who had been friend and employer for five years. When Baggy tried to follow into the lift Alan told him to stay, he was the last thing he wanted the paramedics to see.

They arrived in less than three minutes and took John directly to the Memorial Hospital.

An emergency trauma team met him at the ambulance and took him straight into the operating theatre.

Keith Boscik screamed into the car park four minutes later, dumped his car in front of the accident and emergency entrance, threw off his jacket as he ran, bundling staff out of his way into the prep room.

"What have we got?" he asked his assistant as he offered his hands for scrubbing, the theatre nurses were dressing him as he stood.

"Multiple dismemberment, explosion, it looks like it was some kind of anti-personnel device, not much damage to the torso though. We've staunched the blood as much as we could, there's not much left of his arms and his legs have been badly lacerated . The pieces have been brought in, they're in ice over there but by the looks of them they have probably suffered too much to be of use. It was a clean cut with what looks like some sort of razor disc but the explosion damaged his lower arms."

"How long ago?"

"Twenty minutes, max."

"Let's go."

He burst through the double doors and stopped dead in his tracks when he saw who, what, was lying on the table. Blood was flowing from transfusion tubes, clips, drips, everything conceivable was leading to and from the body of his friend. It needed all of his professionalism to keep from crying out at the pitiful sight that lay before him.

"Okay, let's see what we can do."

An hour later Keith was talking on a phone that was being held to his ear by one of the theatre assistants, calling his own house.

"Suzie, I need you to come to the hospital, I have a problem here, that I think only you can deal with. I've sent my car for you, it should be there in a couple of minutes."

"What is it? Shall I call John?"

"No. Just come, I'll handle the rest."

It took her less than ten minutes to arrive from the end of the phone call.

She was met at reception and led through to a waiting room on the same floor as the theatre.

"Suzie, sit down. What I am going to say to you is going to be a hell of a shock, but there is no easy way to do this."

He sat down with her on a comfortable upholstered bench seat and put his outstretched hands on her shoulders.

"What's happened? It's John isn't it? My God, what has happened?"

She was as white as a sheet, the pain in her face couldn't have been worse if a knife had been stuck into her.

"There was an explosion at your lab this morning. It appears that some kind of device was delivered this to him. It went off while John was carrying it down in to the construction room."

"Oh, no. He's still alive isn't he?"

Keith nodded his head.

"Just."

"Is he going to live?" she was sounding desperate.

"We can keep him alive, and he will probably be able to recover fully, all of his vital organs are fine, there is no brain damage as far as we can tell and very little damage to his body."

He lowered his head.

"What then? What has been damaged? Oh God, you said he was carrying it. His arms!" she wanted to scream.

"Not just his arms," he said softly "his legs are badly cut as well, but I think that we can take care of those. It seems that the explosion was designed to maim and not to kill, it looks as John has suffered the maximum intended damage."

"What can I do? Can I see him?"

"Potentially there is a lot you can do, but you can't see him yet. I am going to need all of the help I can get but first you have to tell me what's possible and what is science fiction."

"Okay."

She felt her control returning, it was the only way she was going to be able to help.

They discussed the artificial limbs that they had been working on and the animals they had built, but the drawback was that none of the new technology had yet been applied to human or living beings, that was still a few months away. There was no guarantee of success.

"At the moment I have two choices, I can either terminate his limbs where they are, which will mean collecting his nerve endings and embedding them in what is left of his flesh or we can try and use your technology, if it doesn't work then we have lost nothing."

"If we produce a plate that we can use like a plug and socket arrangement can you connect his nerves to it so that we can create continuity between his body and the replacement limbs?"

"I don't see why not, we can attach the prosthetic arm by osseointegration, using titanium pins, effectively bolting the new arms onto his bone, just below the shoulder. What about blood supply, will you need it?

"No they will operate independently, electrically, taking the stimulus directly from his brain. It's just the nerves that need continuity for control. If we can design a plate that can connect his tissue to then it is no problem for us to build the new limbs off those plates."

"The alternative is for us to remove his arms back to the shoulder and you provide complete units. That has its risks in so far as once it has gone there is no going back."

"That would mean remaking the shoulder joint, I don't fancy that right now. As long as we make the unit totally separate then we should be able to design it so that we can update and improve it without needing surgery each time."

"You mean to make a completely dry joint?" he couldn't see how it could possibly work.

"Yes, if we use the plate to connect the tissues like an electronic clutch we can keep the connection tight and contiguous and still be able to release it when we need to. The plate will be fixed and won't need to be acting as a pivot point. The only doubt that I have is whether you will be able to connect live tissue to it. If you can do that then I don't see a problem."

"How soon could you produce it?"

"As soon as you give me the nerve map, we'll work around the clock until it's done, maybe two days, three at the outside."

Keith sat up straight and breathed in deeply.

"It looks as though it's down to me then, and I thought that you would be the one with the problems!"

"We work with machines, we can design, within certain limits, more or less whatever we want, you are the one that is limited by the human condition, you can't change or improve what you have to work with, we can. But what we have not considered yet is the impact that all of this is going to have on John. He is mentally very strong, but what this will do to him, I just don't know," Suzie said.

"John is a fighter, nothing can change what the bomb did to him, all we can do is to try to give him the best chance at life afterwards. I don't think he would want to spend the rest of his life seriously disabled if there was something that we could do about it now," Keith replied.

She knew he was right, but that type of decision was normally a joint one with John, she was being forced into making a decision on his behalf, something that would affect the rest of his life, if there was to be one.

"Can't we wait for him to come round, our part of the operation can be carried out almost any time, he can then be part of the decision."

"No. If we leave it we will have to seal off the wounds and that will make it much more difficult later on. It could be days or weeks before he comes round, if at all."

"Hobson's Choice then," she replied, wondering if they were biting off more than they could chew.

"If you are confident about your own abilities, you know that it works, if we do it now then we can save him a lot of pain and further shock. If we allow him to heal and begin to come to terms with what has happened to him he will then have to go through the trauma all over again while we pull him apart to rebuild him. There is a good chance that the shock could prevent him from consenting to the operation. I know it is denying him the choice, but there is only one option if we are to do the best available for him, you have to look upon it as an extension of your artificial limb development program, you have the opportunity to take a major leap forward and the benefit will be going to your closest friend."

"You're right, I suppose that I just needed some help to make the decision."

She returned to the office where Alan was dealing with police, bomb squads and all manner of public officials. The one thing she hadn't wanted was publicity.

The media were there in force. Suzie drove straight into the underground car park, the doors closing behind her as she entered, with reporters running a short distance behind, but not close enough to get through the doors.

She went up in the lift to reception and then down the stairs to the construction lab where she found two men in nylon boiler suits sifting through the wreckage. Alan had taken Baggy up into Suzie's office, he didn't want the aggravation of having to explain his existence to them, he'd never be able to get rid of them.

"Excuse me Miss, could you tell me who you are?" a uniformed officer approached her with a list on his clipboard.

"I'm Suzie Fielding," she said flatly.

"Oh, right thank you."

He turned to one of the boiler suits and said quietly, "Miss Fielding's here, sir."

He looked around and took in her appearance, slightly unkempt, definitely under stress, but still very attractive. He decided that he would try not to add to her problems.

"Miss Fielding, I understand that this is a very difficult time for you, but I would like to ask you a few questions, if I may?"

"Yes, I suppose so."

"Thank you. Until we can contact Mr. Ayres we're flying blind. The most obvious question is, do you have any idea who would want to do this?"

"You said Bob Ayres as though he is involved somehow," Suzie looked disbelievingly at him.

"Well, the package was addressed to him. It appears as though Mr. Hylton was inadvertently caught by a bomb that was intended for Mr. Ayres."

Suzie was quite shocked, she had assumed that the bomb had reached its intended victim, it hadn't occurred to her that it should have had a different purpose.

"I'm sorry, I can't help you at all, there's no earthly reason that I know of why Bob would be a target. How did it happen?"

"That's something we are working on at the moment, there is plenty of evidence here, we have to run some tests and identify the trigger. We know it wasn't triggered by opening it as he was carrying it at the time. It doesn't look like a timing device that went wrong, so it has to be something else. The only saving grace is that there were hardly any people here when it went off. If it had exploded on Monday morning when we assume it was suppose to detonate, there would have been more people here and probably more casualties. What we do know at the moment is that it was designed to damage people, not buildings. Do you have any idea where we can find Mr. Ayres?"

"If Mr. Fisher has given you his home address and telephone numbers, I can't help you more than that. I'm sorry."

"Alright, thank you Miss Fielding, but if you do think of anything, please call me," he said, handing her a card with a name and number, no address.

She was totally confused. She didn't mention her reason for her return from Africa. Let him follow his line of enquiry and see what it throws up. She went upstairs to the lab where Alan was doing his best to keep his temper with an officious young detective who was insinuating all sorts of things about his potential involvement.

"Excuse me for interrupting, but I have to talk to my colleague, please wait outside."

The detective reluctantly withdrew.

"Yes, certainly, please don't leave, I haven't finished yet," he said as he stood in the doorway.

He didn't wait for a response and left for reception.

"Snotty little sod wasn't he?" she observed.

"Yes, I could do without him at the moment. How's John?"

"He's in a stable condition, but we don't know what the shock will do to him, that could be the worst of all."

She went through the discussion and conclusions that she had reached with Keith, and when she finished, she said, "Well, what do you think?"

"It's a big step from what we have achieved so far but there is no doubt it is something we would hope to be doing in the near future anyway, I just wish that we weren't going to have to experiment on John, but at least he will understand what we are doing and shouldn't be frightened by it."

"Thank you, you've just made it easier. We have to start straight away. Can you produce the interface between our work and the nerves when Keith gives you the nerve map?"

" No problem, but we are going to need Bob and Sally as soon as possible. Bob's gone off somewhere for the weekend, but Sally should be at home from what she was saying yesterday. Do you want me to call her?"

"No, you've still got Sherlock Holmes to deal with, I'll call her from my office. Thanks. This is the most important job we will ever have to do."

She squeezed his arm as she stood up and tried to smile, it wasn't easy.

The police and their forensic team didn't leave until after two o'clock, much to Suzie's frustration. Alan was on the verge of thumping the young detective as he continually tried to score points by suggesting, in different ways, that Alan was keeping information from him or might be somehow involved. He considered letting Baggy meet him, or, preferably, eat him.

Chapter 22

Dee-Dee's return was something that Suzie hadn't thought about. The call from the airport to the office at seven fifteen on Sunday evening came like a bolt of lightning.

"Suzie, it's Dee-Dee, where's John? Why are you working late on a Sunday? What has happened?"

"John's not here at the moment" she said truthfully, "we've got a problem that we have to take care of. Wait there, I'll send Alan to collect you. I'll tell you all about it when you get here."

Dee-Dee relaxed a little, but was still concerned when she arrived.

She was shown into Suzie's office. They sat down on the easy chairs away from the desk.

"It's John isn't it, has something happened to him?"

Suzie was more worried that she may get hysterical than anything else, she had thought for forty minutes of how to break it to her.

"Yesterday morning, John took delivery of a package..." Suzie paused.

The colour drained from Dee-Dee's face, she instinctively knew,

"...it wasn't even addressed to him, but for some reason while he was carrying it downstairs into the construction lab it exploded."

Dee-Dee sat there like a stone, not a flicker.

"John is still alive and he will pull through. He is going to have to go through a long operation tomorrow morning, it is quite complex but his life is no longer in danger."

Suzie was becoming concerned, Dee-Dee was just sitting, looking at her, she wasn't certain that she was even listening to her.

"I realise that this is as much a shock to you as it was to me when it happened yesterday morning but we are doing everything we can to repair the damage."

She seemed to switch back on again.

"And just what is the damage?" she said without a shred of emotion, almost detachment.

"He lost his arms in the blast and and his legs were quite badly cut. From what we know, the bomb contained sixteen razor sharp steel discs, it was designed to maim or kill people, the device was targeting someone, the police don't think that it was even aimed at

John, not that it makes it any easier."

Dee-Dee was totally calm. "When can I see him?"

"It won't be possible until after the operation, it would probably be better to wait until later on Tuesday."

At least by then, she thought, he should have some arms.

"I would like to see him tomorrow," she said in such a way as to leave no room for argument.

"Then you had better talk to Keith first, he's the operating surgeon. Look, do you want to stay here tonight, we have spare beds set up for those of us that are working through the night, we are going to try to catch some sleep whenever we can."

"I'd like to help you if I can. I know that I can't do much as far as your work is concerned but I can keep you fed and watered, at least I can make things a little easier for you.

"That would be very much appreciated."

It surprised Suzie completely. She had taken it exceptionally well.

Later on it occurred to Suzie that she was not a stranger to violence and death, her mother had been murdered and her father had almost been killed in the most horrific way. Yet she wasn't made of stone.

The next twenty four hours flew by. By Monday morning the whole of the workforce were involved, the neural interfaces had been manufactured and the moulds for his bones were being printed. Dee-Dee delivered the interfaces to the hospital late on Monday night. She took the opportunity to talk to Keith about John and he told her that he had scheduled the operation for six a.m. the following morning.

"Can I see him now?" she asked.

"We have him in an isolation unit, ensuring that there's no chance of infection. I doubt that he will regain consciousness for some time, even after the operations have been completed. We aren't in control of that side, he is."

Chapter 23

As his spirit faced the all embracing light he heard the words that were not spoken but came from within him. He knew that his time had not yet come to return to the light. A light that no living eyes would be able to withstand, yet he was able to face it without pain or fear.

John was also reaching a decision, to leave the light and return to darkness. The light began to recede, it didn't dim but became more distant.

At the point at which he could no longer perceive the light, he became aware of the voices, human voices that were not within but around him. He was listening, assembling the information he was receiving from the voices, learning about the problems with his body that others were having to contend with. He was perfectly calm and detached. Not his problem, the work was for the others to do. His work would begin when theirs ended.

He lay there for several days in darkness, unable to move, listening to the voices, unwilling to return from his unconsciousness. Perceiving yet not partaking.

It was the period which he knew was necessary for the reconciliation of soul and body, and for his mind to achieve the adjustments that were essential for his successful reunion and to commence the rest of his life.

Chapter 24

The eventual report from Keith, who was totally exhausted, was that the operation that had lasted over fourteen hours had been a qualified success.

"Why do you say that?" Suzie asked him.

"Only because I have nothing to check the results against, until you are in a position to attach the arms I just won't know whether everything is correct. As far as I know, at the moment, everything has gone according to plan, but in this case I am only the middle part of the project, whereas I am used to being the final piece of the jigsaw, it's a strange feeling."

"I can understand that, but without you this wouldn't have been possible. How did the adhesion of the plates work out?"

"Far better than I expected, the adhesion is tremendous, how do you come up with these compounds?"

"As Edison once said, ninety nine percent perspiration and one percent inspiration. We continually experiment and when we've found something we modify it time and again. Trial and error. Sheer monotony most of the time."

"Whatever it is I only hope that the rest of the job goes as well as it has so far. When will you have them ready?"

"We are on target to get finished sometime later tonight, maybe the early hours of the morning. They are modifying the fuel cells at the moment. Because we are not powering the entire body we are having to incorporate the cells only into the bone structure, the only problem being that we don't have much space to work with, so we are modifying them to incorporate a charging point, probably located in each of the smallest digits. We may be able to change it later but at this moment in time it is the best we can come up with. I would like to come down in the morning, if we're finished, and fit them. I can't get my head around it though. I'm scared to death of what John's reaction will be when he finally comes to."

"The only advice I can give you is that if he were to wake up without any arms and he would have a far harder time coming to terms with it than he will getting used to the fact that his arms aren't his own. If it all works, then it will soften the impact. I'm sure that he will be able to cope with it better this way."

He was trying to talk her up, but he was really hoping that the shock that was still waiting for John wouldn't affect him permanently. It was one thing fixing a damaged body, it was something quite different fixing a damaged mind.

Early on Tuesday morning Dee-Dee put a call through to her father who was extremely shocked to learn of the weekend's events.

"I wonder if this has got anything to do with Suzie's conversations with him last week. She spoke to him twice before she left. In fact it was the second call that made up her mind to leave. She told me that John had a problem that he was unwilling to discuss with her. She was very worried about him, she said she had the impression he was either feeling threatened or being threatened, either way she said she had to get back home."

Eric was becoming more convinced that there was something sinister going on, something somebody was keeping quiet about.

"But the parcel wasn't even addressed to him," Dee-Dee protested.

"Then it was probably sent as a warning that went wrong. Think about it, if you wanted to frighten someone with a bomb, but not actually harm them the logical thing to do is to either set it off when there is least chance of anyone being there or place the bomb and send a warning so that the area can be cleared. My guess is that it was sent on a Saturday when they knew that there would be someone there to receive it and then the intention was to detonate it when everyone had left, but maybe the timer was set wrongly and it went off early ro there was a malfunction of some kind. That is something the police should be able to discover fairly quickly. Keep your own counsel, speak to no-one until you know more about it, but please keep me informed, I will help wherever I can."

It was a side to her father very few people knew existed, it had very rarely surfaced since her mother's murder. His gruff and sometimes very rude exterior was his way of preventing other people from getting close to him. Insulation, she called it.

It wasn't long before the police were back. The previously boiler-suited detective returned with Sherlock Holmes, much to Alan's disgust, but he was held in check by the older man, Detective Sergeant Oliver Small (disrespectfully referred to by his colleagues as Dick).

He was anything but a small man, at six feet four and over sixteen stone, fit not fat, his presence was quite dominating which he found quite helpful when questioning witnesses and suspects.

When he arrived shortly after nine, he was disappointed that Suzie wasn't there to see him. Barbara showed him into her office, offered him a coffee, which he gratefully accepted and waited for Alan to arrive. He arrived before the coffee.

"Good morning, Sergeant. I'm afraid Miss Fielding will be out for most of the day, she's at the hospital."

Alan ignored the detestable Sherlock and sat down behind her desk, Sergeant Small sat opposite him.

"How's the patient?"

"He's still under heavy sedation for the time being, until we've sorted out his limbs."

Alan felt awkward about telling him, but it was totally unavoidable. Small knew that John had been dismembered, and he would very soon be talking to him to find out what he knew about the events of Saturday morning.

"Tell me, was there anything unusual about Saturday morning?"

"In what way?"

"Apart from the delivery. was it unusual for you to be the only ones in the building?"

"Yes, there are usually three of us working until lunchtime, John, myself and Suzie."

"Why wasn't she in?"

"Suzie had only just returned from Kenya in the early hours of the morning, we weren't expecting her until Monday."

"Would you say the delivery was expected?"

"Sorry?" Alan was puzzled.

"I mean, was Mr. Hylton expecting a delivery?"

"Do you know what triggered the device? You seem to be looking for specific information," Alan said defensively.

"I'm afraid I can't release that information at this stage, but I need to know what you know."

"I'm sorry, but there's nothing more I can tell you. Now if you'll excuse me I have a lot of work to do."

Alan got up to leave.

"Please sit down, Mr. Fisher."

Small motioned with his head to his sidekick to leave.

"Wait in reception, see if you can find anyone interesting to talk to."

Alan sat down, Sherlock left the room.

"Okay, can we trade? This is strictly between us."

Alan nodded his agreement.

"We know that the bomb was triggered by some sort of sensor device. Whatever it was designed to detect, it found it while Mr. Hylton was carrying it. We know that Mr. Ayres was not due in, so we can rule out both of them as the intended victims. Whatever set it off, we think, should have done it when there was no-one else around. If they had wanted to kill or injure Mr. Hylton it would have been addressed to him and more than likely exploded when it opened. This was carefully planned, but we don't know what the actual trigger was, it would make life a lot easier if you could help."

Alan was confident in the sincerity of the big policeman, he had been around a long while and wasn't too proud to ask for help.

"Before John arrived, I took delivery of a package that was addressed to him. When I told him about it he was very reluctant to open it, he was asking all sorts of questions, like 'who delivered it', 'how heavy is it', where's the paperwork', it seemed as though he thought someone might send him something, but he wasn't expecting it. When he did open the parcel it turned out to be something he had ordered earlier in the week and he felt a bit foolish about forgetting it. But something was definitely worrying him. He'd had a couple of lunchtime meetings earlier in the week, that I would imagine could be connected, but I have no idea who it was that he met, or what the meetings were about, you'd have to ask Barbara about that."

"What do you think could be the trigger?"

"There is only one thing I can think of. How's your imagination?"

"Pretty good."

"Prepare yourself for a shock. Follow me."

Alan stood up and went out to the lift. Small followed close behind.

They went up to the top floor. Alan went into the cinema, they went in and Alan locked the door behind them. He opened a small panel to the left of the doors and switched on the house lights.

"Baggy, come," he called softly.

Out from between the first and second rows of seats came

Baggy.

"Holy shit! Let me out."

Small turned round to the doors and tried to pull them off their hinges.

"It's alright, calm down."

"Bugger that for a game of soldiers, let me out."

His voice was getting louder and more desperate.

"Baggy, come here and sit down." He did precisely as he was told. He sat three feet in front of Alan and looked up at him as though he was the only person in the world.

"My God, now I've seen everything."

"Not quite... Sleep, Baggy."

Baggy lay down and closed his eyes.

"What is this? Cheesus, this isn't real is it?"

The disbelief was total and written all over him.

"Oh, he's real, but not as an animal. He's our little pet. Or more accurately he's John's pet. Before John took the package downstairs to the construction area, I asked him if he wanted me to take it down for him, he said he would do it as he hadn't said good morning to Baggy."

"And this is Baggy?" Small was beginning to calm a little, but his blood pressure was still sky high and making him perspire profusely.

"Yes, he's our own creation. He was slightly damaged in the explosion, he was no more than three feet away from John when the bomb went off."

Everything clicked into place in Alan's mind.

"Got it. Come with me."

Alan unlocked the door and was off and running.

"It'll be a pleasure," he said taking a last shuddering look at Baggy.

They took the lift back down a floor and walked quickly to Alan's lab. "I should be able to show you the moment of the explosion."

"How?"

"Everything the animals see while they are activated is recorded and stored in the servers."

Alan selected Baggy from the menu, tapped in the time and date, scanned back ten minutes. "Here we are. You see Baggy had switched off the previous evening, and here he is, nine thirty three,

Saturday. He's heard the footsteps on the stairs, he's waiting for the door, now he's off to see John."

Small was watching with his mouth wide open. It was quite incredible. The sort of thing you only saw in movies.

Baggy got closer, the bomb went off, silver flashes sped across the screen, and John crashed to the floor. The pictures made them both feel ill.

Small was the first to speak. With a dry mouth he asked, "Can you play back the moment of the explosion in slo-mo?"

"No problem."

They watched it again, frame by frame. They saw the razor sharp discs burst through the box from all four sides of the box, in identical directions, two diagonally up, two diagonally down from each side.

"Okay, I've seen enough for the moment," Small said, professionalism returning. "Would the cat have greeted everyone that way?"

"No. John is the only one that he comes to without being told. He would activate though when he detects any indication of movement, sight or sound."

"Would he normally wander about down there without anyone being around?"

"It depends on whether he has been shut down or whether he has been left to his own devices. If he has shut himself down, in accordance with his programming, i.e. he goes to sleep, he will wake up the same way and behave as though he was in the zoo, he would 'wake up' and pace around in the same way as the panther in the zoo does, that's where we got his programming from."

"I see," he said, not quite sure that he did. "So if you had taken the parcel down and Baggy had not been shut down the previous night, you could have taken it to Mr. Ayres station and left it, without Baggy coming to see what you were doing."

"Yes, that's right."

"So he would then, more than likely have wandered around the room on his own."

"Yes, he would have been disturbed and would automatically revert to program as soon as he was on his own."

"What powers him?"

"Lithium fuel cells."

"Would they give off anything that you could detect?"

"There is a very low level of radiation, far less than we get from the sun even in mid-winter."

"So the sun could have confused the device?"

"No, it's a different type of radiation, I just gave you that as an example."

"So it is quite possible that Baggy would have at some point, after he was disturbed, walked around and come within range of the package."

"I'd say there would be a very good chance of it, yes."

"So it would lead us to believe that it was some sort of warning that went wrong."

"I suppose so, but whoever sent the device had to know, one, that Baggy existed, and two, what the power source was."

The implication was almost impossible to believe.

"That points to an inside job," Small said, putting his detective's hat back on.

"Maybe we are looking for someone in here," Alan agreed.

They stood in silence for a while, Alan not wanting to believe what he had just heard, Small waiting for a reaction.

Alan was the first to speak.

"That doesn't make sense. If someone that worked here wanted to plant a bomb there would be a lot of opportunities to do so without sending one in by courier, no matter how clever the device it still leaves an element of risk. It seems to me as though someone might have been trying to blow up Baggy, but that's ridiculous," Alan said, shaking his head.

"I think you have just hit the nail on the head. It would make sense if someone were trying to demonstrate how much they knew about your little project. How many more of these have you made?"

Alan looked unsure.

"Strictly off the record."

"Okay. Three so far. Two rhinos, Rhoda and Rhonda, and an elephant called Elvis. We're also working on a couple of chimps and a giraffe, but they don't have names yet," Alan said, grinning.

"Are you serious?" Small was trying not to laugh, it was still an attempted murder as far as he was concerned.

"Absolutely."

"Can I see them?"

"I'm afraid not, the rhinos and elephant are somewhere in East

Africa at the moment."

"I shan't bother asking you what they are doing, I think I have had enough unbelievable stuff to fill a fiction library already."

"Some other time."

Alan was finding that he was beginning to like the big man.

"So the possibilities for involvement go a good deal wider than the people that work here then."

"Not really, there are probably only two others outside of the company that have any real knowledge, one is John's girlfriend, Dee-Dee Sampson, the other is her father who is out in Kenya with the other animals."

"I suppose, realistically, that rules them out. So that brings us back then to an inside job. We are going to have to do it the hard way."

He looked at his watch, just coming up to eleven. "Can we use Miss Fielding's office to interview everyone here?"

"I think you had better use Mr. Hylton's, Suzie will be back later."

"I am going to need your help. The key seems to be the radiation from the fuel cells, I need to know who could know about that."

"Virtually everyone here, it's common knowledge, not particularly technical."

"I'll still have to talk to everyone, find out what their movements have been, do a bit of fishing. I think our best chance is going to be Mr. Hylton himself, but that may take a while yet. Can you get someone to give me the employment records of everyone that works here, we might be able to get somewhere from those?"

"I'll get Barbara to pull them out for you, or I can access them for you on the computer in John's office, whichever you prefer."

"Paper's better, I get more feel for it that way."

The morning at the hospital had been nerve-wracking to say the least. There had been no problem fitting the limbs, apart from the fact that the joints were visible, something Suzie promised herself she would work on as soon as possible, the worst part was waiting for him to come round. The nurse, working under Keith's instructions, had reduced the sedative drip to allow John to regain consciousness at his own pace. Keith thought that he should be coming round sometime late morning or early afternoon, provided that there were no other problems.

Suzie didn't ask what the other problems could be, she was too afraid of what the answers might have been. She sat by his bedside from the moment they finished the fitting, just watching and waiting, and occasionally praying.

At three twenty four, John's eyes flickered, at three twenty six they slowly opened. Keith came quietly through the door, the sensors attached to John's head had alerted the nurses station and they in turn paged him.

Keith leaned over him and gazed into the open but apparently unseeing eyes. He stayed like that for what felt like hours, until John tried to speak. It was an inaudible whisper at first, Keith leaned over with his left ear close to John's mouth in an effort to hear him. He whispered slightly louder, "Baggy."

"What did he say?" Suzie asked.

Keith stood up with a broad smile on his face.

"Baggy! After all he's been through and his first concern is his bloody mechanical moggy! I think he's going to be alright."

"Well, that's John for you," Suzie said, laughing and replacing Keith by the bed as his page went off, summoning him elsewhere.

It was another twenty minutes before John said anything else. He just lay there, mostly with his eyes closed, staring straight up at the ceiling when they were open.

At three forty six he turned his head slightly towards Suzie, and without any facial expression said quietly, "It's okay, I know what's happened. I've seen everything. I know you've done your best, the rest is up to me now."

Suzie went as white as a sheet, she didn't know what to say, all she could think of was to say, "Later, just rest, everything is going to be alright."

John nodded slowly, closed his eyes and drifted back off to sleep.

Suzie reluctantly left the room and called Dee-Dee at the office.

"He came round briefly, he's sleeping now. I think it would be best if you were here when he comes round again."

"I'm leaving now."

Tuesday morning had been quiet for the three animals, although Elvis had been the subject of some animated attention from some locals who appeared to think he was going to damage their village somehow. He was the biggest elephant they had seen in a long time and as lone bulls had something of a reputation they didn't want to take any chances.

After that, Jerry made sure that Elvis kept well away from the villages and crops, but at least he had been seen.

All had been quiet for Rhoda and Rhonda since their escapade with the pit, and they hadn't heard of any reports of poaching since.

The news from Dee-Dee changed the atmosphere on the plane completely, Jerry said very little, the shock appeared to hit him the hardest, to Eric it looked as though he had drawn himself into a shell, he didn't ask any questions or show any interest at all. He simply sat and watched the screens and ate his meals in silence.

When Dee-Dee called late into the night, it was to give them some better news.

"John's awake now, he's still very weak but he knows what has happened to him. He hasn't reacted in any way that we can tell. He only talks a little, but the police think that they may have a lead on a man called Lorenzo Lanfranco. Keith, John's surgeon who also is a good friend, was trying to help him find out some background information last week on him for John. They are going to see if there is any sort of link there to the bomb."

"Lanfranco is a nasty piece of work, I've never had any personal dealings with him but he has a certain unethical reputation. I've not heard about him using this sort of thing though, it may just be a coincidence. If it is, it would be a mighty big one," Eric replied.

Jerry was listening to one end of the conversation and at the mention of Lorenzo's name he suddenly felt quite ill.

He excused himself and left the plane, went out to the back of the workshop at the rear of the airstrip and threw up for all he was worth. Ten minutes later he was still shaking like a leaf and praying that what had happened was not relevant to his own connection.

Chapter 25

Maria brought Michael Lanfranco into Dan's study, the walls were lined with dark oak panelling and shelves full of unread books, at least by Dan, they came with the house when Dan claimed it in lieu of a very large gambling debt three years before.

Dan stood up and took the proffered hand. "What's happening?"

"The news is not good. The device went off while Hylton was actually carrying it."

"Oh shit!" Dan winced.

"It blew him apart, literally. He's going to live, but the police are crawling all over the place. The connection has already been made, we are expecting a visit any moment now."

"What's going to be done?"

"We are getting ready to move house."

Dan nodded, he knew what it meant.

"But he wants to take some insurance with him."

"You're joking."

"No, I'm not. We've got a week to get things sorted, he wants you to get the artworks stored safely away, the other preparations are being made and we want to make the collection and for all of us to be out of here by the end of next week."

"I would prefer to stay. I've got quite accustomed to the lifestyle. I like living here."

Dan was openly showing his dissent, a calculated and dangerous risk.

"We suspected that you might, but I'm afraid you don't have a say in the matter. You would be a loose end. You knew when you joined us that you were exchanging your ragbag existence for all this and you knew there would be a price to pay. There are only two ways to pay it."

Dan knew that it wouldn't be Michael pulling the trigger, he didn't have the guts, but he knew who did and life was preferable.

"When do you want me to leave?"

"The replacement works are already in place. You leave tonight for Hong Kong in the Gulfstream, you will be met at the airport, the goods will be received, the plane will be refuelled and you will return one and a half hours later. You will be back here on Friday morning in the early hours, collect what you need and come to the house. Leave Maria, tell her nothing."

"Is she going to be okay?" Dan asked but didn't really want an answer.

"The decision hasn't been made yet. If you get back safely she will most likely not have any problems."

That could be interpreted in several ways, Dan thought, but to warn her before he returned would put the seal on both of their fates.

Dee-Dee had spent Tuesday night and all day Wednesday with John. She only left his side when she absolutely had to. He was awake for more of the time, but said little. She held his hand, aware that he probably couldn't tell, but it was symbolic more than anything. To her it felt almost like the real thing, but the most important part was that she was holding him. Real or not, he was alive.

Sergeant Small came to the hospital twice during the day, the first time he was refused permission to speak to John, the nurse was quite insistent.

"Come back later this afternoon, you will have a better chance then."

The news had spread around very quickly, the media had certainly done their part and the flowers and cards had been almost non-stop since it had been released that he was off the danger list on Monday evening.

Suzie and Dee-Dee had asked for the flowers to be distributed around the rest of the hospital, there were far too many for John's room alone.

The second appearance of the big policeman at the ward reception was greeted with inevitable resignation. The look on Oliver Small's face was one of apology, but they all accepted that he had his job to do and John had been the victim of a murder attempt, so they led him quietly to his room.

"Hello Miss, I'm sorry to disturb you, but I do need a couple of answers from Mr. Hylton, if it's possible."

"Yes, I'm sure you do. He's said very little today, they think he's still very weak and suffering from post-traumatic shock. You can ask him, but I can't guarantee you'll get an answer."

She stood up from her chair and leaned close to John.

"Darling, there's a policeman here, he needs to ask you

something. I'm not leaving you, I'll stay in the room."

She kissed his forehead and moved away.

"Thank you Miss," he tried to smile at her, but it didn't work very well.

"Mr. Hylton, I only want one question answered, if you can. If you can't speak, please indicate to me any way you can."

John didn't move or do anything.

"Do you know who was responsible for the bomb?" Small said quietly.

John didn't move.

"Do you think you might know who did this to you?"

John turned his head slightly towards him, Small wasn't sure whether that was supposed to be an answer and started to ask him again when John whispered "Lanfranco" and closed his eyes.

"Thank you."

He stood up.

"We'll need to talk to him again tomorrow, hopefully for longer, if he's able. I'm sorry miss, I really am. I will look forward to putting the bastard that did this away for a very long time."

"Thank you, Sergeant."

She returned to her position at the bedside, leaned over him once again and kissed his cheek.

John turned his head towards her, and opened his eyes. She couldn't be certain but they seemed to be somehow a little brighter. She knew he was coming back to her when he gave her a very faint smile, and closed his eyes again.

Lanfranco received his visitor with more deference than would normally be accorded to someone with the lowly rank of sergeant.

"Come in, would you care for a drink?"

"No thank you, I just need the answer to a few questions, if you wouldn't mind, sir."

Lorenzo invited him and Sherlock to sit down on the leather sofa that faced the 'Hockney' over the fireplace. The firm seating was surprisingly comfortable. Lorenzo sat in one of the two matching chairs.

"Fire away," he said, smiling easily.

"Have you heard about the terrible explosion at Animagination on Saturday morning."

"Yes, most unfortunate, one of my associates was talking about it earlier."

"We understand that you had some meetings with Mr. Hylton last week. Can you tell me what they were about?"

"Yes, I had approached Mr. Hylton with a view to commissioning some machines for me."

"And how did your negotiations proceed with Mr. Hylton?"

"It's too early to say, we are really only talking in vague terms at this stage. Our total time together was probably only just over an hour and a half. We hadn't even got down to anything specific."

"So how do you see your negotiations proceeding in the future?"

"That's difficult to say, it depends on how quickly and how well Mr. Hylton recovers."

"Is his recovery essential to you then?"

"I think it is very important, I doubt that my proposals could come to fruition without him. His injury could be quite a setback to my plans if it takes him a long time to recover."

"So you have nothing to gain by Mr. Hylton's incapacitation?"

"Heaven forbid, that is the last thing I would want. I was prepared to offer him a very substantial sum of money to execute a project for me. Without him I don't think that the project could go ahead."

"And what is the project, sir?"

"That I'm afraid I cannot tell you. It has no part in your investigation, Mr. Hylton doesn't even know what it is yet."

"If you say so, sir. You are not planning on going anywhere for the foreseeable future are you sir?"

"No, feel free to call me if you think I can be of assistance."

They all stood up and the two policemen left the house.

"Get Tom Fredericks on the phone, I want to speak to him now!"

Michael did as he was ordered.

Dee-Dee was still with John when Suzie came in to see him. Dee-Dee didn't hear the door open, she sat in the chair with her head on the side of the bed, fast asleep. She had hardly left his side in almost two days.

John was awake. Suzie half smiled at him and went around to the far side of the bed and sat in the other chair next to his bedside cabinet.

She didn't know what to say and didn't know what to expect.

He whispered, to her.

"Persuade Dee-Dee to go and get some sleep, she's totally exhausted, I'm going to be fine."

He closed his eyes for a few seconds, as though he was trying to gain some more strength.

The tears streamed down Suzie's face, all of the tension of the past few days was released, she doubted that she had ever felt so happy in all of her life. It was just so typical of him, he's been blown to pieces and yet he's more concerned about someone else.

He opened his eyes and looked at her again.

"Can you move at all," she asked.

"I haven't tried," he said honestly.

"Please try, try and move your hand towards me."

He closed his eyes, more to summon up the confidence to cope with the failure that he was convinced was bound to follow. Slowly, his hand slid across the bed to her.

"Lift it up," she instructed, he still had his eyes closed.

He lifted his arm without any apparent strain, then he suddenly dropped it as a grimace appeared sharply on his face.

"What is it, what's wrong?"

"With the arm, nothing. The pain is searing through my shoulder."

Suzie pressed the alarm button at the side of his bed. Within seconds the nurse burst in, waking Dee-Dee in the process.

"What's wrong?" the nurse demanded.

"We need you to fetch Dr. Boscik, now, there's a problem with his shoulder."

The nurse did as she was requested.

"Suzie, when did you arrive, what's happening?"

"I've been here about ten minutes. It's his shoulder, he moved his arm and got a lot of pain for his efforts"

The pain had gone by the time Keith arrived two minutes later.

"He moved his arm, at my request, I'm afraid and he paid for it."

"Great, that's wonderful, not the pain, but if he managed to move at all at this stage, it couldn't be better." Keith appeared very calm.

"But what about the pain, aren't you going to look at him?" Dee-Dee was confused.

"No, it's simple bruising, nothing more. I expected it, but I didn't expect him to move as soon as this. Another couple of days and the tissue attached to the joint will be far less tender. When he moves his arm, he exerts pressure on the other side of the joint, which is still sore from the operation. He shouldn't feel any pain when the bruising has gone.

"John, it's good to see you. I think we'll have you out of bed for a short while tomorrow, if you're up to it. I'll see you later, I have other patients that need me more than you do. Brilliant, well done!"

He was quite effusive, it put a real spring in his step.

"Ladies, if you'll excuse me."

They looked at each other and then at John who was smiling softly, but still with his eyes closed.

Keith motioned with his head for Suzie to follow him. As they stepped outside the room into the antiseptic corridor Keith's expression changed.

"It is inevitable," he said quietly "sooner or later, that the shock of all that he has been through will catch up with him. It is just not possible that a human being can suffer this level of injury without the mental trauma that accompanies it."

"How do you mean? I thought he was making tremendous progress."

A feeling of unease was creeping slowly through Suzie.

"He is making remarkable progress physically, but he is going to have to come to terms with the fact that his life has changed completely and irrevocably. No matter how successful the prosthetics are I don't know how he will handle the situation emotionally. The most likely signs will be mood swings and irrational behaviour patterns once he has mastered his arms. His cuts on each of his legs are already healing well but will be sore for quite a while. The cuts were more superficial than we initially thought as the discs went across his legs, rather than through them, but we should be able to take the bandaging off early next week, the stitches the week after."

"What can we do?"

"When he leaves here you will need to keep him occupied mentally, focused, try to keep him from thinking about himself. If you can, find a project that uses his new abilities to do things that others cannot but do not under any circumstances make him feel like a guinea pig."

Suzie nodded, but felt slightly depressed. Until that moment she had just been so grateful that John was alive and would be able to lead some sort of normal life. She realised that his life would be anything other than normal.

Chapter 26

"Master, Master, wake up, wake up."

The boy was shaking the shoulders of the sleeping man. Waking him was going to be difficult, the sleep had been aided by the hashish that had been smoked the night before. After several more minutes of cajoling he was stirring.

With a groan and a reluctant prising apart of his eyelids he greeted the world. The sun had only broken through an hour before and yet the village was already full of life. Traders were coming in with their oxen, mules and camels fully laden, hoping to scratch out a living for yet another day under the hot Sudanese sun.

"What do you want?" he said angrily, lurching his feet onto the floor in an attempt to sit up on what purported to be a bed. It was more like a freestanding shelf a foot off the floor, there was no mattress, just a jumbled collection of blankets on some wooden boards propped up by four short legs.

"I have been told that "The Big One" has returned."

"Rubbish. I'm not paying you for fairy stories."

"No, Master, it is true, he has come back to Turkana. It has to be the same one, very big, his tusks are ten feet long, many people have seen him."

The boy was very enthusiastic, although he hadn't seen the elephant himself.

"A likely story. Get out of here, leave me in peace."

Deflated the boy opened the lockless door of the ramshackle room and walked out.

"Wait," he bellowed. "Come back here."

His head was starting to clear. At least with the weed, heads didn't feel like thunder boxes afterwards.

The boy sheepishly poked his head around the corner, half expecting to get something thrown at him, "Yes Master?"

"When was he seen?"

"He has been wandering around the north shore of Lake Turkana for the past four days. The message came in with the fish traders this morning."

"If it is him he has come back to die."

"How can you be sure of that?"

"Because I will kill him. It is Allah's will, he has brought him to me to avenge my son. If it is not the same one, then Allah has brought him to me for another purpose and I shall kill him anyway. We will leave tomorrow. Mtoto Abdebele will make the devil beast suffer."

The news on John's progress was warmly received by Eric and especially by Jerry, who was feeling guiltier than Jack the Ripper. Life had been very pleasant for a while, there had been no trouble at all and they hadn't heard of any poaching anywhere. They were all sure that it was too good to last, but at least there were several poachers who wouldn't be coming back. By Thursday afternoon everyone was relaxing, they had let all of the animals roam free, with the exception of Elvis whose only restriction was to stay within twenty miles of the north end of the lake.

Jerry was even considering the possibility of returning home at the end of February; there would be no shortage of willing volunteers to take his place for a week or two.

Thursday afternoon was a momentous occasion for Dee-Dee and John. Keith came in to see them at three o'clock.

"Hi, how's the patient?" he said cheerfully.

"The patient is doing fine, feeling very nervous but apart from that, pretty good, all things considered," John replied.

Keith thought John was putting on a brave face, it would take him a long time to get used to the idea of his changed state. He wasn't a psychologist but there was no doubt that he would be affected in some way.

"Good. How do you feel like getting out of bed for a while, nothing energetic, just a ride around in a wheelchair, give you a change of scenery?"

"I think that would be quite a good idea. What d'you think Dee-Dee?"

She was hiding a huge grin behind her hands and was grateful that Keith was standing behind her.

"Yes, I agree, you need to start the physiotherapy."

"Right, then I'll fetch the nurse and we can see what you can do."

Two minutes later he returned with a nurse and a wheelchair.

"Now then, if you'll just give us a little space, young lady, we'll help him out of the bed into the wheelchair."

They pulled back the covers and as Keith put his hand out to

John to help, John rolled away from him and gingerly stood up on the far side of the bed. Keith couldn't believe it. John slowly walked round, he was very uncomfortable, but not in serious pain.

"What are you going to do for an encore?" Keith said, amazed at what he was seeing and thought he was going to have to pinch himself.

"Go for a ride in a wheelchair."

John lowered himself gently in to the seat.

"You knew!" Keith said to Dee-Dee.

"Yes, but he hadn't walked before that though. It's wonderful isn't it?"

"It's quite incredible."

"Hey, what about me? I'm still here you know," John said with mock offence.

"Okay, let's go for a tour, and don't grab the pretty nurses as you pass them or we'll switch your arms off!" Dee-Dee said with a laugh.

"Have all of the preparations been made?" Lorenzo asked.

"Everything will be ready by tomorrow morning," Michael replied.

"Good, I want you to pick up the girl on Monday morning, you will take Dan and Sonny to the offices, use whatever force is necessary. You will bring the girl back here. I want there to be no doubt as to who has taken her, no masks, only use tear gas to aid your escape. I have prepared a letter which will explain what I want them to do, you will leave it in the reception for them to find."

"Do you think they will capitulate and build what you want?"

"No, I can't see any way that they will do that now, I want the girl to come with us, she will have the ability to construct what we need, if we provide her with the equipment and people she requires. If everything goes to plan we should be able to get the results we want."

"They won't just sit back and let you take her out of the country, they'll come after her."

Michael knew how they were going to leave but couldn't understand how kidnapping the girl, Suzie, was going to help them get away.

"Precisely, they will make it work for me."

"What are we going to do about our four troublesome friends?"

"Their respective employers will be receiving letters by the end of next week giving details of the crimes that have been carried out against them. The police will do the rest. The others who are not causing problems will receive letters also warning them that they are not free and will be contacted when the time is right, they will also be instructed to watch for news in the media of the four. It will serve as a warning to them."

"Is there anything you haven't thought of?" Michael wished he had half of his father's ability.

Lorenzo wished his son had even half of his father's brain.

Oliver Small visited John in the hospital on Friday morning, not looking particularly happy.

"Hi, I don't know whether you remember me, I'm Detective Sergeant Small, I talked to you briefly on Wednesday."

"Yes, I'm sorry I wasn't more use to you."

"Well, I don't know that there's much I can do, unless you can give me some definite information, I'm in a blind alley."

"What about Lanfranco, have you seen him?"

"I'm afraid so. I must admit that I would love to get after him, but at the moment, apart from your suspicions and your meetings with him last week I have nothing to go on. Under normal circumstances, I would investigate him fully, but unfortunately these aren't normal. I have been told that unless I can get positive evidence linking him into the explosion, then I'm to keep away from him. My boss received instructions from way above," he said, looking up at the ceiling.

"Surely that tells you something?"

"Apparently he has supported police charities for many years and they don't want to upset him. If there's nothing more you can tell me that I don't already know, we'll have to hope forensics can come up with something."

John was reluctant to tell him about the potential blackmail with the photographs of Elvis and Rhonda boarding the plane, there was no guarantee that it would help and it could cause more problems than it might solve.

"No, I'm sorry, I have nothing firm to go on, I didn't receive any threats and I had no witnesses to the meetings that I had with him. It looks like our man has friends in all the right places."

"I'm going to continue investigating him, quietly, where I can, but there are no guarantees I'll be able to find anything much with my hands tied. The only thing that puzzles me still, though, is where he got the information to give him the trigger for the device. It had to come from somewhere. I've spoken to all of your people apart from one, Jerry Grossman, and come up with absolutely nothing, not one of them had heard of him before and I got no indications at all that someone may have been lying. What do you know about Mr. Grossman?"

"He's worked for me for a while, just over a year, he's never been a problem. I don't think he has any money worries. When we asked him to go to Kenya he was reluctant at first, which was understandable, then he changed his mind and leapt at the chance, but that was before I had any dealings with Lanfranco."

"When will he be coming back?"

"Probably in two or three weeks time, it's up to him really, I think he's enjoying himself, he's certainly had some adventures since he's been out there."

"Oh well, I'll check with you again next week if that's alright with you."

"Yes, but I won't be here, they're letting me out today, as long as I take it easy. My joints are healing well, still a little sore but sitting around in a hospital bed isn't going to change that. Call me at the office, I can rest there as well as anywhere," he said with a smile.

Dee-Dee took John home at eleven o'clock and stayed with him, trying to make sure he relaxed. The hard part was making him behave himself.

John was lying on his settee in the living room with his head in her lap and looking up at her he said, "Do you know how much I have to thank you for?"

"You have nothing to thank me for."

"You stayed with me when I needed you more than anything. Without you I wouldn't have been able to cope with this," he said raising his hands. "I still feel like a freak, but you have shown me that it really doesn't matter. The only thing that matters is that we are together, I would rather be a freak with you than normal without you."

"You aren't a freak, you're the same person I fell in love with, you're the same person I want to spend the rest of my life with."

She bent down and kissed him gently, he responded with passion.

With a wicked glint in his eye he asked "Do you think the doctors would think it therapeutic if we...?"

"They didn't test that part for damage, so I think that we ought to make sure it works, don't you?"

"Oh, it still works I can be certain of that!"

Chapter 27

The journey from the hills of Liwan in the south eastern corner of Sudan to Ilaret on the shore of Lake Turkana was relatively uneventful, travelling in the early hours of the morning to avoid the worst of the sun took almost four hours. The most difficult part was crossing the crocodile infested waters of the River Omo in Ethiopia. Abdebele shot three crocodiles which kept the others occupied in a frenzied thrashing of tails and the snapping and ripping of powerful jaws while they forded their way across. The old, battered Landrover was well used to making such journeys, it must have made it a hundred times before without complaining even once. It had been a very faithful servant. It had been the only one to remain with him for anything more than a short time after the events of fifteen years before.

It was the first trip for the boy, Salim Akbar, who at the age of fourteen, was untouched by the rumours and fears of his elders. The prospects for such a boy in Liwan were limited, on the edge of the southern swamps there was little or no work for anyone without a family business to go into, such as goatherding, but the one thing in his favour was that he was a survivor, an opportunist. For three years, since his parents had been killed in the tit-for-tat cross-border raids with Ethiopia, he had lived by his wits, often playing two sides against each other and informing for both. It was an increasingly dangerous game, but one that he played with considerable alacrity for one so young.

For two months, he had been the eyes and ears of many people, an information gatherer, but the one that he considered afforded him the greatest opportunity for escape, adventure and reward was Abdebele. The pay was good for keeping the bandit poacher in good quality information concerning game sightings as well as ill-protected travellers, but the greatest reward would be for information on 'The Big One', the Devil-beast. Salim had been surprised at the speed with which Abdebele had moved, nothing else had stirred him so quickly. That elephant meant a lot to him and Salim would be paid what, to him, was a very large fortune indeed should the information prove to be correct.

The adventure was the start of a new life for Salim, with the money he would make from the trip he could start a proper business of his own, or even not have to work at all for many years, such were the big dreams of small boys.

They stopped for rest and shade once they had crossed the river, leaving their arrival in Ilaret on the shores of Lake Turkana until late afternoon, an hour before dusk.

Abdebele stopped half a mile outside the village, pitched their camp for the night and sent the boy in on his own to glean what information he could.

His return, after two hours, held no firm knowledge, only that a huge bull had last been sighted two days before heading east back towards the game reserve. The best information was that the elephant seemed to be wandering without purpose, as though his travels were complete. Various people had seen him over the course of the past few days, first by the lake's edge next ten miles inland, returning in the direction of the lake, sometimes north, sometimes south.

Nobody in the area would have anything to do with Abdebele. His reputation as being crazy and murderous went well before him. Salim was worth his weight in gold, as he was able to go where others would fear him treading. Abdebele's reputation had been well earned, he had killed probably as many men as he had killed animals. The price on his head had grown over the years to be more than the total earnings of a village like Ilaret, but also the legends. He could see in the dark, he could smell game (and men) better than the hyenas could smell a kill, he never slept and his eyes were sharper than a fish eagle.

None of which was true, but he was totally ruthless. He had killed nearly half of the men that worked for him for no more than disagreeing with him and killed almost as many for attempting to cash in on the rewards that were offered for his head. Until only boys would work for him, always for bounties far in excess of their normal value to him.

If the reports were true though, it could be the final hunt. It could be the elephant that killed his son. From the description, even allowing for exaggeration, it could be the one that would allow him to finally sleep peacefully at nights. The bounty from the ivory would be enough to see him to the end of his days in comparative luxury. All he had to do was wait.

The following morning, Salim set off at a trot to gather his information, he returned an hour later running as fast as his legs would carry him.

"Master, Master, we have to leave now, he has been seen."

"What? Where?" Abdebele's mouth suddenly went dry.

"The elephant! He was seen last night heading back towards the Lake. He was seen by the fishermen as they were returning with their catch, three miles south of the village. We must go now, before he leaves again."

"It makes sense, but he would more likely be heading back to graze, there are few trees alongside the lake. We will follow the shore until we find his tracks."

Ten minutes later they were loaded and kicking up a dust trail that a herd of zebra would have been proud of. It took less than an hour to find the trail that Elvis had left behind and only another half an hour to gain their first sight of him, walking steadily amongst the lush vegetation and trees of the bush, nonchalantly plucking at leaves and branches as he went on his apparently aimless way.

The adrenalin was pumping through Abdebele's body, thrashing through his veins as violently as Victoria Falls. It had been fifteen years. Time distorts the memory, but it was big enough, its tusks were long enough, even longer, but the shape, the curves, seemed different somehow. There was only one way to find out the truth.

They sat in the plane, Eric and Jerry, watching. They had heard the sound of the approaching Land Rover, still too far away to tell whether it was friend or foe. They could see a man and a boy but they were too far away, even with the magnification available to them to gain an identity. They would wait. Elvis half turned towards the intruders to allow a better view.

There was no movement in the vehicle, the man was sitting, peering through his binoculars. Nothing to be learned. Continue to browse and to watch. Wait. Gamewatchers, move on.

"They're following us," Eric said, uncertain of the situation.

Jerry was interested but not concerned. Man and boy, probably his son, no threat.

"Let them follow, it may prove enlightening."

The Land Rover held a constant distance of about four hundred yards for a little under half an hour. Moving steadily, still watching.

"He appears to be waiting for something. Shall we stop?"

"No, turn back, walk towards him. Make something happen," Eric instructed.

There was a short pause.

"He's getting out."

"But he's not armed. Nothing to worry about. Do we carry on?" Jerry asked.

Eric was puzzled, it was neither the action of a poacher, a ranger, nor a researcher and definitely not a tourist. "Is he limping?"

Eric thought he might be imagining it.

"Probably the rough ground, not easy to tell. If he is, it's not pronounced."

"Wait. Pull his face onto the screen. I need to see his face."

Eric's pulse was quickening. It could be the day he had looked forward to for so long.

The face was drawn into the screen in front of him. Very clear, twenty five times magnification, only seventy yards from Elvis. Eric could see him as though he was less than ten feet away. Couldn't be sure. He expected him to be older, but the man looked twenty, no thirty years older. He looked at least sixty. Could it be his man? Possible, but the actions certainly weren't those of the destructive creature that had murdered his wife and almost succeeded in killing him as well.

Elvis and Abdebele were standing less than fifty yards apart, warily watching each other. Elvis was swaying slightly from side to side, his trunk swishing lyrically at the flies that clustered around his great head.

Abdebele stood and watched, waiting for any sign of recognition from the elephant. He was certain that if it was the beast that robbed him of his son's life, then it would remember. The beast had turned the hunter into the hunted for just a few brief moments and had as devastating effect on him as any hunter's bullet could ever have had. Still unsure, he turned his back on the elephant and walked back to his Land Rover where the boy waited, captivated by the scene in front of him.

"Master, I have loaded your rifle, you can kill him easily," he shouted out to him. Salim was thinking only of the huge reward that would be coming his way on their return to Liwan.

Abdebele's pace remained the same.

"Did you hear that? They're definitely there for a kill. Look! He's definitely limping. He's favouring his right leg, no doubt about that now."

Jerry was getting excited

"Let him know that we know him."

Elvis trumpeted loudly and angrily, flapped his huge ears, shook his head from side to side and stomped forward slowly.

Abdebele half turned with a knowing evil grin on his face. It was him. There was no doubt about it. The devil beast was going to pay dearly for coming back. "I don't want that gun. Give me the other one."

He could feel an awesome power flowing through his body.

Chapter 28

John ventured into work with Dee-Dee driving. He was still feeling a little stiff and sore, but the improvements were happening at a pace that never ceased to amaze anyone. Keith had called in early that Saturday morning to see how his friend was progressing, even he was astounded to see him walking almost normally around the house.

The cheer that went up when he walked proudly into the computer lab was vigorous and loud even though it was only raised by Suzie and Alan. It was hard to believe that it had only been a week since the 'accident'.

"Thank you both, without you I wouldn't be here today. This has certainly crystallised what our long term projects are going to be. The sensations are strange and it is going to take me a long time to come totally to terms with what has happened and at some point in the near future I am going to have to give some serious thought as to how to deal with Mr. Lanfranco, but for now I am happy to express my gratitude for the hard work you all put in on my behalf."

"But if it hadn't been for you in the first place we wouldn't have been able to have done half of it," Alan countered. "If you don't mind me probing can you tell me what it feels like?"

Alan felt that it was a question that he would rather not have asked of a friend.

"In the interests of science," he smiled, "it feels strange, being able to move and react in almost exactly the same way as I did before. The most noticeable difference is the power. I have to consciously limit what I do as there is no noticeable effort on my part. Everything responds exactly as I want it to but I have to watch what I am doing with my hands, rather than feel what I am doing. We are going to have to develop that side fairly soon for the touch to be right."

"Can you tell how much power you are putting into your hands at all?" Suzie asked.

"Only by sight. If I want to pick something up, that isn't a problem, but if I want to apply pressure, that is difficult, if it were to be something breakable I would only find out when I had broken it that I had used too much, I wouldn't know for sure that I was getting close to the breaking point.

Alan and Suzie looked at each other, Suzie said "Neural receptors not providing intelligent feedback. The smartware isn't functioning properly yet."

John agreed.

"Not surprising really, so far it hasn't been a requirement but at least you have an in-house guinea pig to work with."

Suzie winced at John's choice of phrase.

"When will the chimps be ready to go out into the big wide world?"

"They're pretty much ready now if you want to let them loose individually. Unless Bob has any more that he wants to do with them, you can ask him on Monday morning."

The situation was beginning to feel a little surreal to Alan, here was a man that only a week ago was virtually blown to pieces and in less than a week they had rebuilt him, not perfectly admittedly, and he was standing there before them calmly discussing the merits and demerits of their achievements as though almost nothing had happened. Weird!

"Good, where's Baggy?"

Alan and Suzie looked at each other again.

"He's, er, sleeping," Suzie answered.

John nodded.

"Any objections if I switch him back on again? It wasn't his fault. If Alan had taken the box down and not me it may not have exploded straight away, but it could have been worse. It could have gone off with the house full."

"No objections, we just weren't sure what your feelings about him would be. He's downstairs."

Alan swivelled in his chair, hit a few keys.

"Ready and waiting boss."

He wasn't so sure but he needn't have worried.

The moment John appeared at the door at the bottom of the stairs he came bounding over to him. They couldn't work out which one looked the happiest. John bent down and gave him the biggest hug. Baggy was definitely smiling and didn't leave his side for the rest of the morning.

Dee-Dee called through to her father as soon as they arrived and was told that everything was quiet, but they thought that Elvis was being watched, but not by anyone that represented a threat. The exchange of news was welcomed by both but in view of the interest being shown at present the call was kept short.

"How's your father?" John asked.

"He's fine, he's got something going on with Elvis at the moment, nothing bad but he'll call back later."

The rest of the morning passed off with a mixture of bonhomie and technical discussion and ended up with John taking everyone out for a celebration lunch.

"What is he doing?" Jerry was puzzled.

"He's loading a tranquilizer gun. Good God, what does he think he can achieve with that?" Then Eric answered his own question. "The evil stinking bastard! There is only one reason someone like him would use that, he wants to have him alive when he carves him up. He is truly sick!"

Jerry couldn't believe what he was hearing.

"You actually believe that he would do that?"

"No doubt about it. Don't forget that this man killed over two hundred animals just because he couldn't find one elephant. Let's play along with him, we'll give him the biggest and nastiest surprise of his miserable existence."

Jerry watched as Elvis slowly tramped towards the Land Rover, totally transfixed. He watched as the rifle was raised to the shoulder, the trigger pulled, the dart dispatched, the impact in the shoulder, the instruction was given for Elvis to stop. Then to slowly kneel down, front legs buckling first. The needle still hooked into Elvis's skin, but penetrating no further, the sedative spreading harmlessly into nothing vulnerable, as Elvis lay slowly down.

Abdebele, pleased with his work, put the gun back, jumped in and drove to the prostrate elephant. He reached into the back of the Land Rover and pulled out a small chain saw and a two foot long machete.

The look on his face came straight from the depths of hell. Jerry shuddered at the sight of it filling the screen in front of him.

"First I will cut out his eyes," he said with relish to the boy, then I will cut open his belly, and then as he dies, I will cut off his beautiful ivories. We will be paid handsomely for this. This is the best work I have done in years, and I am going to enjoy every second of the pain that I can inflict on this devil."

"But the drug? He is unconscious, he will feel nothing."

"He is not unconscious, he has been sedated, he will hear and feel everything, he will just not be able to do anything about it."

He walked towards Elvis, saying to him "You took the life of my son, he had many years to live and died quickly. You would not have many years to live, so you are going to die slowly. Enjoy it while it lasts."

Jerry looked at Eric as they saw Abdebele walk towards Elvis. He was lying on his right side as he approached from the front raising the machete ready to strike into the offered left eye. Eric nodded, Jerry spoke softly to Elvis and the response was instantaneous, His trunk which was lying immobile on the ground to the right of Abdebele flicked across the dusty ground and thrashed into the back of his legs, fetching his feet clear off the floor, Abdebele landing heavily on his back, winded.

Elvis rolled onto his feet, lashed out with his trunk again as Abdebele struggled up on to his knees only to receive a rib-crunching blow across his back. Elvis, on his feet, roughly nudged him over onto his back, then carefully lifted and placed his right front foot onto the poacher's chest, the pressure was light enough not to damage but heavy enough to prevent any movement. They held him there for what seemed like an eon.

Salim who had been standing in the open topped Land Rover, watching, not daring to move, slowly reached down for the rifle that lay on the floor behind him. The gun was too big for him to handle, it was made for someone far larger than himself, but struggling he managed to lift it so that it came to rest on the top of the windscreen. He pulled back the bolt on the rifle, and took careful aim at the massive bulk some twenty yards away, he couldn't miss. It occurred to him that if he did manage to kill it, he would also be killing Abdebele at the same time. The greed flashed into his head. My career, he thought, this is my chance, Allah has presented me with such an amazing opportunity!

He slowly squeezed the trigger, closed his eyes in anticipation of the explosion and harsh reaction of the dealer of death. The recoil from such a large gun was far more than he had ever experienced before, the butt smashed into his shoulder and threw him into the back of the vehicle. Gingerly, he stood up, rubbing his right shoulder, grateful it wasn't broken, disappointed and amazed to see that Elvis was still standing, not having even noticeably moved, ears still flapping slowly.

He picked up the gun again, placed it carefully on top of the windscreen once more, he would not miss again. He also knew what to expect from the rifle. He pulled it tight into his shoulder and leaned forwards into it, negating the recoil. He calmed his breathing.

"Why aren't you shooting this devil? You skinny little bastard! Shoot him now! Get him off me!" Abdebele screamed.

Salim, did as he asked, carefully squeezing the trigger with the centre of the elephant's head in the cross-hairs.

Eric sat staring at the screen, listening to the sound of the shots and the thudding of the bullets hitting Elvis's head.

He was looking down his trunk, dangling towards the terrified face on the floor, a man awaiting execution, he knew that it was his decision, to apply the coup de grace. For fifteen years he had waited and prayed for the moment to come, and yet, when it came to it, all of the certainty and hate was deserting his body through every available pore.

When it came to the crunch, the final truth, Eric Daniels realised that years of bitterness and lust for revenge was not built into his body, it had been artificially created and maintained, and every animal's death at the hands of the poachers had carefully nurtured and cultivated it. And suddenly he found that the roots were not embedded in his soul, but had only been drawing sustenance from the surface. He couldn't do it.

Eric slowly stood up from his chair and turned his back on the face of his tormentor, the murderer of his wife. "Let him go. This is cold blooded murder. It makes me worse than him. I have lived with death for fourteen years, I don't want to live with it for the rest of my life."

Jerry whispered the instruction to Elvis and he slowly took the pressure off the poachers chest. Jerry was horrified to watch the face change from terror to disbelief, to relief to evil in the space of a few seconds. As Elvis's foot travelled up over his body and over his head, Jerry typed in just two four letter words, and the last thing that went through Mtoto Abdebele's mind was an elephant's foot.

Eric turned as he heard the clicking keys, to see, the boy in the Landrover kicking up a huge cloud of red dust as he frantically drove away and the words emblazoned across the screen - FOOT DOWN.

Chapter 29

Sunday was a quiet day on the airfield, nobody talked much at all. The three animals were allowed to wander wherever they wished, Jerry sat and watched or stretched his legs fetching golf balls that he had hit with indifference to the far end of the field. Fong had found an ancient set of hickory shafted clubs in a backstreet bazaar in Nairobi on one of his frequent shopping trips. Jerry hadn't played golf before but he made the most of the diversion.

Eric hardly set foot outside his cabin all day and when he did he didn't say a word. Jerry wasn't sure what to say, so he decided that to say nothing would probably do the least damage.

For Eric it felt almost like a death in the family following a long illness. His emotions were scattered on the winds, he felt relief and at the same time felt remorse. The remorse, he was surprised to find, was not for the death of the poacher-murderer but because it finally closed the book on his wife. The last chapter in that story had now been written and after fifteen years it was difficult to come to terms with. All his waking thoughts were of his wife. He had loved her with a passion that had always stayed with him. Until yesterday. The passion was extinguishing. That was subject of his grief. He had never grieved over her death, he had only ever felt anger. He could now grieve for her properly.

Sunday was a difficult day for John, there were so many things he wanted to do but Dee-Dee, acting under orders from Keith, kept him from doing most of them. He was, however, very pleased to be alive and enjoying the simplest things in life. Everything was taking on a new meaning for him. He had been very close to losing his life and things that he had always taken for granted were now so much more important. He also realised how important it was to help others who, through no fault of their own, had found themselves in a similar situation. The difference was that he had been in position for something to have been done about it almost immediately. New priorities would be set for the company in developing 'real' limbs. He conceded to Dee-Dee that had it not been for his own accident that the project would not have advanced as far as it had during the next two years as it had in the past week, and that while improving his own quality he would be significantly advancing the project at the same time.

"Every cloud has a silver lining?" she said, accepting the irony.

"I would have to agree, but out of choice I would rather have had clear blue skies," he said.

Monday morning for Eric felt a little brighter but he still didn't feel like talking. He was beginning to feel as though some time away from Africa would be a benefit.

Jerry hadn't had any problems with being a murderer's executioner, to him there had been no choice. The man was pure evil, he would kill, kill and kill again. He would only have tried again to kill Elvis, but what then when he found that it was impossible? Jerry hadn't got an answer for the question. He had no doubts, it was the only way. Bring on the next one.

For John, the day started easily enough. At just after nine thirty, they arrived for what they had decided would be a relaxed day, a long lunch and a short afternoon. An easing back into routine.

He went down to the construction rooms with Suzie to find Bob, leaving Dee-Dee with Alan, who was shortly to contact Jerry on the plane to catch up with the weekend's events.

Barbara was sitting in her usual place at the reception desk when three men walked briskly in.

"Good morning gentlemen, how can I help you?" she put on her professional smile in spite of a feeling of disquiet.

"We would like to see Mr. Hylton."

"I'm sorry, but Mr. Hylton isn't seeing anyone for a few days, perhaps you would like to make an appointment to see him sometime next week."

Michael moved quickly to her right with his left hand in his pocket,

Dan smiled at her.

"No I think we'll see him now."

She reached under her desk for the alarm button but before her hand reached its destination Michael's hand had shot out with a black plastic device with two short stainless steel prongs at one end. He pressed them against her arm and squeezed. The electric charge that hit her body took away all control and she slumped, eyes wide open, forward on to the desk, body still quivering.

Dan skipped round to the back of the desk, plucked her easily out of her chair and carried her to the back of the hall to the scanner at the side of the staff only door and dropped her onto the floor like an unwanted rag.

Michael and the other thick set man, Sonny, followed. Michael took hold of her left hand and placed it on the scanner, the door opened with a hiss. They marched through the corridor. Looked at each other, nodded and entered the infra red beam that opened the door to the computer lab.

They walked smartly, silently to where Alan and Dee-Dee were sat.

Alan was the first to react, "Who are you? You're not allowed in here."

He stood up and was confronted by Sonny, who snaked out a fist towards his head, Alan reacted almost too late and took a glancing blow to the side of his cheek, "What the...?" he didn't say any more, he pivoted to his left and came up with all of his immense strength and planted a right uppercut squarely on Sonny's strong jaw. Not strong enough. The splintering of bone was heard by everyone, and Sonny slumped to the floor with blood coursing from his mouth.

Michael was the quickest to respond with the taser, he pressed it to the back of Alan's neck and before Alan could do anything about it five thousand volts were pouring into him. With an almost superhuman effort he spun round and violently elbowed Michael in the stomach, they both dropped to the floor, pole-axed by the blows they had received.

Dee-Dee had tried to retreat to the far side of the room, the other side of the computers, but Dan grabbed for her and pulled her to the floor. He yanked her hands behind her back and slipped an electrical plastic tie over her wrists and pulled tight, too tight, but that wasn't his problem. She had been shouting and screaming but there was no-one else on the floor to hear her. He quickly ripped off some packing tape from the roll he had in his pocket and clamped it over her mouth and shoved her face down to the floor.

Leaving her, he quickly went to Michael, picked up the stun-gun and gave Alan another dose, his trembling body arched upwards as though dragged upwards by an unseen hand and collapsed back as though the weight proved too much.

Michael was struggling to find both his breath and his feet,

Sonny was conscious but incoherent. Dan helped Sonny to his feet, produced a book of matches from his pocket, struck one, blew it out and waved the resulting smoke under Sonny's nose. His eyes became clearer and although unsteady on his feet and in serious pain from his shattered jaw, was able to stand.

Michael was trying valiantly to breathe deeply and forcing his bruised torso upright managed to indicate that he would be alright. A few seconds more and Dan was sure enough to fetch Dee-Dee. The four of them lurched towards the door they had come in through, opened it and gave Barbara another shot to ensure that she wouldn't be raising the alarm for a while and continued the journey out through to the waiting car outside.

Bundling Dee-Dee into the boot, they flopped into the car and sedately, confidently moved away.

It was eighteen minutes before Barbara recovered sufficiently to raise the alarm. Alan was still unable to react even when John, Suzie and Bob arrived upstairs.

"What on earth happened?" John asked.

Barbara tried her best to explain but she couldn't identify anyone other than to confirm that one of the men had been here before.

They all realised at once that Dee-Dee was missing and a frantic search took place of all of the offices. Alan, recovered sufficiently to play back the film from the reception security camera to see what they were all beginning to fear. She was being hustled out to the car waiting on the forecourt.

"Oh Jesus!" he shouted. "John!"

Seconds later he and Bob appeared, Suzie moments after. Alan replayed the scene for them.

John reached for the telephone, "Anyone know Sergeant Small's number?".

The telephone rang.

"Hello."

"Mr. Hylton, how nice to speak to you again. I can confirm your fears. We do have your partner, in fact I should be meeting her very shortly."

"I don't know what bloody game you're playing but you are going to regret it for what little is left of your miserable life."

"Let's not waste our time with idle banter and empty threats,

Mr. Hylton. Please also do not contact the police or try to find her. She will be perfectly safe, provided you do exactly as I tell you. Do you understand?"

"I hear what you say Lanfranco, but the only thing I will guarantee is that if you harm her in any way I will rip you apart and feed you to my cat."

"Now, now, I am sure you can behave better than that, After all, I only want to do some business with you. My offer still stands. The only difference this time is that you will accept the terms and be grateful for the return of Miss Fielding as a bonus. I will call you again tomorrow morning. Please be absolutely certain that if you contact the police I will know about it within the hour. We will also be watching your every move. Don't do anything Miss Fielding will regret."

The conversation over, the connection terminated.

"Well, there's no mystery now. But we have two problems. Firstly, he's got Dee-Dee, secondly he thinks he's got Suzie!"

"Oh, shit!" Alan looked at Suzie, trying to work out the implications, his brain was getting back to its normal state. "When they came in, they didn't mess about. I hurt one of them, badly, permanently hopefully, but they just took Dee-Dee. If they had only wanted a hostage they could have taken Barbara. Why would they think they had Suzie?"

"God alone knows, but if they were being specific, taking Dee-Dee could be not only a mistake but a dangerous one for her if they find out the truth."

One of Alan's computers came to life. Jerry was FaceTiming from the plane.

His face appeared blinkingly onto the screen. "Afternoon, morning, whatever it is where you are. Hi, Alan how's life in the big city?"

Jerry was as bright as the African sun, and just as out of place as in the mid-winter they were still enduring as his demeanour was in the current atmosphere.

Alan tried to be brighter, "Good morning, Jerry. You've picked an awkward time I'm afraid, we're right in the middle of something right now. Can you call back later?"

"Yeah, sure. It would be helpful, I think, if Dee-Dee could be there when I call back, we've had a bit of an eventful weekend. I'll call back in a couple of hours. Okay?"

"Yes, that'll be fine. Thanks, Jerry." The screen went blank again.

"Bugger it. What do we do now?" Any excuses Alan could think of would be little more than barefaced lies, and he didn't feel like telling any of those to a man like Eric Daniels.

John drew in a large breath, held it for a few seconds and let it out slowly. Everyone was looking at him, waiting for some sort of pronouncement. And waited.

"I am in need of inspiration. At the moment, I have little or nothing constructive to offer. Can I suggest that we go to our own offices for half an hour, individually or together as you wish. Bob, send Baggy up to me, please. I'll be in my office if anyone comes up with a brilliant idea."

He trudged off slowly, carrying the entire weight of the world on his shoulders.

When the door had hissed to behind him, Suzie said "This will either make him or break him completely. Bob, go and fetch Baggy please. I for one would prefer some company, bounce some ideas around."

The others all nodded their agreement.

"Barbara, lock the front doors, meet us up in the refectory."

Bob flew downstairs and ran back up, three at a time with Baggy bounding up effortlessly behind him.

Suzie let him through into the corridor and he disappeared into John's open door, where he was gratefully received.

Suzie, Bob, Alan and Barbara, the only ones who knew that the attack had taken place, went up in the lift together, helped themselves to coffee and sat at one of the tables to contemplate the future.

John rocked back in his chair. Baggy may not have been real flesh and blood but apart from Dee-Dee he was more comfortable with him than anyone or anything else. He closed his eyes, stroked Baggy's head and prayed.

"I can't see how we can tell Daniels his daughter has been kidnapped. He can't do anything about it from where he is. He'll go out of his mind," ventured Bob.

"If it was my father," Barbara countered "and it was me that had been kidnapped, I would want him to know. He may or may not be able to help but I think he has a right to know."

"If we don't tell him and she ends up getting killed if it all goes wrong, what would we tell him then? Alan hit the nail on the head.

"You're right. We have no alternative. He has to be told. Any volunteers?" Silence. They all knew that John was the only one. God help John. After all he had been through, he didn't need that at all.

Dee-Dee was driven up to the house on the clifftop. The boot lid was raised and before her eyes could adjust a bag was dropped over her head. She was pulled carelessly out and set upon the tarmac drive.

Stumbling, she was assisted by Dan and Michael into the house. There had been a brief stop at Lanfranco's hospital to drop Sonny off to have his jaw wired and set. Safely inside, the bag was removed.

"I apologise for the theatrics, Miss Fielding. The blindfold was completely unnecessary. There is no secret about where you are. You will be unable to escape and your partner knows who has taken you. At the moment he doesn't know where you are, but I shall save him the bother of finding out by telling him tomorrow morning anyway. Now, if you would do me the honour of indicating your agreement to my terms, your bonds will be released and we can behave like civilised human beings. All I require from you at the moment is an assurance that you will not waste the time of my men in trying to escape, nor that you will attempt to draw attention to yourself in any way. Do I have your agreement?" Lanfranco was very pleasant.

Dee-Dee nodded her head.

"Good."

Dan cut the plastic tie from her wrists, which she instantly brought in front of her. Her hands were cyanosed and her wrists were extremely sore but the skin was not broken and with considerable rubbing and flexing of fingers they gradually regained their proper colour.

Dee-Dee was very confused. She had been convinced initially that she had been taken deliberately, but subsequently found that she was the subject of mistaken identity. It could be either an advantage or a disadvantage to her but as Lanfranco seemed quite satisfied that he had Suzie, she concluded, for the moment at least, that she was safe and chose not to enlighten her gracious host.

She was escorted across the hall to the room where Jerry had first become acquainted with Jacqui's charms, as she entered Dan pointed out the camera that was aimed at the door from the wall opposite.

"There are eighteen cameras in and around the house. Each camera has its own screen. Each screen is watched twenty four hours a day. In addition to that, this particular camera is fitted with an audible alarm so that if the door opens, we will know about it instantly. You will note that the window will not open and the glass is bullet proof. We will not spy on you in the room, you are free to read, play music, sleep, whatever you wish. You will have total privacy while you are in there.

"Should you wish to use any of the other facilities of the house you will press the bellpush on the wall to the left of the fireplace and someone will come for you. Meals will be brought in for you at suitable times, if you have any particular preferences please let us know and we will try to accommodate you. Lunch will be in two hours. It is pointless trying to escape. It would be impossible for you to even reach the front door. Your stay here, we hope, will not inconvenience you too much and you will be released from here by the end of the week. You have my word on it."

Dan's speech was over. Every word of it was true, although the last assurance was not received with any credulity.

The door was closed behind her and as if to emphasise her predicament, it remained unlocked. She didn't feel frightened, nor did she feel angry. She accepted that she was certainly safe for the time being. What about being released by the end of the week? Puzzling, but she had no doubt that it was meant to reassure her. It had to mean that whatever purpose she was there for had to be completed by Friday. She was also comforted by the thought that however clever Lanfranco thought he had been, he still had to deal with John. God help him if he had misjudged the situation.

Meanwhile the conclusion had been reached that Eric must be told the truth. Straight. No hedging around and just deal with the reaction as it happened.

When FaceTime was restored it was Eric that appeared. He looked older, drawn, almost lifeless. John began to reconsider his decision.

A thin smile came to Eric's lips.

"John, it's good to see you. You look far better than I had imagined."

And feel far worse than you could imagine, John thought.

"Yes, well things have changed a little since we last met. You don't look too good though."

John wanted a lead, some guidance from the old man.

"I'm fine, I have just been through some changes as well. For years you think you are one thing, only to find you are something quite different. It's just a little difficult to adjust, that's all," he chuckled. "In a perverse sort of a way it would appear that we have both undergone a metamorphosis during the past few days."

John was concerned. It wasn't the man who took him without a second thought for a trip to the dark continent. He was a shadow of that man. His eyes were dull. Almost dead. How was he going to take it?

"If there is any way in which we can help you, we will, but at the moment we have a considerable problem here."

John waited again for a reaction.

"Does it concern me?" the reaction was almost pathetic.

This is either going to make him or break him, John thought.

"It concerns Dee-Dee."

A light seemed to flicker in Eric's eyes, but he said nothing.

"Less than two hours ago, three men forced their way in here, using stun guns, paralysed Barbara and Alan, bound and gagged Dee-Dee and carted her off. Alan seriously hurt one of the men but was unable to prevent them from getting away."

John paused to let it sink in. Eric's face muscles were beginning to tense.

"We know who has taken her, but they think that they have Suzie, not Dee-Dee. Somehow they have mixed the two up and taken Dee-Dee in error. She is not in danger at the present time, we are convinced of that. I also know what they want. It is the same deal, so they say, that they offered me before."

"But you can't possibly give them that. It would be tantamount to giving them a nuclear bomb."

"I would give them the secrets to the origin of the universe if it were within my power to do so if it meant getting Dee-Dee back safely."

"Well, I will be back with you tomorrow. My work here has

finished for the time being. The three can wander around keeping out of trouble for a few weeks while we come back to visit."

John thought that Eric suddenly looked fifteen years younger. His original impulse was to make sure he stayed where he was, but the fire in his eyes was returning, he didn't think he would be able to keep him away.

"Okay, let us know your ETA and I'll get someone to meet you at the airport."

Eric turned away from the screen.

"Jerry, get things packed away, we're going home and we have work to do."

If John could have seen Jerry he would have seen him age twenty years and the colour drain from his face as though it had been wiped off with a high pressure hose. Jerry was feeling quite sick.

John spent the remainder of the day in his office with Suzie and Alan. They kicked around all sorts of possibilities, but the one thing that they kept on coming back to was how Lanfranco could be sure that even if John produced two cybers for him, how could Lanfranco guarantee that they wouldn't turn around, lock him up and call the police once Dee-Dee had been freed, and as far as committing any crimes with them? John simply wouldn't allow it. Lanfranco wouldn't be able to use them for anything that John wouldn't agree with.

The whole exercise seemed pointless. They concluded that Lanfranco must have a completely different agenda. Why had they picked Suzie? Why not John or Alan. They could all produce cybers. Was that what he wanted. It would take months to put together the facilities, write the software, produce the final article. It didn't make any sense. None of it. They certainly couldn't hold Dee-Dee for months. No there had to be something else.

The following morning, the three of them sat silently waiting for the phone to ring. At nine forty two Barbara put through the call that they had been waiting for. Alan was grateful, another ten minutes and he would have chewed his nails back to his elbows.

"Hylton."

"Good morning. I trust that you slept well."

John refused to rise to the bait.

"Of course. What do you want?"

"Tsk, tsk, such impatience. My request is quite simple. It will not take you too long to comply. It will cost you nothing. It will guarantee the life of your partner and you will still be paid, although in view of your reduced obligations the amount will be reduced by half. Still an attractive proposition, I'm sure you agree."

"As I don't know what the proposition is I can't express an opinion, but before we discuss that I want to talk to Suzie."

"Of course, that is entirely understandable."

A few seconds later, Dee-Dee's voice appeared on another extension.

"John, I don't know what they have told you, but I am fine. I am being looked after quite well. I don't have the freedom I would like but other than that I am being treated like a guest in his house."

"Yes, well I am quite sure that Mr. Hylton could have worked that out for himself. Thank you Miss Fielding. You see Mr. Hylton, I am trying to be honest and above board with you. I want to harm no-one."

"What do you want then?"

"I want you to bring all of the software, compound formulae, the case studies for your apes, construction details, in short, everything I will need to build my own cybers. Except for the materials and labour. That I will achieve from my own resources. You have forty eight hours, Mr. Hylton, to call me and confirm that everything is ready for delivery to me."

"What if I don't agree."

"Would you like to say goodbye to her now, or leave it until Thursday?"

"I'll call you."

John put the phone down and switched off the external speaker.

"Bastard!" John was angry. "If we do as he wants, he'll have the ability to produce his own, as and when he likes. If we supply him with duff information just to get Dee-Dee back he'll only come back, harder next time."

"Surely, though, once we have got her back we can go to the police with the tapes of her being abducted, the evidence for the bomb and get him put away and we have our problems solved."

Suzie believed it. John didn't.

"It's a nice thought, but I am afraid that this man either has good reason not to fear the law or, at least locally, owns a big chunk of it. Even if we could have him arrested, he has already shown us that he can divert the law for long enough to remain free. No, I think that we have to assume that we have to play it straight, at least for the time being. If we can work out a way of getting Dee-Dee out of there safely then I think we should explore the possibility of getting her out without giving them anything.

The phone rang again, "Yes Barbara?" He listened. "Okay, put him through. "Hello, I presume you aren't far away."

"That's right, we should be landing in about ten minutes, clear of customs et cetera in about an hour. I have some interesting information for you."

"Good, I'll send a car out for you, it'll bring you back here. Have you eaten?"

"We're a bit out of sync I'm afraid, we're looking forward to lunch, where I suppose you've not long since had breakfast."

"Don't worry, we'll work something out."

John put the phone down.

Chapter 30

Ever since Eric took the call about Dee-Dee, Jerry felt as though he was sitting on the point of a knife, one slip, whichever direction he went was only going to be painful and now it looked like he was responsible, at least in part, for Dee-Dee's abduction.

When would the nightmare end?

After careful consideration, he decided that he had very little choice other than to confide in Eric and hope that he didn't end up being target practice for the rhinos.

As they were sitting in the lounge area of the plane, somewhere above the eastern Mediterranean, Jerry gathered up as much courage as he could find, surprisingly little, and threw himself on the mercy of the man who had been like a father to him for the past five weeks. Eric had been deep in thought for the first half of the flight, only breaking the silence to thank Fong for the regular offerings of refreshment.

"Mr. Daniels?" Jerry began nervously.

Eric looked up, slightly surprised at the formality.

"Can we talk for a moment?"

"Yes, I'm sorry, I haven't been good company for the last few hours."

"I'm not quite sure where to start."

His courage was leaving faster than a heard of migrating wildebeest.

"Try the beginning," he offered without cynicism.

Jerry took a deep breath. "I think you will probably want to open the door and ask me to walk home after what I am about to say."

Jerry was hoping for a crumb of comfort or encouragement. He didn't get any.

"I think that I may be responsible for everything that has happened during the past few weeks."

He blurted out everything over the following two hours. Every little detail. Well, almost every detail. Not once did Eric say anything critical. He simply sat, listened and occasionally prompted or asked a question when he hadn't quite followed Jerry's thread.

The relief in Jerry was very evident. Although he waited for the threats and promises of the foulest things that his future could hold for him, he considered that he could face that uncertain future with the certainty that he could unravel some of the tangled mess that he had been responsible for creating.

"How old are you Jerry?"

"Twenty three, sir."

"Going on sixteen. Don't call me sir."

The reprimand was given and received in all seriousness.

"It would appear that the major cause of all of our recent problems has been greed, lust and a puerile quest for excitement. Wouldn't you agree?"

The face was stern. Jerry couldn't look at it.

"Yes sir. I mean yes, Mr. Daniels. Sir."

"Look at me when I'm talking to you."

Jerry lifted his head as though a tower crane were necessary to assist the effort.

"What you did was stupid in the extreme, and incredibly naive. Did it never occur to you that Lanfranco might just have had a reason for wanting all of the information which you so easily gave him? I suppose that at first you talked about your work to build up your self-importance to impress the girl."

He was wrong, but it was a fair assumption under the circumstances.

"And once you had started it I suppose you had to continue to maintain your position."

Jerry couldn't let all of this pass without comment, stupid and naive he could accept, but vanity and a need to impress had not been part of the repertoire.

"No, I'm sorry. I think you have misunderstood. It was Jacqui that picked me and saved me from what would probably have ended up as bankruptcy, but what she did was simply to make me available to her father. I answered his questions truthfully because I had seen what had happened to Jones and I understood from Jacqui that he was one of many such people. I couldn't see that anything that I was telling him would be of any use and I was only trying to demonstrate to him that I was worthless to him. It was only when Jacqui's interest in me was wearing off and she started treating me like a possession that I started to think about what I had done and that maybe there was another program of events that I didn't know about."

"And then you ran away to Africa."

The comment was scathing and cut right through to Jerry's

soul.

"Yes, sir. I really am sorry for everything that I have done. If I could undo it all, no matter what the cost, I would do it tomorrow without a second thought."

Jerry was on the verge of tears. The interrogation was the worst thing he had ever had to endure. The realisation was that he was the lowest thing to have ever had the misfortune to have walked or crawled on this earth.

"Thank you. Well, I have no doubt that you might just get that chance. If there is any consolation for you in what you have done, at least you have not tried to justify any of it. That would have been a grave error. Hopefully, what you know about the house and its layout may enable us to get Dee-Dee back safely. Now, I want you to draw a plan of the house and grounds and detail any security measures that you know of, the number of men normally on patrol and any other information that you think may be useful.

By the time Jerry had finished, Eric thought that he might be able to find his way around in the dark without any difficulty.

He stood up clutching the sheaf of papers that Jerry had used and set off for the cockpit, they were approaching home and he needed to call John.

The car was waiting for them as promised and whisked them off at an illegal speed to where their arrival was nervously anticipated.

Suzie greeted them in the foyer.

"I'm sorry that we should have to meet again under these circumstances. Please come through. John's waiting for you in his office."

She turned to Jerry, "I should imagine you have some stories you can entertain the others with for a while, if you want to go downstairs."

"Thank you," he said, relieved.

"I think it would be better if Jerry came in with us, Suzie. He may be able to help."

Eric wasn't going to let him off that easily.

"Whatever you think, she said, puzzled.

They exchanged greetings with John and settled into the chairs around his desk. Jerry took the chair between Suzie and John, located at the left end of his desk, Eric sat opposite John. Jerry felt a little safer, but he wasn't sure why.

John began.

"Just before you called from the plane, I was speaking to Lanfranco. He is demanding enough information and software to produce his own cybers. He no longer wants us to build anything for him, but he is still willing to pay fifteen million just for the information. He also said that if we comply then he will release Dee-Dee... or Suzie."

Alarm bells started ringing in Suzie's head, she became quite agitated.

"No. He didn't say that. My God, it makes sense now. We have to get her out of there. If we don't, she's as good as dead."

"What do you mean?" Eric demanded.

"It's so damned obvious, no wonder we didn't spot it before. He wants the information because he thinks that he has me. And with me and the information he can build the cybers! He didn't say that he would release her, he said that he would guarantee her safety. We assumed that he meant he would release her. We have to get her out!"

"Hold on, there's something here that doesn't make sense. We know who has taken Dee-Dee, we know where she's being held, he wasn't bothered about us finding out about that. Dee-Dee certainly wouldn't have told us she was in the house if she was being held somewhere else."

John was trying to think of other alternatives.

"She may have thought that she was at his house, she could have been anywhere," Eric said.

John picked up his phone and asked Barbara to check the number that Lanfranco called from. She told him the number, he wrote it down and asked her to see if Sergeant Small could check it against his address.

"No need to. It is one of his home numbers," Jerry interjected.

"How do you know?" John asked.

"Jerry knows quite a lot of things, I think you'll find," Eric interjected.

Jerry gave an abridged version of the story he told Eric. Suzie and John sat riveted to their seats, hardly believing what they were hearing. When he finished they simply sat and stared at him.

"I drew a plan of the house and grounds while we were flying back. It won't tell you where she is being held, but it ought to help you get in there to find her."

Eric pulled the sheets of paper out of his inside jacket pocket and spread them out on the desk.

Jerry went through the drawings with them, explaining the symbols he had drawn.

"There are no fences around the house? That doesn't make any sense."

"They don't need them. The nearest neighbour is over a mile away. There are few trees, there are a few scattered bushes and shrubs. The flower beds would not give any cover and nothing is allowed to grow above three feet in height."

"Why not?"

"Because they have a ground radar system, which operates from a distance of about seventy-five yards from the house to pick up anything within half a mile that is more than three feet high."

Eric asked "Why then do they have men patrolling the outside?"

"Comfort, I suppose, and a visual deterrent for any of the people he has cheated in case they get some funny ideas. Jacqui told me about the radar when we were out in the grounds after I asked about several strange looking sensors I saw around the house."

"What about the cliffs? Is there any way we an approach could be made that way?" John asked.

"Doubtful, you would have to come straight off the sea. There's no beach down there. The sea comes straight up to the cliff face. Unless the sea were dead calm, you wouldn't be able to get anywhere near without getting banged about. I think you can forget about that."

"That begs the question then - if he has her there, and we know she is there, then how could he possibly hope to get her out of there to keep hold of her? He couldn't just drive her out, unless they plan to fly her out?"

John looked at Eric.

"Could you get hold of a small plane and fly over the house, see what you can find? Take Jerry with you."

"That shouldn't be a problem," he said, taking his phone out of his inside jacket pocket."

Two minutes later it was arranged.

Eric and Jerry disappeared. Jerry was feeling better about himself once he was doing something right.

John looked at Suzie.

"How are we going to get in there without the place lighting up like Disneyland?"

She looked down at Baggy who had been lying quietly at John's feet, "It's a pity we can't send him in to fetch her out."

"Yeah, a shame he can't open doors... I wonder if he could carry me in?"

"Half a mile riding on his back? If you could stay on you'd do well, but you'd be bound to get picked up by the radar."

"Baggy, stand up." John fetched a tape measure out of his desk drawer. Just under three feet to the top of his head.

"Alan, can you make a saddle for me to lay on his back?"

"Sure, that should be simple enough. Baggy's long enough for you to be able to do that."

"The only risk would be a short blip on the radar if we briefly go over the three foot limit. I doubt that the radar would set off an alarm so easily."

"You could be right. A large bird landing would do the same thing," Suzie offered.

"I want the chimp as well, Alan," John said, growing in confidence. "We can use him for getting into the house and finding Dee-Dee."

"That should work, we'll have to work him from here though."

"What about you, John? You're not fully healed yet! This could set you back weeks," Suzie said.

"It will set me back more than weeks if I don't get Dee-Dee back safely."

It was clear that he couldn't be deterred.

Eric and Jerry returned three hours later.

"There is something under a green canvas cover on the lawn at the rear of the house that wasn't there before. It looks as though someone has made an attempt to camouflage it, but my guess would be that there's a small helicopter under it."

Jerry was feeling better within himself.

"Well it all adds up, doesn't it? The plans, Suzie, the helicopter. But where could it be intending to take them?" John said. "We can only assume that he has something planned. The man clearly has been very careful, and I suppose he couldn't have expected us to have taken a peek from the air at his little hideaway, could he?"

"Less of the little. Even if you manage to get in to the house, it could take you some considerable time to find her in there."

"We're going to use the chimp to do that."

"Oh, wow, good thinking!"

John was less concerned with that than being able to ensure that they didn't get a chance to get to use the helicopter."

"One other thing that we noticed, it may not be relevant, was a large ship, anchored about four miles off shore. It would be big enough to land a helicopter on deck. The flag was Panamanian, not that means a great deal, but it is always possible that they are planning to fly out to the ship," Eric added.

"If we can deal with the helicopter, or even if we can't it wouldn't be that difficult to get the navy or the police to board the ship. It can't get away that quickly," John said thoughtfully.

"That's always assuming that the ship is their destination. It would be better to do something about the helicopter to prevent it getting off the ground if we can," Jerry observed.

"I'll take care of the helicopter," Eric said.

"That's settled then. We will go along with Lanfranco to the point where he thinks I am going in with what he wants, and then, on Thursday night, I can slip in with Baggy. It sounds too simple doesn't it?"

"It would be for Batman," Jerry said, enjoying the intrigue at last, "but this isn't a movie. If it was, we'd have to call it Animan!"

The rest of the day was a flurry of activity. Bob and Sally designed and made the leather saddle so that it could be removed with just two quick-release clamps. Two knee supports and two hand grips either side of Baggy's chest would ensure that John would be securely transported. He was going to have to ride Baggy prone, with their heads next to each other to keep under the radar.

After they tried it out in the underground car park, John was wincing a little.

"It's not going to be comfortable, that's for sure, but it will do the job," John said, patting Baggy on the head.

Suzie and Alan spent the day programming and testing the chimp ready for the incursion. They'd need sight and sound or the task of finding Dee-Dee would be impossible.

By nine o'clock that evening, everything was ready.

At ten fifteen the following morning, with his office packed with people, John called Lanfranco.

"It's so nice to talk to you again, John. I presume that you are ready to do business now?"

"We've done the software and the structural materials, but we are still preparing the tissue samples at the moment. Everything will finally be ready by this afternoon."

"Good, I'm sure you won't regret it. Now, the procedure is quite straightforward. You will come out to my house at five o'clock this afternoon and bring everything with you, you will be given fifteen million in cash and you will leave."

"Not without Suzie."

"I'm afraid that we will need her services for a short while longer, just to ensure that you have not given us the details for something entirely irrelevant. When she has convinced us that it is genuine she will be allowed to leave."

"I'm sorry but I can't agree to that. Look, why don't we make a swap, me for her?"

"No. She is quite comfortable and she is in no danger as long as you keep your side of the bargain. I will expect you no later than five o'clock."

"I have just been told that we won't have everything ready by then, I'll be there at six."

They needed darkness, five o'clock would be too early.

"Very well. Please be quite careful. You will be alone in your own car. Any other vehicles within sight and she will be extinguished, do you understand me? The slightest problem and you will take her home in a plastic bag."

The threat was deliberately over the top, but made the point.

"You will drive up to the house. You and your car will be checked when you arrive. Anything out of the ordinary and you will regret it."

"Understood. But if you break your bargain..."

"Your threats are empty, John, don't waste your time. Six o'clock. Don't be late, or the party will start without you."

No further elaboration was necessary, all those present felt the chill.

John looked around the gathered throng.

"Game on then."

By five o'clock the night was drawing in. At five forty when Alan drove John's car towards Lanfranco's house, the lights were piercing the gloom in the distance. Just over three quarters of a mile from the house Alan slowed down to allow three shadowy figures to slip out onto the grass verge at the side of the road. John, dressed all in black like a ninja, slipped the saddle over Baggy and climbed on board, while the chimp scurried on ahead.

Baggy and his jockey slipped easily away into the blackness.

Alan waited for instructions from Suzie while the they raced across the flat grassland that lay between them and the house.

Chapter 31

Baggy eased silently and elegantly across the lawns to the house. It was an incredible experience for John. They had covered almost a mile in less than three minutes. The lights either side of the central front entrance were glowing, the rooms to the right of the door were also lit, shafts of light showing through the thin gaps between the curtains. John elected to use the left side and remained in the darkness.

He slipped off Baggy's back and unclipped the saddle, leaving it up against the house wall out of sight.

"Suzie," John said quietly, the transceiver in his ear making the connection, " there are no guards outside. Can you find out what's going on here. This is not what we expected at all."

"Will do. Are you okay? Ride not to bumpy?"

"I'm a bit sore, but it was a great ride, very smooth. I'll get the chimp inside in a minute."

Baggy loped off round to the rear of the house, following Suzie's instructions. She was watching two screens, the chimp's, so she could keep an eye on John, and Baggy's. She was also talking to Alan, keeping him informed of the progress.

Jerry was talking to Eric who, with Fong, was in a rented helicopter heading in the direction of Lanfranco's house. He was scheduled to arrive at five past six, but could be called in sooner if needed. He would be holding his position a mile off shore, coming in over the sea with the cover of the cliffs.

"John, I don't like this, there's nobody outside."

"Then we'll have to be careful," he replied.

Baggy had gone half way round the house and had not seen anyone. Suzie used him to look under the canvas and confirm that it was indeed a helicopter and sent him on his way again around the far side of the house.

John sent the chimp scurrying up the vines on the outside of the house and in through a window on the third floor. It was closed and locked, but the chimp easily broke the glass and climbed through.

Dan dropped quietly out of the dining room window a few feet behind John, pointing a 9mm Sig at the back of his head. John turned at the sound.

"Well, now. What have we got here?" Dan said with

considerable malice.

He switched on a small torch he held in his left hand. He moved easily and confidently away from the house and around to John's right.

"We thought that you might try to pull some sort of a stunt. In fact we were relying on it, but I didn't think that it was going to be this easy to catch you."

"This isn't going to end well for you, you know that don't you," John said confidently.

"Everything will be just fine, don't worry about me, I've got a gun and I'm not going to have a problem using it. We have all we need inside."

"Well, if you are going to kill me perhaps you would answer a question for me. Something that has been puzzling me."

"Sure. Whatever you want. Last request and all that."

"How did you get your hooks into Jerry?"

"That was easy. We heard about you from someone shooting his mouth off in a bar. The barman belongs to us. The guy was telling unbelievable stories about tricks with rhinos and other things. He thought it could be of interest to us. We did a little investigating and came across Jerry and his poker games. I set him up and, well, as they say, the rest is history. Just like you. But I don't want to kill you just yet, so let's go around the house where you can be of use for the last ten minutes of your life."

Dan motioned to his right.

"I hate to tell you this but if you don't put down the gun, you won't live to pull the trigger."

The phrase was like an icicle hanging in the air. Sharp and cold.

"What are you going to do? Hit me with your mechanical arms? Are they good enough to catch bullets then?" Dan sneered.

"Hmm, I guess you don't believe me and now you're out of time and luck."

Dan vaguely heard the low growl behind him, a shiver went down his spine. He half turned into the darkness peering to see the impossible, black in black. Even with the torch he couldn't see the danger that was circling around him. He turned back to face John, pointed the gun at his chest.

"Whatever it is out there you'd better call it off or I will shoot you!" he snapped nervously.

"Really? Okay. Baggy, come!"

The response was swift and deadly. Dan felt the incisors perforate his throat and spinal cord. Baggy shook his head with Dan's neck firmly embedded between his jaws as he fell to the ground. He was dead before he landed.

John tried not to dwell on what he had just seen, Dan hadn't stood a chance. Suzie had guided Baggy back to the front of the house, the rest was raw instinct, but even she was shocked at what she saw... first person execution on the screen, but it wasn't a video game.

The dining room window was still open, John climbed onto the sill and slipped quietly inside. He left Baggy patrolling outside in case there were any more nasty surprises. He looked at his watch, one minute to six. Alan would be making his entrance in sixty seconds. John opened the door to hall, he looked carefully around and saw the camera further down facing another closed door. He remained in the room. Closed the door and went back to the window.

"Suzie, anything from the chimp?"

"Nothing on the top two floors," the reply came back in his ear.

"Okay, then take him back outside and make as much noise and distraction as you can manage. Hold Alan off until he's back inside. Go."

The chimp scampered off. Something was wrong, where was everybody? What did Dan mean when he said he was relying on it?

Ten seconds later he heard the sound of breaking glass, the outside of the building instantly lit up and bells and sirens seemed to pour out of every corner of the building. John moved quickly out into the hall, it didn't matter if the camera spotted him now. The door was locked, he kicked hard at the door, the shock that went through his healing wounds was immense. Even worse, the door didn't move. He concentrated for a second and gave it everything he could find with his arms either side of the lock. The door frame ruptured and John fell into the room surprised at his own strength. The room was empty. There was a note on the table in the middle of the room.

It read "If you are reading this, you have twenty seconds to get to the back of the house. Goodbye Mr. Hylton."

John turned and ran out into the hall, turned left through an archway into another lobby. The first explosion ripped apart the dining room, walls collapsed and the ceiling and furniture from the bedrooms above came crashing down. He burst through another door: library, empty. He turned again, opened the door to the billiard room, empty, he ran again across the house, into the kitchen, the library exploded, then the billiard room, the explosions seemed to be chasing him through the house, almost guiding him. He heard another explosion, but it was outside, he could see the remains of the helicopter under the burning canvas billowing smoke and flames.

Fong and Eric had arrived. They settled their helicopter down on the grass, Fong dropped a long tubular object as he jumped out.

John leapt out of the kitchen window and ran over towards them.

"Have you seen anyone out here?"

"Nobody has been out since we arrived."

John turned and looked at the back of the house. The right side of the house was almost in ruins, the roof was collapsing and flames were beginning to catch hold. The left side was still untouched. He could see shadows moving inside beyond the swimming pool.

He shouted as he ran, but his words were lost on the explosion as the kitchen became the latest section to fall victim to the discriminating violence being reeked upon the building.

John didn't wait to find an opening to climb through. He launched himself fists first at the pair of large sliding doors that looked out over the pool. John crashed through, leaving the room blind in one eye. Michael Lanfranco was holding a gun to Dee-Dee's head as he stood with his back to the massive fireplace.

"Get down!" he screamed at John.

It was no time for heroics, John did as he was ordered.

Lanfranco entered the room from the door to his left and looked at John squatting on the floor. "Just in time to witness our escape Mr. Hylton," he said, smiling at John. "Not that you will be able to tell anyone about it, but that's a minor detail."

"You're going nowhere. Your helicopter is burning your grass."

"Never mind, we'll be burning your ass in a minute," he laughed.

John thought he was mad.

Then an explosion brought the wall and ceiling in from the left, and the chimp who had been skittering around above came tumbling in, Michael took his eyes off John and turned the gun on the chimp. John took his opportunity and sprang up, fast, hard and high, crashed his fists into Michael's face and dragged Dee-Dee away from his crumbling grasp. Not hesitating he lifted her up in his arms and ran for all he was worth out through the jagged glass that once was a door.

As he ran towards the swimming pool an almighty explosion lifted him off his feet and carried him the last ten feet into the pool. The entire house seemed to collapse in on itself as explosion after explosion ripped through the house, debris cascading into the night like fireworks at the greatest show on earth. John and Dee-Dee swam carefully to the far edge of the pool, staring in awe at the inferno that they had only a few seconds before been standing in the middle of.

Alan ran over to the pool and picked them both out as though they were driftwood.

"It looks like the cavalry wasn't needed," Alan declared, laughing with nervous relief. "I'm pleased to see everyone out safe and sound. Or at least those that mattered," he said with a grin.

"Thanks, unfortunately our friends didn't quite make it. Nor did our chimp," he said, feeling a little sorry for his saviour.

"Are you joking? He was out of the door faster than you were. Look!"

John turned towards the crowd gathered by the helicopter as they made their way to safety. Eric and Fong, and Baggy with the chimp sitting on his back. All of them with smiles wide enough to swallow a battleship.

Dee-Dee noticed the blood on her hands, but couldn't see where it had come from but then saw it on John's as well.

"Oh, John, your arms are bleeding!"

"Yeah, I took a bit of a pounding, going through the glass door, hurt like hell, but I'll be fine, a bit of TLC from Keith and his crew is needed I think!"

The explosions were still popping off all over the house as they departed, Alan took the animals back in the car, John sat in the front of the helicopter while Eric and Dee-Dee sat and hugged each other in the back. They could still see the orange glow of what was left of the house lighting up the long after they had left.

"I think we changed their plans a little, don't you?" Eric called to John above the noise of the rotors.

"Put it this way, we gave them a bit of a shock. But what I can't understand is how calm they all were. They seemed to be waiting for me to arrive."

"I think they just knew that it was all over, there was no way out from there and so wanted to take you both with them."

"I'm not so sure about that, I don't think that Lanfranco is the sort of character to give up so easily."

As the helicopter landed noisily at the airport, another craft was silently propelling itself away from the subterranean cavern towards its secret rendezvous. The undersea doors of the Panamanian ship cranked open to allow the surreptitious penetration by the thirty foot long submarine.

As they emerged into the safety of the bowels of the vessel Michael said, "That was one hell of a way to die!"

They climbed out of the hatch on to the steel platform that ran the length of the docking bay to be greeted effusively by Jacqui, who threw her arms around her father.

"There were so many explosions we were convinced you weren't going to make it."

"We very nearly didn't, if everything had gone according to plan we would have had plenty of time and we'd have brought the woman with us, leaving Dan and the freak to witness our demise. As it was we only just got the elevator in the fireplace moving down in time as the chimney came crashing down above us. The charges in the top of the lift shaft exploded seconds after the gate closed in nicely above us as we planned but it was definitely touch and go."

"Where's Dan and the woman?"

"I'm afraid Dan stayed behind to feed the cat and the woman escaped with the freak. It's a shame we didn't manage to bring her with us but, if at first you don't succeed, have a go some other time."

"How long do you think it will be before they know what has happened?" Michael asked.

"With the explosions going off at irregular intervals for the next two weeks, I think it will be quite some time before anyone might want to venture back there. Hopefully they'll never find the shaft down to the cavern. The lawyers should be able to keep them away as well, so with a bit of luck we should be well established in Hong Kong before they even start to suspect that we may have escaped."

Chapter 32

Three weeks had passed since the 'Big Bang'. The sun was high in the sky, the temperature was creeping inexorably into the nineties, the sun flashing off the water in the ornamental lake as the vivid pink flamingoes disturbed the placid surface. Every table surrounding the lake had at least one occupant, the background hum was created by a multitude of conversations. The atmosphere was calm, the setting was perfect, the booking of tables required either a great deal of luck, enormous fame or being a personal friend of the Maitre D'.

John sat at his table on the far side of the lake, almost invisible from the entrance to the island's most exclusive watering hole. He was dressed in a cream linen suit and a pale blue linen open necked shirt, the parasol casting a shadow over him, keeping off the worst of the sun. Ten minutes had passed since the arrival of the appointed hour. Not enough to cause concern, but just enough to heighten the anticipation.

A hush fell over the restaurant, he could see unaccompanied men turning in their seats and watching with admiration in their eyes, those that were accompanied were watching for longer than was good for them.

She was wearing a simple short white sundress suspended from her golden shoulders by pencil thin straps, tailored to hug every inch of her perfect frame, long tanned legs supported on white strapped shoes with three inch high heels, long blonde hair cascading freely down her back. There was a light in her eyes that was putting the sun to shame.

As she moved languorously through the tables, she glanced at each of the men, and with a smile and a nod of appreciation for the compliment; she dismissed each one in turn.

She was in his view. Their eyes locked across the remaining tables, no longer glancing at the other tables, she moved like silk over glass towards him, all the heads turned away as he arose from his chair, the conversation around them returning to normal level.

He held out his hand and, as she took it, she leaned forward to kiss his cheek.

"That was the most spectacular entrance I've ever witnessed, even the flamingoes looked pale in comparison."

"Thank you, but you didn't have to pick a table so far away," she chided gently.

"Haha, oh, I wanted to savour the moment and that worked out perfectly!"

Despite the food being prepared by the best chef on the island, it was consumed without a second thought as they talked and laughed and lost themselves in each other.

By four o'clock the temperature was slowly returning to a more comfortable level and the town was coming alive for the final session of the day. They walked around the shops, sometimes looking, sometimes trying, sometimes buying, but always with a smile. Everywhere they went, heads were turning in admiration for the happy pair.

By six thirty they had exhausted all of the shops and made their way down to the beach.

The beachside eateries were starting to make up their charcoal grills to cook the day's catch. They chose a small elevated restaurant with wicker chairs and tables and white table cloths. They were on a wooden platform raised a few feet above the sand, sipping long cocktails. As they sat looking out over the calm sea, the sun sank slowly over it, casting a red glow on the water ,with just the merest hint of ripples disturbing the mirrored surface.

They danced until the lights were going out around them; they were the only ones left.

They gave their thanks to the owner-cook-waiter and slowly walked off down the beach, arms around each other, talking quietly.

They were out of sight of what had been a vibrant beachfront when they sat down on the cool soft sand. He was gently tossing small stones into the sea when she put her arms around his neck and pulled him gently down.

They made love sensuously and gently on the sand with the water lapping softly at their feet.

As the sun rose from its dreams and scattered fresh life all around them with the birds breaking the silence of the night, John was the first to stir and remembered where they were.

He gently awoke Dee-Dee with a kiss, she leaned on his chest, stared into his eyes and gently said "Thank you for the most beautiful honeymoon anyone could ever have."

"It's a pleasure."

"And by the way, the parrots could smell fish!" she said, laughing.

The End

Other books by Antony E. Green:

Noah's Secret: The Beginning

Coming soon:

Noah's Secret: Fall From Grace

Printed in Great
Britain
by Amazon